The Struggle is Real

Alyssa Huckleberry

Preface

Every day, battles take place.

We see them splashed on news feeds online, the details of the conflict in neat, Times New Roman print beneath oversized pictures full of emotion. Civil wars. Persecution. Discrimination. Human trafficking. Drug abuse. The headlines, captions, and heavily-connotated verbiage make it easy to discern the two parties engaged in conflict, and you don't typically have to look further than the strategically-shaded image to determine which party is the villain (because the "bad guys" in life always come shrouded in shadows and black, didn't you know?). These battles feel far away and impersonal; the kind that you lament but never truly engage with. You feel sorry for the people involved, and you may take some small action to offer support or financial aid, but you don't really understand. Cognitively, you get it, but scrolling through highlights of the conflict on your iphone doesn't quite bring to light the full impact of the events. The 4.7 inches of backlit, pixelated news might as well be a 45 foot cinema screen featuring a Marvel movie- you're as likely to engage with the conflict overseas as you are with Thor or Ironman.

Then, there are the battles that by nature seem benign, impersonal, and bureaucratic. These conflicts aren't as compelling, and they don't come with the giant, splashy images. Laws. Corporate lawsuits. Politics. You have an opinion on many of the matters, but you rarely feel personally involved with the conflict, and you may even doubt your role and ability to make any lasting impact. You skim just enough of these issues to sound well-read and articulate at company functions and to commiserate with your barista with an aptly-placed sigh or nod of approval, and you may attach your signature to an initiative in a sign of support, but you rarely get involved on a deeper level. Not out of a sense of superiority, but because of a perceived lack of ownership- it doesn't feel like your battle to fight, and you doubt that any efforts you may take on would make a difference, anyway.

The battles that we claim ownership of are the ones that take place in our own backyard- the conflicts that arise in our work, at school, in our relationships and our ability to carry on in daily life. The client or colleague that seems determined to single-handedly bring about your demise, the task that feels impossible, the unfortunate unfolding of a sequence of events that seem to be a cosmic conspiring of doom focused solely on you (how many successive red lights can one take?!). The neighbor who plays his music just a little too late in the evening, the dog that barks incessantly, the family member who always seems to twist your words or doubt your intentions. These conflicts aren't featured on the front page of *The Wall Street Journal*, but they're featured in conversations, in silent rants, and, for the particularly introspective individual, in the pages of a journal. Some of these conflicts are resolved, some are accepted, and some simply get tucked into the pages of life, never to be consciously addressed, but still claiming their role in the shaping of identity and character.

And then there are the invisible battles. The battles that are so silent that they roar with deafening white noise. Conflict with oneself; self-loathing of unparalleled degrees, matched with self-doubt, anxiety, and fear. Fear of the future. Fear of action. Fear of inaction. Resistance to change. The burning desire to make a change, but paralysis when it comes time to actually do so. Negative self-talk that may masquerade as a silent thought but which shouts as though through a megaphone straight to the very soul. We fight these battles using a myriad of weapons: some elect to disown the conflict by denying it, dismissing it, or placing it on a dusty, forgotten shelf to be addressed later (or never at all). Others determine to fight back by countering the voices and pushing themselves to argue with the thoughts and suggestions made by the negative self in the hopes that these fears and anxieties might one day disappear. The symptoms and surface issues are tackled, but the source may or may not be addressed.

Then there are those brave enough to confront the source, working to reshape and rewire years of destructive thought patterns and habits, usually at the prompting and encouragement of loved ones. Those that venture into this undefined mental space face the trickiest battle of all; one in which there is often no defined enemy and no clear path to victory. The journey is abstract, fraught with roadblocks, and snakes indistinctly through the desert. With no clear compass leading the way, it's easy to get lost.

But to end the discussion of conflict there would be to overlook the greatest source of conflict, an entity so often overlooked. Where does conflict come from? How does it grow from an annoying, niggling episode of self-doubt to full-fledged anxiety? How do we truly disarm our opponents and claim victory in the battle? The first step is to acknowledge the mental space in which these conflicts truly sprout roots and grow; the place where wars are truly waged.

~1~

Change sat huddled with Fear, watching the scene unfolding before them with great interest.

"Is it time yet?" Fear asked, eyes fixed on the hospital bed below.

"Soon," Change offered without making eye contact. He, too, was concentrated on the delivery room. "When Theos gives the word."

Fear nodded, but fidgeted with anxious energy. It was easy for Change to dismiss time; he had a greater margin with which to work in. Fear couldn't afford to be late. It was important that he be ready at a moment's notice- the wrong timing had the potential to be disastrous.

"It's time," Change announced, jolting Fear back to reality. Without waiting for a response, Change departed, leaving the airspace for the hospital room. Fear hurried to catch up, noticing with little interest that Anxiety, Distress, and Panic had materialized during his mental reverie.

In a second, Fear hovered above the newborn child, feeding the babe the typical messages.

Where am I? Who are these people? What is going to happen to me?

Fear yawned, then signaled to Distress and Panic that he was ready for them. The initial excitement gone, Fear found himself bored. He wasn't sure if all characters felt the way he did, but he detested the early stages of an assignment. Newborns all reacted in the same way- there was no variation in response. The behavior was predictable, his messages were pre-planned, and there was little challenge or variability in his work. Theos was often private about the particular nuances each new assignment presented, leaving it to the characters to determine the unique capacities and predispositions each human embodied. Some characters complained about this, but Fear found it exciting.

Early in his career, he had found this stressful: he was in a constant state of watchfulness, living up to his name in feeling lest he miss an imperative clue about the disposition of his assignment. Now, as a veteran, he looked forward to witnessing the subtle signals of personality, the clues that, when correctly interpreted, helped him to realize his full potential within the human.

That was all they were trying to do, really- reach their full potential. It was dull in the beginning, except for the clues- there wasn't too much to work with, and it was largely lonely work. Characters were experienced in isolation, with little overlay. Later, as the human developed, he would have the chance to work with many more characters, often in interesting combinations that spoke to the human's complexity. This was where the fun came in- and where Fear was able to show off his repertoire of skills.

"Fear? Did you hear Anxiety?" Distress asked, a slight edge to her voice. Fear silently chided himself- the newborn stage might be easy, but he couldn't lose his focus. He turned apologetically to Anxiety, noting and ignoring the raised eyebrows on Distress's face.

"I think we're okay for a while," Anxiety repeated. "She's asleep. Distress agreed to stay in the room, but there's not much work to do at the moment. Peace came a moment ago; we won't be as effective with him here."

Fear nodded, watching Peace with interest. From across the room, he seemed to emanate light and warmth. His glow was currently focused on the mother and child, who lay nestled against her chest.

"Peace is getting stronger- I wouldn't be surprised if Love gets here any minute," Distress said baldly. "It would be a good time to take a break, Fear. Anxiety will go with you- Change and I will stay here as long as we're able to see if we can inject any more feeling. We're going to need you when she wakes up- you'd better rest now."

Fear mustered a slight nod, signaling his agreement, then vanished. He didn't particularly care for Distress, and he was annoyed with himself for taking orders from her. The only ones he took orders from were Theos and Abaddon- it annoyed him when other characters tried to boss him around.

***

Back at headquarters, Fear made his way down the familiar, brick-lined corridors towards the East wing of the building. As long as Fear had lived there, Headquarters had looked the same. The imposing, romanesque buildings showed no sign of wear and tear save for the occasional singe mark documenting the wrath of Abaddon. Fear cringed- despite passing these marks daily, they were a very real testament of the power and destruction Abaddon was capable of. He was thankful that he had not been the target of one of Abaddon's fits of rage- a thought that should have brought him comfort. But Fear knew the truth- only the influential, the strong characters could capture Abaddon's attention; he was not yet at that stage. Did he ever want to be?

Fear rifled through the most influential characters in his mind- they had all been showered with prestige, honor, and privilege, but he couldn't think of a single one who had not also experienced a spectacular fall. Was this an inevitable byproduct of work as a character, or did this speak to Abaddon's nature? Fear didn't know. What he *did* know was that he was content enough in his current role- he didn't feel the need to break out as a star character, but he didn't want to get called out for a lethargic, unproductive performance, either.

As Fear neared the edge of the eastern boundary of headquarters, he glanced into the western realm. A large plaza separated the two wings, a giant fountain resplendent in the morning sunshine.

Rainbow prisms reflected off the umbrella of water and onto the succulents encircling the fountain, stray drops splashing onto the neatly-manicured gravel pathways. Fear made his way down one finger of trail and found a seat on a marble bench in direct sunlight. From his vantage point, he could observe the characters mulling about, many hurrying to or from assignments. He could imagine the assignment based on the age and swagger of the character: the experienced, seasoned characters were almost always assigned to the most influential humans, as determined by Theos or Abaddon. They quite literally had a "presence" about them- a cloud of feeling that emanated from their very character, enveloping all around them in a thick wave of emotion.

These were characters that often had the opportunity to work with the most humans- all important, prolific individuals. Fear had never had the chance to work on such an important assignment- he'd always been assigned to typical humans.

Not that there was any such thing as typical, Fear reminded himself. Each human had proven to be a unique challenge, wonderfully complex with an overwhelming cocktail of emotions, feelings, and nuances that could only be understood by Theos himself. His involvement in a human's life depended on the personality of that given individual- Fear had worked on humans who quite literally depended on and fed off of his presence, and others who only occasionally required his presence. He was thankful that these assignments tended to be variable- there was no rest when he was assigned to one of the former type, and it was only after their inevitable death that he would be reassigned to a new human. His last assignment had been cut short as a result of a car accident- Fear still smarted over the fact that he had hardly been able to realize his full potential in that human. Brian, as he was known in the human world, had had many dalliances with Fear, but none that showcased Fear's best work. Fear had felt he was making real, new progress when Brian's life was cut short- one fantastic, short-lived finale of firework fear later, and Fear's assignment was complete.

He hadn't had to wait long for his next assignment- and as much as he dreaded the drudgery of the early days of a human assignment, he knew this one had real potential. He could tell by the fact that Theos himself had requested that Peace and Joy be present at the birth- that wasn't always the case. Predictably, once Abaddon had caught wind of the importance of this human through Theos's dictate, he had arranged for a host of characters such as Anxiety, Fear, and Panic to also make their presence known. Fear could tell that this human had real potential- what else could explain the interest both Theos and Abaddon had taken in the little girl? With this knowledge came a tingling sensation that danced through Fear's limbs and up past his neck. He wasn't sure if this assignment would be a blessing or a curse- he certainly had reason to be nervous. He couldn't afford to cruise through this assignment, or to daydream as he had earlier.

"Fear?"

Fear looked up into the face of Angst, a longtime friend.

"Angst. Please," Fear motioned, moving over on the bench to allow room for his friend to sit.

"Remember when we were young characters?" Angst asked, nodding towards the classrooms adjacent to the plaza. Through the large window, Fear and Angst could see the eager pupils focused on the instructor, an old, grizzled character standing behind a podium. Fear shook his head, a small smile on his face.

"It's not often I feel old, Angst- but you sure know how to make a character feel his years," Fear joked. "That feels like a lifetime ago."

Truly it did- Fear could remember with distinct clarity his days as a student- days spent learning the complexities of his emotion, the many character combinations he may experience within any given assignment, and how to maximize the human's experience of his emotion using any number of tricks and tactics. The facts had been simple enough; it had been the practical experience, traveling with experienced characters to witness firsthand the infusion of emotion, that had been riveting. Fear remembered the awe he had felt as a result of that first experience; the overwhelming sense of importance at the role for which he had been created. He had vowed in that moment that he would take his job seriously- he would not be a "career" character, operating solely from a place of duty- he would make this his life's work.

It was sometimes easy to forget that passion, that flame of a focused, intense purpose. He had been young, naive, and he hadn't been associated yet with either Theos or Abaddon. He'd learned about both in his classes, certainly, but he hadn't been marred by others' perceptions or expectations.

"Remember learning about Theos and Abaddon?" Angst asked, as though reading Fear's thoughts.

"Clear as a bell," Fear replied, eyes glazing over as he envisioned his own grizzled instructor coming down from behind the podium to address them with solemn, baleful eyes.

"I was scared stiff," Angst chuckled, leaning back on the bench and stretching his legs out in front of him, casually crossing one ankle over the other. "I remember thinking that I would be instantly incinerated if I met either one- and I walked around terrified that I'd be called out or summoned for destruction."

"I think we all felt that way," Fear mused. "I think that was their intent- to inspire fear, and respect."

"They certainly did their job well," Angst joked, shaking his head in amusement. "Little did I know that I'd never personally interact with either one, seventeen assignments later."

"Do you wish you had?" Fear interjected, suddenly intent. "Do you wish you'd met Theos or Abaddon?"

Angst seemed to notice the shift in Fear's attitude and straightened up. There was a thoughtful silence before he answered.

"After the initial fear wore off, I used to wish that I would. Now- I'm not so sure. I've gotten close- I've seen Pneuma a number of times, and I think we've all seen Yeshua, Theos, and Abaddon at each of our assignments' deaths- but that's been enough. I'm not sure what would happen if I actually had to interact with them or take direct orders. If I'm being honest, they intimidate me," Angst admitted.

Fear nodded but didn't otherwise respond. He knew exactly how Angst felt- he, too had witnessed the work of these rulers- but he had never been a direct part of their work. It felt like a lot of pressure- and it put a character under direct observation.

"Why do you ask?" Angst probed after a prolonged silence. Now he shifted uncomfortably, uncrossing and then recrossing his ankles in an attempt to get comfortable.

"I think my next assignment is going to be an active one," Fear said as neutrally as possible.

Angst cast a sharp look in Fear's direction at the word "active"- that was the word used to describe an assignment that included direct involvement from the rulers.

"What makes you say that?" Angst asked, eyes glued on Fear. Fear sighed, relinquishing the worries that had piled up subconsciously in the past day.

"There's already been involvement," Fear explained. Angst raised his eyebrows, then whistled.

"*Already*? Wasn't today the birth?" Angst queried. Fear nodded, and Angst's eyebrows shot up and down once more, a rollercoaster of thoughts communicated in a single muscle movement.

"I know," Fear sighed, acknowledging Angst's unspoken concerns. "There doesn't seem to be anything unusual about this human so far," he added, answering Angst's question even before he asked.

"I guess there wouldn't be, this early," Angst offered. "What are you going to do?"

The question was a stupid one, and they both knew it.

“What can I do? This is going to be a test,” Fear spoke to himself more than to Angst at this point. “I’m not going to get to rest with this assignment, I can already tell.”

“Maybe you’ll get a chance to interface with new characters,” Angst tried to cheer his comrade up. “Or you might get a plum position as an instructor after this,” he went on, on a roll now. “You know, you’ll get so much experience and learn so many new things, they’ll probably want to tap you to train the new recruits. You can share your *personal* experience about Abaddon and Theos, without relying on the scare tactics our instructors employed.”

Fear nodded, but suddenly felt far away. If his instincts were correct, and this assignment brought the challenges and connections he imagined it would, then his entire way of life was about to change. Fear appreciated Angst’s attempts to look at the positive side, but he knew his work was going to be much more complicated than what Angst surmised. This wasn’t going to be the pathway to a prestigious teaching position, or the opportunity to interact with interesting new characters. This was going to be a lifelong battle, the extent of which he had never experienced. He needed to prepare for war.

-2-

"She's perfect," a soft voice murmured, holding the newborn close to her heart. The newborn was having none of it- her fists clenched and swung wildly, her legs kicked, and her face turned variant shades of red and purple as she screamed her lungs out.

"She's certainly got a healthy pair of lungs," the father mused, leaning closer to his wife and placing a loving hand on her shoulder as he peered towards the infant in wonder.

"The sign of a healthy baby!" an attending nurse exclaimed with a chuckle. This was the part of her job that never got old- although she'd worked in the maternity ward her entire career, the miracle of birth never lost it's luster- especially as witnessed through the eyes of new parents.

"Is she healthy?" the mother asked anxiously, tearing her eyes away from her precious child long enough to make eye contact with the nurse. The father followed her gaze, searching the nurse for answers.

"Healthy and strong," the nurse confirmed, an easy smile spreading across her face. She was thankful for moments such as these, when she could assuage parents' concerns with the knowledge that their offspring was safe. She needed a deep arsenal of such moments to counter the awful times during which she had to impart distressing news.

Relieved, the parents turned back to their child, instantly oblivious to any activity not directly associated with their newborn.

"Shhhh," the mother whispered in hushed tones, rocking the child gently as she leaned in close. "It's okay. You're okay," the mother repeated.

The father sat on the edge of the bed, drawing close to kiss the child on the forehead and to smooth her fine hair to the side of her head. The infant drew a deep breath, suddenly exhausted from her fit of screams. Her large eyes opened wide enough to take in the sight of these two new humans whose voices registered with a sense of familiarity. Her delicate features contorted in confusion, unsure of whether to continue on screaming or to calm down.

"It's okay. You're okay, Leiala," the father chimed in, recognizing the potential for a peaceful transition. He slipped his pointer finger within grasp of her tiny, strong fist in a silent pact of love and trust. The mother leaned in to kiss Leiala on her head, and the transition was complete. Leiala's furrowed brows relaxed into a neutral position, and her pouty mouth settled into a neat line. Grabbing onto her father's finger, Leiala took in the scene around her with her round, watchful eyes before settling in against the familiar smell and cozy warmth of her mother's chest.

"Leiala, huh?" the mother whispered to the father, careful not to alarm or disturb their daughter.

"It was one of the names on our list." the father whispered back defensively.

"I'm not arguing!" the mother laughed, swaying Leiala gently in her arms. "I'm just surprised. That isn't like you to make a decision without consulting me."

"Sorry," the father replied, even though he could tell his wife didn't require an apology. "It's just that now that we've met her, I can't imagine her with any other name."

The wife smiled, wrapped her arms a little tighter around Leiala, and closed her eyes to capture the moment of utter perfection.

***

Theos nodded with approval at Pneuma and Yeshua. "That was done well," he offered.

"Abaddon was there," Yeshua pointed out.

"Did that surprise you?" Theos asked. Yeshua shook his head, glancing quickly at Pneuma before responding.

"No- I expected him to attend. He can't pass up any opportunity- especially when he knows we'll be there," Yeshua sighed. He wasn't complaining, but he did find the behavior annoying. It was utterly predictable, if nothing else.

"He knows she's significant to us, but he doesn't yet know why," Theos replied wisely.

"You can bet he's got his minions on the case already," Yeshua agreed. "And you had to have noticed the number of characters he already enlisted."

"There were a number, yes. But that doesn't have to be a bad thing, Yeshua," Theos spoke up. "The characters don't solely work for Abaddon. They work for us, too- and they can also take their cues from the human."

"But the human can be heavily influenced by Abaddon," Yeshua countered, not in defiance, but in respect for the work that lay ahead of them. "And you know Abaddon will not let this one go."

"He doesn't let any human go until the final moments of life," Theos agreed. "But don't undermine the influence we can also have on this new life. Pneuma will be instrumental," Theos added, nodding in Pneuma's direction. At this, Yeshua nodded, and all three fell into silence, quietly contemplating the events that were to come.

"This is going to be an active one," Theos mused quietly. "Abaddon's not going to like the work we have laid out for her."

Yeshua was quiet, silently bracing himself for the battles to come. It wasn't that different, really, from the billions of battles they fought every day. Some trivial, others of great magnitude, they were all of supreme consequence ultimately. Every battle took a human one step closer to their final resting place- to Theos's dominion, or Abaddon's. For every conversation or strategic meeting they had regarding one human, dozens more could take place. Knowing the ultimate destination mattered little- the battles would still be fought, and there would be carnage either way.

While the suspense was taken out- Theos literally knew the exact details of every human's life- Yeshua still found it fascinating to watch the human make any series of decisions that led them to their final home. He could empathize; relate to the humans, and he didn't envy them for their journey. If anything, he felt distress on their behalf- he knew the trials each would face, some greater than others. That the ultimate destination was predetermined did little to soften the emotions of the moment- the agony and uncertainty were very real and very painful, Yeshua remembered that well.

This was where Pneuma came in. Yeshua marveled at his ability to meet unspoken needs, to anticipate weaknesses, and to inspire and create support before it was even asked for.

Pneuma would be instrumental for this new human, Leiala- they all would be. For if Abaddon's first move had hinted at what was to come, he wasn't going to let this new life slip out of his reach without a war.

***

Fear was still sitting on the bench when he felt himself summoned. It was a strange feeling, the summoning- one he had never gotten used to. It felt similar to a foot falling asleep, Fear thought. The tingling pinpricks didn't hurt, but they hummed with irritation, buzzing up through his legs and into his core. If you didn't answer the call early on, the buzzing grew in intensity, but it would ebb with time if neglected. Fear knew from talking to other characters that there were some humans who were limited in their capacity to experience emotion- for some, this was a result of heavy medication, but for others, this was the consequence of unresponsive characters. The interaction with the human and his or her characters had never been cemented properly- and from this, the human was never able to experience the full range of emotions.

This was the danger that came from playing it too safe in the early stages- and Fear was not about to learn that mistake the hard way. He had no way of knowing, but he imagined himself to be especially sensitive and responsive to the summoning- he had learned to respond quickly, no matter how tired or illogical the summoning seemed.

Like in times past, Fear surrendered to the niggling sensation, allowing himself to be carried away from the sun-dappled plaza back to the hospital bed.

***

Leiala stirred and whimpered, her tiny clenched fists waving as her mouth puckered in protest. Fear noted that Irritation had already made her way to the side of the bed- she gave Fear a friendly nod, then got back to work. Fear acknowledged Irritation and assumed position himself. He was familiar with Irritation- a few humans back, he had worked closely with her. They didn't often collaborate, but their work was complementary- Fear could tell that Irritation had laid the groundwork to make his job easier.

He waited respectfully for Irritation to finish her work- then he would move in and begin his. Fear never got the chance.

A dark cloud came over the room as two new figures swooped in. Fear bristled, stepping back instinctively as the figures approached. He didn't have to see faces to know that these were not characters he typically encountered. He was vaguely aware of

Irritation making a quick exit as he himself edged towards the corner of the room.

He had never been in such close proximity with Abaddon's workers so early into an assignment. He'd seen them before, certainly- but typically only one at a time, and never before his assignment reached puberty. He was trying to work out what their presence meant when the more imposing of the two figures turned to face him.

"Fear, is it?" the worker asked, his countenance set in a permanent scowl. He had an intimidating presence, but was not terrifying the way some might expect. In spite of himself, Fear felt proud to be acknowledged by the powerful worker. He nodded with certainty, waiting to hear what would be asked of him.

"Don't let us disturb your work," the worker told him. The words were respectful, but the tone was flat, suggesting to Fear that there was more to this interaction than met the eye.

With great hesitation, Fear made his way back to the side of the bed, aware that his every move would be scrutinized by the two new arrivals. He felt self-conscious as he bent towards Leiala- the words he had whispered dozens of times now felt foreign and thick on his tongue. Swallowing hard, he worked to push the workers from his mind as he set to work.

Where are you? Who are these people? What are they going to do to you?

Once the first words left his mouth, Fear relaxed into the work he knew so well. This part of his job was gratifying. To the unschooled character, his work might look trivial and perhaps even frivolous- but Fear knew better. He was building a foundation of Leiala, establishing healthy fears and warning systems that would serve her well if she listened to them. That was his job- to equip his human assignment with proper fear- a lack of this emotion could mean disaster.

As little Leiala squirmed, her crystal blue eyes widened in alarm and then squinted in distress as she looked around frantically for a familiar face or element to ground her. Fear took a step back, waiting for Logic or perhaps even Comfort to step in. These were the typical characters to follow- they taught a young human to rationalize and prioritize fear.

One second passed.

Two seconds.

Three.

At this point, Fear looked over his shoulder, chiding the characters in his thoughts. Logic was typically very prompt, and Comfort was nothing if not overbearing- Fear usually had to plead with her to wait her turn before descending upon a human. Every second they stalled was a second that Leiala lay alone with fear that could quickly go irrational without the proper balancing characters. As it was, Leiala began to cry in short, agonized screams that spoke to her distress.

Fear bristled as he saw the two workers barring Logic and Comfort from approaching Leiala. He noted with discomfort the distressed expressions on both characters' faces and the severe manner of both of Abaddon's workers, who clearly communicated through their wide-legged stance and crossed arms that neither character was going anywhere near the infant on the bed.

Summoning his courage, Fear cleared his throat and spoke softly.

"I've finished my work- it's time for Logic or Comfort to take over," he announced, knowing both workers were well-aware of the natural progression of order. Fear made furtive eye contact with Logic, who glanced down at his feet uncomfortably, then dared to look up at Abaddon's workers.

"Only your presence is required," the smaller of the workers sneered. Fear figured he liked the other worker better- his figure was imposing, but he still managed to conduct himself in a business-like fashion.

"She's just growing more fearful," Comfort lamented, peering over the workers' shoulders at Leiala. The misery on her face was evident as she took in the wriggling babe.

Fear shifted uncomfortably from one foot to the other. He had never been in a situation quite like this- and he wasn't sure what to do. He knew the hierarchy of order: Theos was ruler of all- Yeshua and Pneuma worked with Him. But Abaddon- Abaddon was incredibly powerful and influential, and ruthless, too. He certainly had authority over the characters and his many workers- but to what extent? Fear knew that the current situation defied what was supposed to happen, but what he did not know was his role and obligation in setting things right. He didn't like the situation, and he resented the fact that he felt he needed to take some kind of action. What was he, a lowly character, meant to do in a situation like this?

A bright light flashed into the room and Fear exhaled in relief. It wasn't Theos- such an honor would only come in the most dramatic or important of situations- but it was one of his workers. Dressed in white and armed with a sword that seemed to reflect prisms of light all over the room, the muscular man took one menacing step towards Abaddon's workers.

"Be gone," he announced with authority, but he hadn't even finished the sentence before the workers had departed.

"Thank you," Logic said gratefully as Comfort rushed to Leiala. Fear stood back, taking it all in.

"You're some of the characters assigned to this little one?" the man in white asked.

Fear exchanged a look of camaraderie with Logic, then nodded.

"You'd best get used to these types of interactions," the man said seriously. "Leiala has been marked."

"Marked? What does that mean?" Fear blurted, forgetting his reverence for the man. This was not a concept that had been covered in his character classes so many years ago.

"She's been *marked,*" the man said again, this time pausing for emphasis. "By Theos himself. Leiala is destined for great things," he continued, chest swelling with pride as though he were somehow responsible for the accomplishments to come. "This also means that Abaddon has her marked- he is waging battle early. He knows he may not win the war, but he's afraid of the damage she may bring to his kingdom."

Fear kept his gaze locked on the man, taking this new information in. He had suspected as much, but hearing his thoughts confirmed by a reliable source was nerve-wracking.

"What should we do?" Logic asked, ever-rational. Fear noticed that Comfort had missed all of this message, her sole focus on soothing Leiala. And Leiala did seem to be winding down- her cries were no longer earnest, her breath now coming in ragged shudders.

"Keep showing up," the man instructed somberly. "You will not be able to control the appearance or disappearance of Abaddon's workers, or Theos's, for that matter. But it's important that Leiala still receive all of the characters. Even with our best efforts put forward, she's going to have an unconventional arsenal of emotions. There's no way of knowing the outcome of the battles, but Theos has a plan. Our job is to keep showing up."

The way he said the last bit worried Fear. *Show up?* That didn't sound difficult- that's what he'd spent his entire life doing. But the man made it sound like a great challenge; like something that would prove to be very, very difficult. Fear had a feeling that he was about to discover just how much he really had learned over the course of his past assignments.

-3-

Leiala stood in front of the bathroom mirror, sucking her stomach in. Turning to one side, she scrutinized her middle, pushing at the flesh just above and below her belly button. A wave of despair passed over her as she took in the image reflected in the glass before her. Her stomach didn't protrude- she was thankful at least for that much- but why did it seem so *thick*? Her fingers traveled up to her ribs, which seemed to be wider than most girls her age. She took another deep breath, this time with palms pressed aggressively against her ribs. She pushed as though her life depended on it, the desperation evident in her urgent, relentless fingers. Her face turned red from the effort as she both sucked in her breath and simultaneously pushed. Glancing once more in the mirror, her face dropped and her breath exhaled in an agonized sob. Her fingers flew to her mouth then, anxious to cover any sound that might escape. She did not want to call attention to herself, to make anyone aware of this melancholic diagnostic.

Allowing her eyes to travel the full length of her figure, Leiala at once noticed the furrowed, frustrated brows and wide, sad eyes. Her hair was beautiful, or so she was told often enough. Her forehead was too big, and her cheeks were too chubby. She had too many freckles- not the cute smattering across the nose and forehead, but the pervasive sort that seemed to dot her face like constellations. She liked the light, sky-blue color of her eyes, but lamented the fact that they were fringed with blonde eyelashes- ugly, embarrassing eyelashes. Her nose was neither an asset or liability- and her mouth was fine. Although, if she were honest with herself, she should admit that her smile was marred by the braces covering her teeth and cutting into the insides of her cheeks.

Moving down, Leiala did not yet know to criticize her arms and shoulders for lacking definition, but she would soon enough. She did note that she was not as curvy as some of the other third-grade girls she knew, except in her hips and thighs. This was the greatest source of concern to Leiala-her soft stomach and curved hips and thighs.

Her nose wrinkled in disgust as her eyes passed over her thighs nestled against one another- where was the two-inch gap her friends possessed? The soccer shorts tan line that hit mid-thigh seemed to accentuate the largeness of her legs, and Leiala quickly averted her gaze.
Her calf muscles were too big, but this strangely did not bother Leiala- rather, it pleased her. Secretly, this was a body part she took great pride in- a body part that spoke to the power and strength in her legs.

Finally, she reached her fingers and toes. While her fingers were too stubby and had horrible nail beds, her toes were perfect. Unfortunately, Leiala thought, her toes were also rarely seen- so it seemed to be a wasted blessing. But she knew they were there- and that they were cute.

But none of this analysis brought her comfort or helped her to discern how to approach her current situation. It was Macy's birthday party, and it was a pool party. The party would be at a giant hotel pool, and most of the popular girls from school and *all* the girls from her soccer team would be there. They had of course all seen her in shorts and a soccer jersey, but they hadn't seen her in a bathing suit. Leiala had been careful to keep her midsection covered, but some of the girls on her team who did not exhibit this same concern had ventured to wear tank tops or form-fitting shirts that had exposed slim tummies lined with ribs. Their profile was slender, and Leiala guessed some of them were literally half of her width. These girls had legs like sticks, long reeds that seemed graceful, ladylike, and pretty.

It wasn't fair, Leiala shouted in her mind as a pod of tears forged a trail down her cheek. She saw what these girls ate for lunch- pizza and soda and chips, sometimes with Oreos for dessert. But when Leiala envisioned their tiny bodies, she couldn't imagine where the food went- surely not to their stomach or thighs. And what did she eat? Leiala thought of her healthy lunches, the peanut butter and jelly sandwich on wheat bread, with an apple and carrot sticks as a snack. She didn't have Oreos in her lunch- but she might occasionally have a fruit roll up as a treat. And this was how her body thanked her? With *this*?! Leiala slapped her thigh in anger, silently cursing the healthy pink flesh that seemed to taunt her.

You're strong, Leiala. Think of all that you can do.

The thought popped into her head suddenly, arching through her brain like a seagull riding a current of wind. It lingered, floated, then soared on by. For a moment, Leiala felt a sense of peace, of acceptance. Her body was able to do amazing things. She could run faster than any of the girls on her team, and she was strong, too. She never fell over when she was tackled- but lots of other girls did. She could hold a plank for longer than anyone she knew, and she always played the entire soccer game without coming out for a break.

The moment was broken as Leiala's gaze returned to her figure in the mirror. *Who cares?!* she thought bitterly. *Who cares if you can run fast or far or have strong abs or strong legs if it means that you look like this?* She turned her head away, repulsed and angry. Her body was a disgrace. It let her down. There was clearly something wrong with it, it was defective. How else could you explain the things her body was able to do while taking in its appearance? After all she did to take good care of it- to put in good, clean, healthy fuel and to exercise properly- this was the thanks she got?

Which is more important: to be healthy and able to do great things, or to look a certain way?

A second silent thought made its debut, but this one was quickly, harshly silenced.

"To look a certain way," Leiala hissed aloud, glaring at her reflection. Her fingers continued to push and prod, the sculptor growing more and more pessimistic as she took in her work. Well, she wasn't going to achieve the image she wanted- but she might be able to mold an acceptable look.

Later that night, Leiala sat quietly on the edge of her bed. She thought she'd done well at the party- she'd been careful to keep her tummy sucked in at all times, and she hadn't eaten all the junk food the other girls had. *They* might be safe eating pizza, cake, or chips- but Leiala couldn't afford to indulge that same way. If this was what her body looked like when she tried hard, what would happen if she *didn't*? The thought was terrifying. No- NO- she would not let that happen.

You'll just have to work harder, Leiala. Your body isn't good enough, and you're not as pretty.

This thought was matter-of-fact. It didn't float through Leiala's mind, and it didn't bring her peace. But it was clear, and Leiala appreciated the no-nonsense way in which it presented itself. What's more, she agreed with the thought- it seemed to speak truth.

Don't worry.

Leiala felt herself relax as she listened desperately for what might come next. The other thought had been too happy, too peaceful- it wasn't realistic. It didn't take into account all of Leiala's faults- it seemed to just accept her as she was, as a disgusting mess. This one seemed to understand her situation, and it seemed ready to offer her a solution.

You're not good enough right now, but you can be. You know how to work hard, Leiala.

Leiala's heartbeat slowed, and she felt her tense body start to relax just a bit. It was true, she did know how to work hard.

We can work to make this better. You can achieve a lot, if you're willing to sacrifice. How badly do you want to be beautiful?

"So badly," Leiala breathed, scarcely aware that she was speaking aloud. "More than anything."

Smart girl, the voice praised. *If you're beautiful, then you'll be wanted. You'll have friends, and you'll be loved. Beautiful, successful people are the ones that are loved the most. We can work together to make you like that.*

“Okay,” Leiala whispered, her voice tiny and determined. She wasn’t a fool- she knew that she would have to work hard to achieve what the voice suggested to her. These things didn’t come naturally- she’d learned that much already- but she could work to make herself better. To make herself tolerable. To earn the love and respect and admiration of those around her. Yes, she would work to obtain these things. And the voice had said *we*- she wouldn’t be alone.

Leiala breathed a sigh of relief, thankful for some sense of direction. It was terrible to lack direction, to be a ship cast haphazardly in the ocean. This was a gift, a white-sailed ship come to pull her from the storm. She accepted the invitation.

***

“She’s eight years old!” Innocence roared, pacing the floor like a caged animal. “This is *so* inappropriate!”

“What do you suggest we do?” Joy asked irritably, her fingers pushed up against her temples in frustration. “Do *you* want to be the one to approach Abaddon? What do you plan to say? You don’t think we haven’t had these same thoughts?”

“We have to be able to do something,” Innocence spoke, but some of her passion had diminished as she looked around the room hopefully. The characters just stared back at her, obviously deflated.

“I’m afraid Joy is right,” Peace said calmly. “Abaddon has made his mark on Leiala, and he’s been diligent in sending his workers to influence her.”

“*Diligent*? More like *obsessive*!” Joy cried, hands flying into the air in open-armed exasperation. “He won’t leave her alone. Every time I try to impress myself upon Leiala, I’m held back. Only when Theos’s workers or Pneuma are present am I able to squeeze in any kind of feeling at all. And then it seems I’m immediately overruled by some negative impression from Abaddon. This girl is going to be ruined!"

"She's not ruined," Fear spoke up without realizing it. All eyes turned to face him, and he swallowed, trying to quickly collect his thoughts. "I mean, she's stronger than we're giving her credit for. Theos hasn't forgotten her- He always goes to her, and Yeshua and Pneuma, too. She's not lost to Abaddon."

"She's not lost? What do you call her thought patterns?" Innocence pressed. "You don't think her thoughts are pretty dark for an eight year old?"

"I do," Fear agreed, finding his voice. "But I think this is part of her journey." As he said these last words, he was aware of how cheesy they sounded. *Part of her journey?* Even he wasn't sure what he meant by that. But he had said it with conviction, and he meant it. Leiala was under fire, but she was somehow still strangely on track.

"And where does this journey end?" Anxiety asked. It was the first question that was asked without any emotion lacing the words.

"I'm not sure," Fear answered honestly. "But for all of Abaddon's influence, Leiala still finds her way back to Theos."

"She doesn't even realize she's serving them both," Joy complained. "She's a puppet on strings."

"Only one string pulls, and the other beckons," Innocence said wisely. "Abaddon has her working herself into the ground out of fear- but Theos whispers comfort to her."

"I don't see how she can miss that," Peace mused. "How is it that she doesn't realize what's happening?"

"Abaddon," Fear said simply. "He's sneaky, and powerful. His influence comes from his skill in deception. He wouldn't dare parade around as himself- he's only spoken to Leiala in subtle ways that seem to her to represent her own thoughts and ideas. It's the only way she could be duped into serving two masters."

"It *is* interesting that Theos allows it," Anxiety thought aloud. "Theos is typically jealous- he doesn't like it when loyalties lie in more than one place."

"Fear is probably right- it means something," Joy admitted reluctantly. "But how long must we be edged out while this little girl suffers?"

"To be fair, she doesn't know she's suffering," Innocence pointed out. "She thinks she's acting out of determination, and that she's working towards a goal. She's not aware of the damage that's being done."

"Is that better?" Peace asked. "The road she's walking is a painful one- the darkness might not feel oppressive now, but when Theos does decide to shine the light...it won't be easy."

"Easy? It will be *crippling*," Joy said through gritted teeth, tears welling in the corners of her eyes. "How can we let that happen to Leiala?"

"*We* can't do anything else," Anxiety stated with confidence. "You're forgetting that we're just characters. Theos is running this show- and He has Yeshua, Pneuma, and an army of workers at His disposal. When He decides that the timing is right, we'll have our chance to correct things."

"Too late," Innocence whispered, haunted by the very thought of what might happen to the little girl they all held close to their heart. "These thought patterns run deep, and they can't be easily undone."

"My heart breaks for her," Joy agreed, also in a hushed voice. All the characters seemed resigned to the inevitable outcome that might befall Leiala, but none of them felt peace about it.

"Theos loves her the most," Fear blurted.

Again with the comments! He wasn't sure where these thoughts sprang from- they seemed to have a life of their own! It was a truism he'd learned in his very first class, and the truth and weight of this single sentiment had been heavily impressed upon all the characters. As much as they might come to care for their human assignments, Theos's care would always outstrip their feelings.

It was hard to imagine at times- Fear didn't always come to sympathize for his assignments- some seemed to embark on foolish expeditions that welcomed hardship and destruction. Others were just generally unhappy, selfish people. But when you got an assignment like Leiala- well, it made everything more complicated. Fear had a feeling he said the words aloud as much for himself as for the other characters.

"You're right," Joy agreed, shoulders sagging. "I just wish He would choose to show up sooner rather than later. This wait is agonizing."

This was something all the characters could agree on. Leiala was maturing, but not in all the healthy ways they would have liked to see. But this was not their battle, and they could not fight. They could only wait and watch.

***

Abaddon sat on his throne, his long, slender fingers curled over the armrest of his oversized, ostentatious chair. A satisfied, wide grin smothered his face. He silently reviewed the work he'd been able to accomplish in Leiala's life with growing pleasure. He'd really managed to make a mess of things.

Leiala served him, but she had no idea. She listened to his voice, to his suggestions, to his ideas. She took comfort in having him as a teammate. She believed that he was there to help her. Oh, she actually thought that he would save her! He'd managed to cultivate multiple idols in her life, tangible and intangible things that Leiala desperately sought above all else. Above Theos.

And Theos- well, Theos certainly wasn't pleased, and Abaddon noted with irritation that He hadn't abandoned Leiala, but He also hadn't put an end to Abaddon's influence. Abaddon wondered for a moment if this wasn't on purpose, but dismissed the thought with the surety of a reigning champion. His swollen ego chose to believe that Theos couldn't fight his work- and if Abaddon kept it up, he was confident he could permanently separate Leiala from Him. He wouldn't reveal himself- not yet. His position was too sweet- he had too much power. It would be better to guide Leiala farther down the path, to convince her that she was fine, and that she was only following Theos.

Abaddon made a mental note to speak to his workers about influencing her to read the Bible and to spend more time in prayer- and then to force Anxiety on her. Abaddon's tented fingers wiggled in delight at the mere thought. Oh, yes. This would further convince Leiala that the voices in her head were from Theos himself, that they could be trusted. If she trusted and obeyed the voice now, to what length would she go if she believed the voice was that of Theos himself? He could play this game for a long time- take Leiala far down the path, until the time was ripe for her destruction. And then, when the true origin of the voices were revealed, she'd be too far gone to save herself. Too far gone even for Theos to save. There wouldn't be anywhere to turn except into Abaddon's open, waiting arms.

***

Leiala lay in bed, wide awake. It was closing in on 10:00 PM, and she'd had a big day. She *should* have been exhausted. Instead, her eyes focused on the creamy-yellow path of light coming from the crack in the door. Her eyes traveled the length of the light angular shape, then back again as she worked to quiet her mind.

Right. As if that would ever be possible. Her eyelids fluttered in exasperation as she took a deep breath. Was there an off button for her brain? She didn't think so, but she was hoping that she'd get better at silencing the voices in her mind. It had to get easier when you got older, right? It was probably a matter of *maturity*, something that would happen to her when she turned eighteen, she thought wisely. She couldn't imagine her parents, teacher, coach, or any adult, really, engaging in the tumultuous mental struggle that had seemed to become second-nature for Leiala. It was something she'd grow out of, she told herself hesitantly at first, then again with false confidence.

Stop it! Leiala shouted to herself internally, shifting her body weight angrily so that she rested on her side. Her right cheek rested gently on the pillow as she pulled the covers aggressively closer. With every good intention, Leiala felt sleep become more elusive. Her efforts to calm herself were not only failing, they were counterproductive- Leiala could feel her blood pressure rising and her heartbeat quicken.

It hadn't been a good day. Her mind was tempted to believe it had been a horrendous day, but that wasn't quite true, either. Logically, Leiala knew that. Nothing disastrous had occurred. She was still healthy, safe, and *happy*? The last adjective was somewhat of a stretch, its fragile state confirmed by a single tear that rolled down her cheek. Why did happiness feel so *hard* sometimes? Like work- something she had to intentionally focus on- and still she often felt as though she came up short.

The pancakes. It had started with the pancakes. Squeezing her eyes shut, Leiala gave in to the replay of the day's events that had commenced without her permission.

Sitting at the kitchen table, enjoying one pancake. Two. Three. She was still hungry. So...four.

"You're eating a lot of pancakes!" her younger brother Tommy had exclaimed innocently. Leiala forced a smile and swallowed the last of the fourth pancake along with guilt.

At school, misspelling the word "tomorrow," and getting eliminated in the spelling bee to watch her best friend Katie spell it right. Never mind that she'd made it to the final round and out-spelled the rest of her classmates...*failure* was the word that flashed like a firework in her mind as she cursed her stupidity, ridiculing her former confidence (had she really believed she was smart?), and calling into question her friendship (what did Katie really think of her? How could she stand to be friends with someone so dumb?). She had smiled in what she hoped appeared to be a graceful gesture, heat rising to her cheeks and turning them a bold, candy-apple red as she quickly, ashamedly took her seat and watched Katie accept the spelling award.

Recess, watching her friends eat potato chips and Oreos while she ate graham crackers and apples. Which wouldn't have made any difference, except that Leiala couldn't help but notice the flat stomachs and stick-like legs of her friends as they cartwheeled on the grass. Her stomach didn't look like that. Her legs didn't look like that, either. She was confident in this fact, but made a mental note to check in the mirror when she returned home that afternoon. It must be the pancakes, Leiala thought hopelessly, her mind galaxies away from the laughing group of girls.

Math- a difficult problem written on the board up front. Heart pounding out of control as hands shot up like popcorn; Leiala struggling to remember the procedure her teacher had taught her just minutes before. Shame and anxiety creeping in as it took longer than it should have, the blood pounding in her ears, roaring so loudly that it drowned out any hope for cognitive ability. A classmate answered, and the beating of her heart subsided enough for her to follow the logic, which wasn't as tricky as she'd imagined. More ridicule: *that* had been challenging? What was wrong with her? Had her friends noticed that she hadn't raised her hand? Had her teacher? They must think that she wasn't smart.

Soccer practice, running drills with her teammates. She came in first on the sprints, and her defense was on point. But her skills were lackluster: she couldn't chip the ball properly for her corner kicks, and she missed two shots on goal, aiming just wide of the side railing. Her teammates didn't say anything, but Leiala was sure they were disappointed in her- they were probably worried that she might perform similarly in their upcoming game that weekend. You'll have to work harder, she told herself. You're getting sloppy.

And then for dinner: her favorite dish, a Mexican pasta salad. She was hungry, and the food tasted good- so she served herself seconds. Remembering too late that if she wanted to be ladylike and delicate and slim like her playground friends, she couldn't go back for more food.

So now she lay in bed, questioning her beauty, intelligence, athleticism, and friendships. *You're going to have to do better tomorrow*, a voice whispered. *I can show you how. You need to work harder, do more, if you're going to have friends and be successful. You can be the person you want to be, but you need to put in more effort. Is that worth it to you?*

Yes! Leiala whispered aloud. *Yes!!* She may have failed that day, but she could do better tomorrow. She would *have* to do better. With this new resolve, Leiala snuggled her cheek into the pillow. Tomorrow would be a new day.

***

Fear shifted uncomfortably as Leiala finally succumbed to sleep. His work was becoming increasingly dark, and he didn't like it. Not that he had a say in what his assignments looked like- but if he had, he would've asked to be relieved of some of his current duties. But maybe that wasn't accurate, either- Fear really enjoyed Leiala, and he wouldn't really want to leave her. But he didn't like what his role had become. He was summoned constantly- not only in truly dangerous situations that called for fear, but in nearly every situation. He wasn't partnering with many other characters, and the ones that he was partnered with were getting on his nerves. Perhaps it was the lack of rest, perhaps that the characters were forced to work more closely than ever before, but he was sick of Anxiety and Panic, Shame and Guilt. He could anticipate their actions before they even interacted with Leiala, and he was annoyed with their behavior even though he knew they were simply doing their jobs.

He also felt confused: he had anticipated Theos, Pneuma, and Yeshua to play more of a role in Leiala's everyday life. As it was, Abaddon's workers were a constant presence. So were Theos's workers, but they didn't take action as often as Fear would have liked. He felt frustrated on behalf of Joy, Hope, and Peace, who were often held back in situations that typically would have called for their comforting touch. They weren't permanently sidelined, but their appearances were irregular and, if Fear was allowed to offer his professional opinion, poorly timed. This was all Abaddon's doing- it was out of the control of the characters.

Fear recalled with unease his early education, where he had learned the dangers that came from absent or late characters. Intended to ensure that the characters were reliable and prompt, the instructors had explained that when a character was late to show up or worse, failed to show up altogether, faulty thought patterns were ingrained in the mind of the assignment. These neural pathways were unfortunate and disconcerting when they occurred once- multiple episodes resulted in permanent damage to the thought processes of the assignment that would negatively impact the individual in greater ways than the character could imagine.

Fear knew the warning well, but he'd never seen the effects of such a phenomenon firsthand until now. Looking down at sweet Leiala, he felt sadness swell in his chest. He didn't feel it was fair for Abaddon to interfere this early on- and he couldn't understand why Theos was allowing it to take place.

Theos's workers were present when Abaddon's workers confined Joy, Hope, Peace, and Comfort from approaching Leiala, but more often than not, they stood back and observed. There hadn't been any big confrontations yet- another fact that surprised Fear.

Glancing now at Peace and Comfort as they were allowed to approach Leiala, Fear felt a sense of relief. He hoped the respite would not be short-lived, as some others had been. Shaking his head, he quietly departed for headquarters. He needed to rest- it wouldn't be long until his presence would be required once again.

***

Theos looked down on Leiala, his heart breaking.

"Why are we letting Abaddon get away with this?" Yeshua asked. He wasn't angry, but perplexed. He saw Theos's distress over Leiala and felt it himself. It didn't have to be that way, he knew- they could overpower Abaddon without much effort.

Pneuma sat quietly beside them, taking it all in. He was a man of few words, but that didn't mean he lacked feeling. If anything, he was the most compassionate of all, so skilled was he at communicating empathy and understanding with nothing other than his presence.

Theos sighed now, looking over at Yeshua with solemn eyes.

"Abaddon isn't getting away with anything," Theos began steadily.

"Right- we're *allowing* him to do this to Leiala," Yeshua agreed. "Why?"

"Leiala is being refined," Theos answered, aware even as he offered the brief explanation that it would not satisfy Yeshua.

"She's being *cut down,*" Yeshua clarified. He wasn't arguing, but stating the bald facts. "Her confidence is plummeting, and she's developing dangerous thought patterns."

Pneuma looked thoughtfully at Theos, wondering if he would be sent down to Leiala. Theos caught his gaze and shook His head softly.

"This needs to happen," He offered simply.

It wasn't much by way of explanation, but it was said with confidence that appeased Pneuma and Yeshua. This wasn't easy for any of them to watch- Leiala was a favorite of theirs, a sweet girl with a big heart, eager to please. Her struggles were painful to observe, and the three felt her anguish personally. But until Theos said it was time, there was nothing they could do but wait. They might not always understand Theos's timing, but knew based on past experiences that His timing and plan were always perfect.

***

On the opposite end of headquarters, a similar discussion took place in Abaddon's lair.

"Does it worry you that Theos hasn't taken action?" a worker asked Abaddon, couching the question as casually as possible. He knew it took little to make Abaddon irate where Theos was concerned.

"Why should it worry me?" Abaddon asked, haughty as ever. These were of course not his true feelings, but he was too proud to reveal any insecurity.

The worker shifted on his feet uncomfortably, looking around at the other workers in the room in a desperate plea for help. They all avoided eye contact- they, too knew about Abaddon's terrible temper.

"I mean, it seems possible that Theos is planning something with Leiala," the worker continued timidly, choosing his words carefully and drawing out the words.

"Of course he's planning something," Abaddon acknowledged sharply, casting a derisive and condescending glance in the worker's direction. "Is that what they teach in Strategics now? That Theos occasionally comes up with plans?" he added sarcastically, earning chuckles from some of the surrounding workers as he referenced an entry-level class. The worker swallowed his shame, hurt that his fellow workers would do nothing to support him.

"I meant something we should worry about," the worker persisted, aware now that he was on dangerous ground. There was a good chance that this would push Abaddon over the edge- but his pride wouldn't allow him to stop there.

"What are you suggesting?" Abaddon snarled, swinging his head to glare at the unfortunate worker.

The worker knew instantly he had taken things too far. He wished he could backtrack; take back his comments and rewind time two minutes. There was no way to win this conversation now.

"I'm concerned that we're being lulled into a false sense of security with Leiala," the worker began, knowing it would be far worse if he cowed now. "Theos's presence is markedly absent, and we know He has a special interest in the girl. He's not indifferent, but He's letting us proceed without any struggle whatsoever. It makes me wonder if we're playing into His master plan," the worker finished, speaking quickly to get all the words out.

An uncomfortable silence hung like a saturated rain cloud over the room. The worker was aware of his heartbeat quickening and the heat in his body rising, but he did not take his eyes off of Abaddon. If ever he was in danger of a sudden, painful death, the time was now.

Surprising everyone, Abaddon didn't lash out- instead, he took a deliberate seat in the oversized velvet chair positioned in the corner of the room, his body folding down onto the thick fabric as he crossed his legs and leaned back with a sigh.

"I've thought the same," Abaddon acknowledged. "But it's too early to declare war- we haven't put in enough time yet. She would be an easy win for them now, if we forced Theos's hand. We need to continue to develop the thought patterns and establish ritual behaviors. I don't know what Theos has planned, but we're gaining ground every opportunity we have to influence Leiala. We've already made excellent progress."

"Should we double up efforts?" another worker eagerly cut in, hoping to win the approval of this most-fickle leader.

"No, you idiot- that would completely defeat our purpose," Abaddon spat. "We don't want a war, and we don't want to take any action that will generate attention. Our goal right now is to fly under the radar. Keep Leiala engaged in all the same things, and slowly continue to increase her feelings of insecurity and anxiety. No major movement- we don't want her to recognize that anything's changed. Slow and steady progress, that's the most effective kind. If we do our job well, by the time Theos decides to take action, she'll be too far gone."

Having spoken his piece, Abaddon rested the back of his head, palms cupping the wooden arms of the chair. Surveying the room with a judgmental sweep of his eyes, he nodded.

"Yes, that's what we'll do. Leiala may be marked, but that can't keep us from doing some serious damage. We'll see just how loved this princess is after we've worked our magic."

-4-

Leiala's heart pounded in her chest, threatening with each beat to break loose and tear off like a horse out of the race gates.

I don't know. I don't remember. Quick, think. Think, Leiala! THINK!!!

Palms sweaty, Leiala instinctively took a deep breath and shifted her weight in her seat. She knew she needed to calm down if she had any hope of recalling the answer- the hysteria building in her chest would do her no favors.

You don't know. How could you not *know? This is English- you're* supposed *to be good at this subject. Maybe you're going downhill...maybe you're not as good at reading as you thought you were. You probably lost your touch- or maybe this was never a strength. Maybe all of your success up until now has been a coincidence. Oooh- after a poor grade on this quiz, no one will* ever *think you're smart- you'll be exposed for what you really are: dumb. You can't let that happen! What do you think will become of you if you lose your perceived intelligence? What will Mom and Dad say? They'll be so disappointed. They'll fake it, and pretend they're proud of your "best effort"- whatever that means- but you know they'll be upset. They have to keep you, because they're good parents, but they won't want to. Especially after that lousy performance in that soccer game over the weekend- how could you have missed that shot? And since you're not pretty and slim like the other girls, you need to make up for it by at least being smart and athletic.*

No? Still nothing? Leiala!! You can't afford to fail. Think of something- anything- to protect you from this potential travesty.

Look at the questions again- maybe there will be a clue to help you. Think. Think!

Oh...Jason's quiz. It's sitting there. Right there, easy to peek at. It wouldn't even really be cheating, the way he has it pushed to the side, so easy to read. It would almost be his *fault if someone cheated off of him- he's practically waving the answers around for everyone to see! Just one glance, and you might remember. It's not cheating if you take a quick peek to jog your memory.*

That's it....bingo! See? There was no danger in that, and you remembered everything! Another perfect score coming your way, Leiala- well done. That was a close call, but you preserved your reputation.

Relief flooded through Leiala as her memory came back to her, and with it, the answers to the reading quiz. Her pulse slowed and her heated palms turned cool and clammy as she neatly printed the answers (complete with detailed explanations that Jason had not included on *his* quiz) onto her paper. Tucking her hair behind her ear, she worked diligently, no visible sign of distress present. But with the relief had come a new feeling: a squirming, slimy feeling of discomfort and guilt. She might have dodged an unfortunate quiz grade, but at what cost?

***

Pneuma watched Leiala carefully, waiting for just the right moment to step in. Fear, Anxiety, Logic, and Panic were crowded around the little girl; Comfort and Peace held back by Abaddon's workers in the way that had become standard practice.

Time.

It was a gentle whisper, little more than a dandelion seed tossed in the wind, but Pneuma was more in tune with these quiet promptings than anyone else on earth, and the message from Theos was received clear as a bell. In a single swoop, he approached the scene unfolding below.

***

Comfort stood anxiously watching Leiala beat herself up. She fidgeted uncomfortably, her distress clear for all the characters to see. Abaddon's workers were unmoved by this display of compassion: they didn't so much as look Comfort's way. They stood rooted in position, barring both Comfort and Peace from nearing Leiala.

Comfort felt frustrated, but she didn't know what to do. This was typical now: Comfort was used to Abaddon's workers' presence. It wasn't her job to strategize or take inventory of the bigger picture, but she had enough experience to know that Leiala was too heavily serviced from certain characters- she was not maturing in a balanced manner. This upset Comfort, who was kept from reaching her full potential in Leiala. And yet it wasn't her battle to fight- all she could do was continue to show up and hope that she would be allowed to access Leiala, and to make sure her interactions with the girl counted when she was allowed to approach. Abaddon's workers were polite enough; gruff but not aggressive or rude- but Comfort hadn't given them any reason to behave otherwise.

Comfort hadn't discussed her thoughts with the other characters assigned to Leiala, but could tell by their body language and demeanor that they felt similarly. There weren't any amateurs assigned to Leiala- all the characters involved were experienced professionals that should have been able to cultivate healthy complexity in the girl.

Pneuma's sudden appearance jolted Comfort from her thoughts. Comfort's first reaction was shock: Pneuma had certainly visited Leiala before, but rarely in moments such as these, when certain characters were held back from influencing her. In fact, Comfort couldn't recall a time when Pneuma had visited the girl with Abaddon's workers present- a thought that was affirmed by the surprise that registered on Abaddon's workers' faces.

Pneuma was not intimidating in stature, but his presence was matched only by Theos and Yeshua- one look at Pneuma, and Abaddon's two workers backed away. For a moment, they took it all in: Pneuma, Leiala, and the menagerie of characters- but then they disappeared. Pneuma never so much as glanced at them.

Comfort looked hesitantly at Peace, whose face mirrored her own surprise. The two characters waited, unsure of how to proceed. Pneuma walked with steady, deliberate steps to Leiala, and for a moment, all the characters froze in awe of Pneuma's pervasive presence. Pneuma never appeared flustered, rushed, or in a hurry- but he never dawdled, either. He was intentional, focused, and confident- Comfort never tired of watching him work. As he moved forward, he acknowledged Comfort and Peace with a quick nod that somehow communicated that their presence would be welcomed, needed even, but not quite yet.

Without any words or gestures, Fear, Panic, Logic, and Anxiety backed away from Leiala, making a clear path for Pneuma. This was how it usually worked when one of the three approached, so significant was their appearance. Comfort watched in awe as Pneuma leaned over Leiala, whispering in her ear as he wrapped his powerful arms around her body in a warm embrace.

***

It was two minutes until recess, and Leiala's thoughts were far from the teacher's instructions. Ever since she'd cheated on the quiz, she hadn't been able to focus: she'd traded one problem for another as she'd evaded a failing grade but had inherited a new sense of insecurity and fear at having cheated. The guilt was overbearing, a loud distraction from any new learning or thinking.

You're okay.

It was a simple thought, but it landed on her parched soul like water in the Sahara desert. She clung to this thought firmly, prepared to fight against the onslaught of negative thoughts and logic that were certain to follow such an optimistic sentiment.

You're okay, and you will be okay.

Leiala let the words sink in, surprised by the lack of rebuttal. How could she be okay? She'd just cheated on a test! But the words hadn't been misspoken, and they weren't conditional: they said that she *was* okay, right then. No strings attached. No conditions. Leiala's mind quieted, a real rarity, and she felt her body relax. She hadn't been aware of her tensed muscles and shallow breathing, but this new sensation was most welcome. Perhaps it hadn't been that big of a deal- she'd only glanced at Jason's quiz to help her to remember. That was't really cheating, was it?

You know what you need to do.

Leiala exhaled sharply, her hope deflated. Just when she'd thought she'd caught a break...

You don't have to do it. But you know it's the right thing to do. This isn't who you are, Leiala.

I know it's not! Leiala shouted back in her mind. *I won't do it again*, she bargained, her hopeful thought floating into space like an untethered helium balloon.

I hope not. But that doesn't fix this current situation.

It doesn't hurt anybody, Leiala argued angrily, her ego thankful to battle someone other than herself. Her pent-up anxiety was more than ready to take on an opponent. *No one is affected by my mistake, and it's just easier to leave things as they are. I've learned my lesson, and I won't do it again.*

No one gets hurt? YOU get hurt, Leiala. No one else might suffer, but you will. You don't really want to take that on.

Leiala's heart raced. Just when she'd thought she'd caught a break...

The bell rang, and Leiala jumped. Her tongue felt thick and heavy in her mouth, and her limbs felt weighted like bricks. As her classmates poured out of the classroom, she lingered in her seat, searching for the words to say.

I'll help you. You can do this.

Leiala prepared to lash out, to remind this voice that he wasn't always there to help, to list the numerous blunders she'd committed all on her own, but her resolve deflated. She wasn't sure what kind of help she'd receive, but she wouldn't turn any down. Unsure of what she might say, Leiala pushed herself out of her seat and walked to her teacher, who was wiping down the board in the front of the classroom.

"Mrs. Farmer?"

The teacher turned and smiled down on her attentive, well-behaved student. Afraid she might lose her nerve, Leiala pressed on,

"I cheated on the quiz," she blurted, not daring to look Mrs. Farmer in the eyes. "I couldn't remember what happened in the last chapter, and I looked at Jason's quiz. I saw his answer, and I remembered, and- well- I don't deserve a perfect score."

The words tumbled out, somersaulting over each other in a race towards the finish line. Once they were spoken, Leiala felt a ten-pound weight lift off of her chest. She had done her part. Surprised at how good she felt, she realized it didn't even matter what Mrs. Farmer said in response- she had done what she needed to do. Looking now into Mrs. Farmer's eyes, she was met with affection and respect- two things Leiala had not been expecting.

"Thank you for your honesty, Leiala," Mrs. Farmer said gently after a thoughtful pause. "That took courage to come and tell me that. You're a good student, and a good reader. I think we'll let you keep that perfect score."

Leiala opened her mouth to protest, but Mrs. Farmer shook her head softly in a way that told Leiala any protests would be futile. Leiala felt her heart swell with gratitude and thankfulness towards Mrs. Farmer. She wasn't a failure! She hadn't destroyed her reputation! She'd admitted the truth to Mrs. Farmer, and her teacher still thought she was a good reader- a good student, even!

You are loved. You are always loved. You don't earn love.

Leiala felt warm inside, and her heart bulged. Her earlier fears and anxieties banished, she felt light as she hugged her teacher and skipped out to recess. Could it really have been that easy?

***

“Well done,” Yeshua acknowledged at Pneuma’s return.

“It wasn’t difficult. She’s responsive,” Pneuma offered humbly.

“She listens well for now,” Yeshua agreed. “But if Abaddon keeps crowding us out with all his noise, that may prove to become more difficult.”

“That was a lasting thought pattern,” Theos interjected, shifting the conversation back to the episode that had just taken place. “That will have impact on Leiala in the years to come. I daresay that was more powerful than a dozen of Abaddon’s encounters.”

“And Abaddon has certainly made dozens upon dozens of encounters,” Yeshua cut in. “I’m glad you made that interaction count.”

“Abaddon won’t be happy,” Theos went on. “We should expect increased presence from his workers.”

“Are we going to defend Leiala and increase our presence as well?” Yeshua asked, surprise in his voice.

“Not necessarily,” Theos responded carefully. “I’m hoping we won’t need to make a big play this early. But an increased presence would be wise.”

“I’ll let the workers know,” Yeshua said at once, eager to protect their beloved charge.

***

“What happened?” Abaddon asked the second his workers returned.

“Pneuma,” the first worker sputtered, unable to articulate anything more coherent.

“Yes, I know,” Abaddon replied irritably. “What I don’t know is *why* he came.”

“We don’t know, either,” the worker answered, shaking his head in bewilderment.

“Should we have stayed?” the second worker asked meekly, anticipating a verbal lashing- or worse- from his master.

“No- not necessarily,” Abaddon responded thoughtfully, deep in thought. “I don’t want to do anything rash yet- what I want to know is what Theos is up to.”

“What should we do?” the worker pressed, eager to please Abaddon.

“Watch carefully,” Abaddon responded curtly, casting a meaningful gaze at the two. “Don’t be so quick to leave. You don’t need to interfere, but take note. We need to learn what they’re up to.”

“Yes, sir,” the worker replied, overeager.

Abaddon rolled his eyes dismissively, and the two workers fled his presence. Left alone for a moment, Abaddon considered the scenario once more. He’d had uninterrupted access to Leiala-Theos, Pneuma, and Yeshua had visited Leiala too, but had not yet competed for an audience. Today, that had changed. But *why*? What had been particularly important about that afternoon? Abaddon simultaneously felt anticipation and irritation flash through him: he was eager for a good sparring match, but only when he knew the cost. And what was it that had prompted Theos to interfere? Abaddon was determined to find out.

I never arrive uninvited. It's funny how you accuse me of this very action, when the reality couldn't be further from the truth. Despite what you might think, I'm a perfect gentleman. I court you slowly, test the waters with caution, and only proceed when I'm given the green light. You might not notice the plethora of cues, but whose fault is that?

It's true- I'm not a very polite houseguest. I'm quite yielding and flexible in the beginning- before I make it into your home, and even after I've first arrived- I'm skittish, easy to kick out. But after you've let me in, you see, after I've taken off my shoes and put my bags down and gotten a tour of your lovely home- well then, after you've given me something to drink and offered me a seat on your couch....then, it's not so easy to get me to leave.

You don't really seem to mind at first- you hardly even notice I've taken up residence. I don't make a lot of noise, I don't make a giant mess- I'm pretty considerate that way. But over time, I start to take a toll on you. I start to invade more of your rooms; I start to leave remnants of myself all over the place. My unwashed socks appear under your bed, toothpaste residue lines your sink and splotches your mirror, and dirty tea-stained mugs sit out on all your tables. It's gradual enough that sometimes you don't even notice- you can't even remember what your house used to look like, before I arrived.

And while I don't take up much of your energy in the beginning- not to say you were excited to see me, as humans rarely are, but you also didn't turn me away- I start to require more and more sustenance to live. Your windows go unwashed, and your bed stays unmade during my stay. I help myself to food in your pantry without asking for permission, and I often deplete reserves of your favorite foods. I wear out your best clothes and use your fine china and take the best spot on the couch- but by the time you realize that I've overstepped my boundaries, that **somehow** I've managed to become master of YOUR own house- you don't know how to get me to leave.

You try, of course. You yell at me and you push me and sometimes you even call in reinforcements. Sometimes I laugh at you, and stay right in my spot. You **really** think you're going to get me to hand over the remote to the television, when I'm splayed across your cushy leather couch, munching on kettle corn and drinking diet Coke? Other times I hide for a spell- it's easier to let you think you've been successful in ridding yourself of me...especially when you've called for backup. It's strangely satisfying to watch you celebrate your supposed victory, only to discover minutes-hours-days later that I never left at all.

After a while, you give up. Every human does. You don't want to keep bothering your friends, who might think you're wishy-washy or unconsolable or even just annoying in your neediness. It's embarrassing to you. You read books and watch programs and seek counsel- but it's never successful. You wanted a life without me? Well, you should have thought about that before you opened the front door! I'm no capricious character- I don't appreciate change. I'll stay with you just as long as I possibly can...perhaps that should bring you some comfort.

In a world that changes by the second, a world where rules are made and then broken, principles discovered and then disproved, I'm a constant. People will leave you and fail you and break you, but I won't. I'll never leave you. And I have no interest in breaking you- I just choose to feed off of you. For all your worries about appearing needy, it's me who's needy. I NEED you to live, you see. My sustenance is your emotion. I can't survive without you- I need your shelter, your protection, the good food in your home and your comfortable bed to sleep in at night. It's not my concern that your home is overcrowded, that you don't have enough food for both of us, or that you sleep in a twin-size bed. I think you know who will, over time, end up sleeping on the floor.

I'm sorry it's hard and uncomfortable down there. I'm sorry there's only stale bread and half a jar of peanut butter left in the kitchen. Sorry that you can barely make it down the hallway without sneezing and coughing from the dust and the grime. I really am sorry- just not sorry enough to leave. I don't know what else to say- but- you should have thought all of this through before you opened the door to me in the first place.

-Despair

-5-

Leiala sat expectantly in her chair, waiting for her name to be called.

"Christine. Blake. Samantha," Leiala's English teacher announced, walking around the room as he distributed graded exams.

"Well done, Leiala," the teacher praised as he paused in front of Leiala's desk. "I'd like to keep yours as a sample for future classes, if you're okay with it," he added. The words were spoken in a soft tone, meant only for Leiala's ears, but Leiala squirmed with pleasure as her classmates overheard the accolade and eyed Leiala with envy. Leiala couldn't keep the excited smile from spreading across her face, but she was careful to control her response.

"Of course," she replied sweetly in words that were carefully measured- not too rushed. If she were nonchalant but pleasant about the whole thing, people might assume that she was accustomed to these types of commendations. That was *exactly* what Leiala wanted. She reviewed her teacher's comments carefully, the loopy red scrawl praising her ability to infer the underlying tone of the passage and make powerful connections to classic literature. Now safe in the assurance that her exam had been expertly completed, Leiala read over her responses once more, admiring her own phrasing and ability to go deep within the text. She did this in an aloof manner; she didn't want to appear *too* interested.

Once she was satisfied, she set the exam to the side of her desk- leaving her space to work but keeping the perfect A+ in plain view of her classmates' wandering eyes. She herself took in a sea of B's and B-'s around her...solid work, but not quite up to her level.

Sitting straight in her chair, she was attentive and engaged for the rest of class. She was only too happy to answer questions about the plot and character development- in a way, it was her duty to share her *dazzling*, brilliant thoughts with her less-talented classmates. But nicely. It wasn't their fault that they weren't as smart as she was. Maybe they would improve from observing her example.

Before the second period bell rang, the teacher announced: "Next class, we'll begin our group project. Start thinking about who you might want to work with!"

A ringing C flat incited a mass exodus of students, but not before a number of them made their way to Leiala's desk.

"Leiala, do you want to work on the group project together?" one asked.

Leiala smiled and nodded, happy to help but even happier to be noticed and recognized as special. Her chest swelled with joy as a couple of the hopefuls were boys- now *that* was something new. No matter how hard she tried to play things cool, the opposite gender intimidated her. Maybe even terrified her. She would have to make sure she wore something special tomorrow- maybe something green to show off her hazel eyes. Who knew what might happen working in a small group for fifty minutes?

***

Third period brought more good news- Leiala received her second perfect score of the day, this time on a math test.

"We had one perfect score on the unit test," Mr. Sparks announced, winking in Leiala's direction. "I think Leiala's established herself as the one to beat," he added playfully, referencing Leiala's string of perfect scores.

"Seriously?" Brandon muttered, shaking his head at Leiala. "You're making the rest of us look bad," he griped.

When Mr. Sparks called her name, Leiala straightened her shoulders and retrieved her test, perfecting her humble-yet-grateful demeanor as she accepted her exam.

"I'd like to talk with you after class, Leiala," Mr. Sparks muttered as he passed Leiala her test. Leiala smiled easily and raised her eyebrows agreeably as she nodded her head.

***

Thirty-five minutes later, Leiala stood in front of Mr. Sparks's desk, textbooks balanced on her left hip as she waited for one of her classmates to wrap up his conversation with the well-liked teacher.

"That was a challenging test," Mr. Sparks stated when the boy had left. He took his glasses off with one hand and leaned on the edge of his desk, hands clasped casually as he looked at Leiala seriously.

Leiala blushed with pleasure but didn't respond. What was she supposed to say? That it wasn't that challenging to her? She didn't want to insult Mr. Sparks- she really enjoyed his class, and she thought he was a fantastic teacher. She glanced up shyly at him, hoping he would get to the point.

"I don't think you're being challenged enough in this class," Mr. Sparks went on. Leiala's heartbeat quickened. This was a compliment, to be sure- a *huge* compliment- but it also hinted at a change. She wasn't quite sure how she felt about change- most of the time, it frightened her. Change meant something untested, unknown. It meant a lack of predictability and a lack of control- two things that Leiala worked very hard to protect.

"I've talked to the school counselor about moving you into my fifth period math class- advanced Algebra. You'd be with the seventh graders, but with the mastery you've been showing on our foundational concepts, this shouldn't be too much for you. You'd have to change PE classes, but the counselor assured me that such a change was possible. Of course, this decision is up to you. I just wanted to put the option out there, and give you time to think about it. Obviously, it's better to make any changes sooner rather than later. Talk it over with your parents and let me know," Mr. Sparks finished.

"Thank you," Leiala sputtered gratefully. The words seemed flimsy considering the giant honor Mr. Sparks had just bestowed on her, but she couldn't think of what else to say. "I'll definitely think about it and talk it over with my parents."

"Good. Now, do you need a pass? You've only got another two minutes to make it to your next class," Mr. Sparks pointed out as he rubbed his glasses on the corner of his shirt, put them on, and glanced at the clock on the wall.

"I think I can make it," Leiala said cheerfully, moving towards the door. A quick wave, a smile from her teacher, and she was gone.

Buoyed by such a stellar morning, Leiala had enviable confidence during Science class and was more outgoing than usual as she sat with her small group of friends eating lunch.

"What did you get on the math test?" Kelly asked, opening a bag of goldfish. Leiala waited patiently for the rest of the group to answer. She was delighted Kelly had asked the question- she couldn't wait to announce her perfect score- but she didn't want to give this away. It was much cooler to *wait*, to feign indifference.

In her intelligent group of friends, the majority had received A's, with a couple of B's.

"Leiala got a perfect score," Becky announced for Leiala, a playful smirk on her face. Becky knew Leiala better than anyone- and she would have guessed the game that Leiala was playing.

"Again?" Tracy asked, eyebrows raised in surprise. "That's three in a row now, Leiala."

Tracy, Leiala's other best friend, was just as competitive as Leiala. While she would never admit as much, Leiala knew her perfect scores irritated Tracy.

"Geeze, Leiala," Kelly complained. "I know who I'm studying with next time!"

Leiala almost spoke up to tell Kelly that might not be an option, but stopped herself. Becky noticed Leiala's hesitation and called her on it.

"What?" she asked.

"*What*?" Leiala repeated dumbly.

Becky rolled her eyes and gave Leiala a knowing look.

"What's that look for? You're holding something back," Becky accused as she bit into her sandwich.

"I don't know. Mr. Sparks wants me to change classes," Leiala told them. There was no pretense at this point- a fact that her friends were quick to pick up on. She really didn't know what she was going to do- she was so flattered by Mr. Sparks's suggestion, and of course was tempted to enter the more challenging class, but she also worried that it might be *too* challenging, that she might be in over her head.

"What class does he want you to go to?" Tracy asked. Leiala knew there was envy buried in Tracy's words, but she was too good of a friend to show it. She might have been competitive, but she also cared deeply for her friend.

"Fifth period. With the seventh graders," Leiala told the group.

"He wants you to *skip* a grade?!" Kelly blurted incredulously.

"I know," Leiala intoned, agreeing with the unspoken thoughts her friends' expressions effortlessly communicated. This was unheard of- they didn't know anyone who had skipped a grade.

"Wow." Becky was the first to respond. "That's a big deal, Leiala."

Leiala smiled gratefully at her best friend. She could always count on Becky to respond without judgment, and to let her come to her own decision. Becky was a top student, too- but somehow missed the competitive gene that Leiala and Tracy both shared.

"What are you going to do?" Tracy wanted to know.

"I don't know," Leiala responded truthfully. "I'm worried how hard it might be."

"Hard? Yeah right, Miss three-perfect-scores-in-a-row," Kelly teased, rolling her eyes in mock exasperation. "I think you should go for it. Who knows? You might end up sitting next to a cute seventh grade boy." These last words were spoken with reverence- in Kelly's mind, there could be no greater honor.

***

After school, Leiala couldn't wait to share the news with her mom. She sat quietly in the car on the way home from carpool, envisioning the surprise and pleasure she anticipated to find on her mother's face when she shared the exciting proposition.

"Hi Honey! How was your day?" Mom asked, looking up from the kitchen table as her firstborn daughter walked in. Leiala noticed her younger siblings had started their homework for the evening as they enjoyed apple slices slathered in peanut butter.

"I had a good day," Leiala smiled. "I got a perfect score on the English test, and my math test, too," she announced proudly. "And Mr. Sparks had me stay after class to talk to me- he thinks I'm doing so well that he wants to move me to his advanced Algebra class. He wants me to *skip* a grade." The words shot out of her mouth like moths to an open light, but Leiala slowed down to emphasize the final part. Her mother raised her eyebrows and pulled her head back in surprise.

"Wow! That sounds like a big honor, Leiala," her mom congratulated her. Leiala smiled, drinking in every subtle sign of pride her mother showed. Had she made her mom proud? Was she special? Worthy of love? This update made her think the answer was yes.

"Is Dad home yet?" Leiala asked, knowing already that it was unlikely. Now that she'd seen Mom's reaction, she was eager to share the news again, to receive a second dose of that validation and affirmation.

"Not yet," Mom told her. "But wait! I want to hear more about what happened."

Leiala smiled, shrugged her backpack off, and sat down at the kitchen table. Relay every detail about her stellar day? Oh, why not?

***

"How does it feel to have a day off?" Panic joked to Fear.

Fear shook his head, at a loss of how to respond. He'd had so few days off that he found that he didn't know what to do with himself- he'd ended up bumbling around headquarters aimlessly. He felt irritated- he'd wasted a perfectly good day- but he'd been on edge the entire time, sure that he'd be summoned any moment. After all, he was Leiala's most loyal character, the one that spent the most time with her. It was rare and unprecedented to go an entire day without visiting at least once.

"I know, I know- the day's not done yet," Panic added before Fear could say anything.

"It's certainly unusual," Fear said gruffly.

"I noticed Abaddon's workers were still in full force, even for a good day," Panic went on.

Fear nodded curtly but didn't say anything. He didn't want to encourage Panic- he wanted him to leave, to stop verbalizing all the things Fear had noticed and was now trying to catalog. Abaddon's workers *had* been in full force, and Fear had witnessed some interesting character combinations that day: Joy and Pride had been the main attractions, with cameo appearances from Attribution, Superiority, and Entitlement. Fear had stood off in the wings, relegated to the bench as a third-party observer when he had grown accustomed to center stage. It wasn't that he was irritated that his presence wasn't required- he knew that to be standard practice for all characters. It was that he couldn't surmise what it all meant.

He had seen Abaddon work hard to keep Leiala in a place of self-doubt and insecurity...he couldn't understand the sudden transition to achievement. He knew Abaddon to be intentional and crafty- there was no way this was an accident. But what did it mean?

~6~

Leiala chewed on the inside of her lip anxiously. The winter dance was still three weeks away, but it held the center of attention in Leiala's mind. Now that she was in middle school, she felt very grown up, sophisticated even. There hadn't been any school dances in elementary school, and the boys hadn't taken too much interest in the girls. Leiala had a feeling that was about to change. Amanda had been asked to the dance during lunch that day in a very public display of roses and a glittery poster. Leiala had taken it all in with hawkish eyes: Amanda's blush of embarrassment but also pleasure as she tucked her chestnut hair back behind her ear and dug her hands into the pockets of her cut-off denim jeans. The boy who had asked her was another sixth grader Leiala only knew by reputation: but he was cute, tall, and athletic. Nothing else really mattered, did it?

The asking had been the talk of the school for the entire afternoon, with every girl hopeful that she might be the next to be asked in an extravagant manner. Some girls pretended not to care, but Leiala felt sure this was just to cover their own personal insecurities and fear that they might not get asked. The boys may have been oblivious, but romantic whimsy was thick in the air, and Leiala could not help but notice the increased hair flips, lip-gloss applications, and airy giggles that came from her classmates. She herself looked around with new eyes, taking in the boys in her classes. There were always the boys that *all* the girls liked- but now she looked hard for other prospects, boys who might not catch every girl's eye but who were contenders nonetheless.

All of it was terribly exciting to Leiala. She didn't have many male friends- and by *many* she meant *none*- and her experience of the opposite gender was limited to what she had been able to learn from her younger brothers- hardly the ideal subjects to study. And while she didn't have any reason or hope to suspect that some boy might ask her to the dance, the hopeless romantic in her desperately wished for there to be some dashing young man who had taken notice of her- one who was already busy plotting his grand romantic gesture to ask Leiala to the dance. These were hopes she never shared, of course- how mortifyingly embarrassing to admit to such ridiculousness- but they were nestled in the very deepest recesses of her heart.

In the mornings, she selected her outfits a bit more carefully, brushing her hair until it shone. She curled her hair once that week- not too often, then her antics would have been obvious- but her friends had noticed and she hoped that some of the boys had, too. She'd brought out her darkest hue of lipgloss (her parents were of the firm belief that adolescent girls should not wear makeup, leaving this as her only option), and she'd forked over precious allowance funds for a glittery, tropical body spray from Bath & Body Works.

She had to be noticed now, right? She knew she wasn't the prettiest girl in her classes- there were plenty of popular girls with creamy skin and long, slender limbs that hinted at the trim bodies hidden underneath their Abercrombie & Fitch gear (bodies that they didn't work for, Leiala noted with frustration, considering her own healthy diet and frequent exercise that somehow hadn't transformed her body into a stick-like build)- but she hoped now that someone would notice her. She worked hard in school and got excellent grades, and was athletic- she was proud that she could run as fast and complete as many sit-ups as most of the boys in her PE class. She was also kind, and thoughtful- surely these were qualities that the boys had noticed, right?

On Tuesday, a giant banner hung over the entry to the school, asking Meredith to the dance. On Wednesday, Julia was asked to the dance by a seventh grade boy who wrote a song and sang it to her in the middle of the quad. On Thursday, Stefanie was surprised by a sixth grader who made a public announcement over the school's intercom system. On Friday, Alexa was asked by a sixth grader who had written "WIll you go to the dance with me?" on his stomach using paint- he lifted his shirt during PE class in a show of bravado that was quickly quashed by the administration, but not before Alexa had a chance to say yes.

Later that day, Leiala watched as her classmate Margo received a single flower in every afternoon class- at the end of the day, her suitor waited outside the classroom door with a giant teddy bear. For every grand gesture, there were countless small acts- boys who asked girls in cute or nondescript ways that evaded the public eye. Leiala, like many of the other girls, loved hearing these stories- she loved the long, detailed versions that highlighted the unexpected nature of the asking, the romance, the effort it had taken the boy to ask. Every nuance seemed to scream, "You are worth it! You are special. I've noticed YOU, and I think YOU are the most special girl." It was enough to make any girl swoon.

Leiala listened to these stories reverently, graciously asking the right questions that helped the chosen girl to linger on her special moment. She genuinely felt excitement for each girl- what a wonderful thing, to be noticed- and she waited patiently for her turn to come.

One week until the dance, and conversations had shifted to dance attire- discussions centered around the "colors" each date had chosen for the event, dress styles, and speculation over what type of corsage the date might select. Groups were created for the pre-dance dinners out, and Leiala even heard of a couple of parties that were to take place after the dance. By now, most of the girls had been asked- and some resorted to attending with a male friend just to get the full "dance" experience.

Leiala had not been asked, nor was there any hint that she might be. She still dressed each day with the thought that someone might take notice of her that day, but without much expectation. She daydreamed, but scolded herself for doing so. She could be logical, and she knew that at this point, any invitation was highly unlikely. But she couldn't give up hope, could she? She was an avid reader, and how many of her favorite novels had featured heroines who were swooped up and romanced in the eleventh hour? That was the way it happened, and it could still happen for her!

That final week leading up to the dance, she studied the girls who had been asked- studied their appearance, their demeanor, their dress- what did they have that she didn't? It had to be scientific, procedural- Leiala figured there had to be some common denominator amongst the *asked*. They were all thin, Leiala thought, and they were pretty. No pimples- but some had braces- and not all of them were curvy. Most wore form-fitting clothing with casual anklets and chain necklaces- and most wore makeup. This Leiala had no control over, nor was she willing to engage in some of the flirtatious or reckless behavior that some of the girls were known for. But she *could* mirror their hairstyles, and the style of clothing they wore. And she could strive to mold her body into the rail-thin figures she so admired.

***

"She's spinning like a top," Comfort groused, sinking into the cafeteria chair beside Fear. "I don't know how she can keep up her exhausting pace."

Fear nodded at Comfort in what he hoped was polite acknowledgement as he struggled to swallow his mouthful of food.

"She's working, working, working, and thinking, thinking, thinking, but so little of it's productive," Comfort went on. "And since I'm not allowed to interfere, it's just getting worse."

Fear listened politely and wondered what to say. It was true, Comfort hadn't been allowed much access to Leiala- neither had Grace or Perspective. Instead, Fear had watched, fascinated, as Envy and Judgment shadowed Logic's every move. Leiala had been exposed to Logic early on, but now her interactions with him were flavored with the added presence of Envy and Judgment- and only a fool could miss the impact this had made on Leiala. Leiala's "logic" was becoming less and less so- she was starting to adopt an unhealthy perspective and expectation. Fear had noticed with interest that this had cultivated a curious sort of drive in Leiala- not something he'd seen before. To be sure, Leiala's experiences would be ones written up in textbooks- already Fear had witnessed a number of unusual phenomena that he knew would be documented for the benefit of new characters.

Fear realized the effect he had on Leiala; he'd noticed the change he aroused. Leiala was perceptive and intuitive, by most accounts, a human sponge. Fear had noticed with distaste that he was often summoned along with Judgment at these moments of reflection-as Leiala considered the world around her, she took in a substantial amount of fear and judgment. From this, Fear had seen different reactions. Common reactions included despair, a sense of hopelessness, frustration, despondency...Fear was familiar with them all. But Leiala didn't respond that way. Fear wasn't sure if it was her drive for achievement or perhaps her need for acceptance or possibly even a fear of Fear- but Leiala came alive in these moments when he visited her.

The first time Leiala had responded this way, Fear had been taken aback- the second time, he had studied Leiala closely, curious to learn if she experienced any other character before transitioning to action. As it would turn out, she did- as soon as the slightest hint of fear crept into her awareness, she short-circuited into panic mode, relied on Logic for a quick solution, and threw herself into action working to make that solution a reality. It was quite fascinating to watch, actually- the transitions took place so quickly that they'd be missed by anyone not carefully studying Leiala's behavior. It was impressive and productive, but Fear wondered where the other emotions were being stored. Even with Abaddon's workers running interference on some of the characters' visits, he knew Leiala to be more complex than she was showing. The question was: would this significantly alter Leiala? Would she develop into a balanced, healthy young lady? It wasn't Fear's place to worry, but he did.

***

"It's the night of the dance."

It was a comment, not a question, and it lay awkwardly, suspended in the air like clothes on a line. No one bothered to discern who made the comment, but it was Yeshua who responded.

"When do you plan to visit?" Yeshua asked Pneuma, who had looked heavy-hearted for most of the afternoon. "This is going to be a painful night for her."

"Soon," Penuma answered vaguely, but without any dismissive quality to his tone. "Theos will know when the time is right."

Theos nodded grimly, and Yeshua's jaw set in a firm line. It was interesting, how much they all cared for the humans, their children. At any given moment, they managed billions of human souls, all ripe and overwrought with real, raw emotion. By the human standard, Leiala's troubles were woefully insignificant: an eleven year old girl without a date to the school dance. But they weren't in the business of judging by the world's standards, and this wasn't any ordinary girl. This was *Leiala*. Leiala, an eleven year old girl who felt crushed by a pervasive sense of insignificance and unworthiness. Abaddon had done his work well: Leiala felt the brunt of society's false expectations and had judged herself harshly. Her perspective had gone askew, and she didn't know it. The heaviness of his heart towards Leiala was profound, and his only consolation was that Pneuma experienced the extent of this emotion through him. As if reading his mind, Pneuma slipped away and down to earth, to Leiala.

***

Leiala swallowed each bite of food, the substance thick in her throat. She cut her food into small square bites with her fork, spearing each bite and then navigating it up and towards her mouth with mechanical gestures. She was quiet, thoughtful, and subdued- she didn't add much to the dinner conversation, but she worked to make her face pleasant enough in the hopes that she'd avoid suspicion. As the oldest of four children, this was sometimes successful: in the organized bedlam their household frequently represented, she could escape notice for little chunks of time.

"Leiala? We haven't heard about your day," her mother cut in kindly. Her tone of voice made it clear to Leiala that she had not flown under the radar that evening- a quick glance up from her plate confirmed her suspicions: her mother's eyes were scrutinizing, her eyebrows arched high in an unspoken question.

"Not too much happened today," Leiala answered with forced optimism. Aware that she now also had her father's attention (and, to some degree, the attention of her younger siblings), she hit what she thought was the perfect level of animation. "It was kind of boring, actually. We had a quiz in English, we reviewed a test in Math, and we learned about sedimentary rocks in Science- I hate this unit," she added, aware that details made for a more convincing story. “Oh, and we started Scottish dancing in PE- have you ever heard of such a thing? We had to take our shoes off in the gym, and some of the boys had holes in their socks!” Leiala pushed herself to be upbeat and peppy- if she could pass muster here, she could afford to fall apart later, in private. But not if her mom suspected what she was up to. Thank GOODNESS she didn’t know about the school dance- there was no way her dad or siblings could know, either. Leiala cringed just to think about how the night might pass differently under those circumstances- for a brief moment, her placid smile sunk into a grimace.

“How big were the holes?” Tommy asked, raising one foot up onto his chair and unlacing his shoe.

“Tommy! Not at the dinner table,” Mom announced, gently nudging Leiala’s father.

“Tommy, keep your shoes on,” Dad pronounced with authority, and Tommy’s mischievous smile dissipated into disappointment.

“I bet I have a big hole in one of my socks,” he told them all seriously. Leiala smiled- this time, for real.

“I’m sure none of us doubt that, Tommy,” she teased, shaking her head.

***

An hour later, Leiala lay in bed, thoughts racing through her mind faster than a bullet train. She had made it through dinner- she’d eaten, helped wash dishes, and excused herself without anyone probing for further details. She’d lied and said she was tired when her family suggested they watch a movie to allow for some private time in her room.

Why wasn’t she wanted? Why didn’t anyone want to take *her* to the dance? Everyone else had been able to find a date!

Well, not *everyone*, Leiala chided herself. If she was going to have a pity party, she needed to at least carry it out with authenticity.

But she'd so hoped to be asked! She'd dared to dream that she might be swept off her feet- or maybe just get asked by a classmate. It wasn't even the dance itself that mattered so much- Leiala wasn't too fond of dancing, and if she were honest with herself, the thought of dancing in front of her peers brought on a whole new set of fears and insecurities- but it was the *asking* part that mattered. The *being wanted* part that mattered. She wanted to matter to someone that she didn't *have* to matter to- someone outside of her family members.

A single tear dribbled down Leiala's cheek miserably, taking its time in a slow, lethargic path that zig-zagged towards her nose and then down and away towards her mouth. But even before it had a chance to revel in company, the feeling passed. In its place, a cloak of peace blanketed Leiala. She felt warm, like a fire had been stoked deep in her belly. Her circumstances hadn't changed, and it still mattered that she didn't have a date to the dance, but with these stagnant facts of life came a new sense of peace. A certainty that as pitiful and unsavory as things seemed in that moment, it would be okay. In that singular moment, the depressive energy that had snowballed disintegrated, a snowball crashing without having met its intended mark. Overcome with gratitude, and exhausted from her flurry of emotions, Leiala snuggled into the folds of her pillow and stared into space. She would be okay. She *was* okay.

-7-

Leiala stood at the front of the small chapel, her hands raised as she poured her heart out in song. The past week had to have been one of the best of her life: never had she felt so accepted, so understood. And it had been fun! Up on the mountain with her best friend at camp, she'd spent the past five days ziplining, horseback riding, kayaking, splurging on milkshakes, talking into the wee hours with her cabin-mates, and engaging in epic games of lightsaber tag with the boys at midnight. Add to that the camaraderie of new friends and daily uplifting messages from the Bible and goodness, she felt as though she were floating through camp.

That particular morning, she'd elected to rise early (before most of the rest of the campers) to take the short hike up the hill to the quaint chapel. With only twelve pews encompassed by floor-to-ceiling windows, the chapel felt intimate and magical as the sun rose and shot rainbow prism patterns all across the robin's-egg blue carpeting. Leiala felt the sun's warmth on her closed eyelids and relished in the sensation- just like the sun waking the world to a new day, she felt herself awakened to new life, new purpose. She'd grown a lot even in just one week: her sense of purpose had been super-charged, and her self-awareness had been deeply touched as well. Here, at camp, she didn't feel like the shy Leiala, pigeon-holed into a reputation as a constant rule-follower and steady achiever. She felt fun, alive, daring! She'd been giddy over camp pranks, and edgy in her outfit choices on theme days. She'd taken risks on the zipline, and she'd questioned her fellow campers in their thinking as they somehow navigated their way through deep conversations even amidst such tomfoolery. The blood pulsing through her veins felt changed- it was different, somehow. Even a week's worth of lack of sleep couldn't keep

Leiala from belting the words to the worship songs at the top of her lungs- she was *on fire*!

***

"Do you have to?" Joy asked, looking over at Anxiety in annoyance.

"You've got to be kidding me," Anxiety shot back, an edge to his voice. "You've had full reign of Leiala nearly all week!"

"For the first time possibly EVER," Joy countered, not backing down. "You run Leiala's everyday life- let us at least have this moment. Take a vacation or something," she muttered.

Fear merely watched as the two squabbled. For his part, he'd been pretty idle all week- on standby in case a situation called for him. It hadn't. This place was curious- Fear hadn't experienced anything like it before. It was a Christian camp, one filled with multitudes of Theos's workers, but Abaddon had his presence there, too. Abaddon's minions mostly stayed on the fringe of any given scene, but they were always there, lurking about, ready to influence any individual if given the opportunity. Fear had noticed that their presence seemed to cling pervasively to certain individuals, while others appeared to be cloaked in joy and peace. Leiala had seem to shed layers of anxiety, fear, expectation, and judgment on her way up the mountain, and Fear wasn't sure he'd ever seen her so free. She seemed so happy- Fear felt guilty for his regular presence in her life. Was this how Leiala was supposed to be? She sure seemed to be the best version of herself...

No, Fear reminded himself. He'd been down this path before- worrying that his influence was a negative one; that his role was depressive and counter-productive to the development of an individual. He'd explored the concept far enough to know that this wasn't the case- without fear, individuals behaved dangerously, setting themselves up for failure. He was *important*- needed, even. So why didn't he feel good about the situation with Leiala?

It was because of a lack of balance, he decided. He visited Leiala disproportionately...he was supposed to influence Leiala and add an important dimension to her perspective. Abaddon's consistent presence banning other characters from flourishing with equal impact meant that Leiala made decisions largely through a lens of fear- he had become the focus, the key indicator as opposed to a contributor. It was fascinating, watching Leiala live differently- Fear hadn't seen this before, hadn't known Leiala was capable of living in such a way. He'd kept close, expecting his presence to be needed, but Leiala had been doing fine without him.

***

"We've let this go on too long," Abaddon groused, pacing back and forth in headquarters like a caged animal.

"What do you propose we do about it?" a loyal worker snarled, lips curled and body tense. This was the posture most of Abaddon's workers assumed- aggressive, restless positions that spoke of their need and desire to haunt, attack, and destroy.

"Infiltrate." The word wasn't spoken loudly, but with resolve and surety that made even Abaddon's workers shudder. There was prolonged silence as Abaddon's workers thought about how that might be accomplished.

"No takers?" Abaddon sneered, his giant head swiveling in rage to take in his thousands of workers.

"Theos's presence at the camp is strong," one of the workers spoke up. "It will take work," he added, lest his first words be interpreted as weakness.

"Yes," Abaddon agreed, turning his back on his workers. There was respectful silence as his workers waited for him to go on. He did not.

"I'll go," the same worker announced, anticipating the favor his willingness would generate with his master.

"I will, too," another announced, and a small multitude of workers volunteered in the moments that followed.

Another moment of silence, and then Abaddon turned around. His face was stern, his features contorted in a way that was horrifying even to his workers. His eyes seemed to glow with fire and spittle had collected in the corners of his mouth. Every ounce of his being seemed to scream of hunger, lust, and mercilessness.

"Theos will show up," Abaddon announced, his words frenzied and catatonic.

"He's been coming constantly, but He hasn't really done much," one worker pointed out. Everyone could tell by Abaddon's tone that he felt this would somehow be different.

"He will show up, and He will fight," Abaddon said with certainty, speaking more to himself than to anyone else. Looking up and over the faces of his expectant workers, he grimaced. "And so will we."

***

Pneuma twittered about anxiously, unable to rest. Yeshua and Theos waited patiently for Pneuma to speak, although they had already surmised what He might announce.

"He's going to fight us," Yeshua stated, watching Pneuma for a reaction.

"Yes. He's summoned quite an army," Pneuma confirmed. He looked up into the eyes of Yeshua and then Theos. As always, Pneuma seemed to convey so much information and communicate so much emotion without saying a word.

"We will fight back," Theos assured Pneuma. "This is our ground, and we will not let Abaddon claim victory over our children."

"Do we have enough support?" Yeshua asked. It was the question they were all wondering. "If Abaddon suspects we'll fight back, he'll be sure to assemble a great multitude."

"He already has," Theos said flatly. "Pneuma will have significant work to do." With a nod in Pneuma's direction, Theos turned to Yeshua.

"This will be the first big battle. We will win, but not easily. Abaddon won't take this loss lightly," Theos said sagely.

Yeshua nodded, frowning. There wasn't much joy in this situation, even knowing that the battle would be won. Yeshua knew that every battle came with a cost- renewed strength meant sacrifice, wisdom came from the experience of pain, and victory was birthed from death.

***

Pneuma hurried to the camp director, rousing him quickly. He didn't have the luxury of time- not now. The camp director woke with a start, glanced at the clock, and groaned. Pulling his pillow close, he tried to settle back into sleep, but Pneuma kept at it. Moments later, the director threw back the covers and sank to the side of the bed on his knees in frustration.

"What? What do you want?" he asked, rubbing the sleep from his eyes and yawning. Pneuma rejoiced and leaned in, whispering to the soft and ready heart. He watched as the director wriggled in discomfort and irritation, then settled in and focused. He absorbed what Pneuma relayed and began to pray.

Pneuma stayed for these first minutes, impressing upon the director the urgency and importance of the situation. When he was satisfied with the director's response, and the strength the director's prayers brought, Pneuma departed. On to the next individual, to communicate the importance of petitioning on behalf of the camp, to muster strength for the battle to come. Even with faithful and dedicated followers, this task was easier said than done- and Pneuma did not rest until he was confident the camp was covered in prayer. Now, to equip those who would be the direct marks- some of whom Abaddon had already targeted.

***

Leiala could not sleep. She'd gone to bed easily enough, exhausted from a full day's worth of activities. Her sleep had been contented and restful, a testament not only to the amount of time she'd spent in the sun but also the healing her heart had experienced in the days she'd spent at camp. Then, sometime in the middle of the night, she'd awoken with a start. She'd felt fear without a reason; she'd felt anxious with no rationale. Her heart pounded in her chest and it took her a moment to orient herself.

Camp. She was at camp. As her eyes blinked into the darkness, she saw the lumpy shapes of her cabin mates as they slept in bunks around the room. Her pulse raced and she searched for an explanation. *Had she had a frightening dream? Not that she could remember. Was there some present danger? A loud noise?* Her mind searched for answers, but came up short. *What time was it, anyway?* Leiala wondered without hope of receiving an answer. The blanketed darkness suggested it was the middle of the night- she'd been roused hours before she needed to be up.

Even before she nestled back into her sleeping bag, Leiala knew sleep was futile. Her body was wracked with tension and she was full of nervous energy.

Breathe. Slow, deep breaths, Leiala coached herself. She needed to slow her heartbeat, to calm herself down. Whatever had frightened her so, it didn't appear to be a danger anymore- but even as Leiala worked to convince herself of this logic, she didn't believe it. Something was amiss- she just couldn't discern *what.* She could try to fight the feeling and go back to sleep, but Leiala knew from experience this would end poorly. What could she do in these moments that wouldn't disturb the other girls in her cabin?

Make sure you run in the morning.

The thought materialized out of thin air, a shooting star rocketed through the ash-gray canvas of her mind. It surprised her, this seemingly random thought, but without any other thought to follow, Leiala indulged the brain trail.

You know, because you haven't worked out at all this week. You're going to get out of shape, and you're going to lose all of your fitness.

Leiala felt her heart speed up again. It was true- she'd been busy and active during the week, but she hadn't done any running. Would she lose her stamina that quickly?

You ate a milkshake, too. And you had pizza for dinner the other night. You need to work that off before you become fat.

True. So true. How could Leiala have overlooked these facts? Along with the anxiety and fear that continued to build, Leiala also felt anger towards herself. How presumptuous she had been! Did she really think she could just go to camp and let herself go? Eat junk food? Stop running? She was slightly incredulous at her lack of discipline- it wasn't like her. How had that happened? The feelings of fear increased exponentially. She would have to be more careful next time- that had been a close call! She was ***so*** lucky that she'd woken up in the middle of the night and realized that...what would have happened if she'd just slept on? She shuddered to think of the alternative.

At least you woke up early. You could have been lazy and slept in- now you'll be able to get back on track. You don't need to go back to sleep- you can just stay up and plan out your day. You can run early, before anyone wakes up. And you'll want to hurry, anyway- you don't want anyone to see you all gross and sweaty without makeup. ESPECIALLY not the boys. Can you imagine what they would think?! These girls seem to like you, too- but that's because they haven't seen the gross parts of you. That's good, Leiala! You've done a wonderful job guarding against that- they've seen the strong, lovely parts of you. We need to continue that.

Leiala's fear abated just a bit as gratitude to this unknown voice overcame her. *We*. They were a team. She didn't have to face the world alone. She would have someone to help her navigate these tricky situations, someone to prompt her when she might accidentally let her guard down. She was so thankful that this voice had alerted her to these potential disasters- with help, she could make sure no one saw those unsavory sides. And she had to agree there were *many* parts to her that she should work to cover- if she wanted to be loved and accepted, that was.

You're welcome. If you really want to earn the love and respect of your new friends, and the approval of your master, you should be sure to read your Bible for an hour this morning. Probably every morning. That's what good girls do. Good Christians. I mean, you might still be accepted if you don't, but you won't really deserve it. You don't want to be a freeloader, do you?

Leiala felt overcome with gratitude and shock. How had she been so blind? She was horrified at her ignorance, and thankful for this enlightenment. Now, she knew what to do. There was no alternative in Leiala's mind- now that the truth had been exposed, it was her job to make sure it was executed. *That was such a close call*, she breathed, her tense body rolling over in her sleeping bag. Her mind traveled to the activities she'd taken part in and the food she'd eaten; in her head, she worked out a spreadsheet of supposed calories taken in and energy expended. Was she safe? Or in the danger zone? It was hard to know.

Laying still in her sleeping bag, Leiala tried to take inventory of how her body felt. Did her hip bones protrude far enough? Her thighs seemed to rub together- that wasn't good. Leiala chided herself for not paying enough attention to these things. This was what happened when she let go- her life was ruined. She couldn't trust anyone but herself- and she needed to be vigilant in setting boundaries and following through with them in order to stay safe. She could keep herself safe. *They* could keep her safe. She hadn't done a good job the past days, but she would make up for that this morning. She would wake early, run far and hard, and watch everything she ate. *Just fruits and vegetables*, Leiala thought happily. That would get her back on track. *Safe*. You're going to be safe, Leiala assured herself before falling back asleep.

-8-

No matter how many times Fear visited the east end of headquarters, he couldn't get used to the vibe. A cluster of Abaddon's workers paced up and down the hallway, backs hunched over as they lunged their way down the corridor. One look in their eyes, and the torment was easy to read: each worker possessed a hunted, anguished expression. The first time Fear had ventured to Abaddon's domain, he'd been a new character, untested and naive. He'd been disturbed by the faces of the workers he'd passed- he'd assumed he'd somehow stumbled into some unfortunate and troublesome situation. Now, years later, he knew these expressions to be permanent fixtures plastered on the faces of Abaddon's followers- and it had nothing to do with any given situation and everything to do with temperament. Everything was miserable in the eyes of Abaddon's realm. Even after centuries of experience, Fear still felt unsettled when he ventured east.

Keeping his head down, Fear walked steadily towards the strategics room. He'd been summoned to this particular meeting, one he knew to be important, judging by the list of attendees. He wasn't certain of the topic, other than that it involved Leiala. As a general rule, Fear didn't reject meeting invitations- despite the stereotype that went along with his character, he was generally an affable, easy-going guy. But he had considered rejecting this invitation. He felt uncomfortable with the role he'd been asked to take in Leiala's life, and he knew for a fact that his presence and influence on her had grown exponentially. He didn't want to be a part of any new measures to take this further, and he would have gracefully bowed out...if the invite hadn't come straight from Abaddon himself.

This had never happened before. Abaddon didn't send out invitations. To be quite frank, Fear had been stunned to see the familiar letters blinking on the face of his device. He'd closed the program and opened it once more, sure that the email would disappear. It did not. At that point, Fear had inspected the invitation more closely, scrutinizing every aspect of text for a sign of tomfoolery. There hadn't been any- and at that point, Fear had started to sweat, living up to his name in feeling.

The way Fear saw it, he had no choice but to attend. Even if the notification was in fact a mistake, Fear didn't think he could risk it- if the invitation did turn out to be authentic, there'd be no redemption from Abaddon. Fear had shuddered just imagining what the consequence might be should he take such a bold, dismissive action. He'd thought then of Theos, marveling at how differently He operated.

Theos never sent electronic messages- He preferred to personalize each note. There was never any confusion when Theos sent a message, although Fear had yet to receive such an invitation. He'd watched enviously as others had received the creamy milk-white envelopes, golden calligraphy emblazoned on the front of the envelope, and a thick puddle of red wax sealing the back. Everything about Theos's invitations screamed intentionality- both words and details were carefully, thoughtfully addressed. The ink was permanent, the words resolute. Theos would stand behind his words and intentions.

Abaddon, not so much. Fear had never been invited to attend one of his meetings, either- but he could have lived without that honor. His thoughts raced, and he was thankful the thunder of his heartbeat could not be heard as he neared the appointed room. He couldn't see a positive outcome for this meeting: was he walking into an ambush? Would he be attacked, set up for failure, or asked to do more? He didn't like any option that passed through his mind.

Nearing the entryway, Fear took a deep breath. Mercifully, he hadn't gotten lost, even navigating this new part of headquarters. He was thankful he'd arrived early- he planned to slip into the back of the room and settle into a seat that would keep him far from the center of attention.

His steps slowed, and he instinctively rubbed the palms of his hands on the front of his shirt. Then, before he allowed himself to worry anymore, Fear pushed the door open.

***

Abaddon glanced around the room, taking in the faces of those he'd summoned for this meeting. There were the familiar faces, those of the workers that consistently did his bidding. They knew better than to look bored, but Abaddon knew they'd sat through enough of these meetings to suspect the agenda.

Then there were other faces- a few new characters in the crowd. Abaddon fed off of the uncertainty and angst that so obviously wracked their frail bodies- they were nothing compared to the resilient, desperate energy that radiated from the figures Abaddon had molded himself. He was a master at spotting weakness, and he pounced mercilessly every opportunity he got.

"Fear, please name the agenda for this afternoon's meeting," Abaddon announced, the room silenced as he spoke the first word. Now *that* was power. Theos could say what He wanted: there was no substitute for the feeling of power- the knowledge that he could get anything, do anything that he wanted. No one would dare to stop him, contradict him, or question him. Except for Theos, that was. The thought triggered a hot flash of irritation that shot up Abaddon's spine and settled as frustration in his mind. He turned his attention to Fear, who had gone stock-still in obvious fright and dread.

"Fear?" Abaddon repeated, this time with an edge of anger, an unspoken threat thinly veiled in the tone of his voice.

"I-" Fear's voice cracked, and Abaddon's workers chuckled meanly as Fear's face flushed and he cleared his throat, looking down at his feet. "I'm afraid I didn't receive an agenda for this meeting," Fear tried again, mustering what courage he still possessed.

"Afraid? I can't imagine *Fear* feeling *afraid*," Abaddon mocked, drawing cruel laughter from the crowd. Fear had made a mistake- he'd shown a chink in his armor. Abaddon never passed up the opportunity to humiliate or shred an individual when lobbed a softball- it would have countered his very nature, the essence of his being. A horrible smile spread across his face- his oversized, straight rows of teeth the object of perfection whilst utterly vile.

He'd really gotten to Fear now- the miserable character literally started to shake. Abaddon felt warmth build in the core of his being, his pulse quickening as he began to salivate. He couldn't help himself- he leaned forward, body tensed like a lion ready to lunge at its prey. The fun was just beginning.

***

Fear's worst nightmare was playing out in slow motion before his very eyes: he had a front-row seat in the cinema, his eyes glued to the horror film entitled "Abaddon devours Fear without breaking a sweat." He was past the point of preserving his pride- that had been flushed down the toilet like an expired goldfish seconds into the meeting. Now, his aim was to leave the meeting alive- a goal that was looking more and more unlikely by the moment.

Fear plunged into new states of shock he'd never experienced: far past fear and even numbness, he now felt stupefied and dumb, so terrified was he in Abaddon's presence. Ribbons of thought patterns twirled through his consciousness and then left before he could fully dwell on any single one, ensuring that Fear could not focus on the words Abaddon spoke.

Why had Abaddon called him there? Was there any meeting at all? Or was it just an excuse to feast on fresh meat? If so, why him? How would this end? Was there any outcome where he left alive?

Strangely, Fear wasn't sure he cared. He felt diminished, deflated, hopeless. He'd heard that Abaddon had that effect on others, that he literally sucked all light and joy and hope from the room with a single breath. Fear had surmised these words to be exaggerations- even knowing the extent of Abaddon's power, he'd doubted how true these statements were.

"Fear? Did I terrify you so easily? There aren't any janitors on duty at the moment- if you soil the floor, it'll be your responsibility to clean it up," Abaddon warned, his velvety voice hateful.

Fear heard the words as though underwater: every syllable warbled and stretched out. He had the faintest idea that he should be shamed, that his face should turn red and he should somehow regain his composure- this did not happen. Fear clung to the words, *clean it up*, a life preserver that suggested he might leave the room alive. He must have said something, a string of words or perhaps just a guttural sound he didn't consciously verbalize, for the room erupted in laughter.

"Yes, you're *right*, Fear. We *are* here to talk about Leiala," Abaddon agreed, his tone animated, over-the-top.

"Abaddon, we're wasting time," a worker dared challenge, meriting a gnashing of teeth from the fearsome leader.

"I'll decide when time is wasted," Abaddon roared, silencing all laughter.

Fear threw up.

Oh, that couldn't have helped, Fear worried. Slowly raising his head, he quietly wiped the corners of his mouth and, aware that all eyes were fixed in disgust on him, made the decision to act as though nothing out of the ordinary had happened. This turned out to be a wise move- his disgusting action served as a welcome distraction that set the meeting back on course.

"Fear, your presence was required because we have a new strategy for attacking Leiala," Abaddon announced abruptly, changing direction and tone as though the past few minutes had never happened. Fear recognized the significance in verbiage- Theos always *requested* a character's presence; Abaddon *required* it.

Fear blinked and nodded dumbly. Abaddon began to pace the room, his movements agitated.

"Leiala is a human of interest to Theos," he began, lips curling at the mere mention of his arch-enemy. "And while Theos has allowed us to interfere in Leiala's life, we have not been able to claim any sizeable victory."

Here, there were groans and growls, fearsome sounds that Abaddon dismissed with a single wave of his arm.

"We're going to insert ourselves into Theos's agenda," Abaddon continued, eyes glittering in excitement. Fear was overwhelmed by a sense of dread- what could Abaddon mean by this? He didn't have to wait long to find out.

"Leiala is a faithful servant of Theos. Her soul may very well be lost to us- by all accounts, this would appear to be the case," Abaddon reported. "While we may not have the opportunity to claim victory in that battle, there are others we can most assuredly win."

Goosebumps sprouted on Fear's arm as he saw Abaddon's workers shift anxiously in their seats, eager to learn more. A screen materialized in the front of the room, and an image of Leiala appeared. Fear, a character not programmed to feel such a breadth of emotion, instantly felt pity for the sweet girl. He hadn't even heard yet what was coming her way, but he knew it had to be horrible.

"Leiala listens to Theos, and she obeys," Abaddon continued matter-of-factly. "But," he added slyly, "she cannot drown out our voices. We will stay as a constant presence in Leiala's life, but with new, targeted measures."

Fear's eyes stayed glued to the screen as Abaddon explained the plan. Images of Leiala engaged in her favorite activities flashed.

"Essentially, we'll twist Theos's edicts and manipulate them into idols," Abaddon stated, the pride in his voice obvious as he unveiled the details of his plan. "Leiala reads her Bible- we'll make sure she does this every day- and if she doesn't, Guilt and Fear will overwhelm her. Leiala likes to achieve things- when she experiences success, Fear-" Abaddon made eye contact with Fear here, glaring at him in what Fear imagined was a look meant to inspire submission and compliance- "will destroy the joy that typically comes from achievement. Instead, Leiala will become obsessed with the fact that the success may have been *accidental*, it might not have been earned, and then we'll fill her with fear that she might not be able to duplicate the efforts. We're going to strip Leiala of certain characters and drown her with others until this transition is complete."

Here, Abaddon paused- to let the magnitude of his words sink in. He looked around the room, surveying his workers, then, once he was sure that he had been heard, went on.

"This must be done slowly. Pneuma will likely try to alert Leiala to our deception- we'll need to influence her bit by bit, so that she'll delude herself into thinking nothing has changed. We must constantly feed her this message, and praise her obsession with rules with success and achievement, which in turn will continue to feed her fear of worthiness."

"Brilliant," a worker heaved, a breathy yet masculine utterance that could not be held in. Fear agreed- the plan was ingenious. Terrible, loathsome, and base- but ingenious.

"Yes," Abaddon agreed, accepting the compliment without any grace. "We'll reconvene down the line to strategize the next steps in this diversion- but Leiala is such a rule-follower that this is bound to work. Theos will work to counter our actions, but if we stay consistent, Leiala will buy into our lies. Oh-" Abaddon pointed at a particularly seedy creature sitting in the front of the room, "keep up the work on the body image. Let's turn up the heat on the food and exercise obsession. Slow and steady," Abaddon warned, "but let's build in intensity."

"We'll ruin her," a worker grinned in delight.

"Yes, we will," Abaddon affirmed. "We may not be able to claim Leiala, but we can render her ineffective as she destroys herself. And that's the best part- she'll do it all to herself. *She* will literally be the cause of her destruction."

-9-

The first day of eighth grade, Leiala was ready. To be specific, Leiala was ready for a change; she was ready to be noticed. She'd felt invisible most of the time- not to her teachers, who seemed to applaud her every effort and insight- but to her classmates, who were marginally impressed with her academic efforts (was it really that special to be smart? Or maybe not even smart- maybe she was just a hard worker...) and athletic ability, and put off by her convictions and discipline.

She was smart, but not the smartest; athletic, but not the most athletic; and she definitely wasn't the prettiest- and that was the thing that seemed to matter most. The pretty girls, they seemed to walk on air- noticed and admired by the masses, they appeared to revel in the knowledge that they were desirable and wanted- their very presence seemed to inspire awe and excitement. Leiala had studied these girls for the past two years, and she felt confident that she would capture notice after this summer.

Her outfit was carefully planned: a new dress in the latest style, which thankfully flattered her athletic figure (and had swallowed a good portion of her babysitting money). It had a simple cut and was deep blue in color, which would serve to complement her eyes and hopefully show off her tan as well. Most importantly, it looked laid-back: it was a far cry from the brash, shiny back-to-school outfits that struck Leiala as grasping and desperate. But even this was insignificant when compared to the real changes that Leiala hoped to make for the year- she wanted to break into new groups of friends, to befriend some *boys*, and to make a mark. Wasn't that what eighth graders did?

Shrugging her backpack over her left shoulder, Leiala glanced once at her reflection in the mirror before scampering downstairs to meet her carpool out front.

“First day of eighth grade,” her mom remarked cheerfully, looking up from the kitchen table as Leiala walked into the kitchen for her lunch. “Where did the time go?” she added, more to herself.

“I’m ready!” Leiala bubbled, and the smile on her face affirmed this statement to be true. To be fair- she felt this way on *every* first day of school- she could never sleep the night before. She traded sleep for a lengthy silent film in which Leiala starred, role-playing an imagined day’s worth of events supposed to be the first day of school. It was predictable, exhausting- but it secretly added a bit to the excitement.

***

First period, and Leiala pulled out a fresh notebook and a brand-new set of gel pens. She intended to stay more organized this year than ever before- each subject would be easily identifiable by a unique gel color, and she meant to make her notebooks into a work of art. Armed with an impressive arsenal of pens, post-its, and decorated folders, Leiala perched at the edge of her seat, eyes fastened on the teacher before her, ready to impress and also ready to copy down the first words of scholarly wisdom sure to escape her teacher’s mouth. So focused was she on the teacher and content, that she forgot about her goal to make new friends.

By lunch, Leiala had set into motion three beautiful notebooks- one teacher had disappointed her by choosing to instead give an overview of the year’s curriculum without any student involvement- but she hadn’t gone out of her way to be friendly with anyone new. Her goal had been utterly forgotten until now, when she moved to find her usual group of girls. She wasn’t even sure that anyone had noticed her or her changes- changes that may not actually have happened, Leiala told herself in dismay.

Lunch went by quickly, the time easily passed as the girls shared schedules and teachers, celebrating their luck in securing favored instructors at the same time they lamented their misfortune in being assigned instructors that had reputations for being difficult, mean, or boring. Leiala laughed along with her friends and shared in their first impressions of their classmates- was there anyone new? Anyone who got especially cute over summer? Leiala hadn't noticed anyone, but her friends seemed to think there might be one or two new prospects.

Fifth period math turned out to be the most exciting: now that Leiala had worked her way through sixth, seventh, and eighth grade math, she was left to pursue geometry. There were a small number of other students in her same situation, so the school had hired a special teacher to come onto campus to teach just one period of this more advanced math.

Leiala loved the instructor immediately: an elderly gentleman named Mr. Barnes dressed in dark slacks, a periwinkle blue sweater, and sensible orthotic shoes. He had a kind smile with wrinkles in all the right places- wrinkles that attested to thousands of smiles and not as many frowns. His soft white hair was combed carefully and seemed ready to blow away in the slightest breeze, and the man's eyes sparkled with genuine excitement as he discussed the structure and expectations of his class. Ten minutes into the class, Leiala was determined to impress this man- she had to win his approval.

But as charming as Mr. Barnes was, Leiala wasn't sure he was the highlight of the class. The other riveting detail, the tidbit that made Leiala replay geometry class over in her mind a number of times, was that she had been noticed. Noticed, by two of the cutest boys in school, who also happened to be high-achieving math students. Leiala couldn't be entirely certain, but she thought she'd seen the two friends stop and look up when she walked into the room- their gaze lingering before they said something (was it about her?!) and then turned their gaze away.

These two events, each carrying significant weight and influence, practically inflated Leiala so that she floated into her sixth period class. Not even the sight of the homely PE uniforms and talk of running the dreaded *timed mile* could bring her down.

***

"That was unique," Abaddon's worker proclaimed, standing up at the front of the room, pointing a remote towards the footage that had just been replayed on the screen.

Fear was stuck in these meetings more often than he cared to admit these days- all at Abaddon's insistence, of course. Well- it wasn't Abaddon himself who communicated this- but his workers made it clear that he was expected to attend these strategic gatherings. Ever since that first meeting, Fear had avoided Abaddon and the east wing of headquarters like the plague. As time had passed, he had been able to forget or push out aspects of that horrendous meeting, but the raw emotion and distaste was tangible and impossible to ignore. Fear didn't contribute much to these meetings, and he didn't offer much of his own input- he sat there quietly, doing his best to appear impartial.

"I hate to say this, Anxiety, but I think you need to take a step back," Abaddon's worker went on to say, surprising Fear. "We'll need your services again, certainly, but it appears as though Leiala is ripe to respond to Pride and Fear. The right cocktail of the two of you-" Abaddon pointed at Fear and then at Pride- "could produce exactly the response we need from Leiala."

Fear swallowed hard. His role was about to *increase*? What had the past five years been? Heck, the past 13 years? His mind raced, trying to imagine what he would be asked to do. How could he possibly impact Leiala further than he had already? And how would that change her? Fear was already of the belief that his influence was too great- what would it be like now? Anxiety elbowed Fear hard, bringing awareness back into Fear's body. He focused in time to hear the worker's last words.

"Pride, we want you to take advantage of every opportunity you're given to instill pride in Leiala. Make sure it's a good, long, dopamine-induced feeling...we want Leiala to become addicted to this pattern of achievement. And we want her to believe that she's accomplished these things all on her own- that she got or did these things all by herself."

Pride nodded curtly, and Abaddon's worker turned to Fear. It was clear by the look on his face that he had a little less faith in Fear's ability to expressly carry out orders.

"Fear, when Leiala approaches any new situation, we want your presence to come on strong. It's best if she's not sure where this fear comes from or what it's associated with. You can start small- just a little bit of fear, so that she barely notices- but it should grow with time. Fear, this should be in any and every situation where there is any possibility for failure or an undesirable outcome," the worker clarified, looking down at Fear.

Was he kidding?! This was overtime work, for sure- and it was without question unsavory work. He was just expected to agree to do this, no questions asked? It made Fear sick! Fear didn't need to look up into the face of the worker to know that this was no joking matter- not only did Abaddon want Fear to carry out this assignment, but he expected him to.

"Clear," Fear managed to get out. Yes, the orders were clear. That part was true. The rest- the rest he would have to work out later. He could only hope that Theos would elect to get involved.

I'm not the same as Happiness. We're not related, and we're certainly not twins. I wish you humans would pay more attention- enough attention to notice the differences. You don't really notice much in the alternative realm, do you? You notice ALL of the latest trends, and how others perceive you- you have no problem focusing on the literal, transient things of your world. But the things that really matter- the things that actually affect your soul and influence your state of being- those things are left untouched, unnoticed, unseen.

If you had brand-new designer clothes hanging in your closet, wouldn't you want to wear them? If you had a sparkling, never-been-driven cherry-red Ferrari waiting for you in your driveway, would you choose to bike instead? But that's what you do! I don't have these silly, literal things to offer you- but the principle is the same. The gift I have to give to you far surpasses any item your limited world has to offer. The greatest treasures you can imagine appear as cheap, useless junk to the alternative realm- effervescent, multi-carat diamonds revealed as the trashy plastic trinkets that they really are. But I won't try to convince you of this- I know how you think, and I know the rules that your world operates by. It would take far more than a simple letter to change such deeply-ingrained thoughts and ideals; I won't attempt the impossible.

I just wish you could see the difference. I'm not trying to change the appeal of your earthly delights...I just want you to see how valuable I am, and I wish you could perceive the difference between what the world has to offer and what I can bring you.

Have you ever seen a fish go after shiny bait? That sparkling, shimmering material that glitters in the light water, dancing through the current as it entices and beckons the unsuspecting fish to come just a bit closer, to taste the goodness and capture the magic that has intoxicated its entire being? And what happens to the fish?

If it's lucky, it's unsuccessful: the bait is removed, another fish captures the bait first, or some other force of nature withholds the glittery treasure. And what then does this fish think? He's angry, upset, frustrated- a precious gem of blessing was withheld, stolen by another, luckier fish or otherwise kept from his grasp. Only the fisherman knows the truth: the fish escaped a close encounter with death. The fish may **never** know- he may hold onto this missed opportunity his entire life, bitter that he missed out on a golden opportunity. How misguided!

Or how about the monkey intent on his sweet? The unsuspecting primate stumbles across a gourd filled with nuts and fruit, and determines to make a feast of his findings. No sooner has his hand plunged inside the narrow hole and grabbed onto the tasty treat than it becomes stuck- the hopeful little monkey cannot retract his hand while it's crumpled into a fist. But does the monkey let go of the nuts, realize that he's been tricked and move along his way in disappointment? No! The stubborn monkey, indignant that he's caught a glimpse of that which he believes he wants above all else, screeches and cries and screams- but does not let go of the food. Escape would be easily won- as simple as letting go- but the monkey will not do it. He will cry out in agony all the way until the human comes to make a meal of him.

You read this and ridicule the fish and the monkey- you think they're base, lesser-than creatures with crude, underdeveloped systems of logic. You might even feel sorry for them, not realizing that you're no different. Do you know that so many of us see **you** that way? You don't understand, can't see the situation you're in properly. You focus on the temporal, the temporary, the sensory details that last for moments at the expense of recognizing that which is eternal. I guess that's what I'm trying to point out in an indirect way- happiness is temporal.

Happiness comes from a well-crafted specialty coffee drink, an athletic feat, a favorite dessert, the praise of a friend, the perfect parking spot. Not to dismiss the pleasure that comes from these things, but is that really what you want to spend your life chasing? Do you understand how fickle, unpredictable, and futile happiness is? It depends entirely on your circumstances- circumstances that, I'm sorry to report to you, will inevitably change for the better and also for the worse. You can't control happiness, and you can't control your circumstances. Oh, you can try- so many of you do try, in vain, with all of your heart- but it's of no use. You're determined to catch happiness, which can no more easily be caught than a rainbow or a fragrant breeze. And in your dogmatic quest to secure happiness, you forget entirely about me.

Me. ME! **I'm** the one that can bring you lasting contentment- I'm the one you really want! I don't depend on the mood of your significant other or the report card of your child or the amount of money in your bank account. I come with the offer of companionship 24/7, regardless of circumstances. I can help you to see the alternative perspective in even the worst of circumstances, and even when it doesn't make sense, I can help you to see the beauty in darkness and feel satisfied even when things look like they're grossly wanting. I can do this. Happiness cannot. And yet day after day, people use our names interchangeably, assuming we offer the same services. We do not.

I want to help you. I want to be your faithful sidekick, your loyal companion that changes your perspective of life. But until you stop confusing me with happiness, this cannot happen. I'm just asking you- begging you- to **try** and look beyond. Just try. You'll be surprised at what you see. The things you value most might just turn out to be less precious than you imagine, and you might discover that you require my assistance to grab hold of those things that truly hold value. Someday you'll know- someday everyone learns. I'm just trying to help you, to save you from the trouble and heartbreak that come from walking the wrong path. Seek me! Look for me! Ask for me! The sooner you find me, the sooner you'll see me as the gift I am- much greater than some temporary emotion- the sooner you'll experience life as it was meant to be lived.

I'm waiting for you...

-Joy

-10-

Time passed. Leiala wasn't sure what adjective to assign to this passing of time- it wasn't necessarily remarkable, and it didn't seem to drag on or speed by. But, as sure as a game of heads up, seven up on a rainy day- time had passed. Now a sophomore in high school, Leiala could *feel* the improvements, the accomplishments, in the very sinew of her bones. She was a success- at least, that's what she thought, most of the time.

Reflecting back on her first year of high school, Leiala mentally ticked off her numerous accomplishments. She'd managed to promote from middle school with a perfect 4.0, and she'd been pulled up to play on a more advanced level on her soccer team. She felt that she'd earned the respect of her classmates, teachers, teammates, and coaches- something she prized above all else. With every verbal affirmation and accomplishment, Leiala felt her value increase. She wasn't sure what she'd been worth to begin with- how does one go about measuring such an intangible thing?- but she knew she was worth *far* more now.

Before, she was a kind-hearted, loyal, and generous girl...that was nice, but it didn't necessarily make her important or valuable. She knew her parents and siblings loved her, and she knew she had loyal friends, but she couldn't just take these things for granted. How many times had she heard the message that people are bound to let you down? She was not going to be the fool- she was not going to give anyone a reason to be let down. Of course, these disappointments were to some degree inevitable, but Leiala determined to strive towards perfection- if she were absolutely, positively perfect, she wouldn't let anyone down, and she could appropriately feel pride in her accomplishments. The very best part was that this was all in Leiala's control- her success ultimately depended on only her. If she worked hard enough, tried hard enough, she could make it happen.

So now, as she walked through the hallways of her high school, she held her head high and her shoulders square, speaking to her confidence. Her steps were certain and unwavering- there was no sign of insecurity or fear. Armed with the confidence that if she worked hard enough, she could make it happen, Leiala plowed forward with every ounce of determination and resolve. This attitude had landed her in a plethora of advanced courses, had elevated her to the role of editor of the school paper, and had won her spots on three different varsity sports teams. She'd worked tirelessly her freshman year performing all the labor required to make this a reality- running every morning and attending every sports camp to ensure she'd be in tip-top shape when any given sports season rolled around: if she wasn't the most experienced or skilled, she could rely on her superior strength and endurance to give her an edge. She'd spent countless hours outside of school studying and preparing for any and every class, staying up late into the night working on extra credit or supplemental assignments that she hoped would give her an edge. Sleep was a luxury- of paramount importance were preparation and hard work. Within this structure of discipline, Leiala thrived. She knew she could count on the results of concentrated efforts, and she clung to this formula like a magnet to a refrigerator.

Leiala was proud of her achievements, and of the unlocking of this formula for accomplishment. She was pleased that she'd managed to mitigate some of the uncertainty of her life- if she could just sustain that formula, she was sure that she could handle whatever might come her way. She couldn't control the situations she might find herself in, but she could control her response- and she now felt more confident than ever that she could emerge victorious in any number of situations. This assurance was responsible for the spring in her step and the pole-like rigidity in her spine. She was Leiala, the girl who could conquer the world.

Attending Homecoming without a date. Limited playing time on her volleyball team. A 'B' in her math class. A "Sweet 16" birthday party of a teammate that it seemed everyone was invited to, except her.

Disappointments began to pile up, but Leiala stayed firm in her resolve to succeed. That was the beauty of this mindset: Leiala chose her response. And with every perceived slight, Leiala determined to work harder. She might not naturally have the skills or gifts to be the best, but if she worked hard enough, she could still earn that number one spot. If she didn't give up and stayed focused, she would at least win the respect and approval of those around her, and her efforts might be palatable. And while every failure drove her to work harder, every success encouraged her to continue on with her efforts. The progress and achievement was addicting, a drug she couldn't do without. Even just a little taste made her hungry for more, left her wondering how far she could go or how much she might achieve.

Volleyball season ended, and the first progress reports went home. Fall had passed; Winter was on its way. Leiala had developed some bruises and scratches, but nothing major. Nothing her system couldn't handle. She remained dogged in her optimism, fiercely clinging to the belief that success and better things would come her way.

Then, basketball season. Leiala felt the anticipation and excitement in every fiber of her being. This was her favorite sport, the one she felt most confident playing. She'd had a stellar season her freshman year: on the junior varsity team, she'd led her team in points, assists, and steals. She liked how she felt when she played basketball: she was strong, capable, intuitive- and she felt the respect and admiration of her teammates, and the confidence her coaches had in her. She was reliable, dependable, relentless. And today marked the first day of try-outs.

Leiala knew she had a spot on the team, so that brought her some comfort. Some. Not much at all, though, if she was being honest with herself. She knew she'd have a spot on the junior varsity team for sure- she'd been the star of the team the past year- but Leiala was hoping (and expecting) to make the varsity team. Although doing so would be a major achievement for a sophomore, and not at all expected of her, *she* expected it from herself. And so it may as well have been written in stone- if Leiala failed in this endeavor, she would have a hard time accepting herself.

Walking into the basketball gym, she feigned confidence in her posture as she joined the other girls as they laced up their shoes on the side of the court. A million thoughts raced through Leiala's mind as she took in the competition (known and unknown), assessed who she might want to associate with or partner up with, and then took in the end of the boys' basketball try-outs taking place on the court before her. Her heart seemed to beat in time with the dribbling, her breath catching with each shot taken. The familiar squeaking of shoes on wood made her pulse quicken. She forced herself to take deep, measured breaths- breaths that sent oxygen to every region of her body, breaths that calmed her.

You're faster than all of these girls, Leiala told herself, surveying the crowd. She knew herself to be in great shape, and unless one of these girls had really put a lot of work in, she knew she'd be able to outrun them. The rest, she couldn't be too sure. She had a sweet three-point shot, but she would be rusty- how rusty? She felt confident in her dribbling, but she might be rusty in this area, too. Panic began to bubble up in her- just how rusty would she be? Maybe she should just forget the whole thing, go home. She could do that. It would only take a phone call to her mom, pretending she was sick. She could explain later that she'd decided not to try out for the team that year- she could say she just didn't want to play anymore.

Stop! Leiala commanded herself. *You're being ridiculous.* As foolish as the thoughts were, Leiala found herself fantasizing about this escape. What would it be like to have free time after school? To have the final bell ring, and to go home? Leiala couldn't even imagine. All she'd known was rigor and structure- and while there was comfort in this known, there was also a certain draw and appeal to that idea of freedom, of possibility.

You're being ridiculous, Leiala admonished herself, silencing this thought pattern once and for all. *You're an athlete, and you've played basketball forever. It's who you* **are**, *Leiala- how can you even think about giving it up? Besides, what would everyone think? Mom, Dad, your teammates, friends- they all expect you to play.*

Leiala reached down to touch her toes, stretching at the same time she exhaled deeply. No, she was going to go through with try-outs...and she'd better not mess it up. Her pulse quickened again as she thought about what she would have to do to prove her mettle. She would be aggressive, ruthless, strong. She couldn't fail- would not *allow* herself to fail.

Shhhreeee!

A high-pitched whistle blew, signaling the end of the boys' try-outs, and the beginning of the girls'. Leiala's heart leapt to her throat.

"Girls, out on the court!" the varsity coach yelled, sauntering towards the top of the key with clipboard in hand. His stride was casual, each step long and relaxed. Shifting his weight from side to side, his gaze swept over the contenders indifferently. His demeanor suggested that he was there to judge, and his posture did nothing to alleviate any of the anxiety or intimidation the girls may have felt. Everything about the man seemed to scream, "Impress me!" Leiala felt increasing resolve at this unstated challenge: he wanted to be impressed? This seemed like a challenge she could work towards- she doubted he could imagine just how hard she could work.

"You're here for basketball try-outs," the coach stated, barely glancing up from his clipboard. "You'll find out within the week if you made the team or not," he went on. "Unless there's someone out here that really surprises me, I already have my varsity team. If you don't make varsity, Coach Kelly will consider if you're up to muster for her team." Here he nodded once in Coach Kelly's direction. Leiala caught Coach Kelly's eye, and her former coach gave her a friendly wink. If she didn't make varsity, she'd still have a place, Leiala reminded herself. Coach Kelly would want her on the team again! She focused in just in time to hear the varsity coach's closing remark: "And I don't really care about anything after junior varsity. I guess some of you might make a freshman team." The apathy in his voice was thick as maple syrup, practically encouraging girls to give up right then.

Not me, Leiala growled in her head. *You WILL notice me.* The varsity coach was a jerk- that was overwhelmingly obvious. Maybe he was even worse than a jerk...Leiala could think of a couple of inappropriate words- words she didn't use- that would aptly describe this man. So why did she want to impress him so badly? His onerous affect seemed to fan the flames of Leiala's obsession to please- she was going to *make* him notice her.

Warm-ups began, led by a returning varsity player, a senior. Leiala smiled at the girls she knew and exchanged friendly greetings, but she was quick to focus. She was casual, easy in the warm-up laps and stretching. She didn't want to try too hard too early- and she didn't want to give herself away. The coach wasn't even watching them, really- he was joking around with the other coaches and scribbling notes on his clipboard. Leiala watched him out of the corner of her eye, never letting on that she was studying him, but figuring the whole time what he might be thinking or watching.

Nerves set in during the first drill: lay-ups. This was technically still part of the warm-up, and it was supposed to be easy- which is what made it so difficult. Leiala had done countless lay-ups, but she didn't feel confident as she prepared to take her first one. There was no glory or recognition to be had in completing a lay-up, but there was certainly a steep price to pay if she missed. A missed lay-up would be a strong endorsement for junior varsity- no varsity player could afford to miss one.

Leiala's strides felt foreign, awkward, as she dribbled towards the basket. She imagined herself as an astronaut on the moon, taking uncertain, strange steps while navigating an unknown land. *You've done this before,* Leiala reminded herself. *Relax. You know what to do. You have to relax.* The basket came quickly, and Leiala's footing was awkward and forced as she shot the ball into the freshly-painted corner of the backboard. The ball bounced obediently against the wood and crashed against the rim, circling once before diving through the netting for a successful lay-up. Leiala felt her face flush as heat flamed from the center of her body out towards her extremities. That had been too close for comfort- she needed to relax! But even as she acknowledged this truth, she felt herself tense even more with expectation. The coach was watching now, waiting for someone to make a mistake. Leiala tried to silence her mind, to center her breathing, and to

let her body take over. It didn't happen. Every lay-up sent a fresh jolt of panic through her, every successful lay-up an overwhelming sense of relief that was quickly usurped when the next opportunity for failure presented itself.
Leiala felt giddy with relief when the lay-ups were over- she'd survived one fraction of try-outs. She made a mental note to practice lay-ups in her backyard at home...she needed to familiarize herself with the movement again. She couldn't put herself through that agony again the next day.

The rest of try-outs went by without incident- Leiala was aware that she wasn't standing out in any of the drills, but she wasn't sure anyone was. There were some who clearly lacked experience and struggled, but the drills didn't differentiate the *good* players from the *great*- Leiala was waiting for this discerning moment. It didn't seem to come. *It's only the first try-out*, Leiala reminded herself. *This was just to get us in the groove*. The thought brought her some comfort and at the same time added a fresh layer of anxiety. She hadn't done anything to secure a spot on the varsity team- she'd only managed to ensure she wasn't bumped from the team.

Later that night, Leiala struggled to find sleep. Her mind buzzed with thoughts and ideas about how the day had gone, how try-outs had been interpreted by coach, and with worry over what the next day's try-outs might include. No matter that she'd run around and worked out, Leiala felt energy hum through her body, shocks of adrenaline keeping her wired and alert. Sleep did come eventually, but it was not fitful.

***

Leiala did her best to focus in class, but her mind continued to wander to the second day of try-outs...she was sure the drills would be more complicated today, designed to separate the players into groups of ability. She tried to imagine what she might be asked to do, and she visualized herself working through a great number of activities in an effort to calm herself. It worked- a little.

1:30.

2:00.

2:05.

2:10.

The final bell rang, signaling the end of school. Leiala was ready. Sports bag slung over her shoulder, she wasted no time walking to the gym, changing into her athletic clothes, and preparing for day two of try-outs. More determined than ever, she was pleased to find herself more relaxed this second day- she still felt anxious as she completed lay-ups and ran through drills, but there was more ease behind her movements today.

Try-outs ended with a scrimmage, and Leiala felt excitement course through her. This was it: an opportunity to set herself apart. As teams were created, Leiala made quick mental notes on which of her teammates were adept players, and which were inept. She'd carefully assessed her competition over the past two days, and had an idea of which players telegraphed their passes, who dribbled with sloppy, inconsistent pushes (easy targets to steal from), and who was likely to airball a shot. Conversely, she thought she'd figured who the strongest competition was- and she resolved to match their level of play.

She started easily- no great plays, no giant blunders as she got into the swing of play. But then, a wide-open shot that she hesitated to take. She could feel the coach's eyes burning in the back of her head, shaming her for her cowardice. Heat radiated through her body as she chided herself: she'd had a chance to be noticed, and she'd missed it! Wrought with fear and ripe with panic, Leiala doubled her efforts on defense and sprinted to be first in position. Shifting the weight to the tips of her toes, she tried not to blink as she watched the point guard dribble down the court. Leiala took in the scene before her, the court laid out in entirety. She saw the point guard glance right, then left, and Leiala saw her hesitate just a moment before shifting her body towards the right. Leiala's body tensed as she poised for attack, a lion ready to lunge. Forgetting about her assigned player, Leiala's body shot forward like a bullet the moment the point guard released the ball.

Her right palm made contact with a smack- Leiala had intercepted the ball. Wild energy pulsed through her veins as she charged forward, pushing the ball far in front of her as she sprinted down the court. *This* felt right. This was what it felt like to be in her element. She was wild, free, unstoppable. Then, fear set in. It was funny how quickly that seemed to happen to her lately. The unadulterated joy she'd felt milliseconds before was suddenly marred by the imposing view of the basket looming ahead. A lay-up. She'd have to complete the lay-up. All eyes were on her, including that of the coach. This was her moment of glory: if she made this lay-up, she'd earn a notch that could very well take her up onto the list of varsity players. If she missed, it would mean great embarrassment- her missed shot would not only cancel out any merit she'd won with her steal, but it would call attention to her inability to perform under pressure.

It was coming too fast. She was sprinting, moving quickly- too quickly. She cursed her speed now, wishing she hadn't put so much space between her and the next defender. Defense would have given her an excuse to pause, to wait to pass the ball to another player- to make *them* take the shot-that-should-not-be-missed. All by herself, it would look foolish to pass this shot up- she would need to take it.

Thoughts preoccupied with worries of failure, consumed with fear of missing the shot, obsessed with the goal of making varsity, Leiala's footsteps came awkwardly as she moved in for the lay-up. She pushed off of the wrong foot, and she waited until she was too close to the basket to shoot. She was sure her movements didn't appear natural, didn't speak to varsity-level play.

The ball left her hands and she kept moving, passing beneath the hoop, her eyes riveted on the basket. Like the climax of a grand adventure film, Leiala couldn't bear to witness the outcome and yet couldn't tear her eyes away. Relief poured through her body as the ball bounced easily through the netting, awarding her team two points. A jolt of pleasure flooded through her as her teammates offered high-fives; she could feel the eyes of the coach on her. She'd been awkward in her approach to the basket, but she'd made the shot. She'd delivered on her steal, and she'd set herself apart. New confidence surged through Leiala as she ran back into place. She could do this. She was going to make varsity.

-11-

Change sat in the Strategics room, waiting for the meeting to begin. He was getting tired of these meetings, of being dragged into discussions where his only job was to sit quietly, to patiently listen to reports on Leiala without being asked his opinion. In the beginning, he'd been considered a viable asset; he'd been instrumental in forming the foundation of Leiala's character. He'd grown accustomed to the limelight, to the adrenaline-laced jobs he was asked to carry out.

It was his own fault for cultivating expectations- of all characters, he should know about how quickly things could change. But he hadn't been prepared for this tapering off, the way his role was increasingly pushed off to the side. His constant presence in Leiala's life had cooled at the insistence of Abaddon- Change no longer got to surprise Leiala with new faces, new teeth, or changes in home environment. He'd been relegated to the sidelines to watch Fear and Anxiety take over. He was still a player in the game, but there was no glory in his work. Abaddon had made it clear that it would be considered a failure should his presence be recognized; he was ordered to fly under the radar, to enact change in subtle, miniscule ways that would lead to substantial change over time. Change supposed that this would prove to be important work someday, but it did nothing to inspire his current situation.

"Change? You still staying consistent?" Abaddon's worker asked in a tone that made it clear he already knew the answer.

Inwardly seething, Change bit the inside of his cheek to refrain from giving a smart reply.

"I am," Change answered. Abaddon's worker didn't even look his way or acknowledge Change's response with a gesture or wave.

"Fear, Leiala still doesn't sense your pervasive presence- that's good. We want to keep it so that she's operating out of a response to you, but without registering you as an emotion."

Change noticed with some small satisfaction that Fear wasn't awarded any glances, either- it appeared that this worker of Abaddon bulldozed over all characters, expecting them to bow to his every whimsy. But for how long? At some point, Leiala was going to have to break.

***

Leiala sat on the side of the court, her legs folded out into the familiar butterfly stretch. This was merely a distraction- a way to keep her body engaged as thoughts fired through her mind at rapid speed. She'd made varsity. She'd managed to secure a spot on the roster, along with two other sophomores. Popular girls who seemed to fit in with the older girls immediately. Leiala worked hard to be part of the group, but she was painfully aware that by most measures, she was a bona fide outcast.
Organically, she wasn't like the other girls. Some of this was in her control, like the fact that she didn't party, drink, or "experiment" like the other girls did. Other differences were well beyond her control, like the fact that the group of girls happened to be beautiful, that they all had boyfriends. Leiala tried not to show it, but she felt intimidated in their presence. She'd been so excited to make the varsity team, but now that she was on it, she wasn't so sure it was where she wanted to be. She'd initially felt such pride in her accomplishment, and she knew this was the place for her to be if she was going to improve and take her game to the next level- but she would be lying if she said she didn't sorely miss the junior varsity days, when she was the star of the team, knew all the drills, and felt confident in her role.

"Hey, Lei- we're starting," one of her teammates called to her, beckoning her over with a wave of her arm. Leiala felt a surge of warmth rush through her body as her nickname was used- a sign that she belonged and was part of an inner sanctum. Popping up quickly, she jogged over to the cluster of girls gathering in the center of the court and followed along during the warm-up. She watched the girls carefully, making sure to smile at the right times, to encourage them when they were in a pleasant state of mind and to stay quiet when they looked frustrated. She worked hard not to irritate them with her presence or her play- she was quick to pass to a teammate when she herself had a wide-open shot, and she hustled on defense more than anyone else...*she* would not be the one responsible for a lapse in defense. She was quiet most of the time, but tried to say enough to establish herself as one of the group. It was difficult, draining work- and this was only the interpersonal aspect of the game.

The actual basketball play was another ordeal. Leiala knew she wasn't playing her very best: she was working her butt off, but she wasn't taking risks. She'd paved a way for herself through her aggression, passion, and hustle- and for her calculated risks. She'd felt comfortable doing those things with Coach Kelly, and she hadn't worried about letting her junior varsity teammates down. Now, however, she felt as though weights had been tied to her ankles- she no longer took these risks. She was too nervous, too fearful of how her new coach might react. He was not forgiving, and he was certainly not playful. If Leiala had missed an easy shot on junior varsity, Coach Kelly would tease her- barbs from Coach Kelly never stung, because Leiala knew how much she counted on her and how much she valued her as a player. She was hard enough on herself- Coach Kelly knew that- and so she never needed to yell or intimidate.

Her new coach seemed to favor an opposite approach- he had no interest in establishing relationships with his players, instead he seemed to focus on flashy, sexy plays that mirrored those that might play on ESPN highlights. Coach Kelly had appreciated her steady, consistent level of play- her new coach couldn't have been more dismissive. To achieve these glorious maneuvers, one had to take risks- but if one failed to deliver on any given risk, the penalty was total and complete humiliation. Leiala had never seen anything like it.

The first official practice, Leiala had been initiated into this new coaching style. One of her teammates had missed a lay-up, and the retribution had been swift.

“You moron!” Coach had shouted, face contorted in disgust. “Your teammate sets you up for the easiest basket in the world, and you miss?! Go run two laps,” he’d ordered, face red.

Leiala’s body had stiffened immediately, her instincts taking over. She’d taken in the protruding veins from Coach’s face, the look of distress on her teammate’s face, and the unquestioned obedience that played out as the girl ducked her head in shame and ran the assigned two laps. Leiala had peeked at the other girls’ faces, but had trouble identifying any sympathy or outrage- two emotions that immediately flared up inside of her. *Was this normal behavior?* It would appear so, judging by the lack of reaction. Leiala felt angry, frustrated by this bully. This bully...and her *coach*. She was to respect and obey authority- as a chronic rule-follower, she did this well. But she’d never been put in a position like this, where the authority figure seemed to abuse his position. She’d watched out of the corner of her eye as the girl finished her second lap and quietly found a place in line. Leiala tried to offer an encouraging smile, but the girl avoided eye contact.

Leiala swallowed hard, aware that her muscles were still tense. Her turn was coming up- she would perform this same drill in just moments. Would Coach yell at her like that if she made a mistake? Leiala couldn’t imagine a scenario in which he wouldn’t.

Her turn came, and she completed the drill without making an error. Her movements were stiff, mechanical- every muscle seemed to twitch with formality as she thought her way through each motion. She didn’t make a mistake, but there was no beauty or fluidity to her performance. It felt rigid and strained, and it didn’t feel nice. But it had helped her to escape humiliation.

“Leiala, loosen up! We’re not a freaking robot convention,” Coach snarled. There wasn’t rage behind the words, so Leiala felt safe. Coach was annoyed, but not outraged. *Safe*. Shyly, Leiala looked around to see if any of her teammates would offer her an encouraging smile or nod, but no one even seemed to notice her. Well, perhaps that was the safest. She could be invisible- she could learn how to fly under the radar. She wouldn’t be the star of this team, that much was certain, but she could negotiate her way to a safe position. Leiala could envision the season already: she’d receive some playing time, probably in the second and third quarters of the game, when a player was tired. She could be relied on to remember the plays, to make smart passes, and to outdo herself on defense. She wouldn't attempt any dodgy plays- that seemed to be the way to avoid the wrath of Coach.

After practice, Leiala lingered. She took her time unlacing her shoes and slipping into her sandals, stalling by rummaging around in her athletic bag for her sweatshirt. She was desperate to connect with these girls, her teammates. She hadn't yet figured out how to make a connection: these girls were cool, experienced, and didn't seem to share her sense of humor or other interests. She was quick to smile- that would make her difficult to hate, wouldn't it?- and to offer sweet words of encouragement when the situation called for it. But for all her effort, Leiala worried that she hadn't made even one meaningful connection.

"Who put the stick up Coach's butt today?!" one girl joked, pulling her jersey over her head. Leiala averted her eyes, but not before she'd noticed the chiseled abs on the girl. She shifted her weight onto one hip, not in any rush to put her clean shirt on. Leiala wasn't sure if she intended to display her toned stomach, or if she just didn't care that she was exposed. She struggled to focus on the girl's words, but found herself distracted by thoughts of what it might be like to feel that way- to be so confident (or so indifferent to the reaction of those around her).

Leiala. She feels that way because she looks like that! You would do the same thing if you had abs like that, her mind was quick to offer.

"What stick?" a senior snapped. "Clearly, you don't know much about Coach. That's what he looks like on *good* behavior."

Leiala cringed, and the look must have shown on her face. The senior rolled her eyes as she tossed her shoes into her gym bag.

"This isn't *junior varsity* anymore," she intoned, voice dripping with disdain. "Just wait until we play our first game. We've got stiff competition- if we're sloppy and make mistakes, we'll be crushed." The way she said that last word, Leiala was sure there would be a penalty to pay not only with Coach but also with this senior if any significant blunders were made during a game. Looking around at the other upper-classmen nodding their heads like marionettes, Leiala acknowledged that she had a serious group of people to impress. She felt dread settle in as she considered the task put before her: a mistake would win her the enmity of her teammates and abject humiliation from Coach. Yes, she was definitely going to play it safe.

-12-

Leiala wasn't sure what was happening. She was exhausted, that much was certain. She felt panic the moment her alarm screeched in the morning- it couldn't already be time to get up, could it? Surely she'd only been sleeping for minutes...at least, it felt that way. She'd push herself up in bed, rub her eyes, stretch, and throw off the covers without fanfare. If it was time to get up, it was time to get up- there was no use stalling or trying to change the inevitable.

Downstairs, she'd quietly eat her bowl of cereal while skimming the front page of the newspaper or reviewing notes for that day's quiz or test. There was some light conversation, but nothing too serious, and soon Leiala would be upstairs in her room hurrying to dress and put on makeup. She was meticulous about double, then *triple* checking to ensure she had everything she needed for the day- gym bag, lunch, all the right textbooks and homework assignments. A quick hug and kiss to her mom, and then she was out the door.

At school, Leiala had settled into the routine of dropping her gym bag off in the locker room before school. This had done wonders for her pre-school nerves: the anxiety that came from wondering if her friends had already been dropped off, or if she might have to stand alone without anyone to talk to, had nearly undone her. Now, she took her time walking to the locker room, thankful for a purpose and destination as she slowly walked across campus, surveying the quad for any signs of her friends. She could adjust the time it took to drop her bag off accordingly: if her friends were already there, it was a quick stop- otherwise, she could linger and take her time in the hopes that when she finished, they would have already arrived.

The mornings passed more easily than the afternoon- Leiala enjoyed her English, History, and Journalism classes. These seemed to be her best subjects that year- there wasn't a pop quiz, test, or project that stressed her out. The classes were smaller, filled with people she knew relatively well, and she was confident in the subject matter. Leading up to lunch, however, a rope seemed to cinch itself around Leiala's stomach, tying itself into knots and twists and bows. Her breath became more shallow; her nerves were on edge. Leiala herself couldn't notice these physical changes, but she would admit that she didn't enjoy her afternoons.

Lunch was fine- not Leiala's favorite, but nothing she dreaded. She had stuck with her loyal group of friends, and a few girls she didn't much care for had added themselves to the mix. Leiala found their behavior annoying and immature, but she never let on that she felt this way- it was a small price to pay to enjoy the company of the girls she truly *did* want to spend time with. At times, Leiala was self conscious of this group, afraid that she might be labeled or lumped together with some of the girls she found foolish and awkward. She'd spent a great deal of time trying to work out how to mitigate the situation but hadn't come up with anything. On the days this feeling ballooned in her chest and threatened to take over, Leiala opted to eat her lunch as she walked circles around the quad with one or both of her closest friends. If she'd had it her way, this would have been the daily routine- but she knew it was selfish of her to pull her favorite people away from their other friends.

By the time the lunch bell rang, Leiala's heart seemed to wilt like a day-old mylar balloon. She would battle this oppressive feeling with any number of positive self-talk strategies or "logical" thought patterns, but the shadow couldn't be discarded. Instead, Leiala walked into fourth period with a slate-gray cloud hanging like an umbrella over her being.

Math.

Spanish.

Chemistry.

Each subject brought a fresh set of fears. Math didn't seem as simple anymore. Leiala had struggled a bit with the advanced Algebra the year before, but the concepts and logic had still made sense. Even when she couldn't solve for the answer, she understood what she was being asked to do. She'd been disappointed in herself when she received the occasional B on her test, but A's still dominated the landscape, and Leiala had clung to the belief that she was good at math.

This year, she was pretty sure she'd proven just the opposite. As she sat in Honors Pre-Calculus, she was struck by how bizarre trigonometry sounded. She did her best to conceptualize what it was that she was being asked to figure, and sometimes she could form a hazy, pixelated understanding in her mind, but it was never clear the way she would have liked. No matter of studying, reviewing, or question-asking seemed to help- and Leiala felt mortified and distraught at her lack of understanding. To admit incompetence would have been the end of the world- and so Leiala desperately searched for any patterns in the logic, memorized complicated formulas and procedures without understanding what she was committing to memory, and relied heavily on her reading comprehension, writing, and logic skills to build arguments that might earn her partial credit on tests. Even more paralyzing was the fact that Leiala was stuck in this class with a bunch of upperclassmen, people she wanted to impress. They were all under the impression that she must be smart- why else would she be in that class with them, learning higher level math?- and to prove she was not up to the task would have killed Leiala.

Besides this general angst that Leiala felt was the very real danger that she might be called on by the teacher to orally recite an answer or work through a problem. The first fifteen minutes of class, the teacher lead with this time of warm-up, calling on unsuspecting students to deliver complicated answers. Offering an "I don't know" was not an option, and Leiala wasn't sure which was worse: being asked a simple question (with the potential to respond foolishly and embarrass herself) or being asked a difficult question that she would have no idea how to solve. And so, even walking to the math building, Leiala found her palms grow sticky with sweat, her forehead and the back of her neck burned, and her pulse throbbed wildly out of control. Her fingers clenched her mechanical pencil so tightly that she'd developed a bruise on her ring finger, and her notebook pages were wrinkled and curled from the moisture of her sweat. She'd do her best to look down at her answers- or lack thereof- with a pensive, contemplative expression, one that she hoped communicated to her teacher that she was seriously considering the question he had asked (one that suggested that he might interrupt a thought train of brilliance if he called upon her). She'd peek at the clock in the corner of the room only when she was sure it was safe, hoping to see that the minute hand had inched closer to the 12, signaling an hour's worth of torture complete. Only after the bell had rung did she feel her shoulders sag in relief- only to tighten again when she realized where she was next headed.

Caught in a place of relief (math was over) and dread (Spanish was next), Leiala found herself stalling to pack up her things. The situation in her Spanish class was not much different: this year, Leiala's instructor required them to speak only in Spanish- no English allowed, no exceptions. Leiala was actually quite good at Spanish, but this rule brought her anxiety. She could follow most of the instruction in Spanish, and she felt pretty good about her written responses that she'd had the chance to think out and prepare for. But she *hated* being called on in the middle of class, when she'd had no chance to prepare or think through what to say. Most of the time she managed to pull together coherent phrases that translated to an acceptable answer, but it wasn't as smooth and polished as Leiala would have liked. This practice irritated her and kept her in a high state of alert for the duration of class.

Then, Chemistry: another subject Leiala felt dreadfully poor in. The rest of the day would pass like molasses, Leiala had learned that from experience. With reluctant acceptance of what was to come, she would settle in for the rest of the day, for hours of monotony, confusion, and spurts of brilliance that she worked so hard to achieve. No- she would never be a brilliant chemist, but she hoped she could work an A out of the class. If Leiala had anything to say about it, that would be the outcome- she knew a thing or two about working hard.

It was hard to say how Leiala felt when the final bell rang. On the one hand, she felt a sense of accomplishment: another day of school completed, another day of learning and achievement and hopefully of progressing towards the straight A's she expected from herself. But while the bell signaled reprieve and freedom to most of her classmates, to Leiala it marked the beginning of a brand new form of imprisonment.

The walk to the gym was never long- a fact Leiala both appreciated and lamented. She was grateful to be one of the first girls in the locker room, to have the opportunity to change into her basketball clothes without too many watchful eyes. She felt out of her element with the older, mature girls- and her insecurities ranged from wondering if she'd worn an acceptable style of sports bra to if she was wearing her shorts at the right height. Mostly she just wanted to cover herself up- the other girls were free in their comments about each other's bodies and seemed to feel totally comfortable exposed- Leiala did not share this feeling. When she got into the locker room early, she got to change and stretch on the court right away. This was a good thing. But- it also meant that basketball practice was just a few minutes longer for her- and basketball practice had turned into it's very own version of a personal hell.

On this particular day, Leiala sat in a butterfly position in the middle of the court, watching her teammates giggle and tease each other as they emerged one by one from the locker room to join her. Leiala smiled at them warmly- how desperately she wanted to make a connection and feel accepted on this team- while also taking in the equipment laid out on the court. Unfortunately, there was nothing present that offered any clues as to what she might be asked to do that day- a reality that caused butterflies to congregate in the center of her stomach. Would they learn any new drills that day? New plays? Would she be good at them? Would she be put on the spot in front of the entire team (never good for Leiala's anxiety) or would she be relegated to a basket with a few teammates to get more repetition in? There was no way to know.

She hadn't been on varsity for very long, but she'd already learned the most important things: making a mistake meant public ridicule and ostracization, offering an excuse or explanation meant a brutal verbal lashing from Coach (without any backup from the other girls on the team, who were understandably concerned for their own skins), and it was never okay to admit you didn't know how to do something. She'd yet to witness the consequence of this last truism- but she'd been quick to pick up on the fact that the girls never dared to admit ignorance or lack of understanding, working instead to try and figure things out as best they were able (and accept the wrath of Coach when mistakes were made).

Leiala was thankful she was so perceptive, that she could discern unspoken rules and read nonverbals. She wasn't sure where she would stand otherwise. At the same time, this made for a very stressful and emotionally draining experience: not only was she working hard to try to close the achievement gap between the senior players on the team, but she was also trying to absorb the culture of the team, the seemingly endless litany of new plays and defensive lineups, and, on top of it all, obey the unspoken rules of the team. Add to this her desire to create friendships and meaningful connections (she was sorely behind in this arena), and Leiala was straight-up drained at the end of the practice. Which was no problem, considering the mountains of reading, homework, and studying that she would go home to complete.

But truthfully, all of this would have been fine, had it not been for the unspoken rules. Leiala had already learned well her lessons in control: of putting on a brave face, of masking her true feelings in favor of the display of a thick skin, and of relentlessly pursuing goals, whether they were goals she'd created for herself or others that had been given to her by authoritative figures.

Coach walked to half-court with an irritated lilt in his step, signaling to Leiala and her teammates that they were in for a merciless practice. Leiala watched carefully without making direct eye contact as he approached the huddle of girls stretching- she knew he might interpret this as an aggressive or challenging act, two things Coach did not handle well.

"Our first game should be an easy one," Coach began, eyebrows raised in sarcasm. "If we had any kind of idea what we were doing out on the court." Leiala chanced a glance at the veteran players on the team, who had gone quiet and were watching Coach with somber expressions on their faces. Leiala followed suit.

“We look like shit,” Coach said baldly, spittle congealing in the corners of his mouth as he became more and more agitated. Leiala hid her surprise and was careful to maintain her composure, but inside she was wondering what Coach was talking about. He hadn’t seemed upset during yesterday’s practice- what had happened since then?

“If we’re going to have a prayer against this team, we need to master the 2-3 defense,” Coach went on. “We’re going to hit it hard today, and we can’t afford to make mistakes. You’ve been warned,” Coach ended, his gaze lingering over each player in an aggressive, threatening manner.

Leiala felt her heart hammer within her chest. The 2-3 defense? What was that? She tried to subdue the panic that rose like a rocket to astronomical levels inside her belly. Had she ever done a 2-3 defense? On junior varsity they’d favored man-to-man defense, and they’d been fond of pressing. She knew how to play zone defense, but Coach was making this sound like something different. Adrenaline shot through her veins, and her senses became acutely aware of everything around her. She would need to sustain this super-attentive state of being in order to deduce what Coach wanted from her.

“No fucking around today,” Coach spat, his lanky figure walking away from them and towards the sideline. “We don’t need to warm up with layups or any of that bullshit- if you miss a layup, the whole team runs a suicide,” Coach threatened, referencing the dreaded running drill of sprinting to and from each line on the basketball court in quick succession. “And if you miss more than one layup, then you might as well kick yourself off the team.”

Leiala swallowed her fear as vague instructions were given. She watched as her teammates spread across the court into assigned positions. As Coach delegated roles, Leiala felt her heart sink. They were diving right into this exercise: offense and defense would practice at the same time. This wouldn’t offer Leiala a chance to hide, nor would it allow her time to watch her teammates to try and catch what it was that she was expected to do.

"Leiala, on bottom of the 2-3," Coach ordered.

Leiala jogged uncertainly towards the bottom of the key, looking to the other players on defense for direction. None made eye contact, but Leiala determined that she was to position herself at the bottom of the key based on the placement of the other girl relegated to the bottom 2-3 role.

Before Leiala knew what was happening, the ball was in play. With all of her nerves super-charged, Leiala lowered herself into position, arms stretched wide, fingertips extended. She sat down into a squat, weight shifting to the balls of her feet. She was ready to lunge, shuffle, leap, or run- whatever might be required of her. Silently, Leiala thanked God that she'd been assigned a defensive position. She was okay on offense- she had a solid 3-point shot and could dribble and pass well enough, but on defense, she had proven herself to be excellent. She was fast, quick, attentive- and she had the endurance to sustain these attributes. She was always the first to sprint back on defense, and she was confident in her ability to shut a player down. Breathing deeply, she positioned her body so that she faced the nearest offensive player. Leiala watched her body closely, focusing on her mid-section like her dad had taught her, watchful for any shift that came from the girl's center of gravity, a clue that would foretell which direction the girl planned to move. Leiala felt power warm her bones as she settled into this familiar posture: she could do this!

"Damnit, Leiala!"

Coach's voice rang out like a brash fire alarm, catching Leiala off guard. Dumbfounded, she turned to face an irate Coach. With a sinking heart, she noticed that most of the other girls avoided looking her in the eyes, and even worse, two stood with hands on hips, their body language mirroring Coach's irritation. Leiala stood facing Coach, her body erect and assured, masking the fear and embarrassment that permeated through her being. She held her head high, ready to accept the verbal whiplash that was sure to come her way.

"Did you listen to even one thing I said?" Coach challenged, his face twitching with spasms that spoke to the level of his rage.

Leiala knew he was not actually looking for an answer, so she stayed quiet. She lifted her chin and squared her shoulders to face Coach, ready to accept the brunt of the lashing.
Coach seemed to interpret this as a gesture of defiance, or else as a sign of submission and acceptance of her incompetence- Leiala wasn't sure which. But she very clearly read his disgust, anger, and the punishing look in his narrowed eyes.

"Everyone on the line!" Coach roared.

Leiala felt heat radiate to all corners of her body as she hustled to the endline of the basketball court. She wasn't sure exactly what she'd done, but it was obvious she'd made an unforgivable mistake (in Coach's book) and she'd let her team down. The embarrassment made her tongue heavy and her throat constricted. She tried to shrug off the sighs and glances of frustration exchanged between her teammates, but she saw them and they stung. She wanted so badly to do well, and she was willing to do whatever was asked of her. She just didn't know what was expected of her!

At Coach's whistle, Leiala took off. By the second suicide, she was a full length ahead of her next teammate- quite literally leaving everyone else in her dust. Leiala's lungs burned, but she pushed herself harder. The stinging in her midsection was an appropriate punishment, her penance for mistake. Harder. Faster. Go.

Leiala finished, heart pounding from the effort. Instead of bending over or taking in deep breaths to recover, Leiala forced herself to stand straight and tall, breathing in slowly through her nose to dispel the build-up of carbon dioxide that threatened to burst from her lips. She wasn't sure why, but it was important to her that Coach think that suicide was nothing- it hadn't had any effect on her. He meant to break her- and she wouldn't give him the satisfaction. Neither would she show herself to be defiant- she wasn't on a literal suicide mission- so she didn't smile or show herself to be flippant. She imagined herself as a soldier, calmly and confidently accepting the punishment meted out to her.

Coach watched her with a stoic expression that failed to offer Leiala any clue of what he might be thinking. When the last girl crossed the line, Coach gestured wildly to the court, anger still very well intact.

“Let’s go!” he barked, and the girls reluctantly assumed their prior positions.

Leiala stood uncertainly in her defensive position, once again facing her opponent. Out of pity or, more likely, in an attempt to avoid running future suicides, her teammate muttered instructions on the 2-3 defense to her.

“Stay on the baseline. Watch for the cutter to the basket. You don’t guard me unless I get the ball,” she whispered under her breath.

“Thank you,” Leiala whispered back in relief, her heart warmed by this lifeline extended by her teammate. She quickly adjusted her position, eager to get things right the second time around.

Leiala got it right the next time, and the time after. Fearful of making a mistake, she didn’t accrue her usual steals, but she wasn’t called out for a mistake again. When it was time to switch to offense, Leiala was careful- she’d taken note of what the offensive players were doing as she’d been on defense, and she moved with cautious, mechanical steps. No mistakes were made here, either. Leiala was strangely relieved when a teammate missed a layup and the team lined up for more suicides- she was not the only failure that day. She hadn’t been the only one to let her team down. It was dangerous to take risks, Leiala realized- the punishment was too great. It was much safer to behave cautiously, to make the deliberate move as opposed to the aggressive one. Leiala hadn’t ventured to cut to the basket or take any shots, instead electing to pass the ball to teammates stuck in positions similar to hers. If *they* wanted to take a risk and shoot the ball, great. Leiala wasn’t going to take that risk herself- the last thing she wanted was to cause her team to line up once more in punishment for a mistake she had made.

And just like that, Leiala signed the notice for her steady and certain path to obscurity.

-13-

Abaddon smiled and leaned back in his chair. It wasn't often that things went as well as they just had- but as he replayed the events of that afternoon, he couldn't help but acknowledge the perfection.

"Well done, Mosity," Abaddon praised one of his workers in a rare and generous move. Mosity bowed and grinned mischievously, basking in the praise. A congregation had formed outside of Abaddon's chambers, all eager to watch the highlights of the day light up the screen hanging just outside. Abaddon didn't need to watch the newsreel to know what had been accomplished that day- he had been behind every successful venture. But that day had been particularly gratifying- enough so that Abaddon determined to watch the video if only to congratulate himself on a job well done.

His workers knew well enough not to approach him without an invitation, and Abaddon registered their surprise and unease as he shifted his great body from its resting position in the chair and up towards the door. The raucous crowd quieted as Abaddon's formidable figure emerged; he was given wide berth as he positioned himself front and center. The unhuman quiet would have unnerved the average individual; at the very least, it would have brought uncertainty and awkwardness. Not to Abaddon. He literally reveled in moments like this, and he felt a smug sense of satisfaction knowing that he was single-handedly responsible for the uncomfortable silence.

Then, the hallway lights dimmed, and a flicker of static on the enormous screen gave way to a high-resolution video stream of the day's top conquests. Abaddon was vaguely aware of the workers surrounding him, their obedient faces tipped up towards the screen like sunflowers in pursuit of the sun. He knew they were expectant, hopeful- they wanted to see *their* work, their assignment, featured up on the screen.

They were a proud and arrogant group, but Abaddon had grown to count on that. It was how he achieved the results he did- by playing one worker off of the next, humiliating or goading each worker into achievement no matter what the cost or sacrifice. There was no such thing as moral scruples- if one (or more) workers needed to be sacrificed in order to bring about the greater demise or downfall of a group, so be it. Abaddon knew his self-centered workers would never volunteer for such a selfless and martyr-like assignment, so he counted on the masses to betray, undermine, and destroy each other.

This culture of distrust and paranoia served Abaddon well- he wasn't looking for endurance in his workers, but rather ruthless spurts of energy and aggression. It didn't concern him if his workers burned out quickly- there were always new workers that would fill the ranks. *Always* new workers. There was quite literally not one worker that Abaddon considered indispensable- save for his own skin, that was. His workers knew that, and they kept themselves in line. They were fueled by greed, lust, and pride- those closest to him shared the greatest spoils. But that position of favor could be lost in an instant, never again to be recovered.

Abaddon shifted his weight and took a half-step back. To be honest, it wasn't because he needed to adjust his footing or because he'd grown uncomfortable- no, it was just to witness the effect his presence had on the minions. A rush of pleasure tickled its way up his spine as the workers nearest to him nearly shoved each other over in an effort to clear space. Certain of his superiority and intimidating effect, Abaddon focused on the screen above.

A little boy, murdered by a deranged teenager.
A woman choosing to gossip and belittle her best friend behind her back.
A little girl, choosing to use a curse word and some choice hateful sentences.
An earnest, loving dog kicked by its owner and tied up outside in the rain without food.

A father taking out his difficult day on his children, belittling them with hurtful words he didn't actually mean.
A mother choosing to silence her loneliness and desperation with alcohol.
A boy cheating on a test.
A sister betraying the trust of her brother by teasing him in front of his friends.
A toddler refusing to eat his vegetables at dinner.
A boy stomping on top of the snails that had come out with the rain.
A girl lying about her homework.
A teenage girl obediently taking in derogatory, hateful statements about herself, adopting them as her own.
A man cheating his client on a business deal.
A woman cheating on her husband.
A boy feeding food to the family dog underneath the table.

The plethora of scenes made their debut on the screen for only a few second each- and even then, not all of the victories of the day could be accounted for in video format. Each sin significant in its own way- not necessarily because of the number of lives impacted or the degree of evil produced, but because of the paradigm shift the sin had cultivated in the heart of the character. Each account represented a departure from morality, from pure and honest actions. Depending on the character, this could be easily accomplished, or could prove to be challenging. In Abaddon's realm, the EGQ (evil growth quotient) was what determined success- not the ranking of a single act in isolation.

The murderous teen might score high after carrying out a school shooting, but the EGQ would be relatively low. The teen would either die in the action (not a total loss, as Abaddon would claim ownership of another soul) or be confined to imprisonment or counseling- seriously limiting the realm of influence and potential future damage the individual could cause. Also, in Abaddon's experience, the most dramatically evil events tended to backfire as they churned up public outrage and an outpouring of love, support, encouragement, and hope. Far more effective was the less-obvious evil action with greater EGQ, such as the man cheating on a business deal or the woman gossipping about her friend. These relatively small actions cultivated a pattern of acceptance and nonchalance in the individual, leading them to believe that their action was no big deal, safe, and perhaps even justified. The neural pathway etched into the brain made future betrayals and aberrations easier to bring about, each time with minor adjustments to the size and impact of the wrong. Over time, these "harmless" acts could ultimately graduate to great acts of evil that would serve as the catalyst to countless other evil acts- this was the prized outcome all of Abaddon's workers strived to achieve. Hence the reverence and wonder on display at both minor and major sinful behaviors, each selected for its high EGQ.

The reel ended, and there was a moment of awed silence. Then, a cacophony of noise as the workers burst into shouts of appreciation. Whoops, hollers, and screams of celebration for the damage they'd been able to accomplish that day. Abaddon's smile never faltered. Oh yes, they were making progress.

***

On the west wing of headquarters, Theos stood alongside his workers watching very similar footage. These workers also faced the screen dutifully and took in the images displayed for all to see, but with a much different reaction. Here, grimaces and mournful sighs abounded, shoulders squared and hunched as though carrying the weight of the world. The pictures that passed over the screen were more than just images- they were souls, souls that Theos felt a duty to love and protect. Both Yeshua and Pneuma stood close by, also taking in the footage- as did some of the characters that had wandered in.

Unlike Abaddon, Theos welcomed the presence of as many workers and characters as wanted to draw near- his energy, patience, and stamina seemed to know no bounds. He, too, inspired reverence and awe with every step he took- but there was no fear of retribution or punishment that came from the unquestioned obedience of all those around him. Rather, it was out of love and devotion that his workers served- their actions and behavior quite literally sprouting from the love and affection they felt for their master. Theos sensed this, and welcomed their worship- there was even a sense of expectation that went along with this adoration- but without the force of threats that Abaddon weighed heavily upon.

When the reel ended in the west wing, there was silence. And then, quietly, without any great announcement or introduction, the pictures on the screen faded away into obscurity. The vivid, unfortunate images seemed to melt away through the application of white hot light that not only drowned out the graphics above but further radiated warmth and heat. And then, when only pure white light emanated from the screen, minds seemed to go blank. As quickly as the day's events had been emblazoned into the minds of viewers, the visuals were pulled out and forgotten, never again to be spoken of.

***

Joy stood in the wings of the western headquarters, watching the news of the day. The footage of sin was not on display for all to see- most of the west wing had no knowledge of sin and the subsequent unhappiness and discontent that it brought- but Joy had made a point to seek out the depressing film and watch it in its entirety. She knew the footage would be played and replayed in the east wing, in Abaddon's realm, but she hardly had the stomach to venture out into the midst of malicious workers. Her stomach roiled at the mere thought- she was certain she wouldn't be welcomed, that was one thing, but even besides that, she wouldn't for a second enjoy the diabolical and hateful attitudes of Abaddon's workers.

But she had to get to Leiala- she had to see for herself what was happening, she wanted an unbiased perspective. She had seen the day's events in real time, but she was eager for a second look. She hoped that another viewing of the day might offer her an alternative perspective, or at least some clues as to what Abaddon's strategy was. Even better, perhaps she'd be able to listen in on some of Theos's conversation on Leiala, to hear what He planned to do in response to Abaddon's acts of aggression.

Joy was sure Theos hadn't forgotten about Leiala- He never forgot about any of His charges- but His perceived inaction and passivity was baffling to her. Access to Leiala had still proven to be elusive, and she worried that Leiala's thought patterns would soon neglect her entirely. Joy had watched with increasing concern over the past weeks as Leiala's characters had all been shut down and sent away. Joy had never seen anything like it- it was no longer an overabundance of a single character, it was now the absence of *all* characters that seemed to define her existence.

Leiala had gone numb. She had closed herself off to the world, short-circuiting to a pattern of repeated behaviors learned to mask her true feelings. Joy questioned to what degree Leiala was even experiencing life- she seemed not to engage with anything around her. Not a happy or sad or upsetting encounter elicited an honest response, speaking to the deep hurt and fear that Leiala harbored but could not pinpoint or acknowledge without also destroying her ego and preservation of self.

This new reality overwhelmed Joy with despair- so anxious was she to enact change that she found herself in the west headquarters watching sin footage in the obscure hope that it might somehow offer insight or inspiration. Her pulse quickened as she watched Leiala's face materialize on the screen- she hadn't known if Leiala and the events surrounding her day might merit display on the big screen, but now, as she gazed into the cornflower-blue eyes set with resolve, she wondered under what circumstances it might have been missed.

Leiala stood on the baseline of the basketball court, her erect posture cloaking the insecurity and fear that wracked her body. Even watching the past unfold- she *knew* what was going to happen! She'd already seen it play out- Joy felt her body stiffen. She watched as Leiala took in a deep breath, tilting her head to one side in a gesture that Joy knew meant she was listening closely.

Voices were muted in favor of the inner dialogue that ran through Leiala's brain. Joy felt her heart sink as she listened once more to the pessimistic thoughts and despairing observations made by Leiala. She took note of every posture adjustment, every shift of weight, swinging of arms, and faux stretch that spoke to Leiala's downward spiral. Although there was no way to measure the extent of the damage done to Leiala in a single practice, Joy envisioned clearly the notches Leiala had fallen.

Then, an unexpected move. The footage shifted from Leiala's negative self-talk and mounting despair to that of the coach. This was a perspective Joy hadn't been privy to- she'd obviously seen and been frustrated by the coach's actions, but she hadn't had any idea of the motives behind his behavior.

Joy watched with interest as Abaddon's workers swooped on Coach, encapsulating him in a blanket of anger, frustration, and hopelessness. She felt a wave of pity as Coach was bombarded, ganged up on- with literally no outlet and no perception of hope, he behaved like a cornered animal, lashing out at anyone within reach. His players. The only ones within reach. Joy watched in disgusted fascination as Anger and Despair hunted Coach, shadowed him relentlessly as he attempted to go about his day. Although Joy didn't see the full footage of his day, she suddenly caught an inspired vision of Coach valiantly attempting to fight off the first onslaughts of negative emotion only to succumb to the constant pressure later in the day.

Then, with increasing interest, Joy watched as Coach focused on Leiala- the one player who refused to back down or show signs of weakness when confronted with his terrible eruptions of rage. She felt sorrow and frustration as she realized the basis of his targeted attacks- Leiala came to symbolize all that Coach could not control, all that he felt unsatisfied with in his life. Leiala was no longer a fifteen year old girl with problems of her own and a heart eager to please, but a culdesac for years of frustration, angst, and disappointment.

Leiala was a basketball career cut short.
Leiala was the wife who did not respect him.
Leiala was the baby that cried and kept him up at night.
Leiala was the job that didn't pay enough to move his family out of the dingy two-bedroom apartment they currently lived in.
Leiala was the college education he'd failed to secure.
Leiala was the strained relationship with his father.
Leiala was the sorry, squished peanut butter and jelly sandwich he'd eaten for lunch while his peers ordered a hot meal.

Armed with this fresh perspective, Joy now understood why Coach continued to belittle Leiala aggressively. But understanding the *why* did little to change the circumstances of the fifteen year old girl who was actively losing herself.

-14-

Fear reflected on his earlier conversation with Joy with much trepidation. Joy had made a number of serious accusations that sounded preposterous, but Fear knew in his gut that they were all true. He hadn't been entirely sure of Joy's mission- he'd been skeptical and wary of accepting the invitation to meet with her and the other characters assigned to Leiala. Not because he didn't enjoy the company of the other characters- for the most part, they all got along just fine, recognizing that each was essential in spite of the fact that they might sometimes annoy one another- but because he was exhausted at the end of each day, and he worried that Joy was going to ask him to do something grand.

Joy had been calm in the meeting- eerily calm, Fear had decided. She'd been the perfect picture of composure, her clothes flat-ironed and pressed neatly against her slim figure, the worry lines and creases of her face softened. Fear's guard went up immediately- Joy might be many things, but she was not usually peaceful and subdued.

"Thank you for coming, Fear," Joy had been quick to greet him, making sure he knew that she'd seen him. There would be no escaping now. Fear begrudgingly lumbered to the nearest table, joining Angst and Panic. *How many characters had Joy invited?* He wasn't even sure what this meeting was all about.

"Do any of us know what this is all about?" Fear mumbled under his breath to Panic. Panic shook his head and shrugged his shoulders, raising his eyebrows in a gesture Fear registered to mean exasperation.

"Who else did you invite, Joy?" Angst asked aloud. Joy turned to their table, a placid smile on her face.

"Just a few more characters," Joy said evenly, her intonation flat and measured. Fear was getting more and more antsy by the second. Joy was acting strangely- Fear got the distinct impression that she was trying to cover something up.

Anger walked in, followed by Confusion, and then Despair. Joy lingered by the doorway, stretching her petite figure out the doorway to peer both directions.

"I think that's it," she announced after a moment, peeking expectantly once more before pulling the door to a gentle closed position. Walking to the front of the room, she planted her feet shoulder distance apart and clasped her hands together, wringing them somewhat anxiously as she looked down at her shins.

"I know you're all wondering why I asked you to come," Joy began, looking up hesitantly, a lock of hair falling over her eyes. Brushing it aside with her fingers, she took a resolved breath and looked up at the characters congregated before her.
"Abaddon's done too much damage," Joy proclaimed. Her voice wavered in just the slightest manner- Fear wouldn't have heard it unless he'd been listening for any evidence of insecurity. But he *had* been listening acutely for any such indication, and it hadn't escaped his notice. Her observation was met with a cough and some interrupted chuckles. Fear felt dread seep through his bones- he'd been right, Joy was going to ask them to do something incredible.

"Joy-" Panic began, but Joy caught him off in an apparent onslaught of fresh courage.

"I know! I know, it sounds crazy. We're characters. We're not supposed to get involved. We're supposed to follow orders, influence our assignments when called upon, and otherwise stay on the fringes," she rushed, her words falling over each other like dominoes in her haste to get them all out without interruption.

"So then..." Despair let the words hang in the air, an unspoken question.

"Well, we can't just let that happen," Joy finished, her voice laced with frustration as she scanned the faces around her.

"Joy," Panic said again, but this time there was no question in the voice. There was a subtle warning, one that was not lost on Joy.

"Just wait until you know what I'm asking you to do," Joy had insisted, placating them with a pleading gaze. Fear had watched the characters around him shift uncomfortably in their seats without offering any reaction himself. He realized now that only the stereotyped "negative" emotions were present for this meeting- was this intentional on Joy's part, or was it a mere coincidence? If it were the former, Fear worried that Joy might ask them to do something involving Abaddon. If that were the case- if Joy so much as mentioned Abaddon, Fear was out. No ifs, ands, or buts about it. He'd made an appearance at the meeting, and he would hear Joy out. But he would not put his neck on the line in such a profound way- there was too much at stake. As it was, Fear felt like he was daily grilled- he lived on pins and needles, perpetually anxious that he might be called upon to carry out some distasteful task or worse yet, to endure some public humiliation over a perceived shortcoming.

"Theos knows about this meeting," Joy randomly blurted before continuing her train of thought. Fear and the other characters immediately relaxed, and Fear wondered why she hadn't opened with that comment. He also wondered why Theos wasn't present...

"He knows I've called a meeting, and He knows what I plan to propose," Joy clarified. "Of course, we can't act as free agents- we have to wait to be summoned. But we can still fight back, and that's what I wanted to talk to you about. I want to learn more about Abaddon's methods, so that we can fight back."

A couple of characters tried to interject here, to offer their thoughts and protests, but Joy held up a hand that commanded impressive, immediate silence. She was on a roll now, and there was no sign of insecurity or hesitation anymore.

"I think you'll agree that your role in Leiala's life has grown too great," Joy stated, not waiting for an affirmative response. "You're spending far too much time influencing Leiala's thought patterns, and some of us other characters are hardly ever able to visit. This is not the way it was designed to be. For the most part, we're stuck operating at the whimsy of Abaddon or Theos, but we do have power we haven't been exercising. We've obeyed without question for as long as I can remember- we don't even know what push-back or power we may possess."

"Do we really want to find out?" Angst asked. "This is Abaddon we're talking about, not Theos. As in, the guy who crucifies his enemies and ruthlessly destroys anyone who so much as hints as disagreeing with him. Not the best individual to challenge," Angst ended sarcastically.

"I'm not proposing any specific scheme yet," Joy clarified. "I agree- we can't make a move against Abaddon or work to undermine him until we have more information. Which leads me to my point..."

"Before you even say anything, I feel the need to point out that you're going to ask *us* to take a risk on your behalf," Anger blurted. "If whatever it is that you have planned goes south, it will be one of us- or *all* of us- who go down. Not you."

"That's true," Joy answered baldly, not trying to dodge the facts. "There's no way I could carry out the task I'm going to ask of you. My hope is that you share my frustration and disappointment in Leiala's upbringing, and that you will be brave enough to try to enact change."

"This isn't our job," Panic pointed out. "It's Theos's job to counter Abaddon- He has the power to do so. Characters don't do this."

"Characters *haven't* done this- it doesn't mean they *couldn't* do it," Joy clarified.

"What do you want us to do?" Fear cut in. He wasn't particularly wild about an idea that involved risk and Abaddon, but his curiosity had gotten the better of him, and he figured the sooner he knew Joy's plan, the sooner he could decide he wasn't willing to participate.

"Simple. I want you to attend a strategics meeting in the east headquarters," Joy said.

"That's it?" Fear scoffed. "Do you know how many of those Abaddon has already forced me to attend? I feel as though I'm a strategics expert by now," he ended with a mirthless chuckle.

"No, no- not that kind of strategics meeting. I want you to attend one of the introductory courses, one that focuses on and literally dissects each moment in time to assess the best avenues to influence the assignment. We need to understand Abaddon and his game, and how his workers are trained," Joy explained.

Fear's eyebrows furrowed, and he viewed Joy with newfound respect. How did she know these details about the east end headquarters? How had she learned of these classes? Fear had only learned of their existence recently, as he'd spent an inordinate amount of time in Abaddon's realm.

"You don't think that will be suspicious?" Angst asked. "All of a sudden a bunch of characters show up in strategics 101?"

"I *do* think it will look suspicious," Joy agreed, catching them all off guard. "Which is why I'm not asking all of you to attend. I only want *one* of you to go."

There was a prolonged silence, which Joy promptly filled.

"It has to be one of you- it would be the most suspicious if one of the positive characters showed up in the east end headquarters. I called you all here because I didn't know who might be willing- but only one of you needs to go."

"I'll do it."

Fear felt the vibration of his vocal chords and heard the distant words before it registered that it was in fact HE who had agreed to go.
YOU?! YOU volunteered?! You've got to be joking- you're already on Abaddon's "most hated" list- you want to put yourself under more scrutiny? What is this, a suicide mission?

An army of desperate thoughts marched through his mind in quick succession, each new thought pushing out the comrade in front of him. He should probably change his mind quickly, he should probably explain right away that he wasn't a good fit for the job, or at least offer some kind of excuse.

"Thank you," Joy sighed, smiling at Fear in evident relief. Fear swallowed his excuses painfully- his pride would not let him back out now. Panic clapped him on the back, and the rest of the characters nodded respectfully in his direction.

"Okay- I'm assuming you can get a copy of the schedule of classes," Joy went on, her words now directed at Fear. Fear felt as though he were underwater- Joy's words were far away, floating towards him and then away as though seaweed caught in a tumultuous current.

"Fear?"

"Yes," Fear cleared his throat, his glazed eyes snapping back into focus in time to see Joy's look of concern. "You will do it, won't you, Fear?"

"Yes," Fear agreed, this time with more resolve.

"Okay," Joy responded, this time uncertainty woven into her words. "We're counting on you," she said softly, shyly.

"*We're*?" Fear asked. Who else besides Joy was depending on him?

"All of us want Leiala to grow into the best human she can be, to fulfill the role that Theos designed for her. So yes, all of us are counting on you," Joy agreed.

"What's Theos's role in all of this?" Fear asked, suddenly suspcious and interested to know how the great ruler fit into the puzzle.

"You know He's always mysterious," Joy began, the frustration subtle in her voice. "I don't know for sure. But I did manage an audience with Him, and He wasn't opposed to my plan. He thought it was a good idea for us to understand how Abaddon operates."

"So He doesn't really approve of the plan," Fear distinguished, irritation rising in his chest.

"What do you mean?" Joy asked defensively.

"You made it sound like He'd approved our mission," Fear accused. "But He hasn't approved anything. He's just said it's not a *bad* idea. Not the same thing."

"This is the first step, Fear," Joy said, taking on a new tone of superiority. Fear was acutely aware of the fact that she didn't address his concern, but one look at her shiny, misted eyes told him not to challenge her further. It was clear that she was passionate about this idea- she truly wanted to do her job to the utmost, and Fear had no argument with that. Besides, the mission he'd agreed to wasn't as dangerous as he'd initially feared. As he thought further on what he'd have to do, he realized it wasn't all that scary. It might even be interesting.

For the first time, Fear noticed that all of the other characters had left. When had that happened? He'd been so focused on his conversation with Joy and fixated on visions of his task that he'd been oblivious to their departure.

"I'll look into it right away," Fear heard himself tell Joy. "When do you want me to report back to you?"

"As soon as you've got something," Joy answered. "We need to stop Abaddon."

***

Now Fear found himself standing outside the entrance to the introductory strategics session. He wasn't as nervous as he'd thought he'd be- he didn't think his presence would generate too much excitement, and he'd been such a constant figure in the east headquarters anyway that he doubted anyone would think twice about his reason for being there.

Not only that, but he'd realized as he walked to the assigned classroom that he would be surrounded by new, fresh workers- those inexperienced workers who had not yet learned to be cruel and ruthless and maliciously brilliant. Not that they needed classes to learn how to be evil- but Fear guessed that he would not be harassed.

When the classroom doors opened, Fear slipped in quietly, sandwiching himself between two swarthy figures and then making a beeline for the back of the classroom. He'd brought a notebook and pencil, but they were carefully tucked away. He wasn't sure of the procedure for classes in the east headquarters- were the workers expected to take notes? Or did they simply commit all learning to memory? Fear had more than just literal academic content to absorb- he was about to learn about an entire culture he'd otherwise been ignorant of.

An instructor shuffled obliquely to the front of the classroom, his seniority evident through his significant belly, wrinkled skin, and weary walk. His footfalls were heavy, and his entire face sagged in disappointment. He didn't make eye contact with any of the new pupils as he made his way to the podium. Fear felt the last bubble of panic burst- he would be safe sitting in this class.

The instructor leaned heavily on the wooden podium, which protested with an agonized groan before the instructor relented, shifting back onto his heels. Fear couldn't take his eyes off the instructor, who resembled a grizzled alligator. His skin was scaly, his back hunched, and Fear could imagine without much effort the thick callouses he felt sure adorned his hands and feet.

"Listen up," the instructor announced with surprising clarity and authority, catching Fear off guard. His eyes flashed up- bright, ruby-red gems that seemed to glow and burn into the faces of his pupils. There was no need for the instructor to say anymore- he had the complete, undivided attention of every pupil in the room.

Fear watched in awe as the instructor pushed a button on the small, pocket-sized device cushioned deep in his oversized palm. Long, pointed fingernails seemed to massage the edges of the device, an action that while simple and relatively innocent, sent creepy shivers up Fear's spine.

In an instant, an image was up on the screen. Fear didn't recognize any of the individuals in the picture- they could have been any human. A mom and her adolescent daughter, standing in the kitchen.

"You didn't eat all of your lunch," the mother stated as she unpacked the tupperware containers from her daughter's lunchbox.

"I wasn't hungry," the girl snapped back.

"You were hungry enough to eat the Chips Ahoy, I see," the mom barked. She held up the ziploc bag holding carrots and celery stalks. "But your vegetables went untouched."

"So?!" the daughter challenged, her body tensing into what Fear recognized as an aggressive stance. The mother didn't say anything, but raised her eyebrows, pursed her lips tightly together, and turned her back on the daughter as she rinsed the first tupperware container.

"I hate you!" the daughter roared, stamping her foot defiantly onto the wooden floor. She burst into tears as the mother turned around in shock, then outrage.

"What in the-?! Go to your room this instant," the mother commanded, face flaming in rage. "You can answer to your father when he gets home!"

The daughter seemed to contemplate pushing back, but turned on her heel and stormed up the stairs, slamming the door dramatically for full effect once she'd reached her room.

Then the image froze, and the instructor stepped forward to address the class.
"What did you notice?"

Not one hand went up. Fear wiggled in his seat uncomfortably. He wasn't sure what happened in east end classes when a pupil didn't have an answer, and he worried that the consequence would be terrible. But the instructor seemed to be expecting this response.

"Watch again," he commanded, pushing the button once more.

The opening scene again materialized on the screen, but Fear noticed that this time there were characters and workers hovering in the atmosphere surrounding the mother and daughter. He couldn't help it- Fear felt himself lean forward in his seat. He'd never seen any such thing before- an image that also included the influence of the alternative realm. The still image alone fascinated him- anticipation built in his body for the footage he imagined he was about to see.

In the kitchen, Frustration, Disappointment, and Insecurity clung to the figure of the mother. Hemming these characters in on all sides were Abaddon's workers.

"You didn't eat all of your lunch," the mother stated as she unpacked the tupperware containers from her daughter's lunchbox.

See? I told you- you're a terrible mother. Your children don't even eat the lunches you pack for them. They don't appreciate the work that you do, Insecurity hissed into the mother's ear.

You should just give up, Frustration chimed in. *Your kids wouldn't care.*

And is this what you got a college education for? Did you give up your dreams for this? You could have been so much more- you could have been someone important- but it's too late now, Disappointment rushed to add.

"I wasn't hungry," the girl snapped back.

Geeze, Mom is already mad at me and I haven't been home for two minutes, Despair was quick to offer to the daughter.

Nothing you ever do will be good enough, Hopelessness added. *Why try?*

She has no idea what a hard day you had! Does she even care? No questions about how your day was, or consideration about how tough your classes may have been. Does she care that your friends left you during lunch, or that you got a B- on that project you spent all of winter break working on? No, she only cares about herself! Anger growled.

And now you have SO much homework to get to, and you're exhausted. The last thing you need is your grumpy mom bugging you, Intolerance shouted. Fear could nearly hear the anger that radiated and rattled the girl's bones, so strong was the feeling.

"You were hungry enough to eat the Chips Ahoy, I see," the mom barked. She held up the ziploc bag holding carrots and celery stalks. "But your vegetables went untouched."

You just showed her who's boss, Pride praised the mother. *Make sure she respects you and recognizes who's in control.*

"So?!" the daughter challenged, her body tensing into what Fear recognized as an aggressive stance.

She thinks you're fat! Insecurity screeched. *OMG, she's actually calling you FAT!*

Well, you are a little fat, Fear whispered. *Your jeans were a little tight this morning.*

No, no- you can't let her get away with that. Protect the ego at all costs, Pride commanded, leaving no room for negotiation.

Fear watched the rest of the scene unfold with the painful understanding that while both mother and daughter loved each other desperately, their personal insecurities, frustrations, circumstances, and dispositions had driven them to lash out at each other and cut each other down. It was hard to watch, to know that instead of the love and acceptance that each longed to impart on the other, each one drove the other to a lonely and disappointed place. The single scene was replayed once more, and Fear listened in a daze as the instructor and then the students identified Abaddon's best tactics and maneuvers.

Fear had always harbored a healthy respect for Abaddon and his work- he knew that he was powerful and intelligent. But there was something about seeing it played out with precision, flawless detail, and commentary that made it difficult to stomach.

When class was dismissed, Fear was careful to leave in the middle of the pack. He hadn't taken a single note, but he hadn't needed to. The impressions of the past hour were burned forever into the recesses of his brain.

Do you have to dismiss me so? Do you think that I lack feelings, that I don't notice or don't care when you sweep me under the rug, denying my presence in your life? It hurts. I'm not sure when I became embarrassing, relegated to the realms of fanny-packs and overaffectionate mothers and eighties dance moves. Your actions suggest that I am something to be ashamed of, but when the audience leaves, you come running to me.

Have you ever thought about how this makes me feel? I'm your closet lover- the one you speak to before you go to bed at night, whispering sweet nothings into your ear as you hold me close and murmur on about your dreams and visions for the future. I feel your heartbeat quicken, feel your desperate need and deep want for me. I'm no fool. So why do you treat me like one? Why, when asked baldly about my existence, do you deny me? Am I so uncouth, so uncivilized as to earn such a salty reception?

Oh, I know not all of you are like this. There are some of you who have forsaken me altogether- I'm completely shut out of your life, and you entertain no fantasies regarding our life together. I feel sorry for you- you have no idea how completely wonderful and euphoric I can be- but I respect your resolve. I know where I stand with you- there are no sneaky dalliances or midnight rendezvous to be had here.

And there are others of you who embrace me with full force, your faces glowing with light as you speak of my character. You're envied by other humans who wish they had what you do. You're criticized by some who are sure that our relationship is impossible, foolish, naïve. They believe such an arrangement is ridiculous, out of the question, and nonsensical. They work to cut you down, to expose your supposed folly to any and all who might point out your peace and optimism. Why? Because they can't bear to imagine that I've shacked up with someone else.

But here's the truth that so many of you choose to ignore: I can be yours, too. You can have me. It's not hard- your human soul is literally created to crave my presence, to feed off my existence. It's kept mankind alive all these years- and yet you occasionally suggest that I am a cruel thing: nasty, deceitful, not to be trusted. You don't really believe that, although you profess to. You minimize my presence, shove me into the closet when company comes, and deny my relationship with you when someone asks. And so I must respectfully ask: when did it become this way? When did it become immature or short-sighted to walk with me?

Your life is better with me in it. And at your very core, you know it. Which is why you can't bear to be apart from me for long. You try sometimes, when you feel awfully disappointed. You pack your bags and give me a long tongue lashing where you cry and wail and kick and scream. And you leave. You slam the door behind you so hard that the resounding boom echoes throughout the entire building, warning other residents of my assumed infidelity.

I know better than to take these episodes to heart. Truthfully, this is my cue to fill up the teapot and set it on the stove, to pull some cookies out of the pantry and settle in to my favorite cushion on the well-worn loveseat. You'll be back- usually within the hour, but sometimes you can make it a night without me. If you're particularly stubborn, you might last a couple of days- possibly a week.

But you always come back. You realize you can't live without me- you see how futile and infantile your attempts to sever our bond were. And when you come back, it's with your tail in between your legs- you sneak in during the cover of the night, slipping in through the unlatched first-floor window or sometimes the side door. As dramatic as your exit was, your reentry is subdued, silent, unannounced. You know where to find me. I am- luckily for you- always waiting in the same place. You never apologize, you never explain. But boy, do you squeeze the living daylights out of me as you pull me tight and vow to never let me go. You beg me to make promises I cannot keep and to give you answers and timelines and outcomes that I have no way of knowing. I'm not sure what to say about this revisitation- I wish I could say that it was pleasant, but I can never really enjoy it. I inherit your desperation, and I know you will leave me again: you prodigal humans always do.

I'm not even sure why I wasted my energy writing this- things will never change. I've accepted my lot in life. Until you cling to me again...

-Hope

-15-

Fear became addicted to the class. At first, he told himself it was out of duty- he'd agreed to do this favor for Joy, and he was committed to fulfilling his word. But as time went on, Fear was forced to face the truth- it was more than duty that brought him to the east end headquarters. It was his own warped, burning desire to learn about Abaddon's methods that drove him to arrive early, never taking any notes as he sat through class fully engrossed in the footage put before him.

For as many classes as he had sat through, he could still not get used to the blasé way the instructor talked about each individual, highlighting techniques in the human's life that were quite literally destroying their happiness and sabotaging any chance for peace. In fact, *everyone* in the room sat and took the lesson in without any emotional response- Fear made a concerted effort to do the same.

Joy had asked about the lessons, and Fear had been happy to offer up all that he had noticed and learned. But he often felt frustrated after these conversations with Joy- he was acutely aware of the fact that he hadn't the words or expressions to accurately portray what went on in the classroom. He would go to great lengths describing the classroom, the attendants, the instructor- he'd even tried to explain in painful detail how a scene was chunked, taken apart by the instructor and then the students to identify all the components that were masterfully achieved through Abaddon's practices. But these were just words, ideas, and static images- they only scratched the surface.

Fear wasn't proud to admit it, but he'd actually tried to numb himself. He'd assumed that to be a skill in and of itself, something

Abaddon's workers might have a natural inclination towards, but still something that could be acquired through practice.

It had gotten easier, but he still wasn't there yet. He could cement his features into place and take full command of his expression, but his heart still palpitated and ached for the assignment he saw up on the screen. He hadn't given much thought to his work in this way before- when he was on an assignment, he was just completing a job. He didn't give too much thought to the repercussions of his work- that wasn't a part of his job description. That was irrelevant, anyway- it wasn't his job to have an opinion. It was his job to follow orders.

But there was something about seeing the bigger picture play out before him that now made his current assignment almost unbearable- it was becoming more and more difficult to report to Leiala and complete his work without also wondering what was taking place in the alternative realm and guessing at how it might affect Leiala long term. It had never been his business to care, but now he did. He always had, he supposed, but he'd tricked himself into thinking that he had no power and that all of his assignments had ultimately turned out fine. Now he knew better, and he could never go back to that state of blissful ignorance he'd enjoyed for so many years.

The days passed slowly and, at the same time, the weeks whizzed by. It was becoming difficult for Fear to live with himself, influencing Leiala while knowing what effect he had. Or what effect he assumed he'd have. In all fairness, Fear didn't know for sure- the only thing he knew for certain was that which he was ordered to carry out. He worked hard to push the other images and hypothetical situations from his mind. Until, one day, he could feign ignorance no longer.

The class began like any other: Fear sat expectantly in his seat in the back room, careful not to attract attention through his over-eager behavior. By this point, he figured the workers had grown accustomed to his presence and didn't give him a second thought- but he couldn't be sure. The instructor shuffled to his position behind the podium in typical fashion that suggested intentionality without any rush, and he gave his audience only a cursory glance before turning the projector on. He began to introduce the scene, but Fear didn't register a word he said. His eyes were riveted to the picture on the screen, and his heart hammered in his chest, his ears burning and thumping and drowning out all noise around him. There, on display for the class to assess, was Leiala.

A litany of thoughts immediately flashed through Fear's mind. First, he was thankful that the scene did not take place in a basketball gym- as far as he knew, those were the worst moments of Leiala's existence. It was most difficult to ignore the deep pain that radiated from Leiala on those assignments.

"The girl has just finished basketball practice, and she's at the grocery store with her mother picking up a couple of grocery items before they head home. The girl is a talented athlete, but she's no longer the best on her team, and she's been pretty shredded by the coach and other players for her style of play and temperament. She's coming into this scene with a disposition that is frustrated and desperate," the instructor intonated.

Fear chafed at his flat tone, and his description of Leiala as "the girl." Leiala was not just any girl- she was special! She was *Leiala*. In this room, she was stripped of all identity and personality- she was just like any other human assignment.

Fear could barely breathe, looking up at Leiala in her basketball shorts, oversized jersey, and flip flops. Her long hair was drawn back in a low ponytail that followed the fashion of the other girls on the team. Fear didn't need the introduction from the instructor to register the irritation and distraction permeating from Leiala's body in the form of tense shoulders and clouded eyes. Fear also noted with some anxiety that this was not a scene he remembered- which meant that he had not been present for that moment of Leiala's life. That alone was pretty typical- characters needed rest just like anyone else, and they couldn't be expected to follow an individual 24/7- not only was that unheard of, but it was unnecessary. No character was needed around the clock- at least that Fear knew of.

Fear was vaguely aware of the instructor pressing "play." And then everything became a blur.

Leiala walking down the aisles of the grocery store, following behind her mother, who was clearly on a mission. Her posture was firm, erect- her head held high, her stride sure and strong.

"See that? Right there?" the instructor paused the video and not three seconds had passed. Nothing had happened. Literally Leiala had walked down half an aisle. Fear looked up in confusion, peeking at the faces of the workers around him. Had he missed something?

The instructor shook his head in exasperation, apparently frustrated with his group of slow learners.

"That walk," the instructor pointed out, rewinding the footage just enough to show Leiala walking down the aisle. "What do you notice?"

Again, the instructor was met with silence.

A hesitant hand rose, and the instructor pounced eagerly.

"Yes?"

"She looks confident," he answered simply, uncertainly. Fear grimaced, anticipating the verbal lashing that was almost certain to follow such an elementary response. To his surprise, the instructor wagged his finger in excitement.

"Yes! She does look confident, doesn't she?" the instructor agreed. "Now, what information did I give to you about the girl before we began?"

This time, the entire class obediently vocalized the answer the instructor was looking for: that the girl had just come from basketball practice, where she was marginalized during her time on the court by both her coach and teammates.

"With that in mind, what do you make of this walk?" the instructor challenged the group.

"She's....compensating?" one worker suggested.

"Oh yes," the instructor gushed. "Majorly. Why?"

Fear felt his heart sink as he saw where the instructor was guiding the conversation. He had a feeling he wasn't going to like what he heard next.

"She doesn't want to be seen as weak," the same worker ventured, gaining confidence.

"She's *learned* not to demonstrate weakness. She gives off the aura of being strong, and others believe this about her. It's admired and respected, but it also keeps people at arm's length distance. They don't see her as someone who needs encouragement or comfort, so she doesn't get that. But as you'll see, she badly needs this," the instructor explained, elaborating on the scene.

The movie played once more, and Fear watched as Leiala walked down the aisle for a second time. This time, the picture showed Abaddon's workers swarming Leiala, flanking her on either side.

One worker dedicated his practice to feeding Leiala images of all of her mistakes during basketball practice. Fear watched as Leiala's brow became furrowed and her shoulders tensed. He could imagine her thoughts as she criticized her play.

Leiala's stomach growled audibly, reminding her that it was nearing dinner time. She looked around at the packaged food on the shelves, and Abaddon's worker wasted no time cozying up to her ear.

You can't eat that. You'll get fat. And the chemicals- you'll probably get cancer. And don't forget about the sugar- didn't you read that article about sugar causing acne?

Leiala kept her head down, eyes obediently fixed on the clamshell-white tiles as she marched past the shelves stacked with unhealthy food choices. As she rounded the corner, she caught a glimpse of a girl from school, a girl who looked awfully cute with her hair gathered haphazardly on top of her head in a messy bun that managed to look feminine and cute while also casual and unpretentious.

You couldn't do that with your hair. It's too long and thick.

Plus, you have a big forehead. It wouldn't look cute.

Leiala tossed her ponytail to the side in a superficial gesture of defiance known only to the crowd watching the exchange on the screen.

"She's focusing on her appearance now- obsessively," the instructor pointed out, freezing the frame once more. "She's spending so much time worrying about how she looks that she's forgetting to engage with those around her. She's getting sucked out of the present moment in her obsession with the future."

Fear stared at the screen, wide-eyed. It was true. The only characters in the past scene had been Panic and Anxiety- he hadn't needed to influence Leiala to have her draw near to a pessimistic outcome.

Play began again, and Leiala caught up to her mother.

That girl was all by herself- she was grown up enough to drive herself here to the grocery store. You're like a little girl, tagging along with her mommy while she grocery shops.

Fear took note of the pursed lips and the arrival of Anger.

"See what happened there?" the instructor pressed pause once more. Fear wished he would stop- it was like a horrific car accident that he couldn't bear to look at, but also couldn't draw his eyes away from. There were too many things to notice- too many pieces of evidence showing that Leiala was under assault.

"Insecurity was summoned at the perfect time- and the girl's insecurity went beyond her concern over her physical appearance to the perception of her situation. Although the insecurity is personal and individualized, it's just been projected onto the mother. The mother doesn't know this yet, of course- but we can see the animosity and resentment building in Leiala by the second," the instructor went on, pointing out Leiala's tense shoulders and the flat line of her mouth and brow.

"What makes this even more ideal is the fact that we are dealing with a self-righteous perfectionist," the instructor gloated, the joy in his voice evident. Fear felt resentment build towards this instructor who was practically singing out his observations.

"She's afraid of letting her mother down, her team down, her teachers down, her friends down- literally anyone she's ever met. So she won't say anything to her mom- she'll just let the resentment build. She believes she's doing the right thing in suppressing this feeling, but she won't be able to diffuse it, and when she snaps, it will be far worse than if she had just verbalized her feelings in the first place."

Eyes turned back to the screen to watch Leiala trail her mother, giving clues of her irritation through passive aggressive sighs and the amount of distance she kept between the two of them.

"She's entered into a critical, dissatisfied state," the instructor vocalized, this time letting the footage roll as he spoke. "We've captured her mood, and any attempts to try to pull herself out of this 'funk' will be futile. This is the ultimate goal for any assignment- once in this mindset, the individual is primed to look for problems, for things to go wrong- they will notice and capitalize on anything negative, which will support their false belief that their life is the *worst* and *everyone* is out to get them. From here, we can convince the assignment to do any number of things. One hundred positive things could happen to the girl right now, and she would literally not even recognize them. She's going to judge everything unfavorably."

True to the instructor's analysis, Leiala rolled her eyes as her mom put cottage cheese and then navel oranges into the cart.

"Can we get tangerines instead?" Leiala asked, a slight edge to her voice. It was an honest request, but Fear could hear the challenge in her words.

“No, I already got oranges,” her mom answered, pushing the cart forward without pasuing to engage with Leiala.

“They both have the same amount of vitamin c,” Leiala argued. “And they taste sweeter. We always get oranges.”

“No one likes tangerines,” her mother said dismissively.

This was the wrong comment to make- Abaddon’s workers practically salivated as she intoned the last of the words and then pounced without hesitation.

She doesn’t care what you like, or what you want.

You have no control. You just get bossed around. You are literally a slave, trapped to do what everyone else wants.

“Well, I like tangerines,” Leiala shot back, this time with evident attitude.

“Leiala, don’t be difficult,” her mother sighed. “Let’s just finish this up and go home.”

Leiala said nothing, but her chin protruded defiantly, and her fingers were balled into fists so tight that Fear wondered if she would strain her muscles.

You’re difficult. Everyone thinks you’re difficult. It’s not even a big deal- it’s literally just a simple substitution of a fruit, but your request wasn’t honored. You’re not worth it. You’re not even worth a trade of oranges for tangerines.

It’s better to know your worth now. Imagine how bad you would feel if you didn’t learn the truth until later on.

Hopelessness entered the scene, accompanied by Depression. Then, just for fun, Despair joined the party. Fear watched as they hovered in the mental space just above Leiala, encouraged by Abaddon’s workers.

You could earn your worth.

A false joy sidled up to Leiala at this point- one of Abaddon's workers, but this time gallivanting as a positive entity. A firework of hope lit Leiala's clouded vision, and Fear wiggled uncomfortably in his seat as he watched Hope shoved close to Leiala's side only to be jerked away roughly by Abaddon's workers seconds later.

You know the girls who are worth the most- they're the pretty ones. The perfect ones. If you were perfect, you would be worth tangerines. You would be worth a starting position on the varsity basketball team, and you would be worth having a crush on.

Leiala's facial expression changed- she was thinking. Fear felt his heart sink like a brick to his toes. He could tell that Leiala was buying into this argument given to her by thieves, murderers, liars.

No sound passed her lips, but Fear didn't need to hear any words spoken to know that Leiala had just agreed with the voice.

"This is the critical moment," the instructor announced, freezing the frame mid-scene. "Every action we've seen Abaddon's workers take in this scene has led to this moment. The girl is vulnerable, in a state of despair. This is exactly the state that we work so hard to create- it is in this position that any human assignment is most likely to internalize and accept the message Abaddon has prepared for them. The girl won't apply logic to her situation- and if she tries, it will wither quickly. Despair and hopelessness have that effect- the emotion that comes from such characters is overwhelming; it dominates any other feeling and impedes all thought patterns that don't serve its purposes."

There was respectful silence in the room as the class watched Leiala trail her mother to the check-out line, where a colorful assortment of women's magazines greeted her maliciously.

Lose 15 pounds in time for summer! one magazine promised, featuring a voluptuous woman with an impossibly tiny waist, all highlighted in a skimpy fire-engine red bikini. Leiala contemplated the cover, taking personal inventory of the woman's figure and comparing it to her own. Abaddon's workers were delighted to help.

Her legs are skinnier. She has chiseled abs. Her arms look skinnier than yours, too- and they're also more defined. She doesn't have awkward tan lines like you.

How tall is she? Leiala's thought wasn't vocalized, but the intention behind it was strong enough that it was impressed upon the crowd.

It's impossible to know- it doesn't matter, either. If you're taller than her, your fat should be more evenly spread out, one of Abaddon's workers was quick to rationalize. *So that's not an excuse.*

Is he cheating on you? Here's how to win him back! This magazine featured a buxom woman scantily clad in a super-tight and short red sequined dress. Leiala didn't have to open the pages of the magazine to know the instructions would include exacting revenge through a perfect body- the poisonous remorse the cheater would feel once he saw his gorgeous former girlfriend.

Leiala rolled her eyes and looked away from that cover- how stupid and degrading- but there was still a little piece of the image that glummed onto her insides. *Hot* girls didn't get cheated on. They were wanted, desired.

Get Noticed Now! The next cover practically screamed with it's massive hot-pink lettering. *From Drab to FAB!* the subtext explained.

That's me, Leiala determined, again with conviction that allowed the class to hear her thoughts.

*That **is** you,* Abaddon's workers agreed. *But it's okay- you can change that. The first step to enacting any change is recognizing that a change needs to be made,* another worker interjected sagely.

Leiala's gaze hung heavy on the magazine promising change, then flickered to her mother unloading groceries onto the conveyer belt. Her family didn't read magazines like that- she was almost certain she'd be made fun of or questioned for purchasing such an item. Not only that, but Leiala seriously questioned how helpful the tips might be.

So true, Abaddon's workers again cut in, praising Leiala's thinking. *You don't need that silly magazine to tell you what to change- you've done a marvelous job figuring out your flaws already. We can do this on our own.*

Leiala smiled, and Fear frowned. No one needed the instructor to infer that Abaddon's workers had been successful. The scene faded, and gray static filled the screen.

"Don't miss what happened at the end," the instructor stated, sharing his final words of wisdom. "If you can make your assignment feel good about themselves, hopeful- in conjunction with your plan for them- that's ultimate success. We want our assignments to register our presence and influence with something positive. Like you just saw happen with the girl. She rejected the magazine's content, which some of you may have thought was a failure, but it was actually a more effective victory as rendered by Abaddon's workers. They took her logic skills and tied them into the messages they'd sent her earlier, making her believe that all of it was her own idea. She bought into it: she felt affirmed in her superior cognitive skills, and she'll be more likely to listen to the workers in the future. We've set a great precedent here."

There were murmurs of agreement and a few workers burst into spontaneous applause. Fear was very likely the only student in the room who was not filled with exuberance, but nausea.

-16-

Fear wasn't able to transition back. He was changed, and, as much as he tried to hide or mask this adjustment, it was obvious that he was different.

He hadn't gone back to the class. He hadn't needed to. For as ignorant as he'd been before, he was wise now: He couldn't even report to his assignment without noting the channels in the alternative realm and recognizing the tactics Abaddon's workers planned to utilize. He sensed things before he saw them, and he found himself attuned to the alternative realm that he'd barely even noticed before. The enlightenment was profound and extensive- and he could not make it go away.

Every assignment with Leiala now was pure torture. Before, he'd felt uneasy about the imbalance of characters assigned to Leiala- and that had been during his spell of ignorance. Now, it was excruciating- there was not a whisper that escaped Fear's notice, not a shoulder sag that Fear could not interpret with frightening alacrity.

His fellow workers noticed, and had been quick to comment.

"What's with you?" Panic had hissed under his breath, noting Fear's squirms and whimpers.

"Is there something we need to know?" Anxiety had asked, taking inventory of Fear's new edginess.

Fear had shaken his head, reluctant to try to explain to his colleagues what it was that had changed. He doubted he had the words, or they the capacity to comprehend what he might try to convey. The truth was, he wouldn't have believed everything that he had seen if he hadn't experienced it all for himself to know that it was true. Even Joy hadn't been able to understand the magnitude of it all, and Fear knew she would be most receptive to his new understanding.

"I don't get it," Joy had responded honestly, the frustration on her face evident. "I want to understand, Fear- but I don't," she sighed, after Fear had tried three subsequent times to explain why things were different now, and how he saw things with fresh eyes. He had so rattled Joy with his fervent words and impassioned speech that she had not pressed him to complete any more tasks, and she hadn't asked for any other details on the classes. Fear took this as a disheartening sign.

He dragged his feet completing each assignment, and he found that he was nearly late to a number of moments that were categorized as "high priority." He knew if he continued behaving in this unusual manner, he would capture the unwanted attention of Abaddon's workers, and then Abaddon himself. But even armed with the surety of this consequence, Fear could not bring himself to behave differently.

He wasn't sleeping anymore, not really. He paced the hallways of either end, his gaze always on the floor ahead of him as he shuffled by with hands in his pockets. Bags developed under his eyes, and his eyes were constantly dry and irritated from lack of sleep. He couldn't think clearly. He tried so hard to rationalize his behavior, to explain to himself why it was silly to invest so much in an assignment that was just that- an *assignment* He would receive a new one when Leiala passed away someday, and all his worry would be for not. He reminded himself that it wasn't his job to worry or care, and that there were others in the alternative realm who had been designated for that position. It wasn't his responsibility.

He knew it. He did. And while he could rationalize his way out of every situation, he could not for the life of him change his heart from hurting for Leiala.

And so, on one overcast, gloomy day, with slate-gray clouds obscuring the sun and light drizzle feeding the puddles on the ground, Fear found himself walking through the west end headquarters. Not aimlessly, like his usual routine, but this time with a specific destination in mind.

It felt right. On some level, he knew he was walking to the only place he had left to go. It should have terrified him, and he should have turned back. He was stepping outside the boundaries, inserting himself into a place he didn't belong. He had no right. And yet, with each shaky step, Fear felt more and more confident about his decision to directly approach Theos.

Fear had never traveled so far into the west end headquarters- he was overwhelmed by the beauty and magnitude of it all. It was rich, opulent, and detail-oriented: white marble with thick black and charcoal-gray veins running through it; gold filigree detail decorating the edges. Lavish jewels and precious stones were inlaid with care, and the entire building was ornate and awesome and yet unpretentious and pure.

Fear noted the lightness in his step, the burden that seemed to lift from his shoulders as he neared Theos's dominion. Like in the east end, no one seemed to question his presence. It was amusing to Fear to realize how insignificant he was- he was always worried about taking some action that would significantly alter all of existence...and when it came down to it, he wondered how many even knew he existed.

Strangely, he knew the way to Theos's quarters without ever having been before. There weren't any signs or maps posted anywhere, but Fear felt his feet guide his way. He was a fish pushed along in the current without resistance.

Reaching the end of the hallway, Fear knew he had arrived. The substantially thick white marble doors were pushed open, and a clear ray of soft yellow light sparkled on the floor, beckoning Fear to come inside. It was strange, Fear realized, that Theos kept His doors open. The ruler of an entire realm, busy and important beyond what Fear could imagine, and yet His door was wide open. Anyone could enter. There weren't guards positioned by the door, like in the east end quarters, and there wasn't any screening process like Fear had grown accustomed to with Abaddon. No, there was literally nothing standing between him and the greatest entity in the world.

“Welcome, Fear,” a kind, authoritative voice sounded. It was loud and clear, resounding through the expansive room, And yet there was nothing demanding or intimidating about it. Fear felt buoyed with confidence- he *had* been right in coming there! Theos knew who he was! The validation was instant and deeply gratifying.

“I was hoping I’d see you before too much longer,” Theos went on. Fear stepped into the threshold and made his way to Theos, who had stepped down off of his throne to welcome and approach Fear. At His gesture, Fear made himself comfortable in a chair near to Theos. Both settled in, and Theos shifted forward in his seat, His full, undivided attention concentrated on Fear.

“How did you know?” Fear asked. The question was dumb, and his voice was small, but Theos didn’t point out either of these facts.

“I know everything,” Theos answered simply, an amused smile on His lips. Though bold, Fear knew instantly that the words were true.

“Isn’t it exhausting?” Fear asked before he could stop himself. This wasn’t what he had come to ask- hardly!- but the events of the past week had generated a newfound appreciation for what it must be like to be omniscient.

Theos chuckled and His smile widened. The warmth from His presence encapsulated Fear and pushed out all insecurities and worries until Fear was left with only a fuzzy glow emanating from his middle.

“For a character, it would most certainly be exhausting,” Theos agreed politely. “But we both know that’s not why you’re here.”

“Right. Well, I don’t know exactly why I’m here,” Fear began, stumbling over his words as he still tried to process the fact that he, the lowly and insignificant character that he was, was talking to the ruler of the universe without supervision, appointment, or time constraint.

“You can start by explaining what’s bothering you,” Theos nudged him gently.

“I went to Abaddon’s headquarters- to the east end- to attend a class,” Fear began, glancing nervously in Theos’s direction as he mentioned his foray into the east end. He wasn’t sure how this would be received from His enemy.

“I was there to learn about how Abaddon’s workers approach any given assignment- to learn their techniques,” Fear rushed on. “I learned a lot- more than I probably should have. I saw my own assignment on the screen, and I’ve seen enough of Abaddon’s techniques that now I can’t undo the images or remove this knowledge from my mind.”

“You want to remove it,” Theos stated.

“Yes,” Fear agreed, fingers massaging his temples. “I see evil everywhere. I see the messages, the lies, the taunts. It’s too much- I’m overwhelmed by it all,” Fear finished with a sob. Covering his mouth in horror, he swallowed the frog in his throat. He had the faintest thought that perhaps he should feel embarrassed for this display, this show of weakness to a great leader, but he felt safe in Theos’s presence.

Theos nodded but said nothing. Fear wished He would interject, say something that would alleviate his concern or push them towards a solution. In the silence, Fear could not help but fill the empty space with words he didn’t even know he had.

“It’s just that seeing that has changed everything. I can’t look at Leiala the same way. I can’t look at anyone the same way. I know too much. It’s dreadful- and it feels hopeless,” Fear finished. This time, he was pretty sure he actually was finished. His body crumpled forward in marked dejection, and his head sagged towards his chest.

“You’re not seeing it all.”

Theos's words were calm and measured, but firm. Fear looked up, sniffling, his expression hopeful.

"I got it wrong?" Fear asked hopefully, desperate to hear that the past weeks had been nothing more than an illusion, a reality that had never existed.

"The evil is real," Theos began, sensing the source of Fear's sudden shift in mood, "but you haven't seen everything. You haven't noticed the good."

Fear's glassy eyes shone as he wiped his nose with the back of his hand. What was Theos talking about? There hadn't been anything good in those situations he'd witnessed- they'd been wrought with destruction and evil.

"You're wrong," Theos cut in politely. By now Fear realized that Theos could read his mind and sense his every thought before it was even known to him.

"What did I miss?" Fear asked. He was genuinely befuddled- he tried to replay the scenes in his mind, this time with a positive spin, and he couldn't.

"We're not letting Abaddon get away without a fight," Theos reassured the character gently. "Our presence is made known to Leiala, too. It's just more complicated."

Fear had a litany of questions, but he didn't know where to begin.

"Why don't all of the characters know?" It wasn't the most important question, but it was the one that popped into Fear's mind first.

"You said yourself that you wish you didn't know what you now know- it's a burden to bear. Most characters wouldn't want it," Theos pointed out softly.

"But they're so oblivious!" Fear exclaimed. "They have no idea the damage that's being done to their assignment."

"No, they don't. Some do- your friend Joy does. But most do not- nor do they need to. The role of a character, as you well know, is to influence the assignment with your particular feeling. You're not supposed to guard and protect the assignments from all danger. I have workers to do that," Theos reminded him.

"Some of them aren't very good at their job," Fear groused before he remembered who he was talking to. He looked up in alarm at Theos, who just smiled patiently.

"Let's take a walk," He suggested. "I'm sensing that you would appreciate a tour of the west end headquarters and the work that takes place here. You've certainly spent enough time in the east end headquarters- why don't you see how things operate over here?"

Standing up, Theos tucked his long white robe behind him, extending an open palm in invitation to Fear. Fear didn't hesitate- he was quick to clasp the large, warm hand with his cold and clammy one. He was vaguely aware of Yeshua and Pneuma joining their small party as they walked in a direction that Fear had never explored before.

Stopping in front of a classroom, Fear peered in at Theos's workers. The doors to the classroom were floor-to-ceiling windows, making it easy to view what was taking place inside. Fear wasn't sure what they were talking about, but he was quick to pick up on the fact that the workers appeared distressed.

"A strategics meeting of our own," Theos offered. "And you're right- they are distressed. Unlike Abaddon's workers, we feel in full effect the pain our assignments experience."

"That's horrible," Fear said aloud without any thought.

"It's necessary," Theos rephrased. "None of the workers would have it any other way. It's Yeshua who understands best. He uses his knowledge and understanding to build that tangible bridge from worker to assignment. We're invested in each person."

Fear said nothing but assessed the taut, tense bodies of the workers sitting before him. He only saw snippets of Leiala's life, and he'd only recently become aware of the extent of her suffering. What would it be like to feel *everything*? He couldn't even fathom.

"We can go inside," Theos offered, noting Fear's interest. Fear nodded, and Theos wordlessly pushed the door open, gesturing for Fear to come inside. He did, self-consciously keeping his body close to the edge of the room, trying to escape notice.

"She needs some encouragement," a worker lamented, his voice agitated and firm. It surprised Fear to hear the strength behind his voice- he'd imagined Theos's workers as kind and gentle- there was an edge and aggression to this voice that caught him off guard.

"Abaddon is doing all he can to keep that from happening," another worker pointed out. "And Theos has asked us not to intervene in a big way."

Fear noted with interest that this comment was made with respect and utmost deference to Theos- no one questioned His decree. But Fear did. From what he had been able to make out, one of Theos's humans had called out for help, and He was choosing not to respond in a way that would encourage and strengthen the individual.

Theos sighed, reminding Fear that his question had been heard. His heart skipped a beat as he peered up into the face of the west end master, hoping that some explanation would be forthcoming.

"It's the hardest part to explain," Theos whispered. His soft voice did not suggest any weakness yet felt thick with sadness and vulnerability. There was a long pause here- so long that Fear wondered if Theos would stop there. It didn't appear that He had anything more to say.

"It has to happen."

Theos looked grieved as He said this, as though He wanted to remove himself from the words.

“Surely it doesn’t have to,” Fear countered. He continued to astonish himself with his boldness- who was he to speak to a ruler in this manner? But Theos appeared to accept- even invite- these questions.

“You mentioned that your job is to influence your assignment in the fullest way you know how,” Theos began, looking at Fear for approval. Fear nodded, and Theos continued.

“My influence is far greater than emotion. I am shaping the human into the person they were created to be. They cannot become that person without struggle- it’s what shapes and sharpens their character.”

“What does that have to do with encouragement?” Fear asked. He understood the point Theos was making- it wasn’t a happy thought, but it made sense- but what did that have to do with withholding encouragement?

“You’ve seen the humans’ machines,” Theos began, looking over at Fear. Fear nodded, imagining the cell phones and computers and cars and other fancy equipment the humans delighted in using. “Before these devices make their way into the humans’ homes, what happens to them?”

“They’re tested to make sure they work?” Fear suggested, getting an inkling of where the conversation might be headed.

“And what is done to precious metal to prepare it to be made into jewelry?” Theos persisted, ignoring Fear’s question.

“It’s put into fire,” Fear answered uneasily, goosebumps prickling his arms at the macabre reference.

“So it must be with the humans,” Theos said with quiet determination. “As they are refined and tested, they become more beautiful, more pure, more malleable.”

"They become better- more valuable," Fear chimed in.

"Not better," Theos was quick to correct. "Their worth doesn't depend on this growth. There is no status or ranking here," Theos explained. "But the human becomes stronger, more resilient, and ultimately receives more satisfaction from their life."

Fear had trouble envisioning Leiala receiving more satisfaction from the trials she'd been put through- as far as he could tell, the only effect it had brought her was misery. He was self-conscious that Theos could hear these thoughts, and he waited for Theos to address them. He didn't.

"The world has problems, conflict, and strife," Yeshua spoke up, catching Fear off guard. He hadn't noticed Yeshua join them. "The humans cannot escape this aspect of life. But while the struggle is inevitable, the response is what separates those who achieve peace and press on from those who surrender to the trouble and choose to live in a constant state of misery and hopelessness."

Fear thought hard about the principles he was given: the logic seemed to defy everything he'd seen to be true. His head started to hurt- he wanted to understand, wanted to believe what he was told- but how?

"Some of it will always remain a mystery," Theos said, His words somehow signaling the end of their conversation.

Fear felt frustration and relief in tandem: frustration over the fact that he felt no closer to understanding what it was that the west end accomplished, and relief that he was not expected to understand that night.

"You should come back," Yeshua said kindly, nodding to Fear. "There's more to see, and that's the only way that things might start to make sense."

Fear nodded, unconvinced. In a daze, he was escorted back to familiar territory, where he split off and walked back to his quarters. He'd been given a lot to think about, and he intended to visit again.

-17-

Leiala woke up in a dead panic. She'd overslept. She must have overslept.

With wild gestures, she flopped over in bed, the sheets twisting around her body as her arms groped for her cell phone. Squinting into the darkness, she was barely able to register the time: 4:33. It was early, she still had time to sleep.

A wave of relief washed over her body and she became aware of the shot of adrenaline that had passed through her. Wild energy pounded through her body: her blood felt on fire, and flames of energy crept up her lower back all the way up to her neck. She felt sweat bead on her back and shoulders, and she took long, measured breaths to try to regulate her heartbeat.

It's okay, she told herself. *You didn't oversleep. You can rest some more- you* ***should*** *rest some more,* Leiala corrected herself.

Well, that wasn't entirely true. She had twenty-seven minutes left to sleep- then her alarm would alert her that it was time to wake up and go for a run. She had to go early if she wanted to exercise before her 8 AM class- and if she didn't get a run in first thing, there was always a chance it might not happen at all.

Just the thought gave Leiala shivers. Skip a run? No way. She knew better- she'd seen the positive results of the past sixth months of militaristic training. Just a month into college, and she was proud of the growth and progress she'd made: already she felt more sophisticated, a better version of Leiala.

She'd managed to survive high school- well, that wasn't the most appropriate adjective. Leiala had done quite well academically, earning exceptional marks in her difficult classes; proving to herself that she *was* smart. Worthy. She'd proven herself a solid athlete in multiple sports, and she'd excelled in extracurriculars that had positively padded her college applications. She'd kept her distance from the trouble-makers and partiers, opting to study and train while others were experimenting with their limits. She'd followed all the rules, and she was better for it. By many counts, her high school years had been a great success.

But. But, she didn't have any male friends. She hadn't had any boys ask her to a dance, or even on a date. There weren't any boys that had crushes on her. On lonely nights, Leiala analyzed her situation from any number of angles- ultimately she'd concluded that there were a number of things about her that just weren't quite right, but her reputation would be difficult to change at a school where everyone knew her well. It was painful, but Leiala had given up aspirations to be wanted, to be admired- instead, she dove headfirst into activities that would secure the best possible future for herself. She wasn't able to change her situation in high school, but she could start preparing herself for a different world in college.

It had started with food. Leiala had realized that her body type didn't naturally lend itself to tiny and slender, the figures that were admired, featured on the covers of magazines, the figures that were dated by handsome, eligible young men. So, she would just have to work diligently for the body she desired.

The first thing to eliminate was fat- no fat whatsoever. She was no nutritionist, but cutting fat was the obvious place to start. And no junk food- not that she indulged often anyway- but that was now strictly off-limits. And cutting back on the quantity of food was important, too- although Leiala didn't focus on that aspect as much. That, paired with constant exercise, had achieved some results. Leiala had noticed her thighs had subtly shrunk (her jeans seemed a bit looser in the legs- she had been ecstatic to go and buy new pants!) and if she just kept at it, she was sure her stomach would start to show the definition she so craved.

She'd always been active, but once summer had hit, she'd adopted a rigid exercise schedule in which she ran every day. She wasn't interested in other activities- she would do them, certainly, but nothing could substitute a run. She'd read the articles- running burned the most calories, and it produced lean muscle. Her research was backed up by the figures of Olympic athletes- Leiala had studied their forms carefully, discerning which competitors had the most beautiful bodies. They were all strong, to be sure, but not all of them would look good in a bikini, Leiala thought harshly. The long distance runners seemed to carry the least body fat, so Leiala determined to become a long distance runner.

So far, it was working out well. She was tired most mornings that she set out for a run, but she was doing it. It got easier, after a while- she would roll out of bed and just start. Her body would take it from there- it knew what to do. There was no question in her mind that it was worth it- all she had to do was look at the past four weeks!

Ignored and irrelevant to all but a few people in high school, she'd already built a name for herself in college. She'd been outgoing and personable from the beginning, chumming it up with both girls and boys to secure a solid friend group. She'd intentionally tanned over the summer, her hair was freshly highlighted, and she'd spent a good chunk of her summer job money on spandex-laden clothing from Forever 21 that accentuated her new, slimmer figure. And it had worked! Oh, it had worked!!

Leiala became giddy when she thought about the transformation that had taken place- she was now noticed, desired, and cool.

This is what it looks like to be worth something, Leiala had practically exhaled in relief. She'd been so afraid she wasn't ever going to be worth anything- what a relief to realize that she'd found the formula to acceptance and security! It wasn't that hard- she knew what she could eat, how often she had to work out, what she should wear, and how she should present herself to make friends. There was absolutely no question- she was way better now. This was how she needed to stay to be somebody. And over her dead body was she going back to the land of obscurity.

She had boys who had crushes on her. Not boy- *boys*. BOYS! Eighteen years without so much as a compliment from a male outside her family, and now she had boys asking to take her out to dinner, bringing her gifts, and complimenting her on her appearance. She worshipped this feeling, this importance- it fueled her to push herself out of bed and out the door when it was still dark outside in the morning. A small sacrifice. A necessary sacrifice.

On some level, Leiala knew this also helped her to manage her stress. She had entered an accelerated and advanced program in her college, and some of her classes were difficult. Very difficult. The language-based classes were always a cakewalk for her: even if it involved copious amounts of reading or an unprecedented amount of work, she was confident in her ability to not only meet the expectation but exceed it. She had the highest grade in two of her classes. The more abstract, calculations-based classes were more difficult. As an accounting major, Leiala would take a number of these classes, and there was one in particular that was really proving to stump her.

Her first test back had been a 'C': Leiala felt the hot flush of shame even now as she recalled the moment the professor had distributed the exams. Well after the test had been reviewed, Leiala had revisited the angry red marks on her paper circling her errors, each time, she shamed and degraded herself for making mistakes. What was wrong with her? She was supposed to be a star student, showing herself to be worthy of her position in the advanced program.

She'd made a point to attend all office hours after that point: to show the professor she was dedicated and committed to success, and to ensure that she took it upon herself to make every possible effort to conquer the class material. If she had learned anything, it was that she could accomplish something if she worked hard: harder than anyone else, harder even than she thought she could.

The thought of failure fueled Leiala, the potential shame burned any thoughts of letting up or taking a break from her mind. She wouldn't even know herself if she failed- that wasn't part of her DNA. People knew her as the smart girl- her family believed she was smart. She wasn't so sure herself, but enough people believed in her, and she wasn't about to prove otherwise! She had to keep the charade up- she had to establish her worth.

She didn't have to do it all at once, but slowly, she would make herself perfect. She'd made progress in her body- that could carry over to other areas of her life. If she just worked hard enough and applied enough discipline, she could achieve perfection. And then, when she was perfect, she'd have more than just a few boys with crushes on her, and more than a few admirers and friends- she would morph herself into the person everyone wanted to be around.

The thought warmed her body and made her drunk with the possibilities. It was hard to believe that just months ago, she'd been naive and worthless. College had opened up doors, opportunities- and Leiala was grasping onto every single one.

***

"She needs to pick a side!" Theos's worker exclaimed in frustration.

Fear was surprised by the outburst- generally speaking, Theos's workers were controlled and only occasionally expressed annoyance or rage- but not the feeling behind it. He himself had wondered at Leiala's decisions.

Over the past few months, he'd spent enough time in both the east end and west end headquarters to know that both were dedicated in their attempts to win Leiala's heart. And both sides were successful, which, in Fear's mind, meant neither were successful. The thought was disheartening.

His time in the west end headquarters had been enlightening and life-changing...and that was putting it mildly. He remained committed (addicted?) to classes in both domains, eager to soak up and understand as well as possible the tactics both implemented in order to win souls. Even Joy had been overwhelmed by the endless reports of information he'd eagerly come to her with- while she hadn't specifically asked, Fear could tell that her appetite for intel had waned, and he no longer shared all of his revelations with her.

It was harder now, to communicate with the other characters. Fear hadn't anticipated that. He'd figured his new learning would marginally impact his life and viewpoint, and he'd assumed that nothing else would change. He'd certainly never imagined that he'd have trouble relating to the other characters. But he found himself consistently unsatisfied and frustrated by his conversations with his colleagues, who didn't seem to understand the extent of the battle taking place in the alternative realm. Fear couldn't understand their lack of interest, their apathy.

On good days, the characters would feign interest and ask questions, but Fear could see the glazed look in their eyes; he could read their indifference. He tried to remind himself of his former ignorance- not long ago, he'd cared nothing for studying this realm (and how many years had he lived that way?). But now that he'd tasted the difference, he couldn't go back.

He was outraged by the east end: their subversive, sneaky tactics launched relentlessly to destroy the assignments. And he was intrigued by the west end: he couldn't understand their seemingly passive attempts to win souls- no force or manipulation was used by the west enders, who instead opted to coax and persuade through their constant, reliable presence and lack of judgment. This frustrated Fear, who saw their patience and how it so often felt trumped by the aggressive maneuvers of Abaddon's workers.

"The end game," Theos had gently reminded Fear time and time again. "We're not interested in winning every battle- but we are certainly committed to winning the war."

"Don't you win the war by winning the battles?" Fear had asked, genuinely interested in this way of thinking. He'd attended enough strategics classes in both headquarters to know that the battles were analyzed, picked apart and dissected in order to identify strengths and weaknesses, not to mention the progress the assignment had made. The battles had to mean something- otherwise why was so much time dedicated to their analysis?

Theos had smiled here, nodding at Yeshua to take over. Fear immediately perceived that his question had been ignorant and naive, and yet there was nothing judgmental or condescending about Theos's smile.

"The right battles," Yeshua had cut in. "We expend our energy on winning the *right* battles."

"Because you need to save your power for when it really counts?" Fear asked. This made sense, but some of the battles he'd seen Abaddon win didn't seem like they'd have been hard to squash.

"Some of the time," Yeshua agreed. "But it's oftentimes more than that. Sometimes it's better for the battle to be lost."

Here, Fear felt totally baffled. It was better for a battle to be *lost*? What, for morale? To falsely lull Abaddon's forces into believing they had gained some momentum, only to decimate them in a later battle? His brain wracked through his experiences to see if he could discern a logical pattern, but he couldn't find one. Yeshua registered Fear's question, judging by His follow up.

"It builds character."

Fear blinked, searching Yeshua's face for clues that might explain further. Yes, he could attest to the fact that character was in fact built during the battles that were lost- Fear had witnessed the strength, stamina, and resilience that had come from a slaying. But- but what about the humans' feelings? Fear had learned during his time with Theos how deeply the west end workers cared for their assignments, the humans that were reverently referred to as "souls." He had felt the care for these souls, he had felt the deep hurt that came when they suffered. And for every battle that was lost, there was gut-wrenching suffering.

"But they hurt so deeply," Fear couldn't help but point out. It was a statement that welcomed a response and begged for an exclamation.

"They do," Yeshua agreed, his expression pained. Fear watched with interest as He looked down at His hands, massaging the palms of His hands gently. "But pain is a necessary component of change, and change is inevitable."

“And it’s important they change in the right way,” Fear finished Yeshua’s thought.

Yeshua nodded. “We’d like the changes to be productive- something that helps the soul to realize its full potential. This growth comes through struggle. A small sacrifice for a larger blessing to come later.”

“The humans don’t seem to appreciate that much,” Fear muttered, thinking upon the tears of frustration, confusion, hurt, and disappointment.

“They don’t,” Yeshua agreed, again with a strained look upon His face. “Don’t think it’s easy on us- it’s not. But we know it’s for the best.”

“The humans don’t seem to understand that,” Fear pushed back. He wasn’t trying to be difficult, but it really didn’t make sense. There had to at least be some way for Theos to communicate to the humans that what was happening was for their own good- that would alleviate some of their stress, surely!

“We try,” Yeshua told him. “That’s Pneuma’s job- He visits the humans and speaks to them- in His own way, that is.”

Fear speculated on this point. He’d seen Pneuma visit humans before, and they did inherit a sense of peace and comfort after His visit. But he wasn’t sure they understood that their suffering was temporary, or that it would lead to a long-term blessing. But he supposed that was part of what Yeshua was trying to tell him- the humans couldn’t know for sure, because that would take a critical piece out of the faith and growth process. Not as much character was created when an outcome was known- it was in the unknown, the mysterious, that true grit and identity surfaced.

Switching subjects, Fear jumped to a different idea he’d wondered about: how it was that the outcome of the war was determined. He understood well enough that battles could be lost in sacrifice for the overall war- but when did the war end? When could victory be claimed?

“The war never ends,” Theos spoke up, sensing Fear’s question. “It endures for the entire life of the soul.”

“So how do they know that they won?” Fear asked, becoming more depressed by the moment. All this work for what seemed like very little reward.

“They can understand the victories in day-to-day life most of the time, especially with Pneuma’s help. But otherwise, they know when they go to their final resting place,” Theos explained.

Fear nodded. This still didn’t seem like a very good deal.

“And Abaddon gives up at that point? He admits defeat and walks away?” Fear pressed, wanting to make sure he understood everything correctly.

“Abaddon never gives up- he just switches to a new target,” Theos corrected. “And he fights in battles even when he knows winning the war is a lost cause.”

This statement caught Fear’s attention and threw him for a loop. Abaddon *knew* he had already lost some wars, but still persisted in fighting the battles? That didn’t make sense.

“But why?”

The question dangled in the air uncomfortably.

“He lives to destroy,” Theos answered simply. “His ultimate objective is to destroy souls, but he’ll take whatever he can get. For those who are already committed to the west end, his objective shifts. He knows he cannot overcome a soul united with our forces- but he can certainly distract, manipulate, and torment. He may not win the soul, but he can inflict significant damage.”

“He uses the souls to hurt others?” Fear asked, brow furrowed.

"Others, and themselves. You know how your job is to help each human achieve their full potential of any given feeling and characteristic?" Theos asked. Fear nodded quickly, eager to hear more.

"Each soul has more than just emotional potential and capacity. At the moment of inception, a soul is given goals, dreams, and passions. Our job is to try and guide the soul to realize these dreams and desires in the fullest way possible. This is a difficult task- one that Abaddon obviously tries his best to thwart. He knows that the souls can do major damage to his cause when they are on this path to enlightenment- and he does everything he can to stop it. Hence, the battles. He might know the soul is a lost cause, but that doesn't mean that the soul can't be driven far away from their full potential, that it can't develop into a paltry shadow of its full capability. And *that* is what Abaddon aims to do," Theos concluded.

"Leiala?" Fear asked. He knew the answer to his question even before the words left his lips.

"Yes, that's what happening with Leiala," Theos agreed. "She has been marked with great potential- and that threatens Abaddon. He won't let it sit- he's going to do everything in his power to distract, confuse, and destroy the girl."

"Will he succeed?" Fear asked nervously, goosebumps dotting his arms.

"That is a decision Leiala must make," Theos answered ambiguously.

"But the battles- will Abaddon succeed in winning some big ones?" Fear pressed. He was fearful for Leiala and the pain that might be waiting for her.

Theos didn't answer, but He turned to Fear. With large, knowing, doleful eyes, He nodded. Fear's stomach turned and his mouth went dry. And he'd thought he'd seen the worst...

-18-

It was funny how quickly Change could appear, how quickly that fickle and feared character could visit and turn a life upside-down. Fear had never really considered he might be as vulnerable and needy as some of the human assignments he'd been given, and yet he found himself in Character Counseling.

He wasn't even sure he knew such a thing existed before last week. He certainly hadn't known any characters who had attended, and he'd never seen the counseling sessions advertised in either the east or west end headquarters.

It was Yeshua who had first suggested to Fear that he might benefit from counseling sessions, apparently at the suggestion of Pneuma. Fear had been baffled, surprised, dismissive, embarrassed. He couldn't keep up with his train of thought, first registering complete shock over the existence of such an entity before progressing towards a place of false self-assurance that he would never need such a service. He finally ended in a place of reluctant skepticism as Yeshua gently pressed the issue.

He knew enough about counseling: he'd seen human assignments attend counseling services in the hopes that their undesirable behaviors and thought patterns might be shifted. It had been a while since Fear had been personally assigned to a human who attempted counseling, but he remembered well how it worked. And how it didn't. And most especially he remembered the incredible amount of activity from the alternative realm that seemed to surround each counseling session.

That was likely the most-missed element of counseling, Fear thought- the fact that so few of the humans seemed to recognize that the battle took place on far deeper ground than the surface-level issues they tended to bring up. It wasn't worthless, the counseling- Fear had seen a number of humans who had really benefitted- but the extent of the healing really depended on how seriously the human addressed the issues, how cognizant they were of the real issues bubbling beneath the surface, of just how pervasive the influence of the alternative realm was.

And now he was being recommended for these services.

He had to admit, he had changed. He was depressed, despondent even, and his self-worth had plummeted. He loathed himself, loathed the influence he had on Leiala. He felt sick to his stomach any time he was summoned to influence her, and he felt nauseous when he wasn't- because that time was spent recounting the moments when he had affected Leiala or imagining how he might be asked to influence Leiala in the future.

In the beginning, he'd casually tried to bring these issues up to the other characters he interacted with on a daily basis- he'd felt sure that some of them would be able to relate, maybe they would even be able to share personal experiences that would cheer him up. That had not been the case.

Most of the characters looked at him blankly, grunting and smiling uncertainly as Fear ventured to share the general details of how he was feeling. Joy seemed to understand better than anyone else- but even she had looked more and more uncomfortable as Fear had opened up.

Unwilling to completely ostracize and isolate himself, Fear had simply stopped sharing. He had worked hard to convince himself that what he was experiencing was not in fact reality- he had dipped his toes into a completely foreign way of thinking and viewing the world, and he could simply draw himself back out of it.

But as time passed, Fear was forced to admit that he couldn't revert back to his original, unadulterated way of thinking. He couldn't shake the thoughts, the visions, or the attitude that hung thick around his being like a cloud of mosquitoes.

Then, Yeshua's suggestion.

"You're not alone, Fear," Yeshua had said gently one Tuesday afternoon as Fear paced the hallways of the west end headquarters. Fear had looked up in a daze- his thoughts had taken him so far away that he hadn't even noticed anyone walk up to him. Tears welled in the corners of Fear's eyes, and he knew then that he needed help. He swallowed hard, pushing down any potential emotional display. He couldn't bring himself to speak, but he looked up at Yeshua with round, vulnerable eyes that he was sure communicated his every thought and insecurity.

"You're not," Yeshua repeated, reading the question in Fear's eyes. "You feel alone- but you're not. You just don't see the others in your same position."

Fear sighed, shoulders slumping forward with such force that they threatened to topple his entire body. He plopped his deflated frame onto the nearest marble bench. Resting his forearms on his knees, he was indirectly aware of Yeshua seating himself gingerly on the seat beside him.

"It's one of the greatest misconceptions," Yeshua voiced, again speaking without prompting. Fear didn't move a muscle, but he absorbed Yeshua's every word like cracked leather greets oil: every nerve in his body was tuned and ready to receive.

"Some of the loneliest individuals are those who are surrounded by others."

Fear moved his head upwards an inch- he hoped Yeshua would recognize this movement as an affirmative nod. It seemed to be the only movement he could generate- he didn't have the energy to put forth anything extra.

He sat in comfortable silence, thankful for Yeshua's presence. His unhappiness still ran rampant and unchecked, but he was able to register that with Yeshua by his side, he didn't feel quite as lonely. There wasn't a need to say anything, and at first, Fear succumbed to the silence that blanketed their figures. But as thoughts and questions continued to pinball around his mind, he found the fuel to engage Yeshua.

"Why don't they know?" Fear asked, voice cracking in marked distress.

"I'm assuming you mean the other characters," Yeshua began, looking sideways at Fear.

"They don't know because they don't want to know. They don't have to know. *You* didn't know for many, many years," Yeshua pointed out.

"Why did it take me so long? I don't see how I could have missed it all. I mean, I knew *something* was going on, and I knew a little bit, but I really had no idea. I've been a fool," Fear admitted sorrowfully.

"Everyone plays the fool at one point or another," Yeshua encouraged Fear kindly. "The greatest fools are those that never recognize their moments of foolishness."

"But the worst part is, I miss it. I MISS IT!" Fear was finding his voice now, and his words no longer crackled with sorrow but with electricity, anger. "I don't want to know- I don't want to be wise. I'd rather be a fool!"

Now, he was standing. His arms waved wildly, and he could feel the spittle that had collected on his lower lip in outrage. Without seeing his reflection, he knew he looked like a madman.
He could imagine his unkempt hair, rumpled clothes, the hunch in his posture, and the bags underlining his bloodshot eyes. The permanent frown and furrowed brows that had seemed to hijack his facial expressions.

"I didn't ask for this. I didn't ask to understand, to be wise. I was trying to do the right thing- I was just an obedient character. I didn't want anything more!" Fear yelled. He was pacing now, not making eye contact with Yeshua.

"I did what I was asked, and I tried to be helpful. I went to the classes I was asked to go to, and I did this favor for Joy. This stupid, idiotic, moronic favor that's landed me in permanent hell."

With each word spoken, the emphasis grew, until Fear was literally snarling the words through gritted teeth, neck veins bulging. He felt light-headed in his anger that threatened to eat away at his sanity like vultures upon fresh meat. This new knowledge, this revelation- it was toxic, poisonous. It was literally destroying him.

"But a part of you knew," Yeshua responded softly.

Fear looked at Yeshua dumbly, staring at him with blank eyes. He wanted to hold onto his anger, he wanted to use this fuel to launch him to someplace more productive, or even just to distract him from the depth of his pain. He didn't want Yeshua to speak to him in a rational, calm tone that whittled away at his rage.

"I didn't know," Fear hissed. He didn't even bother to consider Yeshua's words, so determined was he to engage in a fight.

Yeshua said nothing, forcing Fear to take a step back and think about what had been said. Had there been a part of him that had known? He wasn't sure. He didn't think so. But it was possible. Heck, anything and everything felt possible now- Fear wasn't about to rule anything out. He knew better- he'd just seen a complete 180 take place in his personal life over the course of this current assignment.

"How could I have known?" he asked, this time without bitterness. He really wanted to know.

"On a distant level, you knew there was more. You weren't ready to engage before," Yeshua explained.

"I'm not ready to engage now!" Fear cried. He heard his agitated voice and wished he didn't sound so hysterical. But he couldn't help it. My goodness- he wasn't the slightest bit equipped to tackle the obstacles he'd been presented with. He hadn't a clue of what to do.

"If we waited until we were fully prepared, we wouldn't ever do anything," Yeshua said quietly.

Fear sat in silence. There was nothing to fight back with- he couldn't think of what to say. He hated Yeshua's words and yet he had no ammunition to launch back.

"You're not alone," Yeshua repeated.

This time, Fear absorbed the words. Yeshua had said that earlier- what did He mean?

"It sure feels like it," Fear mumbled. The rage was dissipating, and in its place, the familiar despondency and hopelessness was settling in.

"That's what Abaddon would have you think," Yeshua asserted. "You're more effective to his cause when you think like that. But you're not alone. You have a team behind you- they're just teammates that are easy to overlook."

Fear contemplated the wisdom behind these words. A tiny ember of hope ignited deep within his soul. So insignificant that Fear worried a whisper of a breeze would extinguish it. Could it be? Was there a way to dig himself out of the deep hole he found himself in? Was it possible that he wasn't alone?

"I'm behind you," Yeshua told Fear. "And you're not the only character."

Fear's head snapped up at this last assertion. There were other characters that felt the way he did?

"You should try Character Counseling," Yeshua suggested, going on to explain what Characters Counseling entailed and why Fear would benefit. Fear sat numb, listening to Yeshua's words as though through an intercom. He felt removed from the situation, far away- but this was a familiar feeling by now. At any other point in the conversation, Fear would have shunned Yeshua's words without any consideration whatsoever. But without arguing against his feelings, Yeshua had somehow wheedled His way into Fear's confidence, revealing vulnerabilities that Fear felt desperate to plug.

"When?" Fear heard himself ask.

Yeshua responded with all the information, carefully written down on a notecard for Fear to take with him. Which was a good thing, Fear mused, considering the number of thoughts and worries and factoids tumbling around inside his skull.

He didn't remember Yeshua leaving, or walking back to his dormitory. He could only remember the resignation he'd felt as he'd rested his head on his pillow for the night- a night that looked from every angle to be another sleepless one.

I'll go, he determined. *What have I got to lose?*

***

Fear sat on the plush couch uncertainly, his feet barely resting on the thick carpeting beneath him. He hadn't had to wait long to be admitted into the counseling office- no sooner had he offered up his name than he was ushered into the comfortable room he now found himself in. He had no barometer with which to compare his experience, but he felt fairly confident that the superior treatment he'd received was a result of Yeshua's influence.

"Good afternoon, Fear," a voice rang out as the door opened, announcing the entrance of Fear's counselor. Fear sat on the edge of the cushioned couch, trying not to look too expectant as he craned his neck to get a glimpse of the individual Yeshua had assured him was highly competent and personable.

Pneuma.

Fear was thankful for the thick cushions on the sofa that held him in place- he was afraid he might otherwise have fallen out of his seat. *Pneuma?!* Pneuma didn't have time to listen to Fear's insignificant worries- He had a kingdom to rule! Guilt crept into Fear's gut, and shame wiggled up his spine. He felt heat radiate from his body- there had to be some mistake. He shifted uncomfortably, waiting for the words with which to apologize and explain that he hadn't meant to waste Pneuma's time.

"You're not wasting my time," Pneuma said directly.

The hairs on the back of Fear's neck prickled. He hadn't said anything about wasting time- but he knew Pneuma had access to his innermost thoughts. This didn't always make him feel uncomfortable, but at the moment, it seemed to make him especially vulnerable in a way that Fear detested. Pneuma could sense even this, Fear knew, but He politely didn't comment.

"I don't understand how you have time for this," Fear said carefully, giving voice to the thoughts Pneuma was already privy to.

"This is the most important part of my job," Pneuma told him earnestly.

"To speak with characters?" Fear asked. "I'm sure there are more important things to do."

"You don't think you are important?" Pneuma asked, studying Fear carefully.

The question jolted Fear- it didn't answer his question even indirectly, and yet it somehow cut straight to the heart of the matter.

"Well- uh- no," Fear was forced to admit. "I'm just a character."

"I hate that word, *just*," Pneuma stated with conviction. "It strips every action of it's power and repute. It invalidates and renders unimportant every worthwhile thing on earth. There isn't a thing that is irrelevant. Theos *just* created everything we see before us," Pneuma pointed out.

"I'm thankful He created me," Fear stumbled, worried that Pneuma took his tone to be disrespectful. "I just don't understand why."

"You're looking for a straightforward answer to that question," Pneuma said, slicing straight to a motive Fear hadn't even recognized within himself. "And one I can't offer. The worth of a being can never be summed up in only one or two or even fifty reasons. You're allowing yourself to be paralyzed by the questions. You need to start *living* them."

"*Live* the questions?" Fear asked meekly, repeating the words Pneuma had just said. "I don't know what that means."

"It means you stop trying to make sense of everything," Pneuma challenged.

"Believe me, I wish I could!" Fear exclaimed. "I would give anything to let all of this go, to forget about it and just move on. I don't want to waste my time worrying and stressing about all the possibilities, about all the terrible things that might befall Leiala as a result of my influence."

"You want to, but you won't allow yourself to. You feel guilty letting it go- you feel responsible to hold onto the guilt that's accumulated over Leiala's misfortunes that you claim ownership of. Let it go. Let. It. Go," Pneuma told Fear intentionally, leaning forward to make meaningful eye contact.

"How?" Fear whispered.

"It's both the easiest and hardest thing to do," Pneuma told him seriously. "But now that you're willing, we can begin our work."

The easiest *and* the hardest thing? How could that be? Fear couldn't imagine how it could be so. He had a feeling he was not going to like the work ahead of him- and yet, this was the lifeline he'd been desperately hoping for.

Pneuma watched him steadily, carefully now, waiting for his acceptance. Fear could sense that he wouldn't be bullied into any actions- Pneuma would be the perfect gentleman, waiting patiently for permission to step forward into more intimate territory.

"Okay," Fear agreed. "Let's do it."

As the simple four words left his lips, Fear felt a burden lift from his shoulders. Nothing about his situation had changed, but he felt more optimistic than he had in a long time.

“We’re going to start with your name,” Pneuma began, not wasting any time. “I understand why characters are given the titles they are, but I will not refer to you by the name of *Fear* any longer. You will not be defined by your work,” Pneuma insisted passionately. “It’s impersonal, and it boxes you into a false identity. I want you to think about that before we meet again. That’s your first homework assignment- to come up with a new name. A name that encompasses who you want to be, what you want to do. Try not to label yourself with a noun- think about who you are at the core, what makes you, YOU. You’re more than just a character that communicates fear- your name should reflect that.”

Fear nodded. Pneuma’s words felt like a soft, misty rain descending on parched, dehydrated earth. He had no idea what- who- he was, but for the first time, he felt motivated to find out.

That night, Fear slept. His dreams were vivid, colorful, and exciting. He didn’t wake once in the middle of the night, but when the sun rose with the dawn, he felt rested. His new life was beginning.

-19-

Leiala was beside herself, she was so excited. Ecstatic. Over the moon. So elated was she that the adjectives seemed to pirouette through her mind, twirling and spinning in beautiful patterns that mirrored her attitude towards life.

She'd figured it out- and it hadn't even been hard. The only regret she felt was that she hadn't discovered this secret earlier in life- she could have been *so much* happier, so much earlier!

Everything was paying off. She had to put a lot of effort in, it was true, but when she attended every office hour and exercised every day and watched her diet religiously and prayed every morning and saved enough money to buy the right clothes and budgeted enough time to make sure she checked in with every friend- well, then life was just great! Leiala was on cloud nine. She'd had a perfect GPA the past two quarters of college, she was skinnier than ever, she had a loyal group of friends, and she had boys that were actually interested in her. *Boys*. They liked her. She still couldn't get over it. They wanted to be around her, wanted to be with her. Like, they were bringing her thoughtful gifts. They wanted to spend time with her. They told her she looked nice.

Leiala shook her head. While the thought sent delicious shivers up and down her spine, it also brought anxiety, fear that was hopelessly welded to the wonder and delight of being someone *special*, someone that was noticed.

She wasn't sure how she'd fooled them all, but she had. She'd established a rigid, unforgiving schedule for herself, and she'd been lucky so far. It had all paid off. People thought she was worth knowing. But now there was pressure- she had to live up to the ideas and beliefs people held about her. Leiala tried not to focus on this fact, but it nibbled on her insides like termites on moist wood, threatening to bring the entire structure of her being to the ground. Her mind raced more than usual, and her heart seemed to beat faster. She was excited!

At least, that's how she explained away these new feelings. It was only natural to feel this excitement, to want to continue to impress her friends and teachers and live up to the expectations she knew they held for her. She knew what her life looked like when she didn't put in major effort- and she had no desire to revisit those days. No no no- she was more than happy to spin like a top (but that wasn't likely to be necessary) in order to keep the facade up. This was just the price of importance, of acceptance, of worth. Maybe not for everyone, Leiala was quick to admit- not everyone had to work so hard at it- but it was true for her. And work she would!

Leiala walked with long, assertive steps that showed not a hint of uncertainty. As she neared the cafeteria, her pace didn't waver- she walked right in and looked from side to side, trying to spot her friends.

"Leiala!" a voice called out, reassuring Leiala of her place in the world, of her *wantedness.*

With a casual wave, she readjusted the purse slung over her shoulder and made her way to her friends, tucking her hair behind her ear playfully as she approached the mixed group.

"Hey guys," she said cheerfully, dumping her purse on the empty seat she knew was saved for her.

"Hurry up and get your food," one of her girlfriends whined. "We're trying to make plans for this weekend, and we can't make any decisions without you!"

Leiala rolled her eyes in mock annoyance but inwardly warmed. Yes, she was wanted- maybe even admired. Her ideas were good ones, and her opinion mattered. Her friend pouted to emphasize her point, and the rest of the table just smiled.

"I'm hurrying," Leiala teased, tossing her long hair over her shoulder as she made her way over to the salad bar. She looked disdainfully at the girls waiting for pasta- how *unfortunate* that they hadn't yet discovered the rules with which to live by. They might get away with it now, Leiala thought reproachfully, but soon enough their metabolism would slow down and their free eating would catch up with them. Then she would just shine and stand out even more, Leiala thought with a glow of pride as she passed the generic iceberg lettuce for the nutrient-rich kale and spinach. Each topping was carefully selected and placed on her plate, the end result a mosaic of color. She'd read somewhere that different colors signified different vitamins and nutrients, so she made a point of including at least six. A spritz of vinegar for flavor, and she was back with her friends, aware of the hawkish eyes of the girls surveying her plate of food. No one said a word, but Leiala could feel the guilt and envy of her girlfriends, she could feel them comparing their own daily activities and food consumption with her own.

It doesn't matter what they do, Leiala told herself. Not everyone could endure such a strict regimen- and she didn't care one bit if her friends ate hamburgers or quinoa. She was the only one who would come under such stark scrutiny; she was the only one trying to pass herself off as special. She sat perched on the edge of her seat, aware of exactly how much of her stomach protruded as she sat.

A lightning bolt of anger flashed through her as she felt subtle pressure on the inside of her pants. Pretending to retrieve something from her pocket, she inconspicuously pinched her midsection, desperate to know about how much excess she was carrying. It was hard to manage a grip, but there was enough there to mask the rock-solid abs she was working hard to obtain. *No protein bar for breakfast tomorrow*, Leiala bargained. *Just a banana until lunch.*

"Leiala?"

"Huh?" Leiala asked, her awareness coming back to her friends sitting around her.

"We were talking about this weekend. Did you want to go to the festival?" her friend asked.

"That's this weekend!" Leiala exclaimed, her countenance and tone bright. "We have to go. They're supposed to have live music, face painting, games, and a bunch of crafts and food. Yes, yes, yes!"

As plans were made and logistics arranged, Leiala did her best multi-tasking. The festival would be so much fun- she went through all the activities she wanted to be sure to participate in, then mentally drew a decision tree in her mind that adeptly sorted the "risky" activities from the "safe" ones.

Risky: fried foods, fatty desserts, the pressure to share or split said foods with someone in the group. Also, transportation: she would be stuck there until her ride decided they were ready to leave. And the live music: if the group decided to dance, she might be pressured into joining and make a fool of herself.

Safe: fruit and vegetable stands, face painting, games, shopping for crafts.

It was enough of a balance that it was worth going- she would not need to concoct a last-minute excuse for why she couldn't attend. Most of the risky situations could easily be neutralized, Leiala reassured herself: she could pretend she was full if someone asked to share dangerous food (she needed to remember to throw a protein bar in her purse), and she could print out a copy of the bus schedule so she could get a ride back if she really needed to. She would practice basic dance moves in her dorm room later, when her roommate was out, and she would be sure to stick to safe, controlled movements that wouldn't expose her as the inept fool she knew she was.

"This is going to be so much fun!" Leiala interjected with a squeal, injecting fresh enthusiasm into the group. She felt confident about her solutions to every possible risk- her good mood was authentic, her hopes light and buoyant.

***

"I've literally ruined her life."

Fear shifted on the couch, his hands busy twisting and then shredding the tissue Pneuma had offered him just minutes before.

"Now, wait a second," Pneuma interjected, interrupting Fear and silencing the rant that was sure to follow. "We're going to explore that thought."

Fear rolled his eyes, by now comfortable expressing his true emotions with Pneuma.

"What's there to explore? I was given a terrible assignment- my job is literally to ruin lives and produce insecurity. And somehow I've managed to live with this reality and blind myself to my true role until now. I'm horrible, evil, and destructive. My name is Fear- my very name is on par with curse words," Fear exclaimed in a fit of passion.

"Your name is not Fear." Pneuma's voice was soft but firm.

"We can pretend my name is *Response Regulator*, but we all know what my real job is," Fear argued back, referencing his "new" name. "We're not fooling anyone, especially not myself."

Fear saw Pneuma's jaw tense, but to His credit, He didn't say anything. Fear found that he enjoyed pushing Pneuma's buttons- he wanted to find His breaking point. He didn't understand why Pneuma was wasting His time counseling him in the first place- he wasn't a very interesting character, and his problems were certainly paltry when one considered the major battles taking place in the alternative realm.

"What do you want me to explore?" Fear sighed, feeling guilty. He was being difficult, and it wasn't fair to Pneuma. Pneuma may demonstrate exceptionally poor judgment in His selection of counseling patients, but He was there. He cared. Fear couldn't understand why, but he wasn't so far gone to fail to recognize that he should probably not push away one of the few allies he had left.

"Your role. You said you're only responsible for inspiring terror and bringing destruction," Pneuma paraphrased, His eyes piercing and focused with laser-like intensity on Fear.

"Well, yeah. Do I really have to list out all the evidence? You've seen it all," Fear responded. He was loathe to relive and play with vivid imagery the terror he had inflicted on Leiala especially.

"I think it would be worthwhile," Pneuma parried, somehow without irritation. Fear knew well enough that Pneuma would not push him to do anything he didn't want to, but it was clear that He thought the exercise would do Fear good.

"From the beginning? I don't even know that I can remember them all," Fear exhaled loudly, blowing all the stale air from the bottom of his lungs as he considered the depth to which he would have to climb to acquiesce to this request.

"Chronology is not important," Pneuma dismissed. "I want to know the events that you believe shaped Leiala, or that have been imprinted on your heart- even if you don't understand why they've been put there."

"My heart? Are you sure I have one?" Fear joked, his voice cracking at his pathetic attempt at humor.

Pneuma was silent- He didn't take Fear's bait, instead choosing to wait patiently for Fear's genuine response.

Fear closed his eyes. The blackness of the inside of his eyelids turned into a soft yellow as he relaxed into his mind. The images he worked so hard to shelf descended upon him with elegance and alacrity.

"Leiala is two. Her mom leaves the room, and she screams bloody murder. She believes her mother is abandoning her."

Fear felt the weight of this feeling as he recalled the visit: the stiffness of Leiala's chubby body, the overwhelming, debilitating distress that consumed her every cell. He had paralyzed the girl to the point where she could not process a single thought or emotion other than the fear he had injected. She had screamed and sobbed and kicked in a torrential downpour of distress before her mother returned.

“And you think this event was unnecessary,” Pneuma stated matter-of-factly.

“Yes!” Fear exclaimed, his face and tone of voice indignant. “What good did it do her to worry and agonize over that? It was all for nothing, anyway.”

“That time,” Pneuma pointed out. “But what came from that experience?”

Fear blinked. Was Pneuma trying to trick him? He’d just told him what had come from that experience: nothing but heartache and distress.

“Look deeper,” Pneuma encouraged patiently, leaning forward in earnest.

Fear scowled, trying to recall if there had been any noteworthy after-effect. He shook his head and shrugged his shoulders in frustration.

Wordlessly, Pneuma scooted forward in His chair and rested His feather-light fingertips on Fear’s temples. The pressure was gentle and the fingers cool, but at the same time, the gesture was intentional and solid- Fear instinctively closed his eyes. An aquamarine blue flooded the darkness, then Fear descended back into the memory, this time with an added perspective.

As in the strategics classes, Fear now saw activity in the alternative realm, but he also saw a colorful ribbon that danced throughout the frame of the memory. The ribbon was silky, rainbow-colored, and thick. There did not seem to be any force behind the ribbon, which bobbed up and down artfully. Fear could not see the pattern that the ribbon made, but he was instinctively aware that the single thread was a part of something so much bigger, that it was full of purpose.

For a moment, Fear struggled to focus on the scene playing out before him: he was so mesmerized by the ribbon that changed colors like a lava lamp, the vibrant colors flowing like liquid magma as Pneuma directed the choreography of the cord with graceful and determined gestures, a conductor masterfully manning his orchestra.

But then, Leiala. Screaming, just as Fear remembered her. His heart sank. It looked just as bad from this perspective as it had from his. Fear cringed, his body withdrawing from the scene.

It's not over.

The words were imprinted on Fear's heart without a single syllable uttered aloud.

Keep watching.

Hesitantly, Fear dared to watch the scene unfold. Leiala screamed, and now Fear noticed the balled-up fists, the tight little hamstrings, and the force behind her wails. He'd always known the intensity behind the scene, but now he saw the strength, too.

"She's learning to fight," Pneuma agreed with approval.

Fear watched in disbelief as he took in toddler Leiala, persistent and relentless in her quest to win back her mother's attention. Fear had always registered the great length of time Leiala had screamed as evidence of the depth of her anguish; now he recognized this expanse to be a marker of persistence, determination, and grit.

"And it pays off," Pneuma narrated as Leiala's mother walked back into the room, scooping Leiala up into her arms. "She didn't just experience fear- she learned a healthy response with which to fight it. She didn't cry and then give in- she channeled all that fear and stubborn energy into soliciting a response."

Fear watched, incredulous, as Leiala clung to her mother with superhuman strength, her arms and legs tentacled around her mother's slim frame possessively. Now, Leiala was held in return, her hair stroked and her back patted in reassurance. Fear could feel the love, connection, and trust transcend the memory and seep into the current moment.

"From the fear, a stronger connection," Pneuma pointed out. "Trust was built."

Fear was speechless. Was this true of all of Leiala's "fear" memories? He so desperately wished it might be so, but he knew instinctively that it was not. Was it? He looked up at Pneuma curiously, interested to explore further. How many other memories had he falsely categorized as solely destructive?

Pneuma, sensing his unspoken question, nodded.

"Another," He agreed.

I wish you could see that I'm a good thing, but only in moderation. There's this misconception about me traveling around: that more of me is a good thing. That spending time with me and granting me access to high places and prizing my opinion above that of other characters somehow translates into greater wisdom and self-actualization.

What you don't see is that I can paralyze you. If you spend too much time with me, I suck you in and convince you that you need even more- and then more- and even more of me to make any progress. You start to feel inadequate, and you start walking in circles. If you spend too much time with me, I depress you. I don't mean to, but the memories I can recall most easily are the depressive type, and you humans can only take so much of that in your life. You start to believe you are something you are not, and this not only affects your perception of the past (and might even convince you that you've been living a lie or worse- that your life hasn't held any meaning) but also that of the present- you start to project the past and your faults and errors onto your present situation. From here, you inevitably come to the conclusion that you've nothing significant to live for or look forward to- a great disaster by human standards.

But don't make the mistake of neglecting me. If you ignore me entirely, you run the risk of absolute folly. You will repeat the mistakes of your past, your maturity and growth will be stunted, and then- your life truly won't amount to anything.

It's hard to strike a balance, I realize that. It's difficult to carve out time to meet with me- I realize that, too. I'm not a noisy character that demands attention- I'm pretty shy, actually. You have to seek me out intentionally, win me over with your fervent pleas and petitions that you want nothing more than to spend time with me. I'll show up when I know you're earnest and serious about our relationship- and in appropriate doses, I can work wonders in your life. I can help you to understand yourself better, to make subtle yet significant changes that will alter the course of your life in dramatic ways you can only begin to imagine. Others are likely to notice we've spent time together- I tend to grant peace, quiet self-assurance, and humility to those I meet with.

But don't make me your life. I can't live up to these expectations- I wasn't meant to be your life partner. I'm meant to be your friend, but not your significant other or even your best friend. Those humans who err in this way *end up living in the past, reliving usavory moments time and time again. They believe they're studying their ways and behaviors in order to correct the future, but they're really just wasting the present moment. They become so consumed with what **was** that they don't realize that they're missing what **is**- it's slipping by, soon to be out of reach- a stunted, immature memory that will someday be replayed and scrutinized for its flagrant faults.*

Keep me close, but not too close. Hold me in high regard, but in moderation, never to be prized above all others. I'll help you as I can- but don't expect too much from me.

-Reflection

-20-

Leiala blinked, dumbfounded. She wasn't sure where to go or what to turn to. With trembling fingers, she turned over her Geology exam, read again the 62% written in bold red pen that threatened to undo her. The scantron was crinkled, wrinkled and creased by the marks of sweat that had escaped her fingers as she clutched the test possessively. She stared at the 62%, let it burn angrily into her mind.

She deserved it: she had somehow brought this failure upon herself, and it was only right that she now suffer because of it. She lamented the fact that she did not have the test questions in front of her- she wished to see where she'd gone so terribly wrong. It was disappointing, crushing, to make it this far in the realm of academia only to learn the truth: she was a terrible student sorely lacking in intellect, a sorry excuse of a college undergrad. She'd fooled her instructors long enough and tricked her way through the system for over a decade, but the truth was catching up with her.

What was she to do? The way Leiala saw it, she had only two options: she could give up, embrace the unfortunate truth and admit defeat- or she could double her efforts in the class, attend every office hour, read over every page of the textbook twice before lecture- anything that might help her to secure a better grade in the class. The first option would be easier, certainly, but it would also expose her unfavorably and destroy her reputation- it would ruin everything that she'd built for herself.

Fear slithered into Leiala's soul like a slick serpent, wriggling easily to her heart and squeezing it protectively. The second one! She had to do the second one. There really wasn't an option- she couldn't possibly be happy if she wasn't successful. Leiala's heartbeat quickened as the decision was solidified in her mind, etched in stone. Yes, she would succeed in Geology, or she would die trying.

***

"See? That was a helpful reaction," Pneuma reassured Fear as they relived the recent memory together.

Fear nodded, disappointed that Pneuma hadn't invited him into His perspective again. Pneuma had only offered on a few memories- Fear wished he'd suggest that approach more. It had been magical, watching the fabulously colored thread weave throughout the image as the memory had played out. He'd been meaning to ask Pneuma about the significance, but he hadn't had the opportunity yet.

"Fear?"

Fear snapped back to awareness, looking up into the expectant face of Pneuma.

"Would you rather I addressed your question before we unpack the memory?" Pneuma asked kindly.

Fear shook his head. The questions could wait.

"What did you see?" Pneuma asked patiently, redirecting Fear's attention to the topic at hand.

Fear hesitated, gathering his thoughts as he tried to imagine different perspectives and viewpoints that he might have missed. He knew Pneuma well enough by now to imagine the capacities in which he might fall short, and he now focused his efforts on seeing if he could pick up on any of these elements.

"Leiala worried about falling short, and I influenced her to work harder," Fear began. That part he was confident about. "And she didn't give up."

Pneuma nodded, encouraging Fear to go on.

"So I guess I was helpful in motivating her to keep going," Fear concluded.

"Most definitely," Pneuma agreed. "Without your influence, Leiala might have given up or accepted defeat- you inspired her to move forward. That's no insignificant thing."

Fear smiled. He was relieved to hear this from Pneuma- so far, counseling had proven to boost his self-esteem. He could now see the benefits he brought Leiala!

"And what else?" Pneuma asked, breaking through the silence.

Fear looked up in surprise. Was there some other benefit he had overlooked? One look at Pneuma's face, tilted gently as He watched Fear curiously, told him that this was not the case. He had sugar-coated the situation this time, neglecting to recognize the detrimental effects his arrival had brought Leiala.

Reluctantly, Fear allowed himself to open up. He'd hoped counseling would help him to embrace the positive and discard the negative: so far, it had only challenged him to process and investigate every angle. Fear wasn't sure this was the approach he'd wanted. His self-awareness was continuing to grow, but that didn't always turn out to be a positive thing.

"Also, Leiala now believes she's not enough just as she is," Fear began, the words finding an easy path out of his mouth. He'd known the truth the entire time- he just hadn't wanted to admit it. "She thinks she has to work hard and achieve some tangible measure in order to be considered worthy and in order to be loved."

"Yes," Pneuma agreed. "That was not only your influence, Fear."

Fear nodded. Anxiety had been present in the situation, for one- he knew he hadn't been alone in creating an effect in Leiala. This knowledge did little to make him feel better.

"It's confusing," Fear exhaled, the frustration evident in his tone. "How do we classify this experience for Leiala? Was it damaging, since it reinforced her perfectionist tendencies and affirmed her desire and pursuit for achievement through worldly measures? Because that's obviously not serving her- that seems to be an action straight from Abaddon's play book.

"Or is it somehow a positive experience, since Leiala learned to persevere in the face of failure, since she chose to try again and get back up when so many others would just throw the towel in? Why do these situations even happen at all?!" Fear ended, throwing his hands up in the air in exasperation.

Here, Pneuma chuckled.

"You have no idea how many humans share those sentiments precisely," Pneuma smiled. "Life ***is*** complicated- this one scenario illustrates that. Why does it have to be one or the other?" Pneuma challenged. "It might make it easier to classify and organize our memories and past if that were the case. But you've seen for yourself as we've revisited memories that it simply isn't reality. Most situations have multiple effects."

"So who's controlling the experience?" Fear challenged. Pneuma was right- he didn't like the ambiguity surrounding so many of the memories.

"That's complicated," Pneuma began, earning Him an exasperated sigh from Fear. "I know- you'd like it to be simple. But hopefully by now you're realizing that things are rarely simple and straightforward."

"Yes, I think I've realized that," Fear agreed dryly.

"Theos is in control, if that's what you're asking," Pneuma began. "But Abaddon has a significant influence, and the human has control over the choices they make."

"So it's a giant mess," Fear surmised snarkily.

"It's certainly not neat and tidy," Pneuma agreed, ignoring the attitude in Fear's voice. "But it's still beautiful- and it's *real*. The greatest reward comes from that authenticity."

Fear's mind instantly traveled to the multi-colored ribbon.

"The ribbon," Fear blurted. He didn't know how, but he knew it was connected to what Pneuma had just mentioned.

Pneuma smiled now, a slow grin that moved the joy from His mouth to His eyes, which glittered with brilliance and excitement.

"It's beautiful, isn't it?" Pneuma asked. There was a reverence in His tone that further intrigued Fear.

"Very," Fear agreed, his mind recalling the hypnotic way the cord had glided across the scene, weaving in and out and up and down as it changed color and hue and even luminosity. "What is it?"

"Life. Eternity. Theos's plan," Pneuma stated matter-of-factly, listing the ideas in quick succession.

Fear scowled, trying to make sense of these grand ideas.

"That ribbon you saw is the thread of Leiala's life. The color, movement, and speed at which it moves is all orchestrated by God, influenced by Abaddon, and controlled by Leiala. It's a grand dance which includes beauty, horror, misfortune, and success. It will follow Leiala for the duration of her life," Pneuma continued.

Fear absorbed this information carefully, trying to piece together these new facts and place them within the context of what he had seen. There had indeed been stripes of the ribbon that looked dull or colorless, but this had only served to amplify the beauty of the brilliant colors that had typically been placed right beside the neutral tones. The cord had varied in thickness, and the speed and beauty of the twirling ribbon had changed even within the minutes that Fear had witnessed its magic. What it all meant, he wasn't sure. But he remembered well the movements and appearance of the thread, the way it had almost seemed alive.

"And everyone has a thread?" Fear asked. It was the natural follow-up question, and it made him think back to his previous human assignments.

"Every human has a thread," Pneuma agreed.

"What does it all mean?" Fear probed. "Each human has a thread, but what does it do? What's the point?" As far as he had been able to determine, the ribbon hadn't had any effect on Leiala's life. It had simply existed.

"You won't know on earth," Pneuma explained, His voice suddenly far away. Fear didn't even blink, so riveted was he on Pneuma's words.

"So never?" Fear asked.

"We'll all know someday," Pneuma told him. "But in time."

This response immediately sent Fear into a state of frustration. Time. TIME! Something he seemed to have an endless supply of some days and other days he didn't have nearly enough. Why must he wait to know? He was so sick of being patient!

"You can't rush a masterpiece," Pneuma added, His chiding tone revealing that He had heard Fear's thought.

"A masterpiece?"

"It's all of life, humanity," Pneuma told Fear. "Leiala is a part of that story. So is every other human. The threads don't seem to connect right now, but they will someday. What looks like a mess down here on earth will be revealed as a masterpiece from above."

"And Abaddon's work?" Fear doubted. He so badly wanted to believe Pneuma's words, but he had his reservations.

"Even Abaddon's influence has it's place on the tapestry," Pneuma told him. "Every band of color, every movement- literally every part of every thread- is a part of something bigger."

Fear sat back, considering the weight of this statement. Could it possibly be true? The struggle, the challenge, the evil- was it all a part of something greater? Something he couldn't even fathom?

"You're going to have to trust me on this one," Pneuma said. "But I promise you, it will well be worth the wait."

-21-

Leiala struggled to breathe. Her lungs couldn't keep pace with the heaving gasps that quite literally crippled her, drawing her center of gravity down towards the ground. She didn't try to resist this forward momentum as she crumpled to her knees, her long hair sticking to the wetness of her cheek. An anguished shudder rolled through her body, her spine arched and then sank in obedience like a frightened cat. Her vision blurred, and she was vaguely aware of the possibility that one or more of her roommates was home. Wiping at her eyes with the back of her hand, she was able to focus well enough to ensure that she had in fact closed the door completely.

With the imminent threat of discovery neutralized, Leiala's fear left her, and she succumbed to the heartache that washed over her like a tidal wave. She wasn't low enough- even her elbows and knees couldn't support the pain, hurt, and disappointment that suffocated every cell in her body with hundred-pound weights. She collapsed unceremoniously onto the cheaply-carpeted floor, her cheek irritated with a bright rug burn she could feel but not see.

Good. Let it burn, Leiala thought viciously. It was only fitting that her physical form suffer the way her inner being did.

A fresh sob swirled deep within her belly, spiraling its way up with the ferocity of a hurricane. As it bubbled and erupted from her lips, Leiala silenced the noise by clamping hard on the sleeve of her sweatshirt, her teeth slicing through the worn cotton and piercing the flesh beneath.

Release.

Leiala bit harder, sticky saliva now wetting her sweatshirt as she bit harder, punishing her despicable flesh. *She was so awful. Despicable. Unwanted. How could she have dared to think any differently? She was stupid, stupid, STUPID!*

For a moment, the expansive sorrow melted into anger, and Leiala felt her body tense as a current of power seemed to electrify her being. But just as soon as it had come, it passed, leaving Leiala as she was, a crumpled heap of limbs, saliva, and wayward hairs congregated on the floor. She didn't have the energy for anger. Not yet. At some point, she knew, she could channel this sorrow into her preferred emotion- one she knew how to work with- but not at the moment. Not when it was all so fresh.

Where did she go from here? Leiala didn't know. She didn't want to know. To pick herself up would mean to go on living, and she wasn't sure she wanted to. Could she just disappear? Could she just cease to live? She didn't want to end her life, but she wished someone would end it for her. For a moment, her brain fantasized all the ways she could cease to exist.

Maybe her heart would stop working- she'd read it was possible for a heart to be overwhelmed with sorrow and have a physiological response so dramatic that it ended a life. That would be nice, Leiala thought, and it would be nice and clean. But even in her dramatic state of mind she knew that her current situation wouldn't elicit such a powerful bodily response.

Or maybe she could get hit by a car. That would be quick and relatively painless, Leiala thought. Or someone could bomb the building- that would be dramatic. On some level, Leiala recognized the lunacy of her thoughts, but the fantasy helped her to stomach her current situation, it made her feel somehow in control. It was important to feel like she had a choice, like she had some sense of control over her life. In the most stressful and limiting circumstances, Leiala would remind herself that she had the choice to live. It wasn't that she thought seriously about ending her life, it was having the choice that mattered.

Honestly, the best would be if she could just melt into oblivion like the Wicked Witch of the West. She would be so thankful, so indebted to the person who dumped water on her, ending this insufferable existence she called her life. Heck, she'd even take the role of Dorothy if it meant that three clicks of her red ballet flats would transport her far, far away. A hint of a smile played upon her lips at this literary reference but was quickly shunned by Leiala herself. No, there would be no joy tonight. Not after what had happened.

As Leiala's cries and whimpers died down, her body shuddered, relaxing into the fetal position she had adopted. Now able to control her sobs, the arm was removed from Leiala's mouth, and her clean sweatshirt sleeve was used to wipe the tears and spit from her swollen face. With slow, intentional motions, Leiala pushed the wet hairs away from her face and tucked them behind her ear. A long, slow sigh escaped from her lips, and she felt her body relax into the centimeter-thick carpet scratching at every inch of exposed flesh.

On some level, Leiala realized that she was now in the eye of the storm: the jolting, aggressive onset of the squall had been weathered, but the real work had not yet begun. The fuzzy, incomplete and irrational thought-processing of the past hour were beginning to fade, and Leiala sensed that she would now be able to form a lucid thought.

What had happened? Leiala wondered, picking at the taupe carpeting. This was the second time she had messed up in love- the second time she had blown it big-time. Her stomach dropped and she felt a new wave of nausea as she recalled the painful learning of the past year.

The first time, it had been someone else's heart- not that that mattered. Leiala had felt the pain as deeply as if it had been her own. Why couldn't she be like the other girls in her dorm, the girls who were flippant and dismissive of the feelings of the boys they dated or rejected? Leiala couldn't understand their approach, but she envied them immensely when she considered the weightiness of her own heart. Why must she feel things so deeply? Empathy was a skill she hadn't had to learn- it seemed to have been built into her being, its capacity far greater than most other intangibles.

She had been perceptive even as a small child, reading the bodies, language, and facial expressions of her peers and also adults. Her imagination led her to consider how others might feel in any number of circumstances. Her heart bled for those in pain, whether they be human, animal, insect, or plant. Her heart seemed to break for any marring of beauty, any deviation from that which was intended to be. That was the problem: she saw the limitless potential in any person or situation, but also the sin and circumstances that kept it from reaching its optimal level. Crying babies bothered her. Snack wrappers on the ground bothered her. Vulnerable snails crossing the sidewalk were in dire need of her aid. An untended plant bruised her sweet heart. She wanted to inspire beauty and brilliance- she wanted to nurture life everywhere she went!

Sometimes, this was easy. As a young girl, when her infant brother had cried in the night, she had leapt from her bed, bare feet padding down the carpeted hallway to reach her brother before her mother was awakened. She would spend ten, fifteen, sometimes thirty minutes holding her brother, rocking him and soothing him, whispering love or singing silly songs while making funny faces- anything to ease his mind and lull him back to sleep. She felt fulfilled in these moments, sure of her purpose. She was needed, valued, and she was able to restore the beauty and peace that she so longed to see in the world around her. The next morning, if she felt tired, it was hidden beneath the warm glow of knowing she'd done something to make the world a little sweeter.

She picked trash up from the ground, collected recyclable bottles and even plastic sandwich bags in token efforts to improve the environment, and she never failed to help a snail, rollie pollie, or earthworm that was stuck in a compromising situation. Her strong sense of justice led her to stand up for every outcast or overlooked individual, whether it was the homely new kid, the struggling reader, or the insecure new teacher or unpopular librarian.

But then, somewhere along the way, things changed. Leiala was taught by the world that she could not feel so deeply, she could not function properly, if she allowed herself to feel the way that she felt. And so, being the people-pleasing over-achiever that she was, Leiala adjusted.

Her progress was slow at first, but she learned steadily. She learned to channel her drive towards competition and achievement, and she learned to ignore that which she could not control so that she could focus her efforts on controlling that which fell within her realm of influence. It was impractical and overwhelming to feel to the extent that she did, but she could instead *do* things to show her solidarity with those who suffered. She learned that the actions of crying and mourning were unproductive, made other people feel uncomfortable, and should be avoided at all costs. She learned that there was no value in these behaviors, which only served to immobilize. It was far better to push past these emotions, to target a plan or approach that yielded more tangible, productive results.

Leiala was a good student, in every regard. She took these lessons from the world and integrated them into her being with resolve and passion. She decreased the time in which she moved from feeling to planning, and she learned to mask her vulnerability in a show of strength. And the more Leiala did this, the easier it became. By the time she was in high school, Leiala felt like a pro.

The feelings hadn't necessarily left her, but the sharp edges of emotion had been dulled and controlled. Others often remarked on her determination and her resolve, mistaking her high achievement and polished veneer for strength she wasn't sure she truly possessed. But she felt proud when others made these comments, and she wanted desperately to believe that it was true.

And then, there were moments like the one that had transpired that day that reminded her of her weakness, of her vulnerability, of her failure to numb any feelings at all. A harsh chuckle escaped her lips- what would others think, if they could see her now? Oh yes, the controlled, put-together Leiala, undaunted by any task, lying in a pitiful heap on the ground, ugly-crying and chewing on the string of her sweatshirt? The thought fueled Leiala to push herself up into a seated position. Pushing her hair out of her face once more, Leiala let her arms rest on the insides of her legs as she took a deep breath.

Breathe. Get it together. This is not the end of the world, Leiala commanded herself.

Just thinking in this way gave Leiala a spark of power, a small sense of control. She knew how to do this- how many times had she done this before? She was letting her emotions take over, and she needed to move back into a rational space. Starting with the first wound that had broken open during the day's events.

You didn't mean to do it, Leiala. It wasn't intentional, so it doesn't matter.

Leiala could confirm that her intentions had in fact been entirely pure, but she also knew that this didn't mitigate the hurt that she had brought upon someone she cared about. She winced as she recalled the expression on her friend's face when she had told him that she liked him back, when she let him kiss her. She'd thought she *had* liked him: she knew she loved spending time with him, loved their conversations, and loved the thoughtful gifts he brought her and the undivided attention he gave her. She'd never been in a relationship, or even on a date before, so she assumed that this was enough. Her girlfriends, giddy at the prospective romance and grand gestures of love Leiala had been given, had encouraged her that this was enough, that she *must* be in love. Leiala wasn't sure. But how was she supposed to know? Feelings were fickle- she needed to look at the evidence before her.

And this misguided approach had landed her in an impossibly painful situation. The moment their lips met, Leiala felt it. She knew. There was no rationalizing the reality that was now clear as a cloudless sky: she had no romantic feelings for her dear friend. But seeing *his* reaction, and knowing how deeply he felt, she panicked. Adrenaline pulsed through her veins, amplifying her every sense and instinct.

Mask! Control! Her mind had screamed at her as she threatened to tense and pull back, revealing her true feelings. Her pride had kicked in here, too: how stupid would she reveal herself to be if she admitted the truth just seconds after declaring a sentiment of affection? What would he think? What would their friends think? She had just found her place in college- she had just won a place of acceptance, privilege, and belonging. That could all fly away in an instant, if she wasn't careful.

So she'd smiled, urging her body to relax even as she wanted to run, run, RUN far away. She bit the inside of her lip, counted to ten, counted to ten again, then feigned a yawn and declared herself tired. And then- Leiala cringed to recall it- then, she'd made a bad situation worse.

She'd hid. Literally, she'd hid. She only emerged from her dorm for class, taking long, circuitous routes she knew he would not traverse. She ate meals in her room, ran only in the very early hours in the morning, and avoided their entire friend group to ensure that they would not cross paths and to ensure that she would not have to explain herself to any mutual friends.

She could imagine the pain, the confusion, and the hurt- her own present rejection brought this empathy back in full force. It threatened to cripple her, to undo her now- she couldn't bear the thought of inflicting such pain upon someone else. But she had done it, and it was now in the past. With a pang of guilt, Leiala was forced to admit that she'd never made amends for her wrong- she'd been so embarrassed by the situation that she'd never owned up to her action, choosing instead to hide out for months. She'd acted cool and distant when they'd seen each other next, a grand facade to the true discomfort and remorse that she really felt...and things had never been the same.

She'd cursed herself then, resolved to guard her heart a bit more carefully. That had been a rookie mistake, she'd told herself. She hadn't had any experience with love- that was why she'd acted like a silly pre-teen (and that was a generous description, if Leiala was honest about the way it all went down).

But then, she'd allowed herself to entertain feelings again. This time, Leiala felt more confident about her own feelings, about the attraction on her end. She'd had a number of signs that her feelings were reciprocated, and she hadn't been the one to initiate their times spent together (which she had taken as a clue in and of itself), but when it had come down to it and she had shared her feelings, it didn't appear that the feelings were mutual.

Even now, the sting of rejection hit Leiala with the force of one hundred samurai swords. Coupled with another "C" on the latest Geology test, and the knee pain that Leiala just couldn't seem to shake (keeping her from running), Leiala felt desolate and worthless. Who was she, if she wasn't a good student and athlete? She had just proven herself to be unwanted, and the successive failures that came straight on the heels of this rejection seemed to confirm that she was in fact an utter loser.

On a rational level, Leiala could argue any of these situations away: she hadn't, in fact, been rejected- she just hadn't received the effusive compliments and praise she'd been hoping for as she'd shared her own feelings; Geology was only one class within her burgeoning collegiate career, and her knee would heal in time (if she would only allow her body to rest!). But this was what came from swallowing her feelings- when the slightest crack appeared in Leiala's finely welded armor of control, release came powerfully, pushing her to a place of overwhelming despair.

You'll just have to pick up the pieces and put yourself back together, Leiala told herself matter-of-factly. She didn't mean for the words to sound harsh- this was about self-preservation. This was going to be harder to come back from, Leiala acknowledged, but she could do it. She *would* do it. There wasn't another choice. There weren't any magical ruby slippers or buckets of water lying around- this was all on Leiala.

And as painful as it was, Leiala knew what she had to do. Pushing herself up to her feet, Leiala made her way to the mirror. She judiciously studied her blotchy skin and puffy eyes as she ran a brush through her tangled hair. A frozen spoon applied to her eyelids would reduce the swelling, and a little foundation would even out her complexion. Smoothing her hair back into a low ponytail, Leiala used weary but determined movements to change her clothes, smooth out the comforter on her bed, and organize the few papers on top of her desk. Organization. Neatness. Control.

By the time she finished cleaning the bathroom, Leiala's crystal blue eyes sparkled, and a fresh coat of mascara helped to separate the lashes that had clumped together from her salty tears. Deft fingers smeared foundation underneath her eyes, and a few pinches to her cheeks brought a rosy glow.

Leiala glanced in the mirror once more, this time trying on a smile. It felt unnatural at first, but it soon ebbed into what appeared to be a genuine grin. Leiala could spot the evidence of her true state of being: the teensy branch-like red veins in the corners of her eyes, the lips that protruded farther than usual...but to anyone who might encounter Leiala, she looked fine. Just the way Leiala wanted it.

-22-

Fear woke with the knowledge that it would be a big day for Leiala. He couldn't articulate how this knowledge had come to him, but he knew it with certainty. Months before, he wasn't sure he would have had such a feeling, or if he had, if he would have recognized it. But things had changed since his visits with Pneuma-beyond the counseling, he seemed to know, to *sense* things that he hadn't been able to before.

He dressed nervously, slipping into jeans and pulling on a t-shirt in his haste to make it to the west end headquarters. Pneuma would surely tell him what was going on.

As he rushed down the corridor, Fear wracked his brain for clues. Leiala had certainly had an interesting few months- Fear could attest to that. She had thankfully bounced back from the ego-crushing moment in which she had ventured to bare her soul, although Fear acknowledged that the progress had been slow and the path convoluted.

Fear lamented the fact that Abaddon had influenced Leiala during this time- he had used her anguish and uncertainty to fuel her determination to try harder to attain success. Curiously, though, Abaddon had not usurped total control like Fear had worried he might. Abaddon's focused efforts on Leiala had reinforced faulty thought patterns, but they had not been able to stop her from reaching a point of total surrender: the crushing pain of failure had drawn her into Theos's open arms.

Things had seemed to settle after that, Fear reflected in relief. Leiala had spent the weekend licking her wounds, then she had picked herself up and started putting the pieces back together.

Her planning wasn't always a bad thing, Fear thought- it had helped her to negotiate the pain and get herself back on track. Theos was instrumental in those early moments, too- Fear remembered the way He had soothed Leiala and assured her that everything would be alright.

The problem was, Leiala promptly forgot the unconditional acceptance as soon as she made worldly progress. Fear had witnessed this pattern: when Leiala first fell, she was overcome by a sense of hopelessness and worthlessness. It was in this pitiful state that Theos was most effective in getting through to Leiala, that He was able to convey to her her immeasurable worth and unchallenged place in life. It just didn't last.

The next A grade, the next boy who showed interest in her, the next friend who complimented her outfit, and Leiala was back to believing that her worth was directly tied to her performance or appearance. Fear wasn't sure how Theos stomached it- he was very fond of Leiala himself, but he often felt frustrated in these situations. Leiala seemed to be stuck in a hamster wheel, unable to pull herself out of this repetitive, destructive habit. Theos never gave up on Leiala, Fear acknowledged- and He never showed any indication of resentment towards Leiala as He came near to her to offer her the same comfort He had so many times before.

But that wouldn't be the problem today. Over the past few months, Fear had watched with much trepidation as Leiala appeared to develop feelings once more. He had rejoiced with her, but also felt anxiety on her behalf- he knew all too well the deep, gut-wrenching emotions that had so far come with relational encounters.

Making him more nervous was the fact that Abaddon had been unusually quiet. Fear was trying not to obsess over this fact too much, but it hadn't escaped his notice that his summonings had decreased, and that Abaddon's presence in Leiala's life had been constant but was no longer targeted the way it had been in the past.

This was the first question out of his mouth as he barged into Pneuma's office. Pneuma, to His credit, didn't appear surprised by Fear's unannounced entrance. On some level, this irritated Fear- he'd been looking forward to Pneuma's reaction to his dramatic entry.

"It's intentional," Pneuma confirmed in a matter-of-fact tone.

Fear felt goosebumps prickle his arms- that was what he'd been afraid of.

"What does he have planned?" Fear followed up quickly, chewing on the edge of his fingernail nervously.

"He's hardly held a press conference on his intentions," Pneuma joked, His tone playful as He gave Fear a sly wink. "But I imagine he's working to lull Leiala into a false sense of security, to establish a pattern and rhythm in her life that will draw her to a place of comfort. Then, when he does choose to make his next move, the effect will be that much greater."

Fear nodded. That made sense. He silently cursed Abaddon's ingenuity- he truly was a dastardly, clever being.

"Do you think he knows about me?" Fear asked next, trying to keep his tone even in an attempt to hide the nerves and anxiety that rode on the back of this question. Pneuma sensed it anyway- as Fear knew He would.

"Don't take this the wrong way, Fear, but I doubt Abaddon's concerned with the actions of characters," Pneuma told him steadily. Fear was aware of Pneuma's penetrating gaze fixed upon him, and his cheeks burned self-consciously.

"I don't think he's focused on me," Fear hurried to explain. "I know I'm basically irrelevant to him. It's just that I worry that since I'm assigned to Leiala, and he's taken a great interest in her, that maybe he would feel threatened by my actions."

"Abaddon is many things- intelligent, crafty, powerful, and insidious, to name a few," Pneuma began wisely. Since His gaze had been fixed upon Fear, He hadn't blinked once. "But Abaddon is not Theos. He has his faults, too. He has inflated confidence, and he is impossibly self-centered. He doesn't suspect any character will dare defy his orders, and since it isn't on his radar, he won't detect your true feelings. As long as you continue to follow the summons and don't behave strangely, you'll likely go unnoticed. Abaddon certainly wouldn't suspect you've spent time in the west end headquarters- that type of action is largely unprecedented," Pneuma assured him.

Fear didn't try to hide his relief- his exhale was long, and his entire body seemed to relax with the release of tension he hadn't realized he was holding close.

"That's good to know," he thanked Pneuma. "I've been worried he would be able to tell."

"Over time, your character will show more evidence of time spent in the west end," Pneuma warned. "But it's early yet- you don't have anything to worry about."

This additional information served to deflate Fear just a bit- not because at some point in time he would show physical evidence of his time in the west end and fall under Abaddon's suspicion, but because he was not yet there. While he didn't want his changes highlighted for Abaddon to see, he was disappointed that he didn't already have the mark of a changed character. He found himself wondering what that would look like, and hoping that he would achieve this status someday. Pneuma seemed to sense his feelings but kept silent.

"What's going on with Leiala?" Fear asked, changing the subject. "I sensed the change as soon as I woke up."

"Very perceptive of you," Pneuma acknowledged. Fear waited impatiently for Him to continue, but He was frustratingly mute.

"Pneuma?" Fear pressured impatiently. He knew already that Pneuma would not cave to his demands- that wasn't Pneuma's style- but he couldn't help himself from asking.

"Why are you asking me?" Pneuma asked. "Theos holds the future- not me. That's not my job. And if it were, I still wouldn't spell it all out. That takes all the beauty from life."

"So you *do* know," Fear accused. "It wouldn't take any beauty away- not for me. If anything I will better be able to appreciate the beauty when it comes- I'll be ready for it, and I can manage my response appropriately."

Pneuma smiled as though amused, and Fear knew his plea had done nothing to influence Him.

"You know that's not how it works," Pneuma said simply.

Fear sat in stubborn silence, hoping Pneuma would change His mind. He did not.

"You're welcome to stay with me, to watch it all unfold," Pneuma offered.

Fear looked up in surprise- he had never done that before. What would it be like, to watch Leiala's life unfold in the presence of Pneuma? Would he see the events take place through the perspective of the alternative realm? That could be seriously interesting. He nodded, moving towards Pneuma.

"We'd better move closer," Pneuma told Fear. "There's a good chance you and I will both be summoned for this one."

Fear nodded, his excitement masking any frustration that Pneuma did in fact know what was about to happen, and He was holding out on him.

***

The food was good, but Leiala couldn't even eat half of her meal. She would remember the color of the tablecloth, the sound of the waves crashing against the cliffs, and the feel of the laminated, unusually-tall menu as she held it in her hands...but most of all, she would remember the way he looked at her.

He. The man that sat across the table from her, pretending to look around the restaurant and out the window to the ocean below, but who was really sneaking sidelong glances in her direction. Leiala felt the color rise to her cheeks in pleasure, and she tucked her hair behind her ear self-consciously.

In so many ways, her life had felt like a fairy-tale over the past few months: not just because of the magic unfolding at the table before her, but because none of it seemed real. *Was* it real?

She'd met a man- one that she liked. That she was sure she liked. She'd been careful, slow- even slower this time- to make sure she didn't make a mistake. Their meeting hadn't been contrived, there had been no romantic motives (as far as she knew).

They'd met on a double-date, one where they hadn't been intended for each other. Leiala had to chuckle as she remembered the scenario, one her roommate had talked her into: she was the reluctant double on a date that meant a lot to her roommate- and he had been the second reluctant date, intended for her roommate. Not thirty minutes in, it was clear that plans had gone awry- Leiala found herself giggling and sneaking smiles with the wrong man, much to the chagrin and frustration of both her date and roommate.

From there, things had progressed slow and steady. Leiala found herself more willing to go to parties that she knew he would attend, and she found herself putting more effort into her appearance when she knew he would be around. Their conversations were playful, flirtatious- but never overtly so. Leiala didn't have a forward bone in her body when it came to romance, and he was too married to his freedom and reputation as "uncatchable" to show singular interest in Leiala.

Leiala knew about his reputation, knew about all the girls who had crushes on this handsome football player with a tendency to party too hard and play the field a bit too much- and so she wisely kept her distance while developing a crush of her own. She matched his aura of mystery with that of her own: he left parties early, vanishing into thin air without so much as a goodbye, and she did the same. He feigned indifference to all the female attention that flocked his way, and she pretended not to notice (all while ensuring that she looked her very best). She knew better than to flatter or compliment him- instead, she teased and pretended apathy to his presence. There was no way *she* was going to make a move- she wasn't sure she wanted to, anyway.

But then things had started to change. He'd started messaging her, and they'd talked late into the night. She didn't want to, but she noticed how her heartbeat quickened when she received a message from him, and she registered the disappointment when an afternoon or evening passed without a message. Their playful banter escalated to bets- athletic challenges that offered them the chance to spend more time together under the pretense of competition.

A basketball match.

A soccer game.

A flag football event.

A running race.

The last event ending on an abandoned football field with dewy, kelly-green grass. A subtle breeze swirled under a blanket of twinkling stars as they'd climbed onto the roof of the nearest building, laid a blanket down, and talked about their dreams as they stared out into space. And something changed. Leiala knew it. He knew it.

They'd talked all night, only agreeing to move when the sun rose, bringing the rest of the world back to life. Time hadn't passed sequentially, Leiala remembered thinking- she felt as though she were the featured, magical display inside of a snow globe. It didn't feel real. But it was, and that frightened her. And when he'd asked her to join him for breakfast, she'd said no. Suddenly overwhelmed, afraid, and unsure of what had happened, she had retreated to her dorm.

Later, she would process the night's events and determine that she was okay with things progressing- she was willing to take that small risk. But she would continue to take baby steps- she remembered well what had happened the last time she had ventured to take a chance.

Over spring break (mercifully backed up to this burgeoning romance, giving Leiala the chance to sort through all that had transpired), he had called every day. She hated talking on the phone, but not with him. Somehow, the hours seemed to whiz by, and every click of the cell phone ended with the magnetic warmth of an overworked cell battery on her ear and a similar warmth emanating from the recesses of her heart.

It had all led to this: an official date with him. Him, the man who didn't date or commit to just one girl. But as they shyly ate dinner at the restaurant overlooking the water, Leiala had to admit that he appeared to be pretty smitten.

Later, as they walked the abandoned, tree-lined street down to the pier, Leiala had felt the magic that descended from the twinkle lights spiraling the gnarled trees. She had felt the magic in the soft, salty breeze that gave flight to her stray hairs, causing them to tickle her cheek playfully. And she had felt the magic radiating from the body of the man standing next to her, felt the energy and desire as she nervously kept a good foot of distance between them.

He had asked to kiss her then, and she had said no. Later, this would make her laugh- she had said no, but she had offered to let him hold her hand instead. And as they'd held hands, their warm palms seeming to communicate more than words were able to, he had tried again. He had made an earnest speech, one that Leiala recognized as honest and authentic. He had only *really* liked three girls in his life- there had only been three girls he'd ever wanted to kiss. Leiala's heart seemed to slow down, then speed up as she hung on every word: the crush in middle school, the girlfriend in high school, and now her. He wanted to kiss her.

Leiala was quiet, thankful her long hair made a curtain that covered her face, bought her time to think. She knew she wanted to kiss him, too- but would that lead her down a path she would regret? Her heart thumped wildly in her chest, and she felt the rush of a decision overcome her. She had to do this- she had to follow her heart. It had hurt her before, but it felt safer now.

Aware that they were approaching the end of the pier, she looked out at the reflection of the full moon in the water, the lights of the buildings and strings of lights playfully dancing on the water. Swallowing her gum decisively, she looked up at him with steady determination she didn't quite feel and leaned forward for her first real kiss.

-23-

Fear was dimly aware that Abaddon's tactics had changed. He wasn't able to articulate at first what it was that had changed: he just knew that Leiala appeared to be happy, and Abaddon was allowing her to feel this way. He wasn't summoned as often, and when he did visit Leiala, it was for short bursts of time. Fear could never have imagined himself saying this, but he actually felt like his character was now *underutilized.*

He thought perhaps he was just self-conscious, that he had unrealistic expectations for his character. How had his past assignments gone? Maybe he'd just grown accustomed to the demanding, exhausting schedule that the beginning of Leiala's life had dictated.

He kept these thoughts to himself in the beginning- he didn't want the other characters to think he'd adopted an inflated sense of self-importance, and he wanted to explore his feelings a bit further, to see if there was any validity buried in them.

But as days melted into weeks which melted into months, Fear was forced to admit that the unease was still there. The unease that Leiala no longer seemed to struggle with. Was his trepidation the result of his ego, which demanded recognition and importance on some level? Or was his concern for Leiala authentic, genuine? He knew he could go and ask Pneuma about it- He would offer him a direct answer, Fear felt sure. But he felt sheepish about it all- he worried over the answer he might receive.

He eavesdropped on other characters' discussions, and brought up Leiala's change whenever it seemed natural. The other characters all seemed to share the opinion that this change was beneficial, that it signified the growth and maturity Leiala had fallen into.

They were all pleased that their work appeared to have been productive- Leiala had developed into the balanced assignment they had all hoped she would.

Fear couldn't detect even the slightest hint of hesitation or worry in any of the characters- they all seemed to possess a single mind where Leiala was concerned: she was happy, their workload had decreased, and the tension between Theos and Abaddon had ebbed. This was cause for celebration- but Fear could not join in on the festivities.

And so, one day, Fear found himself walking down the corridor of the east end headquarters once more. This time, he was not there against his will, or on assignment. He was there because he wanted to be, because he wanted to learn.

The change in tone was palpable as Fear crossed the threshold of the peaceful garden patio into the dark, oppressive realm of Abaddon. The air became thick and moist, making it hard for Fear to breathe. His pores seemed to widen instantly as a steady stream of sweat began to dribble down his back. He felt uncomfortable, oppressed. This was in stark contrast to the feel of the west end headquarters- a change that Fear felt strongly after the amount of time spent in Theos's domain.

With direct steps, he walked aimlessly down the corridor, bumping into Abaddon's workers as he moved deeper and deeper into the belly of the east end. Sweat now ran down his forehead, and the heat stirred irritation in Fear, who found he could not move forward more than a few feet without exchanging slick, stank sweat with one of Abaddon's workers. The big, small, and giant- none seemed to take consideration of the other individuals walking the hallways, instead bumping into any figure that impeded their path.

What *was* Fear's path? Honestly, he wasn't sure. He was just following a hunch, an intuition that had nudged him to come, to explore, to wander. He passed classrooms, passed strategics rooms, and the dormitories (although Abaddon's workers never seemed to sleep). None of these rooms called to Fear, and so he kept walking. His pulse quickened, and his step seemed to magnetize his footsteps down a path he had never ventured down before.

And then he saw it, and he knew.

The place he had come to visit.

Annals.

It was written on a beleaguered piece of driftwood, the charcoal lettering inconsistent and sloppy, giving Fear indefinite clues of the value Abaddon's workers ascribed to the dank room. If it was possible, the temperature in the room seemed even warmer than out in the hallways, and the lighting was dim.

Fear ducked to enter the room, which was noteworthy, considering his small stature compared to most of Abaddon's beefy workers. His nostrils stung with the pungent smell of mildew and smoke- an odd combination for what Fear surmised was a library of sorts. He squinted his eyes to try and adjust to the lighting of the room, offered through gothic candelabras, rusted lanterns, and the flickering light of sinister wax candles. Fear's eyes rapidly moved from the rough, uneven wooden surfaces of the tables before him, stained with sticky pools of hardened wax and what Fear worried might be blood. Abaddon's workers sat on stools before these imposing forms, their backs hunched deliberately over the pages spread out on the tables before them.

At once Fear was struck by how small they all were: Abaddon's workers were by and large oversized, giant creatures that communicated intimidation and threat. This room seemed to be where all the inconsequential creatures congregated: Fear took in their small, wiry statures and pointed limbs. Although small, there seemed to be something more sinister about them. Fear could sense intelligence, craftiness that outstripped their larger counterparts.

Not a single head had turned in his direction, Fear noticed with relief, and so he allowed his gaze to cautiously wander to the dusty, disheveled shelves that lined the walls of the room. Every book seemed to have the same leather cover, but Fear noticed that the wear and tear and size of the books varied greatly: there were some books that seemed ready to disintegrate at the slightest application of touch, and others that appeared to be in pristine condition. What's more, there were colossal books that were three feet high and two feet thick, and there were books no larger than a pocket-sized dictionary. But there were lots of books- lots and lots and lots of books. As Fear surveyed the room, he noticed a gaping hole just beyond what appeared to be the librarian's desk.

Pulse quickening, he edged forward to take a peek. He did not want to awaken the interest of the workers around him- he kept his steps light and made as little noise as possible.

Books. More books. Millions upon millions upon millions of books.

The hole was never-ending, a chasm that stretched indefinitely. The shelves were never-ending, as were the quantities of books. A single ladder descended deep into the pit, but Fear couldn't see where it ended. Wisps of smoke escaped from the crest of the pit, and Fear could hear the crackling flames of fire far below. That explained the singe marks and charred bindings on some of the books he had seen.

"What are you doing here?" a sharp voice demanded, electrifying Fear with terror as he jumped a foot into the air.

He turned in what he hoped appeared to be a casual manner, his wide eyes searching for the speaker. His gaze quickly settled on a squat worker with wide, cat-like eyes that narrowed as he took in Fear's form. The worker stood behind the official-looking table that Fear had assumed was the librarian's desk (was there such a thing in this place?), and so he grew even more nervous.

"I was sent here," Fear lied drily, the saliva collecting in his mouth stale and thick.

"You dare to lie to *us*?" the worker asked in genuine astonishment, resting both palms down on the splintered surface of the table in aggressive fashion. Now, Fear had earned the interest of the other workers in the room, who couldn't pass up the opportunity to witness a show.

Help.

Fear wasn't even sure where the word came from, but he was certain that his mind begged for some- any!- kind of aid. What had he been thinking, coming into the east end headquarters? This wasn't the west end headquarters, where an individual's presence was accepted, welcomed. Had he gone soft in the time spent away from Abaddon?

Suddenly, he was aware of Pneuma's presence. Hope lifted like a helium balloon deep within Fear's belly. He wasn't alone.

"Pneuma," he said aloud.

"Pneuma?" the worker challenged, becoming more outraged by the moment. "Now you expect me to believe that it was Pneuma that sent you here?"

Fear checked himself- the workers could not sense Pneuma's presence with him. Words came to him even as he found himself at an utter loss for what to say.

"I am here to check on the status of Leiala."

It wasn't what he would have thought to say- with all the books in the room (Fear wasn't even sure what they were books about), Fear felt he should at least identify Leiala using her last name, perhaps her social security number. But only Leiala's first name had fluttered into Fear's mind, and Fear had the understanding that this prompting had come from Pneuma and not himself.

"You seem to be in the wrong place," the worker charged him, his words suspicious. "There are no *live* humans here." The way he emphasized the word *live* brought goosebumps to the back of Fear's neck at the same time it drew throaty chuckles from the rest of the workers.

"I mean to check on her records."

Again, with the words. Materializing from a place Fear could not identify, but that was certainly inspired by Pneuma.

The worker seemed to consider Fear again. Aware of this reproachful scrutiny, Fear did his best to look self-assured, confident, and powerful. But who was he kidding? Anyone could tell just by looking at him that he was a simple, powerless character.

"Who sent you?" the worker asked again. Fear noticed with hope that the biting edge to the words seemed to have left- the worker appeared to exhibit genuine curiosity.

"Are you sure you have the jurisdiction to ask those questions? How often do you find characters in here?" Fear spoke with authority he did not feel. "That should be enough to tell you that I've been spent by someone with far more influence than you."

Here, he tugged on the bottom of his shirt and squared his shoulders, bringing himself to his full height.

"I'm not here to tamper with records," he added, at the silent bidding of Pneuma.

The worker took his time in offering a response. Fear felt strangely calm in the waiting; he had a certain peace, knowing that he was going to get his way. After a stretch that felt like the equivalent of five minutes, the worker nodded his head in a slow, deliberate movement that indicated he was none too excited about this visitor.

"I'm not done recording!" a worker complained from across the room.

Fear turned to watch a wiry worker lean protectively over the large, sepia-toned pages of what he assumed was Leiala's book. He was intuitively aware that each book represented a human life. He hadn't yet figured what was written in each book, but he knew he was about to find out.

"You'll have to wait until he's finished," the pseudo-librarian barked, eager to regain some of his lost dignity.

Fear nodded and took uncertain steps towards the table where the worker busily scribbled notes. He looked up at Fear and glared, his teeth bared in evident distaste. Fear took this as a warning not to come any closer, and so he waited uncomfortably feet away from the table, shifting his weight from side to side as he considered the room once more from this new angle.

The workers had lost interest in him- they went back to scribbling away in the open books. To call it a library would be incorrect, Fear realized- these were no books of fiction or even nonfiction- most were incomplete. He watched in fascination at the scribbling of the workers with their fountain pens, the ink that seemed to bleed into the uneven paper with every scratch and twitch of the pen. *What were they writing?* Fear wondered.

He didn't have to wait long to find out. The disgruntled worker finished his scribbling, signaling the end of his work by slamming the pages of the book shut with a giant clash. Dust and dirt rose from the table, swirling in mystical patterns caught in the light of the waning candle. Fear knew he would receive no further invitation, and so he walked forward with confidence he did not feel towards Leiala's book.

Leiala's book.

Leatherbound, like all other books, but with rose-petal pink leather that distinguished it from the others. Large, Fear noticed. Thick binding, and what appeared to be singe marks on the front corner. The ragged, uneven edges of the book spoke to the unconventional story Leiala had written for herself, and the sinewy cord binding the pages together seemed to weave and wrap around the book possessively.

"Don't mess anything up," the worker warned with a snarl, shoving the book across the table towards Fear. He caught the large book with his midsection, inhaling sharply as the wind was knocked out of him.

For a long moment, he looked at the book reverently. He wasn't sure what he would find inside, but the mere fact that this was Leiala's book made it worthy of high regard. Fear looked up at the worker in front of him with a dismissive glance, an action that irritated the worker but succeeded in getting him to leave.

It would be impossible to get comfortable in the steamy, minatory room, but Fear did his best, wriggling his bottom onto the squat seat of the stool in front of him. Then, with careful, deliberate movements, he reached a trembling hand out and fingered the leather-bound book before him.

The surface was bumpy- in certain places, charred. Angry black slashes ruined the otherwise pretty pink color, and there seemed to be claw marks in one corner. But it was beautiful. With heightened anticipation, Fear opened the book.

***

Hours later, Fear sat in the same position. His shoulders ached and his spine felt stiff, but he could not, *would* not, bring himself to move.

Leiala's life lay before him. In events, facts, figures, and strategies. Stripped of the romance and wonder of any sentiment or feeling, Fear nevertheless was fascinated at this window into Abaddon's strategy. From the moment of Leiala's inception, there was documentation of the efforts made on Abaddon's behalf to influence, wield power over, and capture Leiala's soul. It was all there. In black and white. The actions and strategies Fear knew that Abaddon used, but that he didn't always recognize in full effect. But the spindly, permanent scrawl in the pages before him left nothing to the imagination- and there was nothing to deny.

Naturally, Fear had started in the beginning.

July 15- Prolonged exposure to fear, stirring of insecurity and need for affirmation. Removal of comfort and joy.

Fear had felt adrenaline course through his body in raging torrents at the mention of his name- *he* was featured in this book! But of course he was featured in the book, he chided himself. He was a character, assigned to Leiala. That was his job, to obediently influence Leiala at the bidding of Theos or Abaddon. But there was something about seeing it in black and white that charged Fear, made him feel guilty. He'd known all along that he was affecting Leiala, but seeing his name associated with events he knew had led to unfavorable outcomes didn't feel good. It was unsettling, and it drove him to read further. His eyes grew bleary and unfocused as he scoured pages and pages of entries, working his way through the years of Leiala's life.

October 19- Amplified sense of fear in soliciting a partner for the game at school. Rejection used to reinforce idea of low self-worth and undesirability. Attribution introduced as Leiala watches more skilled peers field multiple requests for partnership.

November 27- Seeds planted for later body insecurity during dress-up play time with friends. Leiala doesn't fit into the pretty pink tulle dress she wants to wear, realizes this is because she is bigger than her friend who owns the dress. Insecurity visits, joy is withheld. Logic and rationalization team up to produce the thought that beautiful things are worn by smaller girls.

December 29- Leiala overhears strategic conversation of adult women describing their bout of the flu. Women express gratitude that at least the vomiting and lack of appetite helped them to keep off holiday weight; Leiala makes an association with food and fear, recognizes she must be vigilant to avoid disaster.

February 9th- Addressing valentines, Leiala agonizes over the assignment of each valentine. Analysis paralysis: by overthinking the consequences/reactions of each potential outcome, she feels overwhelmed and must walk away from the task. Seeds sown for risk avoidance, giving up even before starting.

May 11- Leiala is called on without warning in class, and freezes. In her panic, she forgets the answer and even the subject matter. Leiala hears a giggle and imagines the entire class making fun of her and ridiculing her stupidity. Firm foundation of insecurity established now; imagines everyone is watching her at all times-

this can now be used to fuel "pretty" behaviors that focus more on appearance than on organic content.

The entries were damning, and there were countless entries for each day. Fear had checked- he'd hoped to see at least one day where Leiala had been left alone.

Every once in a while, Fear witnessed an entry that was written in red ink instead of black. These entries appeared bolder, the thick crimson lettering seemed to shout from the pages. Fear could feel the passion behind the words even before reading them, and he was unconsciously certain that these entries were penned not with ink but using the blood of Leiala herself. Depression descended upon Fear as he prepared to take in the first iron-red entry. He swallowed hard, chewed on the inside of his lip.

August 11- Leiala completes soccer tryouts. She is nervous but uses self-talk to negate fear and build confidence. On a breakaway, she is tackled from behind and falls hard, face-planting and injuring her face, arms, and legs. Bleeding cheek, elbow, and knees, bruised hip and jaw. This is seen by coaches, players, and parents- Leiala feels humiliated, reinforced feelings of hopelessness and worthlessness. Realizes she was tackled by her friend. RIPE.

At first glance, the entry did not appear to be that much different from the multitude of entries Fear had already processed. It wasn't a happy event, but none of the accounts listed in the heinous book were. What made it different?

RIPE.

Fear came back to the single word listed without pretense at the end of each entry written in red ink. There was something malicious about the four letter word, something that spoke to Fear and whispered to him to look again.

RIPE.

Ripe, like a pear in a tree or a tomato on a vine. Like food. Something to be devoured. That final thought brought with it the understanding that that was exactly what was taking place: Leiala was set up to be guzzled, scarfed, demolished, consumed.

Ripe for change.

The thought appeared suddenly, and Fear knew it came from Pneuma. He leaned into this wisdom, quieting his mind in order to hear more.

She's ripe for change, ripe to be influenced. These are the memories that have served to influence her the most, that have marked the climax of her sense of self. The turning points.

Fear felt the words fall like rain on fertile soil. He received the message and knew unconsciously what Pneuma meant. These moments, marked in violent red ink, were the moments that had defined Leiala's path through life, that bled from the very essence of her being. Fear was horrified to realize that it was Leiala's very lifeblood, her soul, that made up the dried, rust-red lettering on the page in front of him. Abaddon had these moments specially documented to mark Leiala's vulnerability, her propensity for influence, her vulnerability for attack.

His premonition was confirmed as he read on. Every scarlet entry was followed by a particularly sinister strategy that exploited Leiala's weakness, exposed her soft heart and unprotected ego.

He had read enough. He didn't need to read every entry written in Leiala's book to know now how Abaddon operated- he had seen enough. Again, Fear was overwhelmed by a sense of wonder: he couldn't fathom how he had made it so far in life without recognizing how much was going on underneath the surface.

With a sigh, he stood up, reverently closing the book documenting the life of the girl who had grown to mean so much to him. His fingers traced the lumpy leather cover softly, in memorial to the girl Leiala could have become, to the many events that might have transpired differently.

It's not over.

The dark cloud that seemed to encapsulate Fear cleared just enough for him to have knowledge of a glowing light- not a spotlight or floodlight, but a bright, burning ember nonetheless, an eternal torch, a flame of hope.

No, Fear agreed, without any certainty of what he was pronouncing. *It's not over yet.*

-24-

Leiala couldn't keep the smile off of her face. She'd done it- this time, she'd finally figured it out *for real*. She couldn't exactly articulate it, but she'd stumbled upon the winning formula to life. She'd worked so hard, so diligently, for this moment. And oh, how glorious it felt now that it had finally arrived!

Classes were going well. Leiala had the straight A's and string of perfect scores and exemplary papers that proved she was smart, successful, and disciplined.

She had determined the proper schedule with which to navigate life: early morning runs bled into class (a granola bar and banana served as breakfast on the go), which bled into part-time work at the college smoothie shop. She worked a daily two-hour shift that offered just the right amount of spending money, and she got to wear a hot-pink uniform with a tropical apron and her hair pulled back in a high ponytail as she created mouth-watering blended treats. The work pleased her.

After her shift, she'd meet her boyfriend on the dappled corner of a nearby lawn, where she'd unpack a picnic lunch and offer him her latest smoothie creation as they giggled and kissed and talked under the shade of a poplar tree. More class, and dinner together with him. Evenings spent studying in one of their preferred coffee shops, always splitting a large caffeinated beverage (a sure sign of their love). Then, nights spent together, Leiala snuggled in the warmth of his embrace as her head hit the pillow- always after a prayer and devotional, of course.

It was everything she had ever wanted. She felt loved, desired, worthy, beautiful, smart, clever, athletic, and accomplished. Her life made sense; she could see the starry, promising future laid out in front of her. Sometimes, she was struck with the fear that it could all be taken away in an instant: she could be stripped of these ethereal circumstances, once again reduced to nothingness. But Leiala shook this fear from her mind and countered this threat by spending more time reading the Bible, more time praying. She wasn't aware of her intentions, but on some level, she was bargaining with God.

See? I'm a good girl. I'll keep doing things for you. You don't have to mess things up for me. I'm thankful! I'm going to stay right where you have me. Thank you, God, for this perfect life. Thank you for this perfect future. I love it. And most of all, thank you for teaching me how to be perfect, thank you for showing me the formula to success. I get it, God. I totally understand. I know what it takes now, and I can do it.

***

"I should have visited Leiala at least four times today," Fear grumbled aloud to his fellow characters.

The characters acknowledged Fear with little more than a cursory nod, indicating their muted tolerance of what had become standard rants on Fear's behalf.

"Seriously," Fear persisted. He was frustrated by the apathy and naivete demonstrated by his counterparts- he wanted to inject them with the same passion and outrage that he now held close to his heart.

"There's nothing we can do about it, Fear," Anxiety pointed out. He was Fear's closest friend, but even he had grown weary of the tirades.

"But maybe we *should*," Fear continued, knowing even as he spoke that his words were falling upon deaf ears.

He looked around in earnest, hopeful that at least one character would share his opinion, or at least express interest in learning more about why Fear was so passionate about the topic. But eyes were averted, downcast, sending a clear signal to Fear that they did not want to engage.

Fear blew out the stale air that had collected in his lungs in a sharp, reproachful breath. Pushing himself up and out of his chair, he walked purposefully to the west end- he knew he would be understood there.

Minutes later, he stood before Theos, Yeshua, and Pneuma- Fear had the rare opportunity to hold audience with all three. Some of Theos's workers were present, too- a detail that did nothing to silence Fear's bold declaration.

"Leiala should be feeling fear," he began, trying hard to keep the accusation from his voice.

"We know," Theos's worker agreed wearily, looking at Fear without any trace of surprise.

Fear was a bit taken aback by this quick agreement- if they knew, why hadn't they already taken steps to fight back?- but shook this thought off and allowed himself to refocus.

"Leiala is dismissive of fear, when she should be heeding its warning," Fear announced, sure of the importance and credibility of his words as he spoke. "She's spent her entire life up until this point living in fear, and now she's completely abandoned it."

Theos's workers considered Fear thoughtfully but did not say anything.

"She's going to get hurt- she's not paying attention to the signals!" Fear exclaimed, pleading for some sort of reaction from his audience.

"She *will* get hurt," Yeshua agreed.

"We're going to let that happen?" Fear challenged. This wasn't going as he'd hoped.

"It's Leiala's choice," Theos remarked slowly, His words laced with heaviness.

"But we can influence her," Fear bargained. "We can show her why she should be afraid- we can inject fear back into her so she doesn't make this mistake!"

"This is a part of her story," Theos disagreed.

"She hasn't forgotten fear," Pneuma added. "She is still very much motivated by fear."

Fear weathered the dejection from the first remark by focusing on the surprise Pneuma's comment brought.

"But I haven't been summoned at all," Fear pointed out. "How is it that she's influenced by fear?"

"It's not fresh fear," Pneuma agreed. "But she has quite the arsenal of reserves built up from over the years. She doesn't need your presence to tap into this."

"Her fear isn't coming from you directly- she isn't operating in a way that suggests she's afraid something will happen. Rather, her fear comes from a place in which she worries over what might *not* happen if she fails. Just as powerful, really," Yeshua pointed out.

"This is still part of Abaddon's plan?" Fear questioned.

He was met with a series of solemn nods.

"And we *have* to let it happen?" Fear followed up.

"We don't have to let it happen," Yeshua countered. "But it's in Leiala's best interest for it to carry on."

"You agreed she will get hurt," Fear accused.

"She will. But this is her choice, her path. It won't mean nearly as much if we forge our way into Leiala's autonomy and hijack her right to make these decisions for herself," Yeshua explained carefully.

"Even when we know it will hurt her?" Fear asked. On some level, he understood what Yeshua was telling him, but he didn't want it to be true. It seemed hard, uncomfortable, painful.

"Especially when we know it will hurt her. We've accepted that this battle will be lost, but for the greater good of the larger war raging," Yeshua told Fear.

"We choose to focus instead on the next battle, on the rebuilding that will need to come from this fall," Pneuma added.

"We just leave her?" Fear asked incredulously.

"We never leave," Pneuma was quick to correct. "We will always be with Leiala. But we won't intervene or force ourselves upon her."

Fear felt the wind in his sails collapse, felt hopelessly deflated. He'd hoped for a battle plan, for a strategy packed with specific actions he could take to combat the enemy. Perhaps even instructions for the subtle undermining of the enemy. But not this.

"You're disappointed," Yeshua commented, addressing the unspoken sentiment.

"I am. I just- I just thought we would do more. This feels like giving up," Fear explained honestly.

"It is giving up- but just in this circumstance," Yeshua agreed. "Never on the soul, but sometimes on a specific action or event."

"Don't give up, Fear," Theos spoke up, eyeing the desperate character carefully. "Leiala is going to need your support more than ever soon."

"It's going to be a big fall, isn't it?" Fear questioned, knowing the answer even before the words materialized. He'd seen enough of

Leiala's reckless, whimsical behavior to know the answer to that question.

"I'm afraid so," Theos affirmed solemnly.

"How long?" Fear countered. The longer this went on, the greater pain Fear could see Leiala encountering.

Fear's question was met with silence, which led Fear to believe that no sudden change was on the horizon. He was also aware that an answer to this question would probably violate Theos's private policy in which He refused to answer direct questions about a soul's future. It was Theos's worker who said the final words, bringing goosebumps to the back of Fear's neck and causing the hairs on his arms to rise in foreboding premonition.

"We can't start preparing for the rebuilding too early," the worker challenged Fear, his gaze penetrating. "This isn't just a stumble- Leiala is preparing to walk off a cliff."

I'm admitting it and owning it right now: I don't bring anything to the table.

I'm not trying to, I don't want to. I thrive off of destruction and insecurity and comparison- all things that lead to certain dissatisfaction and depression. You can't be happy with me. I literally don't possess the DNA to bring you anything but heartache. But still you choose to spend time with me- you can't resist sitting next to me, tasting and trying the feast I offer you. I'll confess it now: the "feast" is just dirt.

You don't realize this at first, so distracted are you by what you see and imagine. But when you do come to your senses and recognize that you've been consuming filth, you don't blame me. You point a lot of fingers, and make a lot of fuss- but it's never directed at me. I'm thankful for this, of course. But I don't quite understand why you let me get away with it. I suppose I'd learn my lesson after awhile, if I was made to. But no one has thrown me out yet.

I'm highly insightful and attentive- I see things that others miss, and I hone in on those characteristics that others overlook. You take these observations to mean intelligence, and you assume that I'm worthy and important, something you should respect. But do you notice the lens through which I look? Have you ever noticed that in my judgments I always focus on those elements that you believe you lack? I'm of a singular mindset, one that negates general observation in favor of highlighting the areas of "need" and "want." I'm really good at confusing the concepts of "fair" and things that are "necessary" versus those that are actually luxuries. I never leave you satisfied.

You presume that I don't have relationships with other humans- you think I'm especially loyal to you. This is false. I visit every human, and my message is always the same.

More, more, more.

More.

More.

I can whisper it in your ear; I can shout it from the rooftops. I'm the cadence that your life begins to beat to, if you're not careful to reject me with force and conviction. I can make you work hard, and I can get you to grab hold of certain earthly victories- but only if you keep your fists tightly clenched. You must always strive with me, and you can never find rest or peace. That's part of the deal- you can never "be" in my presence. To nullify my voice, you must obey and strive and reach and work- and then, I will release you for a little while. But not for too long- because there's always someone new to compare yourself against, always something new to try to procure. It's wonderful and terrible, the great many things that are available on earth. You will never get them all- but so many of you die trying. You think it's possible; you've bought into the lie that worth and value can be bought or secured through effort.

You keep me in business- and oh, darling- business is good. I feast on the juiciest, most tender pieces of meat, supple grapes and warm, rosemary-scented flaky biscuits and chilled lavender lemonade. It's lucky I'm so often on the move, visiting one human after another- what with the decadent cuisine I'm entitled to, it would be very easy for me to grow lazy and rotund- an obtuse blob seated upon a gilded chair. I'm thankful to you- none of it would be possible without your summoning, your willingness to entertain my character. Your tributes sustain my lavish lifestyle and keep me active.

You younger humans are more fun to play with- the older humans seem to outgrow me a bit, although they thankfully never completely desert me. The youth, those fledgling humans- they are where the true gold is. Your supple, malleable minds are truly a delight- so eager to earn, receive, and take hold of that which is not yours. Never mind the blessings you've been given- your eye is trained on another's.

Well, that's all for now. I don't have much time, you see- there's always someone that NEEDS me, that WANTS me to help them, to show them how to get more. How sad for you that I'm the only one who ever earns satisfaction...

Pledged to you until the end,
Envy

-25-

Abaddon sat in the control room, her fingers tented and nestled just beneath his nostrils. A slow smile played over his lips as he sat in solitude, watching Leiala.

It had been easy. Easier than he'd anticipated.

In the beginning, he'd worried about the amount of effort her assignment would require, how much drain on his resources she'd be. He'd considered that Theos's precious girl might have taken serious reserves to immobilize and disarm; he'd believed that committing his resources to Leiala would require significant investment.

But oh, how easy it had been! Lately, he hadn't even had to do a thing- he just sat back and watched as Leiala continued to walk down the path he had laid out before her, unaware of the fact that she was a lamb walking to the slaughter. Theos's princess still wore her crown, but it was dusty and dull. The silver needed polishing, the gems appeared lifeless. It didn't even sit straight on her head, instead angled askew in a posture that suggested it might fall off altogether at any moment.

And the rules! Abaddon almost giggled in delight when he considered how elementary it had turned out to be, how simple it had been to take down this supposed warrior. He hadn't needed his craftiest workers or his most sinister plots- all he'd needed was to introduce Leiala to the safety and security that came from following the rules. How quickly she had found comfort in them, worshipped them, and made them into idols.

No cursing.
No drinking.

No sex.
No gossipping.
No cheating.
No lying.
No skipping workouts.
No sleeping in.
No dessert.
No carbohydrates.
No purchases for herself that weren't absolutely necessary.
No frat parties.
No sleep until all her work was done.
No skipping church.
No skipping prayer.
No skipping a phone call home at least once a day.
No secular magazines.
No rated R movies.

Some of the rules were wise- most were likely to lead to healthy behaviors when adopted for the right reasons- but Leiala didn't adopt the rules for the right reasons. She threw herself into these rules full force, with the abandon of a runaway train. She obsessed over the rules, neglecting the truisms they were created to protect in the first place. And now- now Leiala had shackled herself, Abaddon thought, his glance turning to the thin, golden threads that connected Leiala to her rules. The string, no wider than a fishing line, resplendent in deceptive flaxen coloring that alluded to riches and wealth beyond imagination, strong. Tying Leiala to the entities responsible for her demise- there was no glory to be seen here. The glory was *his*, Abaddon smirked, glancing above Leiala to a trophy case gleaming with idols.

Perfection.

Exercise.

Healthy Eating.

Abaddon took in the imposing form of each trophy; there was no lack of shine or polish here. The trophies seemed to glitter, sparkle, and shine- their glossy sheen beckoning the viewer to come closer, to see what they had to offer.

And the best part was, Leiala had no idea. She thought she was doing so well. She thought she was pleasing Theos, doing his bidding. She was blind to the shackles, the threads, the idols. She didn't even possess the capacity with which to see them, not even if someone were to point them out to her. Oh, Abaddon allowed her the daily dalliances with Theos, allowed her to believe that all was well- that was what made his work so insidious and effective.

But Abaddon slowly influenced Leiala, with the help of his workers, to approach each day with a checklist, complete with items that needed to be ticked off. He allowed Leiala a rush of dopamine for each task completed, the golden thread dipping to release that sweet, natural chemical that led Leiala to believe she was doing so well.

She. Singular. Leiala, by herself. Operating on her own. Gone rogue, far from the folds of the only one who could actually protect her.

And Leiala began to forget that she was just a human. She forgot her place, and her limits. She began to carry the weight of the world, weight that could only be supported by the creation of more of the golden threads, evenly distributing the force of the pressure. Every accomplished item brought satisfaction, a sense of achievement, and worth.

It was an addictive cycle, one that played into Leiala's predisposed weaknesses, and she fell into the game perfectly. The star wide receiver, flawlessly receiving every arched pass with open arms. And Theos? Well, Theos just became another item on the list. Abaddon awarded a rush of dopamine for her time spent with him, but that was it- just a splash of neurochemistry. Nothing greater than what a run or A paper or sensual kiss brought.

And that, Abaddon thought with unvarnished satisfaction, was how you brought a ruler to His knees. He had single-handedly supplanted Theos's prime weapon of unadulterated joy and the gift of Pneuma's presence with a single cheap splash of chemical feeling.

And as Leiala ventured further down the path Abaddon had for her, the feelings grew more numb. It became more difficult to achieve satisfaction from her accomplishments, which seemed dull and unimportant over time. Instead of a sense of achievement, Leiala developed a sense of satisfaction. The things that had once brought her great pleasure and joy now became little more than a handful of characters written neatly on a lined piece of paper in tidy, vertical lettering; things that would yell and scold and chide her if she forgot them, but that brought no pleasure when she engaged with them.

Lest she wise up to the strategy with which he had wielded on her, Abaddon had only to whisper a simple sentence in her ear that fueled her onward: *More. That's why it doesn't feel good anymore. It's not enough- you need to do more.*

And, obedient puppet that she was, Leiala did more.

An A- brought disdain; soon, it was only acceptable if she had set the curve for the class, if she had managed to score the highest mark.

It wasn't enough to run, to exercise- she needed to run farther, train for races, and reduce her mile time. And who was she kidding, thinking she could get away with just running? She needed to incorporate weight training and a core workout to make sure she didn't lose muscle tone.

Food- how had she gotten by eating romaine lettuce salads with *regular* salad dressing, and, heaven forbid- croutons on top? It was horrifying- thank goodness she now had access to kale and lemon juice- all she really needed for a healthy, nutritious meal!

Faith- she'd somehow believed going to church and praying was enough, poor girl. No, no- it was imperative she begin each day with journaling, prayer, and time in the Word- she needed to set her alarm for *at least* an hour earlier.

These, supplemented with the messages Leiala naturally received from her environment on how to be a better girlfriend, better friend, better daughter, how to be *hotter*, more desirable, smarter, more successful- kept Leiala very, very busy. Her ego grew, and her success and star grew brighter, but her soul began to fold inside itself. The little girl who had once prayed earnestly for adventure and a grand story had now resorted to living out a great to-do list.

Every once in awhile, the soul would peek through like the sun on an overcast day, and Leiala would feel a splash of joy that took her back to how her life had once felt. But these pockets of time never lasted, and when they left, Abaddon assured Leiala that the memories were nothing more than sentimental, idealistic ruminations that were far bent from reality; whimsical distractions that only served to pull her from her present list of goals to accomplish.

And the soul withered. The once vibrant plant, fraught with luscious fruit and intoxicating, fragrant flowers dried out, curling up into ugly gray and dirt-brown remains that hung limp and fragile on the end of gnarled branches; dreams that could be cast off and carried away forever with one gust of wind. Alive, but by all other definitions, lifeless.

It would stay that way for almost a year.

***

Leiala lay stunned, wide-eyed in bed. She wasn't even going to try to sleep- she knew she would get no rest. There would be no relief from the pain, the agonizing depths of her suffering- and truth be told, she didn't want there to be. She wanted to feel the dagger plunge deep into the open wound; she wanted to take handfuls of salt and rub it in the mess of blood herself. She welcomed physical pain, sought it out- anything to silence the internal pain that threatened to drive her out of her mind.

How had she ended up here?

You idiot. Stupid bitch, she snapped at herself. *You did this. It's all your fault.*

Leiala agreed with the vicious voices in her head, accepted their truth. It was her fault- she'd somehow lost control. She'd become lazy, she'd neglected to notice what was brewing underneath the surface.

Die. You should die. You'd be better off dead. You wouldn't feel anything then.

It was pitiful, but the final thought brought more hope than Leiala believed possible, and she clung to the morbid idea for a moment too long.

You don't have to be all dramatic about it- you don't have to cut yourself or take pills or something. You could just step out into traffic on a busy street, Anna Karenina style. No one would ever know for sure that it was a suicide.

Either that, or you could leave a note. Ooooh, imagine how good that would feel- then people might finally see your pain, they might see you for the vulnerable soul you really are. You would finally receive the love you want, seeing their pain over losing you.

The myriad voices played tempting scenes in full display in Leiala's mind, captivating her with their compelling arguments. All at once realizing that she was actually considering what the voices were suggesting, Leiala recoiled.

No! That's crazy, she whispered, nervous as though someone may have witnessed what had passed through her mind. *Besides, what good would it do to know I was appreciated and loved after I was already dead?* she rationalized, hoping to quell the voices once and for all.

But if you ceased existing, you wouldn't let anyone down. That's the danger right now- if you keep going, you are bound to let people down. They'll see you for what you are, Leiala- for who *you really are: a fraud. No one loves a fraud. You might as well tap out now, dear, while you still have a few poor souls fooled into thinking you're worth something.*

This was a harder thought to counter. Leiala registered the words as true, and that scared her. Scared her not because she seemed to seriously be contemplating death, but because the inevitability of letting others down was staring her right in the face.

All at once, it was too much effort to stay stagnant in bed. She had no energy and yet she was jumping out of her skin. With a dramatic sigh, Leiala catapulted the covers from off her frame, swinging her legs out to the side and down until they reached the soft carpeting below. She pulled herself down, allowed her body to melt into a heap at the foot of her bed.

There was no escape. She'd worked through every scenario, applied every ounce of logic and fantasy and reasoning to try to devise some whisper of a plan or idea that might remove the oppressive pain or remove *her* from her own life. Nothing. She always came up with nothing.

GOD! Leiala screamed in her mind, her fingers pushing through the thick waterfall of hair to pull at the roots. *Where are you?!* Leiala demanded in earnest, her words seething, desperate, vulnerable.

She didn't give Him time to answer.

What was it she had learned in yoga? Downward dog, deep breaths, the connection of certain postures to peace? In frenzied desperation, Leiala curled her toes under and launched her figure upside down. Her hair hung like dead grass over her as she concentrated on taking measured inhales that matched the length of her exhales. Through the screen of hair, Leiala read the taunting numbers on the clock across the room: 2:53. In the morning. Leiala tried to push the bold, cherry-red reminder from her mind. *Breathe. So simple. Just breathe.*

You're going to be so tired at work tomorrow. This is the third night in a row of no sleep.

I know, Leiala snapped angrily. Would the voices just SHUT UP, just allow her this moment of peace that yoga was supposed to offer? Her mind would not turn off, her body could not find release, and she struggled to keep her composure as she hung pitifully upside-down. The darkness of the room was softly lit by the glow of the moon as Leiala shifted positions, moving now to stretch out the front line of her body. She didn't feel any less tense, but it at least gave release to the abundant energy bubbling treacherously inside of her.

My job. That's just one of my problems, Leiala thought bitterly. She hated her job- she hated nearly everything about it.

It was hard to believe that months before, she'd graduated summa cum laude, the Facebook pictures proving the perfect life she was about to continue as she posed with her family and boyfriend in her cap and gown decorated with all sorts of symbolic accolades.

Feel the hurt. Look. Take it in, Leiala thought as she glanced over her shoulder at the picture thumb-tacked to her childhood bulletin board, one of the few that earned the honor of physical printing in this digital age. Her smile was so genuine, so unknowing, so stupid. *You had no idea,* Leiala chided herself, at once repulsed and empathetic for the bright-eyed twenty-one year old.

The day had felt glossy: surrounded by the ones she loved more than anything, surrounded by the unspoken promises of the life she had worked hard to build, a future she felt sure was within her grasp.

A job in finance, to pay the bills and build experience. She wasn't convinced she would love it, but it would satisfy her (and she would be good at her job, of course!, so she would build a solid community within her workplace) until her boyfriend graduated from college. He'd move down to be with her, propose (they'd already been looking at rings, Leiala reminded herself with stoked self-assurance, and they were part of a pre-marital bible study, soooo...), and once he found his job, Leiala could worry about what she was supposed to do.

His job would be more important, anyway- they'd just want to save enough money to buy a house together before twenty-five, so that they had a nice place ready for the first child, which Leiala believed would come mid-decade. It was all planned, down to the two or three year gap between the three children they would have, ensuring Leiala would be safely done having children by the age of thirty. Thirty was an age that offered safety: an age that capitalized on the existence of healthy and vital, relatively-young eggs. Not to mention the comfort that came from knowing that her body would still be capable of morphing back to a toned and fit shape (she'd heard it got harder the older women got).

She'd of course stay home with the children to spend the days baking homemade bread and cauliflower-crust pizza, reading to the children and engaging their minds with Mozart and Shakespeare and dreams of travel. They'd take old refrigerator boxes and build rockets with which to soar around the world, and they'd play restaurant underneath the fort of flannel sheets, munching on apples and sipping on hot cocoa as they discussed philosophy and their dreams, all the while building an impressive vocabulary and problem-solving logic skills that would lead to total domination of the SAT test one day. They'd run through the sprinklers with their fluffy, well-behaved dog, and play at the park to improve fine-motor coordination and hone gross motor skills, because Leiala was sure she'd produce gifted athletes. She'd have a beautiful dinner spread ready when her husband came home, and they'd all talk about their days before snuggling in for a bedtime story together.

When the children reached school age, Leiala would be in the PTA, she'd be Room Mom, and she'd help to coach their recreational league teams. And she'd do it all without wearing yoga pants or running around haggard with a messy bun and oversized sunglasses hiding bloodshot eyes. It would be the perfect life. Perfect.

The image used to make Leiala swoon, send her heart fluttering with delight and anticipation. Now, it rankled and ruffled every nerve, an iron-hot reminder of the dejection and disappointment she'd been made to face.

Perfection seemed to crumble overnight. The relationship went first, Leiala reflected, her body trembling with a fresh wave of hurt and rejection that had rattled her to the core. He didn't want her, and he didn't want her perfect life. Leiala couldn't fathom this second part, but it was the unvarnished reality: he didn't want to move to her hometown, instead he had sought employment opportunities across the nation. This first chink in the armor had exposed further differences, chasms that Leiala was willing to navigate across, if only he would show his love and commitment. But as Leiala leaned forward, ready to sacrifice for what she believed would be the resurrection and redemption of her dreams of perfection, he leaned back, distancing himself emotionally from the girl who had been ready to give him everything.

It stung. Even now, Leiala felt the pain like a dagger in her side, sucking the breath and the life from her. She'd been slow to give away her heart, but in the end, she'd wrapped it prettily and handed it over, and now it would seem that it was being returned to her. Her pride had led her to make the decision, to call the end of their relationship- but it was no secret that the outcome was not what Leiala had wanted. Confusion reigned, and she couldn't make out what to do with the dilapidated, ravaged heart strewn carelessly in the shoebox of her room. Was it worth reviving? *Could* it be revived? Leiala didn't have much faith.

This had been the apex of her perfect life, the instrumental, foundational piece on which everything else would be built. Now removed, Leiala found herself grasping at the other components of her perfect life, desperate to reclaim that which felt far away.

Her job. The job that was intended to be temporary, only meant to build capital with which to launch their new life together. Now, the job she had for only herself, with no tangible goal on the horizon. And she hated it.

Every morning she drove in standstill traffic, dressed in muted grays and whites, her appearance polished and professional with her matching pearls and neatly-pinned bun as she worked numbers, crunched figures, and created spreadsheets in excel. The early challenge of learning how to operate the various programs had dissipated into mindless drudgery that offered Leiala no relief from her punishing, sadistic mind. The thoughts that refused to leave her be. There was no fulfillment in her work, no promise, no hope for the changed world she'd imagined inspiring.

Instead, she clocked in and out dutifully, quickly securing a position as a top worker as she sat with laser-like focus in front of her computer, working figures adroitly with fingers that danced with familiarity over the keyboard. She left her chair twice each day: once to go to the bathroom, and once to retrieve her lunch from the refrigerator. With the exception of these two five-minute chunks of time, Leiala sat glued to her chair, heels off and legs tucked up underneath her as she stared at the computer screen before her.

Numb. Numb. Leiala begged to feel numb. She tried without relief to lose herself in the numbers, to unplug her mind.

She launched herself into a new reality, one in which she pulled herself from bed before dawn to run- to run until she couldn't breathe, until her sides screamed and heaved, until she was forced to release the pressure in an outburst of tears or a glorious show of vomit.

The pain felt good, Leiala told herself, and it gave her something new to focus on. Then, anxiety built as she drove to work: everything seemed so much more serious, now that it wasn't temporary. Leiala doubted everything about her life, and yet she had no idea how to truly assess her situation and discern her next steps.

And then, her childhood dog had passed. Leiala had witnessed his undoing, the slow, undeniable path to death. She had processed and comprehended each sign: the pervasive blood leakage from the nose that spoke of the tumor lying within, the ragged breaths that became more and more labored, the slow, lethargic movements that served as an undeniable sign of aging. Leiala had forced these negative observations from her mind- they had no place in her perfect life- but she was no fool, either. She knew death was inevitable. And still, she found herself grossly unprepared.

One night, watching her younger siblings while her parents were away. Cody, their sweet, sweet golden retriever, struggling to breathe, taking frantic inhales as he sneezed uncontrollably, an endless stream of blood spurting from his nostrils, drenching everything around him.

Not allowing herself to feel, to truly understand what was happening, Leiala had launched into action. Her arms wrapped gently around the shuddering mass of golden fur, her hands steadily stroking the ribs that quaked in fear. Her movements inspired and determined as she led her best friend outside, to the dew-stained grass that sparkled underneath the light of the moon. A warm, yellow-hued moon that seemed to mock the situation at hand.

With the help of her younger brother and sister, staunching the blood flow with tea bags as they dipped rags into a basin of warm water, wiping the blood from Cody's straw-colored fur. They'd prayed together, read the Bible aloud, and in the face of such a terrifying ordeal, they'd found peace.

Hours into the night, the spasms had stopped, and Leiala was grateful that she had not been forced to take Cody to be put down in the middle of the night. Never had she felt more solidarity with her siblings, who had rallied around her to soothe and comfort their beloved pet, who had helped to bleach the walls that had been splattered with blood, to scrub the carpeting with the same marks, and who had even lovingly helped her wash the blood from her hair and face.

They had laid together, huddled in the family room on futons with Grandma's knitted blankets, surrounding Cody so he would not have to be alone. No, her fear had not been realized that night, but as her siblings found release in sweet sleep, she lay awake, a new corner of her heart cracking open with the realization that she was once again about to have her precious dreams shattered.

Weeks later, she'd been in the room as they'd said goodbye, the falsely-cheerful figures of her family members huddled close to Cody as they fed him Butterfinger bars and whispered words of love and assurance. She'd watched, utterly wrecked, as her beloved dog, trusty confidante and believer in all of her dreams, had taken in the slow drip of eternal sleep and passed on.

Watched, devastated and destroyed, stripped fresh in a way that she hadn't believed was possible. That shoebox heart, sitting in the corner of the room, decrepit and unfeeling? *That* heart could feel? Could still produce such powerful emotion? It was an unpleasant discovery to one who wished for nothing more than to feel numb. And she'd watched, envious, as life slipped from the once-vital body, wondering why the same couldn't happen to her.

That was it: the final lynch pin. It wasn't a fact she advertised, but she slept with Cody's dog toys for months afterwards, so desperate was she for some sense of control, some sense of familiarity. The stale scent of dog breath and fur calmed her, allowed her to trick herself for brief moments that everything was unchanged, that her perfect vision for her perfect life had not been shattered.

Rock bottom.

Leiala became like a ghost, quietly tiptoeing through life without making a mark. She convinced herself that she did not feel, she begged herself not to feel. When the pain of depression felt overwhelming, she pushed herself to physical pain. And she worked to rebuild. On a distant level, Leiala knew that she could not live out her days like this, and so she took miniscule steps to re-establish her existence.

She moved to reduce her life to a science, this time more rigid than ever before. Last time she'd been strict and disciplined, and that had led her to heartbreak still. She needed to tighten up the gaps, she needed to make sure there were absolutely no loopholes this time.

She began to wake up at the same time every day, weekday or weekend.
The same running route, every morning, at the same time.
The same snacks and meals, at the same time every day.

There was comfort in this routine, in the familiarity and control that this cultivated inside of Leiala. Abject depression quelled any appetite, and Leiala found herself losing weight that she hadn't even meant to. And it pleased her, this form that appeared shriveled and inconsequential next to the former Leiala. There was little pleasure to be found, but there was satisfaction that came from knowing she *could* do it- she could work her way down to a size zero, she could eat and exercise herself down to ribs and skinny thighs. If she could not be *happy*, Leiala determined, then at least she could be *perfect*.

And once again, Leiala found herself on the hamster wheel.

-26-

Abaddon scowled; paced the length of the room with agitated, aggressive steps that made everyone around him nervous. He was frustrated, tormented that he couldn't close on Leiala. He was destroying her confidence and ruining the remains of any happiness she had once possessed, but he still couldn't do her in once and for all.

Why? Abaddon asked himself, even though he knew the answer was Theos.

***

Theos waited quietly, watching Leiala from above with tender love and care. Pneuma had approached Leiala moments before, comforting her and overwhelming her with love and peace.

"It's almost time," Yeshua said aloud, narrating what all three knew to be true.

***

Leiala stood in the shower. She had the water temperature turned as hot as it would go, felt the relief as the scalding water scorched her flesh, burning angry pink welts on her chest and arms. Here, in the private rectangular prism of frosted paneling, Leiala could let it go. Her dreams, her hopes...and the control she worked so hard to maintain during every other moment of the day.

The release was sweet, the agony real- it was often hard to stay standing as the full force of the day's events and disappointments hit her square in the gut. Her hands went out in front of her in a desperate attempt to stay upright, her palms sliding, grasping down the pearl-white tiles of the shower as she found her way to bended knee. The punishing jet of water rained down on her head, pounded like white-hot nails into the back of her skull as her hair grew damp, soaking; hung like overcooked spaghetti over her face.

Then, the sobs. It was easier to cry here, where her pitiful whimpers were masked by the thud of pounding water. When it felt like too much effort even to stay propped on her knees, Leiala rolled down into a seated position. Naked, vulnerable, crouched in the fetal position. A perfect representation of the state of her soul, Leiala thought bitterly as she tipped her face up to face the showerhead, felt the sting of the water on her cheeks.

God, how did this happen?

Leiala gave the thought its space; let it breathe. She wasn't really expecting a response- she was just giving her soul a chance to decompress.

Are you really asking?

The voice surprised Leiala. Even though she knew without a shadow of a doubt that she was alone, she still looked up and around her. Yes, she was alone.

Lifting her hand, turning the water off, sitting still and quiet, expectant.

I am. I want to know.

I love you.

It wasn't an answer, but it was what Leiala needed to hear. She began to cry again, but this time it was tears of relief that fell from her eyes, not tears of pain. This promise of love helped her to pick herself up, to towel off in slow, deliberate movements, and to quietly pad to her room, where she methodically brushed out her hair and changed into sweatpants and an oversized sweatshirt. She sat on the ground, waiting.

You have to know that you are loved, Leiala.

It was the same thought as before, but tears still formed in the corners of Leiala's eyes. How badly she wanted to believe it, believe that she was loved, cared for. And in the deep recesses of her heart, she knew it was true. There was no flashing billboard, no fireworks display, but a deep understanding of truth. She *was* loved. She *was* cared for. A sudden unquenchable, insatiable hunger for more truth overcame Leiala. She needed more answers, more understanding, more wisdom. She reached for her Bible and pulled it down beside her. Opening its pages, she immersed herself in the words.

***

"That went well," Yeshua commented. There was a peace about the room, a pleasure that hadn't existed for a while.

"She was ready to listen," Pneuma agreed. "There's been too much noise and distraction up until now."

"The timing was perfect," Theos agreed, affirming Pneuma.

"She's still stuck on perfection," Yeshua added after a satisfied, pregnant pause elapsed.

"One battle at a time," Theos said with authority. "We won't give her more than she can handle. She wouldn't be able to process that appropriately if we brought it to her awareness right now."

"She's struggling to process the changes she's encountered as it is," Pneuma agreed.

"Her dreams have been shattered. She's realizing how hopeless and pointless her plans were," Yeshua spoke aloud, verbalizing what they all knew.

"Her dreams, but not her idols," Theos stated.

"She's relying on us," Yeshua countered hopefully. "This has to diminish her idols."

"Diminish them, yes," Theos responded. "But Leiala cannot truly embrace peace until these idols are destroyed. In the meantime, Pneuma is invaluable as he ministers to Leiala's soul, healing her."

"And we start to rebuild," Yeshua finished.

"We rebuild, and we tolerate the presence and distraction Leiala's idols present- for now," Theos dictated.

-27-

The growl was low, guttural, ravaged. The walls shook from the reverberations of the strong bass, and even Abaddon's stocky workers had to reach out for the walls in order to steady themselves. No earthquake had passed through the east end headquarters- the workers knew better than to imagine something so banal, so simple. It was an unobscured warning from Abaddon- a sign of his great displeasure. The workers nearest to him scurried, their clawed feet scratching and clicking along the floor in evident haste.

Abaddon was in a fit of rage, prowling the room, swiping at paintings that hung on the wall and cutting down the thick curtains that garnished the frame of every door. The workers stuck in the room with him knew better than to try and escape now; instead, they stood stock-still, careful not to move in any manner that might arouse the attention and rage of their wrathful master.

"We've lost ground!" Abaddon roared, his giant head swiveling back and forth aggressively like a frightening Chinese dragon. The workers diminished themselves, sucked in their stomachs quietly and tried to press themselves flat against the wall. They knew what to expect when their master was in a mood like this- if he so much as grazed the corner of their elbow, there would be hell to pay. Literally.

Abaddon could not be calmed, would not allow himself to be settled. In this state, there was no winning- nothing his workers did would allow his outrage to subside. Now, his head finally froze in place, his body tensing and slowing until he held a single crouched posture of defiance, aggression, and suspicion. His red eyes blazed with fire, and his yellow pupils widened with expectation and anticipation.

"No one is going to ask me *why*?" Abaddon growled, his voice controlled in a way that somehow made his next words even creepier. "No one cares to understand what has happened?"

The workers avoided eye contact, their faces and eyes downcast. The pupils in the room were caught without the answer, trapped in the awareness that there *was* no correct response. A heavy, thick moment passed- the profound silence of the room was only interrupted by the ragged shards of breath that came from Abaddon himself, breath that metamorphosed as a hot, pungent cloud of steam even in spite of the high temperature and humidity in the east end.

"She went back to Him!" Abaddon raged, the moment of stillness broken as his body violently mobilized in a lightning-quick motion that sent the unfortunate chair in his path sailing clear across the room, landing heavily upon a worker who whimpered in surprise and pain. Abaddon ignored him as he paced the room once more, daring each worker to look him in the eye.

"The puny, measly, wormy, treacherous little bitch went back to him," Abaddon snarled, his voice murderous. "Who does she think she is? She can't make it without us- ***she's nothing without us***!"

The last words were a pitch too high, the words unnatural. Abaddon was able to squeeze them out before he himself shrieked. The hairs on the back of his neck stood on end, and his body shook as though an electric current had passed through him.

Then, perfect stillness. The workers, stunned into statue-like form far elevated from any lack of movement they'd been able to maintain before. It wasn't often that this happened, but they knew the sign of a west-end attack when they saw one. The invisible, white-hot arrow of truth that seared the very backbone of their spirituous ruler, the only arrow that could bring him to his knees.

Just like that, the workers knew their fate. The imminent death that would soon come to them all: Abaddon never suffered such humiliation without the destruction of all witnesses. He could not, *would not* tolerate any display of weakness, any sign that he was not in fact the supreme ruler of every dominion.

The workers had heard rumors of such episodes, but that was all they were: rumors. No worker had ever shared from personal experience what the workers in the room had just witnessed, the mighty and true shot of Theos himself.

All at once, they began talking. The hopeful and ignorant spell had been broken- now that every worker knew his fate, there was no reason to hold back.

"How did it happen?" the first worker asked anxiously, eager to distract Abaddon from the crippling pain that had humbled him, had brought him pitifully to his knees.

"It happened because we didn't do our job correctly," Abaddon seethed, body trembling with rage. "It happened because *YOU* didn't do your job correctly!"

This second accusation brought with it the first death: a mercifully short death brought about by a ball of flame that engulfed the worker nearest to Abaddon. The workers watched dutifully as the medium-sized figure was consumed by fire. The form wriggled and writhed, screaming in agony. The smell of sulfur and tar wafted lazily through the room, stinging the nostrils of every being present. The workers had little reaction: whether out of deference to Abaddon or merely because they were used to such displays, it was unclear.

But this action had done little to calm Abaddon as the workers had hoped- this first death had seemed to whet his appetite for revenge.

"It happened because of ***HIM***!" he screeched at no one in particular. Him. Theos. Their ultimate enemy.

“What do we do?” another worker asked, desperately changing tactics. Perhaps, if they could just focus Abaddon’s attention on the true enemy...

“What can we do?!” Abaddon spat, coagulated chunks of blood dotting the spittle that flew indiscriminately from his mouth, raining down on anyone within range. A thought seemed to strike him in this moment, something that caused him to pause, consider, and then settle.

“We fight,” he smiled, his knife-like teeth revealed in a cheshire cat grin.

“Matsar!”

The worker summoned was not in their company, but materialized in a cloud of fumes as his name was called.

Matsar was not particularly substantial in form, but his figure was lithe and his color and shape adaptable, capable of changing to suit the context. He was not particularly notable, save for the wide-set, leering, green-yellow eyes that seemed to look far beyond with each slow-blinked gaze.

If you happened to notice his claws, your heart would stop in sudden fear. Never before had such claws been seen. They were long, yes- but that wasn’t what made them so impressive. Shaped like screws, the claws twisted downward with the unquestioned strength of steel, hooked at just the right angle and extended eight inches long.

All signs of formidable strength and horrible trepidation, to be sure. But the real show-stopper was the color of the claws, brought about by the residual blood and sweat and even muscle and sinew that decorated the gnarled claws, staining them and speaking to the depth to which Matsar was able to cling to a human.

“At your service, Master,” Matsar bowed, his voice slithery and lisp-like as he hissed this supplication to Abaddon.

"Yes, yes," Abaddon smiled, taking in the form of Matsar, eyes lingering on the treacherous claws.

"My assignment, sir?" Matsar asked, his unsettling green eyes offering up disdain for every other figure in the room.

"Yes, you are the one worthy of this assignment," Abaddon proclaimed, ignoring Matsar's question.

"A permanent assignment, then," Matsar sibilated, his voice drunk with pride. Abaddon was typically quick to cut down any worker who dared show such pretense in his presence, but he conveniently overlooked this protocol in his excitement over his fresh idea.

"Oh yes, a permanent assignment," Abaddon agreed, the wide smile glowing lantern-yellow through the dark room. "We're going to put those claws to good use."

Matsar smiled in return, clicked his talons together for Abaddon's benefit, showing off his most prized feature. The other workers in the room lit up with envy, desperate to somehow glum onto this worker's success to save their own hides.

"And who is this most lucky human?" Matsar asked.

The sinister ruler never skipped a beat.

"Leiala," he practically sang.

***

"Did you hear?!" Anxiety gasped, pushing open the door to Fear's room without warning. Sweat ran in steady streams down the side of his face, evidence of the long and quick run he'd made to make it to Fear's side.

Fear sat upright immediately, swung his legs to meet the ground in expectation.

"Leiala?" he queried, though he hardly knew why he bothered to ask. Of course it was Leiala! Who else would it be?

Anxiety nodded, head bent down as he worked to recover his breath. Fear tried to be patient, but his heart immediately leapt into his chest, and his throat tightened as though a boa constrictor was squeezing the life from him.

"You heard about Abaddon's fit, surely," Anxiety began, backing up a step to confirm the foundational events leading to his news. Fear nodded eagerly, anxious for him to go on.

"How Theos sent the arrow to remind Abaddon of his place, to punish him for overstepping his boundaries, and Abaddon executed all of the workers who saw it happen," Anxiety said, ignoring the fact that Fear had signaled that he had in fact heard the news.

"Do you know *why* he did it?" Anxiety asked now, his figure leaning forward in earnest. His eyebrows were raised provocatively, inviting Fear to question him at the same time they spelled the answers out as clear as the alphabet.

"Leiala?" Fear asked, now open-mouthed in shock. The war had just escalated to a whole new level, if what Anxiety suggested was true.

"Oh, yes. All because of Leiala. Abaddon was furious." Anxiety was euphoric, disbelieving, and incredulous even as he shared this news with Fear.

Fear sat back down heavily, his eyes moving rapidly back and forth as he tried to process this new information. A million questions materialized and then dissipated in his mind. He wanted to know everything, but he sensed that there was more to what Anxiety had to say. The questions could wait- there was something more important.

"What else, Anxiety?" Fear pushed, beside himself with anticipation.

"She's been assigned."

The three words hung in the air like clothes on a line in the middle of a hailstorm. Drenched, battered, and punished by the fear, hatred, and questioning that immediately swelled up inside of Fear and wiggled out without ceremony.

"Assigned?!"

There was no greater horror for a character. When a human was assigned a permanent worker, little could be accomplished. The worker took over the response of the human, controlled the processing of their emotions and their perception of reality. Characters became obsolete- there was no need for them unless the worker said so.

Temporary assignments were common enough- obnoxious but expected, part of the job. But a permanent assignment was a death sentence to the human- an embossed, already-signed RSVP card that assured the human would show up to the wrong party, at the wrong time, in the wrong place.

"Yes- assigned," Anxiety confirmed, the distaste evident in the way he spoke the poisonous word.

"Who?" Fear asked, a bit breathless at the news. He certainly didn't know all of Abaddon's workers- how could he, there were millions!- but he knew of some of them. The most dangerous ones. And a little inkling had started inching its way up from Fear's gut to his mind, warning him that this was about to become far more serious than he had ever expected.

"Matsar," Anxiety breathed, collapsing into the nearest chair. There- he had said it- he had shared all the foreboding news.

"Matsar," Fear repeated, his tone dull.

An invisible hand seemed to tighten around his heart at the mention of this name. This name, which Fear was reluctant to admit that he knew. *Well, he didn't know Matsar,* Fear corrected his thoughts. But he had heard enough about Matsar to feel like he did know him. And he certainly had heard enough about him to know that he didn't want a worker like that within one hundred miles of Leiala. But- *assigned*? Fear felt the knots form in his stomach. For all the talk of battles, Fear felt confident that the greatest one yet was just beginning.

I hope.

The thought surprised Fear at first, until he took a moment to unpack it. He hoped there was a battle? Where had that come from? He had never hoped or wished for battle before- it was too tricky, too emotionally draining and damaging to his assignment.

But what was the alternative?

And therein lied the heart and soul of this most desperate plea: a battle meant a fight, a clash of power between Theos and Abaddon. It meant Theos showing up. And without Theos...

Fear let the thought die, a fish out of water, struggling to breathe, wriggling in a desperate attempt to return to familiar waters before the moment of certain death. There was no use finishing that thought, because it pointed to a scenario in which Leiala played the role of the fish.

There would be a battle, because there *had* to be a battle. Theos cared about Leiala- Fear had seen that for himself. He would show up and fight for her, Fear knew- but that didn't mean there wouldn't be greater carnage.

-28-

Matsar's presence didn't radically alter Leiala's life the way Fear had worried it might. He'd imagined Matsar immediately materializing at Leiala's side, his talons sinking deep into her supple, unsuspecting flesh. That wasn't the case.

Fear was thankful that so far Theos had been present every time Matsar materialized. During the first encounter, he'd been particularly anxious, watchful of every movement made by every being in the room, whether from Abaddon's or Theos's realm. He'd huddled in the corner of the room, aware of his great insignificance. But mostly everyone just stayed put. He'd anticipated some great battle, some clash of forces- but the moment played out pretty typically, with both sides scrutinizing the other without ever crossing paths.

Fear wanted to feel elated- he was relieved by this turn of events, felt certain it meant that he'd overreacted. But he couldn't shake the unsettled feeling lodged deep within his belly.

"You're right to remain suspicious," Pneuma had told him, affirming his worries.

"I am?" Fear asked, disappointed. He'd really been hoping he'd been wrong.

"Abaddon's taking this slow- he knows any dramatic change would startle and unnerve Leiala," Pneuma explained. "He's studied her character- he knows her propensities and inclinations, and he means to exploit them."

"And Theos will allow this?" Fear asked, a hint of disbelief in his voice. He'd seen the protective way Theos had guarded Leiala's bedside Himself, he'd seen the almighty ruler kneel by her side, scoop her up, and whisper words of encouragement straight into her soul.

"Theos will allow it," Pneuma agreed. "This is part of Leiala's story- it's preparing her."

Fear's mind immediately returned to the image of the colorful cord. He found himself wondering what color thread was being used in that moment- and he wondered what present image or symbol was being woven into the great tapestry.

"But He won't leave her," Fear clarified.

"Never. He will never leave her," Pneuma agreed. "Even when it becomes painful to watch- even when she turns from His presence- still, He will remain."

Fear nodded, silently digesting this information. So little of the alternative realm was as he'd imagined it to be. He'd had so many beliefs and expectations- there had been so many technicalities he hadn't taken the time to consider.

***

The first time Matsar initiated physical contact surprised Fear. It was not a stressful moment, nor was it one filled with anxiety or uncertainty. By all regards, it was a joyful moment, a cause for celebration.

Leiala had dared to change careers, stepping out in faith to leave the comfort and security of a job she despised without knowing where she would land next. That, Fear remembered well- leading up to that critical moment of decision and action, Fear had been working around the clock, speaking to Leiala in any and every capacity.

The actual moment of decision he couldn't speak to- he could only remember a blinding white light, an enormous sword wielded by Theos himself, and the polite but definite exclusion of *every. single. thing.* from Leiala's presence. Only Pneuma, Yeshua, and

Theos were present with Leiala for some moments- when they departed, Fear still had to squint to make out the figures of Joy and Peace through the residual bright light that shone from Leiala's very being.

Afterwards, he was summoned back- but without the force and intensity and frequency he'd anticipated would come on the heels of such a bold move. Fear found himself working alongside Peace and Joy, the major players in the months following Leiala's decision. He found himself accepting cameos instead of leading roles- and he was surprised by Leiala's focus and determination in spite of odds that appeared to be stacked against her.

The year that followed was a strange one: Leiala worked hard to realize the dream that had been put in her heart, the precious pearl of divine inspiration protected by the stalwart clam. She moved steadily towards her goal, weathering a painful year of humility and drudgery with the constant presence of Theos and His enclave of supportive workers and characters. She was exhausted yet energized, utterly dependent and yet determined, her hopes and desires surrendered whilst full of expectation.

And, at the end of the year, a dream realized. An incredible story of hope, of redemption, of an unfortunate, unhappy situation turned into one of unspeakable joy. Leiala taking a major step forward in realizing her calling as she accepted a job that would change her life. It was cause for celebration, jubilation! The storm had passed- that desolate path Leiala had walked along had finally led to greener pastures.

It was in this moment that Matsar stepped forward to make physical contact with Leiala for the first time. Fear watched like a hawk as he leaned in close, rested just one claw on Leiala's right shoulder.

"Congratulations! You did this," Fear heard him whisper, the hiss and whine of his voice unnoticeable.

Fear saw Theos's workers bristle, but no one made a move to stop him.

"This is the first step towards everything you *really* wanted," Matsar continued. "You wanted something false and contrived before, but now you are following your true calling- the calling that *Theos* gave you," Matsar encouraged. As he mentioned Theos's name, Matsar looked up defiantly at the ruler, smiled with mockery and condescension as he twisted his message of pride and self-reliance to include the King of Kings.

Time passed slowly as Fear's breath caught in his throat: he didn't allow himself to blink as he watched Leiala. Would she accept his message? Fear silently willed her to reject Matsar and the message he sent, his body tense with apprehension. Couldn't see feel the claw? Couldn't she see the sharp, corkscrewed talon that was now rested possessively on her shoulder, digging into her flesh?

For a moment, Leiala tensed, and Fear held out hope that she would respond, that she might cast Matsar off in a fit of rage. But then, Fear watched with silent horror as Leiala shrugged her shoulders and went about her business, Matsar by her side. The talon firmly lodged in Leiala, subtle and unremarkable, but undoubtedly *there*.

Fear looked up at Theos anxiously, sure that something more must happen. Theos wouldn't allow Matsar a foothold on Leiala, would he? But Theos made no move to stop Matsar- nor did any other being in his realm. They didn't make a move to leave Leiala's presence, but they also made no move to stop the dastardly creature.

It was the first move Matsar made, and he didn't make another for some time. Instead, he followed Leiala around lightly, tiptoeing alongside her as she went about her day, the single claw cemented in place. Fear was aware of Matsar's tactic, his strategy of ensuring that Leiala became accustomed to his presence, familiar with this feeling, before he dared to enact another change.

And Leiala did adjust and become comfortable with this new standard. Just days later, Matsar pressed inward once more, this time with a new message.

"Isn't this so wonderful? You worked so hard to earn this. We must be careful to protect it- you don't want to lose it. Remember how miserable you were before," Matsar whispered, the words light and seductive.

As he spoke, a second talon appeared on Leiala's shoulder, the sharp edge pushing firmly, testing the yield of the human tissue before possessively sinking in. Leiala stiffened as before, seemed to consider these words, and then ultimately accepted the message. A self-assured smile flickered on Matsar's lips as he shifted just a bit more of his weight onto Leiala.

And this was how it went. Leiala loved her new job: she loved the freedom and inspiration that came to her, the realization of what she was created to do! And yet every day, she worked harder to control and protect that which she'd been given. In equal parts she worked harder and lost joy.

Like a leaky faucet, Leiala leaked the joy and peace that had overwhelmed her in the beginning. At intervals, Leiala would realize and mourn the loss of these intangible blessings- in those moments, Fear hoped she would wake up to the tactics employed against her...but she never did. Instead, the antidote to every problem or insecurity that surfaced seemed to be to work harder, to create a better plan, to become more disciplined. Ideas fed to her by Matsar, of course.

Matsar, who now had all ten claws entrenched in Leiala's shoulders. Who now experimented with the distribution of his weight as he applied just a bit more pressure to Leiala's burdened form day by day. Leiala spent time with Theos- Matsar encouraged her to do this- and she did all the *right* things. Her time was filled with good, productive, life-giving things. And she was blind to the reality that her real life was literally being sucked dry by the beast on her shoulders.

Matsar was a bossy one, Fear realized- he lived up to his namesake. He promised Leiala control at the very same time he worked to take over every aspect of her life. It outraged Fear, the terrible irony- not to mention the naivete and ignorance Leiala demonstrated daily.

“How can she not see it?!” Fear exclaimed to Pneuma, aghast. “It’s so obvious- *he’s* so obvious!”

“To us, yes,” Pneuma had counseled wisely. “But you must remember that we operate in the alternative realm. Not many assignments are able to see that which takes place here. They’re too stuck in the their world.”

“They need to pull their heads up out of the sand!” Fear complained, ignoring the truth in Pneuma’s words in order to release his pent-up frustration and anger.

Pneuma didn’t respond, but Fear felt the anger ebb as he recalled his own ignorance to the alternative realm’s workings- he, a character who operated within its parameters! Empathy flooded into his being as he imagined how much more difficult it must be to live without even this elementary understanding.

“I realize she sees more than the typical human,” Fear agreed with a sigh, sure it was Pneuma who had leant him this understanding.

“Just think of your past assignments,” Pneuma prompted.

Fear obediently reflected on the dozens and dozens of assignments he’d already worked with, the multitude of humans who had barely even scratched the surface of the alternative realm. In truth, it was Leiala who had brought him to this place of enlightenment- for all that she had done wrong, Fear was forced to admit that she had an earnest heart bent on pursuing truth. Her path meandered, snaked in directions that took her to places that Fear resented- but she always picked up her feet and continued walking.

Fear had worked with humans who had given up, who had allowed themselves to stay stuck in desert land for far too long simply because the path became too difficult, or who had stubbornly stayed in false paradises in order to enjoy the pleasures and cheap thrills that these pseudo-realities had to offer. Leiala did none of this. She was frustratingly ignorant, stubborn, and had an increasing penchant for total, obsessive control- but Fear still considered her his favorite assignment yet, and he knew it was because she didn't give up. She was bent on discovering truth, and she sought it out even as she circled the very wisdom she was in desperate search of.

Years went by. Nothing significant changed in Leiala's life, and yet everything changed.

She worked the same job she loved, she lived in the same home, and she engaged in the same activities. She had the same friends, went to the same places, and had settled into a comfortable routine. A routine that unfortunately had grown to rely heavily on Matsar and his oppressive rule.

Fear grimaced when he reflected on the role that Matsar had taken in Leiala's life- he had chafed when Matsar had first come to Leiala, when he had rested a single claw on her shoulder. Now- now Matsar perched protectively on Leiala's back. The full weight of his slender body weighed Leiala down, a metaphysical stunting that served as a powerful metaphor to the effect he had on Leiala's life.

No thought, no decision could be made without Matsar's influence and meddling. Leiala believed she consulted Theos, but it was Matsar who directed her daily decisions. Theos was on the throne, but Matsar was quite literally riding on her shoulders. To make life easier for Leiala, he had created a list of rules to follow in which to keep her safe, rules that would protect her treasured possessions from being lost forever.

Rules for what social invitations to accept.

Rules for how to spend her time.

Rules for how to dress, how to spend her money, what to eat, how often to eat, and when to eat. Rules for what exercise to engage in, and when, and with whom. Rules for what to read and what not to read, for the amount of notes she should take, and what she should share with others. Rules for what must be accomplished before she was allowed to go to sleep, and rules for how much money she needed to save. Rules quantifying the length of time she should spend with family and friends, and how much time she should dedicate to professional development. There was a rule for *everything*, Fear thought resentfully. And rather than feel stifled, frustrated and outraged by the chokehold she'd been caught in, Leiala actually worshipped these rules, praised them with every obedient action she took. Her every behavior suggested the deep gratitude she felt towards these rules that made her life appear safe at the same time it communicated to Fear the deep insecurity and fear that had actually consumed her.

"Pretty soon he's going to be living inside her brain," Fear groused one day to Pneuma after a particularly frustrating day watching Leiala make a series of anxious decisions. She was a hopeless puppet, a marionette ordered to dance and twirl and step at the whimsy of an evil being pulling golden threads that dictated every move.

"He will never be allowed inside her heart, but he already has extensive access to her brain," Pneuma agreed.

"So when comes the part where you fight him off?" Fear asked. "Does this just continue forever?" He didn't know if he could take that.

"We're waiting on the awakening," Pneuma replied mysteriously.

"An awakening? What does that mean?" Fear asked suspiciously.

"The cords," Pneuma reminded Fear, setting the expectation straight off the bat that Fear was not likely to feel satisfied by the response that he was about to get. Fear made a face but remained quiet, hopeful Pneuma would share more.

"The timing is right. Leiala will be shaken up," Pneuma said vaguely.

Fear was quietly contemplative. He hoped for the change, for Leiala's sake- but at the same time he realized that this would likely also mark great turmoil and discomfort for Leiala. He preemptively imagined her pain and grimaced.

“You’re right- it won’t be pretty,” Pneuma agreed, surprising Fear as he vocalized this more personal thought. “But it will dislodge Matsar,” He added, a sly grin warming His countenance.

-29-

For a month, Fear wondered if he had heard Pneuma correctly. He didn't question Him aloud- that would have felt disrespectful- but he doubted what he'd heard. Pneuma had said the timing was right- but he didn't see any change in Leiala. If anything, Leiala seemed to have fallen into a predictable pattern- one that was busy and full of life, but that also carried with it the weight and sadness of a sack of dirt, the unrealized dreams tucked inside the burlap bag without regard. Fear doubted Leiala had accepted this true reality- she seemed to stuff her days with so many activities that she scarcely had time to think. Fear suspected this was an intentional decision on a subconscious level.

Leiala slept fitfully, because she wore herself out. She gave everything she had to every situation she found herself in, and she found fulfillment in this. There was structure to her life, and there was always something she had her eye on improving. Her life didn't look as she'd expected it to, but that was just because she had more that she could work on.

That was it- there was always a reason, an explanation for why things weren't the way that she wanted them to be. It wasn't meant to be a self-deprecating mindset, but simply the way Leiala rationalized the life she found herself living: she had a multitude of things in which to feel grateful, but it didn't change the fact that there was also one big thing that she found missing. When she was honest with herself, she could admit that this was a big driving force behind her never-ending list of goals and her seemingly-endless reserves of energy. It was in part nervous energy, fear that she might never receive that gift she prized most of all.

Why it hadn't happened, Leiala wasn't sure. Why hadn't she been able to meet someone who loved her, who thought she was special? She wanted to believe it was because the timing hadn't been right, but as one year melted into the next, she found it difficult to hold onto this thread of hope. Was it logical to cling to this belief, or was it somehow shirking the truth she couldn't bear to even consider: that perhaps she just *wasn't* special? For as much as she wanted to believe that wasn't true, Leiala also knew well enough to face facts. And the facts weren't particularly gracious, when she considered the one boyfriend she'd had and the scar that had been left in the aftermath of the split.

Some days, Leiala attempted to practice logic- she would carefully walk through her past and thoughtfully consider all the reasons why she had failed to catch someone's eye. She never wrote out a physical list, but the reasons were carefully filed in her mind, confirmed as she intermittently reevaluated her position.

She needed to make herself prettier.
She needed to become skinnier.
She needed to make herself smarter.
She needed to become stronger and more fit.
She needed to become more fun.
She needed to become more godly.
She needed to read more books, books that would tell her how to become a better daughter, sister, friend, and significant other (if the day ever came).
She needed to save more money.
She needed to become more interesting.

At times, the list looked overwhelming. Leiala felt the pressure of its contents pressed upon her chest as though a ton of bricks had been stacked upon her. But when she considered walking away, giving up on her most precious, closely-held dream of becoming a wife and mother, her stomach roiled and she literally felt nausea overcome her. She'd tried saying the words, she'd tried to stand square to the mirror, tried to stare her reflection down with a gaze of steel. Tried voicing the words matter-of-factly: "You're not going to get married, and you're not going to have kids. And that's okay," but she couldn't do it. She would begin with ironclad resolve, but couldn't get halfway through before her lower lip started to tremble, liquid collected in the corners of her eyes, and her eyebrows sloped downward in a dead giveaway of the torrent of tears that were about to break free.

In the aftermath of these more emotional moments, Leiala's determination was greater than ever. She treated this desire of her heart like any other goal on her list: if she created a plan, and worked hard, it was something she could achieve. Thankfully, Matsar had some very specific strategies available for Leiala to utilize.

***

"I can take her farther," Matsar reported with confidence, his posture certain and unintimidated as he spoke to Abaddon.

"It goes without saying that you should do so," Abaddon replied dismissively. He was not interested in inconsequential progress, which was what Leiala's case had become. Things had moved along in a satisfying manner: Leiala accepted every invitation to venture farther down the path Matsar laid out in front of her, and Abaddon was pleased with the firm grip Matsar had succeeding in winning over Leiala.

The claws now deep within the tissue and fibers of her shoulders and back, Matsar's full weight now rested upon Leiala, a literal burden to carry. But through Matsar's crafty behavior, Leiala demurely accepted each new application of weight- she didn't even think to counter it.

Leiala carried Matsar with her everywhere she went, often naive to his very presence. But oh, he had wiggled his way into her conscience, his whispers indistinct from the thoughts that came from her own brain. And, Abaddon thought with no small amount of satisfaction, she trusted him. He was particularly pleased in the situations in which Leiala was forced to choose to listen to one voice: that of Theos, or that of Matsar. He loved watching as Theos's precious human, his beloved daughter, chose to listen to Matsar over the voice of her very own father.

But he wasn't sure what use could come from further movement. They'd rendered Leiala partially ineffective- mostly due to the fact that she was so consumed with her own fears and insecurities and plans for the future that she couldn't fully process and enjoy the moment she was living in. Past that, Abaddon wasn't sure what else could be done about the girl- there didn't seem to be some dramatic next step in which to take her.

"She's reaching the edge," Matsar continued, undeterred by the lack of enthusiasm exhibited by his master.

"Meaning?" Abaddon asked as he looked off into the distance, examining his own set of claws. It was a sign of respect that he bothered to extend the courtesy to Matsar to respond- most workers would have been cast out based off of perceived impudence in pursuing an issue not encouraged by Abaddon.

"Her behaviors are highly controlled- she is listening to every word I give her instructing her to do more. She's at a critical point: we can try to push her to jump to that next level, but it might bring awareness to what's happened to her," Matsar explained.

Abaddon considered this carefully. He'd been in this precarious situation before, where he was forced to decide whether to take a leisurely and lethargic approach to an assignment, or risk pushing them to greater destruction (and possibly wake them from their stupor). The work with Leiala had been an investment- steps and progress made gradually, in painfully-slow increments that had been necessary and productive in guiding her to the place she now found herself in. Abaddon desperately wanted to take her, to shove her, to that next level- but he wasn't sure if that would undo the groundwork that had been laid with such care.

"You're hesitating," Matsar commented assertively, his statement demanding further explanation.

"Theos is too calm," Abaddon responded, again overlooking the challenge in his worker's words.

"And you suspect He has something planned?" Matsar asked.

"I do. There's no other explanation for His silence," Abaddon mused, his gaze traveling back to the slithery worker in front of him.

"Perhaps He believes she is building resilience?" Matsar suggested. He knew better than to suggest that Theos had been beaten- a comment of such epically ignorant proportions would surely get him booted from the room.

"I don't think so," Abaddon responded irritably. He wished that was the case, but his gut told him there was more to it. He had witnessed enough of Theos's work to know that silence usually indicated a great movement. It angered and frustrated him beyond measure to know that just such an event was in the works, and he had no knowledge of it.

As if on cue, a wiry worker came huffing and puffing into the room unceremoniously. Abaddon and Matsar looked expectantly at the small, lithe figure before them, eager to hear the news that had brought the minion forth so boldly.

"It's Leiala," the worker panted in between giant gasps of air. "You're going to want to get back," he added, pointing a finger in Matsar's direction.

Before another word was spoken, Matsar vanished. He didn't need to know what it was that had happened to Leiala- *any* event was an event that he should be there to witness, to guide her through.

Abaddon glowered at the worker. He had been right about Theos being up to something, and he hated it. It wasn't fair- how Theos knew what was coming next. It gave him an unfair advantage, one that kept him perpetually (and sometimes marginally) below his archenemy. He had come to trust his instincts, and he'd become adept at studying Theos's behavior, but this didn't take him farther than anticipation.

"Her dream," the worker spat, aware that if he did not speak quickly, he would find himself eliminated in a fit of impatience and fury. "I think maybe her dream is coming true?"

Abaddon growled, his head thrown back as he launched himself purposefully from his chair. This would not do- this could not happen. He'd made too much progress, he'd invested too much in claiming Leiala's mind and rendering her worthless for kingdom work. He had a thousand questions for the worker, but none that could be answered quickly enough or with satisfying detail.

So, Leiala thinks her dreams are about to be realized? We'll see about that, Abaddon sneered, seething. Smoke curled in loops as he exhaled loudly through his nostrils, the anger quite literally heating his body and the room. It had been awhile since Abaddon had visited a particular human personally, but this was an occasion that called for his presence.

Uncertain of what he might come across, Abaddon felt confident in his ability to find a loophole, a chink in the armor with which to plunge his most experienced talon- a grip he would use to rip any hope or dream or thought of happiness to shreds. He would find the weakness- he always did.

With hatred fueling his every move, Abaddon disappeared in a cloud of fire. If it was a battle Theos wanted, He was about to get it. Abaddon wasn't going to relinquish his hold without the fight of his life.

I'm gradual. I'm sneaky, deceptive, and slow. I'm not like Grief, who makes his presence known immediately with his demanding, aggressive nature. Grief has to steal the spotlight- he can't bear to let any other emotion share airtime. But neither am I like Joy, who takes her sweet time, an effervescent light and warmth radiant about her. Joy's presence is evident; she's not looking to slip one past you. I'm difficult to confront, because you don't often recognize me.

In essence, I'm not evil- but if you overlook my work, your soul may plunge into despair. Do you know what it's like to be me? To cautiously inspire subtle differences until one day, you humans come to the realization that you're a perfect stranger to your own self; that your habits and life situation are utterly foreign to even your own being?

Not all of my work is this dramatic, to be sure, but my job isn't often pleasant. I'm resisted by all, even those who worship me. No one appreciates my work; no one can see what I'm working to accomplish. I'm not trusted- none of you can guess my objective. Will I hurt you? Will I help you? You have no idea. I threaten the equilibrium of your life, your sense of normalcy. To those of you who appreciate structure and predictability, I represent the destruction of all you know and understand. You hate me before you even give me a chance.

Can I tell you a secret? I don't know if I'm going to help you or hurt you, either. It actually makes my job easier, not knowing the outcome. It helps me from taking sides, or from developing feelings or establishing connections that might work against my objective. So I partially understand where your apprehension comes from- you've probably had negative experiences with me, at some point or another.

But do you realize my presence is mandatory? I'm literally woven into the tapestry of life- I'm part of the blueprint that makes up your DNA. You can't live life on earth as a human without walking alongside me. You THINK you can, because you don't recognize my presence on some days. You think you are immune, that you're somehow set apart from the rest of mankind. You don't acknowledge me until I bid adieu and take my leave.

Others of you seek me out, typically for all the wrong reasons. You're fed up, disappointed, angry, discouraged- you know you need me to alter your course. I'm wary of you humans- you call upon me in a moment of desperation, and in your frenzied state of mind you jump ship and grab onto the next thing you see instead of waiting patiently for that which is scheduled to come organically. Sometimes your impulsivity works out for you, and things turn out okay. But sometimes you just make a bigger mess.

Most of you experience me in more than one way- I wonder which you prefer? Oh, I know how you feel in the moment- you always make that very clear- but I mean after everything is said and done. When you reach the end of your days, when you can see why everything fell apart and then together the way it did. Do you prefer when I come quickly, unexpectedly, and dramatically? Or do you prefer when I creep up on you, slowly, hesitantly making my presence known to you? You'd think that after all these years, after all the assignments I've had, that I would have picked up on a pattern or preference, but I haven't. There are too many situations, circumstances, personalities, and ultimate outcomes that play into it all.

One thing I apologize for- I'm not like the others. You have no choice but to accept me- there is no denying my company or influence. I didn't ask to be so powerful, but it's part of my job. It's a strange thing, really, to carry so much weight and yet go unnoticed so much of the time. More than any other, my reception changes moment by moment. Idolized, repelled, cursed, blessed...I get it all.

If I could press upon you one thing, one lesson, it would be this: don't resist me. You can't. It doesn't matter what you want- ultimately, I always make my mark. You'll waste a lot of your life in agony and distress if you choose to battle me. It makes no difference to me- your feeble attempts to keep me at bay never succeed. So I say this truly for your benefit only, that you might live your life fully and truly. Accept me. When I come, let me in. Be graceful, and if you're feeling charitable, maybe even offer me a cup of coffee and a seat in your home. I won't stay long- I never do.

-Change

-30-

Fear was invested. He'd tried to deny it for long enough- it was time to face the truth. He took every affront and attack to Leiala's character personally, as though it was a targeted attempt to undo him. He'd never felt such an attachment to an assignment before, and he was uncertain that he ever would again.

If he ever got another assignment, Fear thought snidely. At the rate things were going, and considering the measure of his attachment to Leiala, he wasn't sure he would survive. Wasn't sure he wanted to survive if Leiala didn't. What a whirlwind her life had proven to be, and it had nothing to do with circumstances. Well, maybe it had a little to do with circumstances- but quite honestly, Fear had been assigned to many humans who had lived through far more trying events. The obstacles Leiala had encountered weren't extraordinary, but the alternative activity surrounding them was. Fear felt exhausted just watching Leiala live- and he wasn't even in her skin.

He knew Abaddon was after her, and that scared Fear. Ironic, Fear thought as he shook his head, that he should be overwhelmed by the emotion he was responsible for cultivating in others. It wasn't just that Abaddon was after Leiala, for in truth, he was after every human assignment- it was the approach that he had decided to adopt.

There was a dedication, a determination to Abaddon's efforts that Fear hadn't seen before. Leiala's work was no longer delegated to his minions- every worker was carefully chosen to fulfill a specific task, and Abaddon himself oversaw the large-scale operations. The book detailing Leiala's life had been opened multiple times, and there were teams of workers now assigned to her case, to identifying and pinpointing every weakness, proclivity, and fault. Fear had seen the teams as they pored over the open pages, honing in on the red print but scouring every color text as they searched and hunted for even the most miniscule of clues.

And the video room- they were pulling up and replaying highlights of Leiala's most influential moments- those that had shaped her into the human she was. Pausing the screen mid-scene as Fear had seen in the Strategics class to analyze Leiala's response and project what her future tendencies might be. Their analyses were thoughtful, complicated, and shockingly accurate. Fear found that these workers were able to pinpoint quirks and patterns in Leiala's responses that Fear himself had never recognized- characteristics that, once they were pointed out, Fear knew immediately to be true. These crafty, clever workers were working hard, working overtime, to build a case against Leiala. To exploit every possible situation, to forge a crowbar in every tiny crevice, to plant splinters and thorns in every square inch of Leiala's flesh.

"It's overwhelming," he tried to explain to Pneuma. "You have no idea how much work they're putting into destroying her. I've never seen anything like it."

"I have," Pneuma said wryly, not in an attempt to one-up Fear but in an attempt to assure him that the battle before them was not lost.

"And you still think we can win?" Fear asked, trying to hide the doubt that still managed to seep through his words.

Pneuma smiled at Fear patiently. "You're uncertain," Pneuma stated.

Fear said nothing. He didn't mean to defy this ruler of the west end, but yes- it seemed very uncertain. The west end appeared to be operating business as usual- as though they were totally oblivious to the frenetic, hate-filled actions of the east end. Pneuma knew they were preparing for attack, but did He really actually *know*? Did He see the size of the workers, the number of workers, the experience of the workers assigned to Leiala? Fear found it hard to imagine that He did- he couldn't imagine He would be quite as confident if He did.

"Despite what you might think, I do know the extent of the preparations in the east end," Pneuma voiced, reminding Fear of His penchant for knowing exactly what he was thinking at any given time without a single word uttered.

"Have you been there?" Fear asked curiously. He had never heard of Theos, Yeshua, or Pneuma traveling to the east end, and it was beyond question that any worker of the east end would be welcomed into the west end.

"I have not," Pneuma answered matter-of-factly. "But I don't have to. Theos knows every single thing that happens on every square inch of the universe- and beyond," Pneuma added for good measure.

"He sees Abaddon and what he's up to?" Fear asked, incredulous. He couldn't imagine such pervasive power- and he wondered why Theos didn't wield this power in more literal ways.

"He offers choice," Pneuma responded, ignoring Fear's initial question to get straight to the heart of the matter. "He doesn't force himself on anyone- that would take all the beauty and the magic from his being."

"Abaddon forces himself upon humans," Fear countered, fully aware that he came across as a petulant toddler whining that something was unfair.

Pneuma allowed the ignorant comment to linger in the air like the stale belch of carbon monoxide from the exhaust of a car. Fear didn't need Pneuma to address the comment- he knew how foolish it had been to compare Abaddon to Theos.

"I just thought maybe He would be more assertive in fighting for those that try to follow Him," Fear tried again, hoping to better articulate the unease that riddled his insides.

"You want Him to swoop in with a force of power, to destroy Abaddon," Pneuma offered.

"Yes!" Fear exclaimed. "Leiala is trying- she's messing up, but she's trying. And she's messing up because of Abaddon! She doesn't know what he's done to her. And she can't get rid of Matsar," Fear lamented, the anguish fresh.

"She's not as far gone as you think she is," Pneuma said thoughtfully, quietly.

"Matsar?" Fear challenged.

"His days are numbered," Pneuma reminded him.

"How numbered?" Fear asked impatiently. He was tired of Pneuma speaking in elusive mysteries, in pretty words that sparkled with wisdom and promised the world but somehow felt so far out of reach. He didn't want to dwell in a land of fantasy and glory- he wanted to see the results, wanted to touch the action and the answer.

"Theos's timing is perfect," Pneuma chided Fear.

Fear was silent, but he did not repent of his thoughts. It was true! Theos worked in an agonizingly slow manner, according to Fear (and, he imagined, every character and human would agree, if given the opportunity). *He* might live forever, but the humans did not- Fear could speak to the truth in their mortality as evidenced through the number of assignments he'd already outlived. Why must the humans wait so long? It seemed to prolong their doubt, add to their fear and hurt- and it seemed so unnecessary.

"You have to trust," Pneuma said gently. "Theos isn't mean or cruel- you know that. He operates in a way that doesn't make sense to anyone else- because He isn't *anyone else*," Pneuma pointed out. "He's Theos. He wouldn't be revered and hold the position of ruler of the universe if He acted in any other manner."

Fear sighed. He knew that what Pneuma said was true, but it did nothing to assuage his fears over Leiala's future. The way he envisioned it, she would be eaten alive!

"I have an idea," Pneuma voiced suddenly, separating Fear from his depressing thoughts. "Come with me."

Taken aback, but filled with curiosity and the knowledge that it wasn't often that Pneuma invited anyone to follow Him somewhere, Fear followed. His footsteps felt heavy and clumsy next to Pneuma's light steps. Pneuma seemed to walk on air, while Fear was painfully aware of his every move. Pneuma didn't move too quickly, but His pace wasn't leisurely, either. Fear wasn't sure how He did it, but He had learned at some point during their sessions that Pneuma was not constrained by space and time the way other characters, humans, and workers were. He was capable of existing in multiple dimensions at a single moment in time- and Fear had learned that He ministered to literally thousands, sometimes millions, of individuals at any given second.

It had been a relief to learn this, Fear remembered. He'd felt guilty for dominating so much of Pneuma, for claiming such a significant portion of His time when his questions and insecurities were petty compared to others. Pneuma had affirmed his importance and need for counsel, pointing out that he didn't have any way of knowing that his need wasn't as great as another individual's. And then he'd been reprimanded for comparing himself to others, which Pneuma explained was the beginning of great disatisfaction.

But for all his authority over space and time, Pneuma still moved with purpose- and He did not tarry in carrying out His intentions. Fear stretched his short legs out as long as they could go, eager to keep pace with Pneuma as they traveled down the pearly-white corridors to a section of the west end that Fear had never been in before. Caught up in the excitement of venturing into a new place, Fear unconsciously slowed down as he craned his neck to look around, to absorb every detail he could.

The corinthian columns supporting the high marble ceilings were white, the color of cumulus clouds on a bright and sunny summer day. The slate-gray veins of the marble snaked across the expansive pillars, adding character to an otherwise unblemished structure.

But soon they came across doors- also heavy marble, but with names etched on the front. The names were not difficult to read, and yet the lettering was thin, chipped into the surface of the glossy marble. Fear slowed down to read them, wondering what these rooms were. He'd never seen (or known) of any such wing of the west end- he had no idea where they'd gone.

"Keep up, Fear," Pneuma prodded kindly. "We have a ways to go. We're not close to Leiala's room yet."

Leiala's room? Fear wondered. *She had a room? For what?* Questions circled in his mind, smoke messages coughed out of a skywriting plane. Fear knew Pneuma could sense his questions, but He chose to remain silent.

Finally, Pneuma slowed. Fear found himself filled with anticipation as his saucer-like eyes took in the careful etching that pronounced the room to belong to Leiala. Pneuma stood outside the door, which Fear noticed had no handle. Without knowing what was housed behind the door, Fear was aware of the great honor he was about to receive- he had the unconscious knowledge and understanding that this was not normal protocol for Pneuma; this was not a place He normally took characters.

Fear watched with wide, reverent eyes as Pneuma blew on the door. Not the pressure of a shoulder or a palm against the marble surface, as Fear had guessed. No- it was a single, seemingly-insignificant puff of air that commanded the impossibly heavy marble door to open. And open it did, without hesitation or effort.

A bright light blinded Fear, and he was overcome by a warm and fragrant gust of wind that simultaneously warmed him to his toes and filled him with indescribable peace. The wind quite literally lifted him off of his feet, lazily dragging him off the ground to ride in the current of the balmy breeze.

In any other situation, this would have frightened Fear, or at least unsettled him- how could he explain floating away in a breeze?- and yet he knew no fear. He was aware of Pneuma's presence close to him, but he could not see anything- the light was too bright.
This was Leiala's room? What did it have to do with Leiala? Fear wondered. It was a wonderful room, to be sure- Fear had just entered and he already was of the impression that he never wanted to leave. But as far as he knew, Leiala had never set foot in this room- how could she, when her shoes and gravity kept her firmly planted on earth?

"Come down," Pneuma commanded, and the breeze instantly subsided, gently whisking Fear back to the ground until his toes grazed physical space again. He felt a wave of disappointment wash over him- he'd felt complete joy and contentment floating through the atmosphere, and he was loathe to let it go.

"See," Pneuma commanded again, and Fear was aware of the light dimming. Whether this was an adaptation of his eyes and their ability to perceive what existed in the room, or whether it was a modification of the room to accommodate his shortcomings, Fear wasn't sure. But as his eyes worked to adjust to the new lighting- still bright, but no longer blinding- Fear felt a sense of wonder creep up through him, a tingling that erupted into existence like a firework and snaked its way up his legs, generating heat at the same time chills passed over his form.

Surrounding him, densely covering every square inch of the seemingly endless room, were shiny white threads, thick cords that hung straight down with intention and prestige. The breeze did not seem to affect these cords- they danced in the movement of the wind, but in a carefree, spontaneous choreography that suggested playfulness over any contrivance. They instantly made Fear think of the cords that he had seen sewn into the tapestry of Leiala's story. Pneuma had told him these were a part of the bigger picture, the larger story that told of all humanity- but these cords were different. Where the other threads had taken on color, had displayed numerous shades and pigments and hues, these cords were all white. Totally colorless.

Fear looked around for Pneuma, captivated by the grandeur and beauty of the cords at the same time that he was desperate for understanding of what they were, what they represented.

Look up.
There were no words spoken. It would have felt abrasive, discordant, to speak in such a pure and beautiful room, Fear realized. He was aware of the thought that transcended his consciousness, and he knew that Pneuma had tapped into His ability to communicate through thoughts.

Obediently, Fear turned his chin up, gaze following the seemingly endless threads that swayed like seaweed in a current. The light reflected off of the threads and they seemed to glow, bright white lights that radiated beauty beyond compare. And at the top of each thread, a bulbous balloon. The balloons also white, opaque flesh that also glowed with the knowledge of a light housed within. Millions, maybe even billions of these balloons crowded the room, densely populating every space.

He was vaguely aware that his mouth was hanging open- that he stood in awe of the grandeur and impossibly beautiful scene before him. He didn't know what he was looking at, but he had the awareness that it was holy, pure, and *special.*

Take my hand.

Fear ripped his gaze from the balloons long enough to search for Pneuma in the room, to intertwine his fingers with the most wise counselor. And then he was moving up, past the sea of milky white cords to the balloons above.

As they neared the top, Pneuma slowed, and Fear again beheld the wonder of the giant spheres. And noticed the calligraphy scrawled on the surface of each balloon- the beautiful, rhapsodic writing that foretold of something wonderful.

Pneuma kindly navigated Fear to the closest balloon, indulging his desire to see one up close- to decipher the writing stretching across the surface of each.

Comfort.
Companionship.
Financial blessing.
Wisdom.
Teaching.
Faith.
Leadership.
Joy.

Fear still didn't know exactly what he was looking at, but he felt overwhelmed by the magnitude of the number of balloons and the innumerable beautiful, hopeful words that were written on each. Tears blurred his vision, so overcome was he by the display he couldn't fully comprehend.

What are they? he wondered, his thought directed towards Pneuma.

Blessings.

Pneuma didn't elaborate, but He graced Fear with understanding that rushed over him like a waterfall, drowning his expectations and doubts in a deluge of love and joy.

They were blessings, all of them marked for Leiala. Intended for her, set apart for her, and *her* alone. Each one, carefully marked and protected. Each one different, promising something new and unique and special and wonderful.

Fear was overcome. Ashamed, that he had doubted Theos's love and affection for the girl. Embarrassed that he had questioned the plan Theos had. How could He want anything but the best for Leiala, when He had stored up so much wonder for her? It was humbling, to see each balloon floating proudly, each unique and unlike any other in the room.

And Leiala gets them all?

If she asks for them, Pneuma explained. *Some are released incidentally, or at the movement of the spirit- but most are accessed through prayer.*

Leiala prays for them? Fear wondered.

Leiala, or another petitioning on her behalf.
And they're all for Leiala? Fear marveled, incredulous at the sheer magnitude of it all. *She won't run out?*

There's no such thing. There are an infinite number.

Fear was stupefied. Was it possible- could it be- that Leiala might access every blessing in the room? He couldn't imagine any human receiving so many blessings.

It's about to rain, Pneuma said, the excitement lacing His words obvious.

Fear was working to process what a storm of blessings might possibly look like when he noticed even more substantial balloons in the midst of the ivory spheres. These balloons looked to be made of pure gold, and the writing atop them was raised, filigreed into the decadent design.

Special blessings. Those that unleash the power of Theos, Yeshua, and Myself, Pneuma explained.

Fear turned to Pneuma in surprise, unsure he had just heard correctly. Theos actually gave away some of His power- to *humans*?! Pneuma simply nodded, His face solemn.

Goosebumps dotted Fear's arms at the knowledge that such incredible power was accessible by human assignments- by *Leiala*! Did she know she could receive these incredible blessings?

*She knows, but she doesn't quite **know**,* Pneuma acknowledged. *Soon,* He added- again in that frustrating way that told of an ambiguous time frame- one that the alternative realm apparently believed would pass quickly. Fear wasn't so sure.

There is a lot of power here, Fear was forced to acknowledge. He was in awe of the enormity of it all- he wasn't sure he'd ever wrap his brain around it.

And this is just the power that Leiala herself can access, Pneuma pointed out with a knowing grin. *You haven't even seen the army amassing on her behalf.*
A shiver of delight crept up Fear's back. Oh, he had been wrong. So wrong. Leiala hadn't been forgotten- there was no way he could believe that, looking into the room chalk full of blessings marked, *designed*, specially for her. He hadn't seen the army, or the other preparations made on Leiala's behalf, but he didn't have to.

The battle would come, and Fear knew that Leiala would be hurt. But the victor of the battle, of the greater war? Fear had only to look at the effervescent, holographic-like bubbles floating about him to answer that question.

Fear couldn't speak the rest of the afternoon. He wasn't sure he could find any words worth the space and time, after witnessing such ethereal perfection. Words felt cheap, wasted. He felt insignificant- not in a way that had him questioning his worth, but that humbly reminded him of how small he truly was in the scope of all that Theos had created. And he no longer felt dread. There was new knowledge, new understanding of what was to come.

And for the first time in a long time, Fear had faith: Leiala would be okay.

-31-

Leiala felt giddy.

Don't be silly and unrealistic, she chided herself. It had been years since she'd had this feeling, and she was unsettled by how quickly she had fallen back into its trappings. How quickly she was drawn into daydreaming, how jubilant she was to welcome back feelings that had been put on the shelf for nearly a decade.

You're just setting yourself up for disappointment, she warned herself. She was hardly the expert at this relationship stuff, but she knew her own track record. It wasn't good. Love was wonderful, and Leiala believed it was real and magical and heavenly. She'd seen it before, had witnessed her friends' beautiful stories and fairytale weddings, had shed innumerable tears of joy as she'd watched the bride, always breathtakingly beautiful, appear at the end of the aisle, ready to meet her groom.

This moment in particular never failed to overwhelm Leiala, no matter if she'd never met the bride before or if she was standing up next to her. It was symbolic of a long wait redeemed, of a story ready to be catapulted into the next adventure: a tale Leiala was sure would be filled with glory and grandeur and magic. But more than all that, it was the hope, the unspoken promise, and the pure, pure joy and love that shone from the trio of faces: the father of the bride as he gazed with pride and wonder at the lovely woman before him, who had one day long ago been nestled in his arms as a mere babe; the groom, posture firm and steady, but face so full of joy and expectation: the lovely woman walking towards him would soon be his wife, a jewel to admire and a safe haven in which to retreat; and the bride- the bride, always walking with confidence, her steps sure as she seemed to gaze right past any members of the audience, straight into the eyes of the one she was about to give everything to. It was poetic. It was moving.

And for all the skeptics and naysayers, Leiala knew that true love could stand the test of time. She'd seen that, too- had witnessed love that lasted for decades, love that grew and evolved and demanded deeper roots. Love that stood still when jobs fell through, when circumstances demanded that a family be uprooted and taken into the unknown, when children were taken from the world too early and when health became a memory and memory became a fickle friend that only materialized on certain days. This love was not fanciful and whimsical and Jane Austen-like; this love was fierce, it was strong, it was BOLD, and it demanded respect.

Leiala wanted all of it. She wanted love that would take over her thoughts with its opulent and fantastical nature, that would make her weak in the knees. But she also wanted the love that would stand the test of the world- the kind of love that sought fortification from within, that promised to be an anchor during times of turbulent storm. Leiala was excited to live the fairytale, but she was also prepared for the fight that she knew would inevitably come knocking on her door. She wanted these things so desperately, and at the same time she was working so hard to convince herself that these things didn't really matter.

She'd made a comfortable, happy life for herself- she recognized that her days were filled with lovely, beautiful things that brought her happiness, sometimes even joy. But that pervasive joy that she earnestly desired was what continued to elude her- there was a restlessness that could not be quelled by international trips and long trail runs and brunches on the beach with friends followed by cozy afternoons sipping on lattes.

It should be enough, Leiala had told herself time and time again. She had more than enough- she'd been richly blessed (more than anyone else she knew!), and yet there were days that she felt so empty. She never begrudged the friend who found her soulmate, or who happily announced a pregnancy marking the beginning of the storybook life Leiala envisioned for herself- she was genuinely overcome with joy for the people around her who found these incredible miracles, who reminded Leiala that these things *were* still possible, that they still did happen. But behind the radiant smiles and giggles and jovial exchanges that took place at a bridal or baby shower was the unvarnished truth that she was millions of miles away from that dream.

The trick was not to think too much. Leiala found that if she hosted one of these events, if she busied herself arranging decorations and refilling champagne flutes and replenishing tea cakes while organizing games, she was okay. If she focused on the event- and on making sure everything was perfect for her friend- then it was all okay.

Usually.

But when a tender moment arose, one in which the heart was demanded: words of relationship wisdom spoken to the bride-to-be, a tender prayer made over the expectant mother- those moments choked Leiala. For all the control she exhibited in her everyday life, these events served as kryptonite ready to unmask every unfulfilled dream and earnest desire as tears welled in her eyes and insisted on parading down her cheeks.

She resented herself in these moments, felt frustrated that even through years of focused discipline and resolve, she could not shake these desires. They shamed her- a public proclamation that she might have blessings in her life, but she could not achieve *this* one. It was her scarlet letter to wear- UNWANTED emblazoned on her forehead.

In the wake of this shame, this disappointment, Leiala was able to channel her sorrow into fuel. She'd learned as a girl that nothing productive came from pity and sadness- so she'd also learned how to expedite this emotion and forge ahead into dissatisfaction that materialized as anger she could channel into a plan, a tangible objective she could achieve.

She could get that blessing she longed for- she just needed to pursue it relentlessly, to give it everything she had. And she'd been offered the blueprint of how to make that happen: more prayer, more exercise, less food, more accomplishments, more things. This would all make Leiala into a better person, a more desirable person. One that would earn the attention of a man, since the person she was now was clearly unworthy.

As time passed, Leiala became more skilled at numbing the pain. She tried not to think about that prized dream she lacked and worked to convince herself that she was fully satisfied with the life that she had. Most days, she succeeded- but only because she numbed herself and built walls around that which was capable of bringing her the greatest joy and the deepest pain: her heart.

Guard your heart, the Scriptures told her, and boy did she listen. There was no such thing as too much guarding: a full patrol was sent out in steel armor, landmines were strategically planted, and the skies were dotted with fiery arrows just waiting to take flight. The softest, most vulnerable corners of her heart were buried within this defense, and Leiala considered this victory. She could endure, she would be okay, if she could just maintain this controlled, measured approach. She had the formula, she had the routine, and she was ready to live out the slightly sub-par days she saw stretched out before her. And it was right in the middle of this predictable flow of life that he came into her life.

So guarded was Leiala that she didn't see it at first. It took multiple people- children even!- sharing the truth that they saw before Leiala even began to entertain the possible validity in the situation- the chance that someone was interested her. Her surprise was genuine, and her response cautious- her heart had been seriously bruised by false hope and unrealized expectations the last time she had invited someone in to hold that place...she would move forward with great trepidation. She doubted, refuted, and challenged every account from every conceivable angle. She dismissed and denied any comments made about the situation- this was the way to protection.

It's dangerous to allow yourself to be swept up into an emotion or a dream, Leiala reminded herself prudently. She was just doing what she was commanded to: she was guarding her heart, taking things slow.

She prayed.

She waited.

She wrote letters, sealed and tucked away in a shoebox- to be read someday if anything ever materialized.

And she prayed a lot more.

And slowly, things began to align. The timing of events felt divine, and Leiala felt comfort, peace, and affirmation of a magnitude that she hadn't experienced in a long time. Her heart remained protected in its shell of armor, but Leiala was acknowledging its existence as she began to contemplate pulling it out. She couldn't explain what was happening, and she wondered if that was because the acts were not of her own doing, but rather something ordained through the heavens.

She confided in one friend. Five days into a girls' trip, in a sunny plaza in Hawaii as they sipped on coconut lattes. Her friend, never one to mince words: "You're an idiot. We're not leaving until you follow up." Leiala, laughing, emboldened by the balmy breeze and the invigorating buzz of caffeine, doing just that. And more things fell into place.

Late-night discussions, held on the dewy grass of their tropical resort watching the explosive sunset atop cheap cotton towels, huddling close together after the sun's dramatic goodbye as the air chilled and frogs began to warble and ribbet. One night in particular, deciding to stay out under the stars even as light rain began to fall. Sitting atop the grassy knoll, whispering fervent prayers under the tent of a sweatshirt. Raindrops glistened on their suntanned arms, the crystal snowglobes highlighting the goosebumped flesh beneath. And then back in the room, another piece falling into place.

It continued like this, even when Leiala returned back home. It couldn't be explained- and Leiala didn't try to.

She confided in two friends.

Three.

With each confidence, and with each brick taken down, Leiala waited cautiously, wondering if everything would suddenly implode in an effort to shame her for believing that *it* was possible. And when she felt steady, she would take another step in faith. And another.

Leiala demonstrated unusual patience, likely due to the extent of her fear and uncertainty in this abandoned realm of romance. But she had hope again, and she felt warmth and peace radiate in her belly and stretch to her fingers and toes- she dared to believe that she might experience that which so many of her friends had embraced.

A series of letters and an international trip later, and Leiala prepared for their first date. How many dates had she begrudgingly agreed to with the excitement of a patient preparing for a root canal? She knew the questions to ask, she knew the right way to tilt her head to feign interest, and she knew exactly how to dress for any given situation: cute but not like she was trying too hard, always ballet flats (height was typically uncertain), and the wash of jeans dependent on the time of the date. And she hated them all. Would give herself a pep talk before, work to convince herself that it *might* be awesome, that she might meet the love of her life- and that ended in tears, every time. Tears of disappointment, acknowledging how far she felt from her dream; tears of frustration that so many of the *promising* young men that she met were utterly boring and vapid and lame!

But not this date. Leiala was excited, more excited than she was ready to admit to herself. Her dress picked out nearly a month before their first date was even set in the hope and expectation that there *would* be a date. A romantic white sundress- one that Leiala worried might be slightly bridal, and that was a cause for some concern- but that made her feel lovely and feminine and that showed off her golden skin in the heart of summer. Her accessories carefully chosen: a thick turquoise necklace and matching stud earrings that she knew drew out the bright hue of her eyes.

No, there was not much use in denying the anticipation leading up to this date- there was so much hope, so much promise- all confirmed by a number of signs that seemed to point to the uniqueness of this situation. There was a bit of fear here, too- the worry that perhaps she was making too much out of it all, that possibly she was setting herself up for disappointment. But in spite of these fears, Leiala still felt optimistic, excited and encouraged that she might be on the edge of a great adventure.

And then the actual date came. And for all the anticipation and nerves that had corroborated to make a dangerous cocktail of emotions, Leiala wafted through the night like a fragrant incense set upon a gentle breeze. She remembered everything, and she remembered nothing. She remembered the glitter of his gray-green eyes, the wide smile that made her heart flutter. The deep tan set off by the nectarine-colored shirt he wore, the muscled forearms that she found so attractive. The easy way he moved, the care and consideration he offered her during every moment during the night that simultaneously put Leiala at ease and left her hungry, greedy for more time with him.

She couldn't remember what they talked about, but she remembered walking along the cliffs overlooking the ocean, watching the sun as it bid adieu through a glorious sunset, and then sharing a bottle of wine over dinner as they lingered in the hidden gem of a restaurant nestled amongst the cliffs. It felt easy, natural even- as they left and drove to the top of a hill to watch fireworks, then back to the house and jacuzzi to submerge their legs in the hot, bubbly water as they talked more.

It was a night Leiala wished would never end. She lost concept of time, and she totally surrendered to the magic of the moment, the conversation that never ran dry. And when the night did end, it was with a gift- something thoughtful and lovely, something that resonated with her soul and that touched her core, a tendril of a plant that curled in between the bricks guarding her heart. A warm hug, and then a goodbye made with sparkling eyes that silently promised that they would see each other again.

Leiala left more certain than ever: this was it. Her fairytale had begun, and happily ever after was on its way. And that might have been true, if Abaddon didn't still rule the earth.

***

Weeks passed, and Leiala began to give up on sleep, that elusive and fickle creature that never seemed to want to spend time with her anymore. Some days, the lack of sleep carried rationale that made sense to Leiala: there was a reason or factor that directly fed into the insomnia. But other days, there was nothing but an anxious mind busily running through and imagining every possible scenario in an attempt to prepare for the unknown.

For years now, Leiala's life had moved forward in a semi-predictable pattern, and she had become quite adept at traversing the myriad of situations with her predetermined responses. She was in control, she knew what to expect, and she felt that she responded with grace and ease. Now, she found herself in uncharted waters. She had no expected path and no way to suppose what might happen next- and this kept her awake at night.

She wasn't conscious of this reasoning, and she couldn't articulate the fears and worries that fueled her nervous energy, but that did nothing to negate the reality of the situation. Added to the unknown was the knowledge that he seemed to *see* her in a way that others did not: he had a way of cutting through the polished exterior she managed to present to call out the underlying issues and mentalities that powered her every move. This inspired awe in Leiala- how wonderful it was to be seen and truly known, to be appreciated and admired in a way that she hadn't felt before- and it also incited a very real fear: how was he receiving this knowledge? How was he able to detect her inner parts, the pieces she worked so hard to polish and gloss over?

This knowledge came through pointed, poignant questions that were spoken in kindness- words that disarmed her, that gave way to a wave of defensiveness before panic overcame her. She'd spent so much effort numbing the noisy, unsatisfied parts of her soul that she had denied the existence of certain parts of her. She didn't have answers to the questions, didn't know anything more than that they pinged her soul and generated heat in her body.

But with a gentle flip of her hair and the thoughtful tilt of her head, she answered the questions articulately, with words that she believed to be true but that didn't begin to capture the roiling lava that swirled within her soul. Later, these questions would haunt her- would be written down in the pages of her journal, the source of constant reflection. Why were these questions so powerful, so meaningful to her? She couldn't put her finger on it, but she knew they touched upon something important, something worth knowing.

And she fell in love. She'd known that she would, and she did. It was warm and dear- the feeling she carried with her- and it roused her to be the very best that she could be. She remembered some of the feelings that came with love, but this one somehow felt new: the motivation and inspiration to live up to being the person that she was thought to be. Most of this sensation was healthy, an earnest desire to realize her potential and share the beauty and love she'd been gifted with the rest of the world. But there was another part that seemed to eat at her, pressure her with added expectations that came fresh with new fears.

She wasn't as wonderful as he thought- as so many thought, and she needed to make up for that. She needed to work *harder* to be *better*, to be the girlfriend that he deserved and the woman that so many believed she was. She wasn't good enough yet, but she would be. She *could* be!

Soon, the sleepless nights began to feel like a gift. It meant that she had more hours each day to accomplish all that she had her heart set on: hours to exercise, to journal, to complete master's assignments, to read the Bible, to write encouraging letters to friends, to clean her apartment and do laundry and prepare healthy meals for the week. Her life became a science, and it reached a level that it never had before: for all the whimsy and flexibility she tried to offer in her job and her relationship, she became more and more shackled to a structure in which control reigned.

It began to consume Leiala- she saw it, but she wasn't quite sure how to fight it. She could see the inflexibility, the fear and insecurity that influenced responses that didn't fall in line with freedom- and yet she didn't feel like she could actually embrace a mindset that rejected that which had brought her such success. Because, Leiala reminded herself, it was that rigid routine that had brought her this far. That had pulled her from the drudges of deep despair to this perfect life. Because it *was* perfect, wasn't it? Or close? Maybe perfect was unrealistic, but Leiala knew she could get pretty darned close.

-33-

Abaddon grinned. There was nothing that brought him greater joy than messing with Theos's children- especially when the humans believed it was Theos's fault.

Looking down at Leiala, Abaddon was warranted in his response of pride. For all of Leiala's painstaking efforts and genuine desire for Theos, she had fallen hook, line, and sinker for the bait he had cast in front of her. Matsar's work had laid a firm foundation from which to exploit Leiala, and the detailed studies of her character and responses had proven most fruitful: Abaddon could correctly identify all the situations in which Leiala would be most vulnerable to attack, drawing her farther along the thorny path he had laid out for her.

And, Abaddon thought with mirth that seemed to bubble from his fingertips and toes, she thought she was doing it all to please Theos! She listened to him, she listened to all of them- especially the voice of Matsar- all the while believing she was pleasing Theos. That she was following him diligently, making him proud as she worked harder and harder to achieve perfection. And oh, were they making ground!

Matsar's claws were buried deep in the flesh of her shoulders by now- Leiala couldn't go anywhere, make any decision without first consulting him. His full weight anchored Leiala to the ground, made her footsteps heavy and cumbersome- but she believed this was simply the product of a perfect lifestyle. After all, it couldn't be easy to be perfect. If it were easy, everyone would be perfect. And Leiala certainly wasn't *everyone*. She reminded herself of this when she felt tired, burned out- when she felt inclined to just give in and relax, to rest and refresh.

Matsar's grasp had proven to be so successful that it was now easier to dispatch workers to speak directly to her. Their voices were not quite as well received as Matsar's, which had become so smooth and honeyed to Leiala's expectant ear that it couldn't even be distinguished as unique from her own consciousness. But these voices now whispered lies to her, and more workers were able to moonlight as guest speakers as they hovered right by Leiala's face, stroking her long hair with smooth, soothing gestures at the same time they offered her violent, abject fiction.

Every once in a while, Leiala dismissed the voice- she saw the lie and rejected it. But more often than not, she absorbed the deception and obediently succumbed to the instructions given to her.

The answer to all of her problems could be found in eating less. Exercising more. Spending less money. Earning more degrees. Winning the admiration of more people. Becoming more beautiful.

And Leiala was nothing if not a diligent over-achiever, the model student eager to please. She worked harder, worked tirelessly, and grew more and more tired. Abaddon helped her, supported her by offering her the nervous, anxiety-ridden energy necessary to power the sleepless nights and endless list of tasks to be completed. And Leiala accomplished more, grew thinner, and won success in the eyes of the world. And, in direct correlation, Leiala's joy dwindled.

She was too distracted to notice. She had worked to make herself numb, but now her life was so crowded with expectations and fears and anxieties and lists that she literally did not have the capacity to recognize joy's departure. She claimed to listen for Theos's voice- she set aside the first hour of every day to spend time with him- but even this had been warped by Abaddon, who had convinced Leiala that she needed to make the most of their time together by reading more biblical books that offered insight into the living Word rather than time spent in the Word itself. Leiala's time with Theos followed a prescribed formula, like everything else in her life- there was no flexibility, no yielding to the promptings Theos placed on Leiala's heart.

And while she believed that her whole heart was before Theos, Abaddon knew better- he saw all the areas Leiala had claimed control over- the many pieces of her life that she held tightly to with clenched fists. She would listen to Him, as long as it led her to make the eating choices she approved of, as long as it meant she could exercise when she wanted, as long as it didn't interrupt with the plan for the day that she had created.

And that, Abaddon preened, was all that he ever wanted. To take Theos's followers, those who believed they worshipped Him, and distort their worship until it was directed at something different altogether- until they worshipped things and dreams instead. Because, as everyone in the alternative realm knew, to worship things and dreams was to worship him- Abaddon- the ruler of all that earth had to offer.

Now that Leiala had bought into the lies, now that she was merrily on her way to a life of stunted dreams and fruitless labor- Abaddon could start to destroy her. She was committed now, and she wouldn't recognize Abaddon as the party responsible for the pain that was slated to come her way. And for as much as Abaddon had enjoyed watching her saunter towards death, he would delight in the suffering and affliction that was at her doorstep.

***

Things weren't going well.

Leiala wasn't sure what triggered this epiphany, or what events had led to her present unhappiness, but she couldn't help but acknowledge that she was in a state. She was doing all the right things, but without any of the happiness she had once experienced. She was working harder than ever, and she wasn't seeing any of the fruits of her labor. She felt frustrated, resentful.

That wasn't how it was supposed to work. She had done the work, she had stayed obedient to the tasks put before her. And she was supposed to reap the benefits.

So what could explain the distance that had been forged in her relationship, the chasm that seemed to widen daily? What could explain the pervasive sadness that had blanketed her day-to-day life, hanging like a gray cloud over her head as she engaged in activities that had once brought her joy?

Leiala didn't have the answers to the questions, but she felt the answer to who was responsible. Theos- what was He doing to her? She was giving Him everything, she was literally working herself to death for Him, and where was He? Where were the blessings? Where was the peace, the joy?

Eat less. If you're skinnier, you'll be more beautiful. Or at least you'll be more powerful. You'll show that you have strength that others don't; you can do things that others can't.

Run more! Run farther. Run faster. That always makes you feel better- you get the endorphins, and then you might be able to have a piece of bread as a treat later in the day.

YOU can do this, Leiala. Look at what you've already done- what's keeping you from more? You just need to focus, to concentrate, and to work harder.

***

"She's not listening!" Fear exclaimed, hands clasped over each ear in distress. "Why can't she hear you?"

It was agonizing, Fear thought, seeing Leiala in such despair, and watching as she walked away from the truth that Theos was feeding her.

"There's too much noise," Yeshua told Fear matter-of-factly. "Pneuma won't stop repeating the message, but at this point, it's futile. She's not ready to listen."

"When *will* she be ready?" Fear asked anxiously. "She's not getting any better, with Abaddon and his crew hanging around her."

"She's going to have to be broken," Yeshua said. The words seemed to bring Him pain- He sighed and shook His head.

"What do you call *this*?" Fear challenged, looking down at Leiala. "I'm pretty sure she's at the end of her rope."

"Not yet," Yeshua answered. "When she reaches the end of her rope, she'll have no choice but to reach out to us instead. And *that* is when she'll be broken- that's when she'll be able to hear our voice."

Fear nodded, not in agreement but in acknowledgement of what must come. He believed in the greater plan, remembered the multi-colored cords and the balloons of blessing- and he knew greater things lay ahead of Leiala. But he also surmised from the tone of Yeshua's voice that things were about to get worse before they got better.

***

It happened. The slow and painful death march of Leiala's relationship ended as abruptly as it had all begin. She'd been led into the relationship, and she now felt led out of it. At the same time that she knew it was right, it brought her great pain. It wasn't just the loss of a relationship with a man she cared for deeply, it was the loss of a dream, of her hope that her deepest desires would be realized.

She wasn't sure how it had all happened, and she wasn't sure that it even mattered. Maybe one day, she would be able to wade through the mess of miscommunication and distance and fear that had suffocated their relationship- but all her brain could register at the moment was pain. Rejection. Failure. Disappointment. Confusion.

What *had* happened? She'd felt so certain in the beginning, penning letters and romantic journal entries she felt sure would one day be read aloud. She'd felt affirmed in her convictions to step forward in faith, to open herself up to love that had lay dormant for so many years.

For as lovely and desirable as she'd felt in the early stages of the relationship, she now felt despised, loathed, worthless.

It's because he found out. He realized you're not worth it.

You should actually just be thankful that someone bought into the lie for as long as he did. It was never going to last- surely in the depths of your heart you knew that to be true.

Leiala, in her pitiful, vulnerable state, had to agree.

You're pathetic, but you don't have to let everyone know. Whatever you do, keep it together. You know what will make you feel better? What will make you feel stronger? Eating less. Running more. You should start training for races again. Make sure you look presentable- it's more important than ever to look polished now. One person realized you for the fraud that you are- let's not have the whole world keen on your secret.

And Leiala obeyed.

The night of the gut-wrenching phone call that severed any last hopes of revitalizing their relationship, she quietly closed her door. Texted her closest friends that she was fine, she didn't need anything, all while she laid on the floor, body shaking and trembling with the ferocious, soul-served sobs. Silencing her cries as tissues piled up around her and her vision became blurry, then clouded, and then entirely black as she couldn't bring herself to open her eyes at all.

Pain. Worse than physical pain- that could be endured with the hope that time or remedies could bring relief. This pain, it was a stab to heart, the fiery dart that plunged straight into the bull's eye of her greatest fear: that she would live her life out alone, that she would never be worthy of another's love. She wouldn't be cast in the role of wife or mother- she wasn't worthy of this honor. There was no remedy for this pain, and there was no hope in this realization. These muffled cries came straight from the heart, carried with them the belief that for all Leiala might experience in her life, that which she wanted most would not be amongst them.

Such realization was paralyzing at the same time it demanded a response. The numbness that Leiala had sought after so desperately failed her now- she could not silence the pain or sorrow that washed over her.

Two friends, ignoring her cool and collected texts, who came over anyway, forging their way into her bedroom, stepped over the mountain of tissues and sat beside her, quietly stroking her hair and holding her hand without saying a word. They knew. They saw her, too. They were privy to the Leiala that most of the world couldn't see, that which Leiala worked hard to make *sure* they didn't see: the Leiala with an impossibly soft heart, Leiala who felt deeply and bled when others weren't watching.

More sleepless nights. Nights where Leiala felt stripped, a mere skeleton of flesh and blood held together by a single, brittle thread. A thread she silently, and then loudly, wished would be severed. If she couldn't have her dream, life wasn't worth living.

And as exhausting as her life had felt before, it felt exponentially more so now. Now that there was no longer a reason to persevere- there was no reason to be perfect anymore. But Leiala still played to the tune of the expectations of others, this time an empty shell that faked happiness she didn't feel. Some knew, they realized the charade- but most were fooled. Leiala was a good actress- she was a master of control, after all- and most were too wrapped up in their own set of issues.

In desperation, Leiala determined that she must go deeper, become edgier to numb the pain, or at least to feel something other than the pain that had so insidiously taken over most areas of her life.

She completed a master's degree, and felt nothing.

She trekked to the top of Machu Picchu following ancient Incan trails, and then forged her way deep into the heart of the Amazon. She felt temporary relief, so far removed from her daily existence that had entrapped her with expectation- but there was no lasting peace.

She bought a home- a place to call her own, a beautiful retreat backed up against mountains riddled with trails. She drank her morning tea by the fireplace watching the bunnies play and the birds sing in the secluded, private park just beyond her patio. The sunlight filtered beautifully through the mature trees, casting magical shadows on the carpeting- something Leiala had always appreciated. And she had the ultimate- that which she'd dreamed of for so long: a walk-in closet. It brought her no satisfaction.

She determined to run a marathon, and spent her free time plotting out a foolproof training regimen- one that would secure her a place in the Boston Marathon. She ran ten, fifteen, twenty, then twenty-five miles in order to prepare. She ran up hills, then mountains, then multiple mountains. She pushed herself to run *harder*, to run *faster*- to take her body past where it wanted to stop. She expected these runs to bring relief, to flood her with endorphins galore. But for all the reflection these three hour runs brought her, the end only brought tears and depression that Leiala couldn't understand.

And in the midst of it all, Leiala worked to confront that which so many had thoughtfully pointed out to her but which she only now was willing to admit: an eating disorder.

It was painful, and humbling, to consider how deeply entrenched her thoughts and attitudes towards food ran. It was shocking to realize how honestly ignorant she'd been to that which everyone close to her had seen.

Her first therapy session, a concession to those who saw her deep depression and pushed her to get help. And from that very first session, the identification of a series of problems that Leiala hadn't been able to acknowledge or see: perfectionism, control issues, a need for achievement- obsessions that had landed her in the open arms of an eating disorder.

Depression that didn't shake, when she realized how far she had buried herself. When she cried over a homework assignment to eat an Oreo, and when she paraded up and down the aisles of the grocery store with tears in her eyes as she surveyed the food items she was supposed to put in her cart, but just couldn't. Fear, when she realized that she had quite literally taken herself to a place where she believed it was better to die than to gain weight, where the ultimate goal was to live out each day without needing to eat at all. And all this, coupled with the staunch, fervent belief that there was no problem- she had everything under control.

Whose control? Leiala wondered.

If the past months had taught her anything, it was that she didn't have any control whatsoever- her desperate attempts to keep things following a safe, consistent pattern had exploded, the shrapnel lodged in every area of her life as an ugly reminder of where she had descended.

Frustration came as she tried to be perfect even in her recovery and failed- frustration that came from knowing what she was supposed to do but then not being able to do it.

It should have been so easy. No one else seemed to struggle with it. Why was it so hard for her? Leiala was desperate for relief, for answers, for any stray ember of hope. She couldn't go on- she couldn't take her life anymore. And it was then- when Leiala reached the end of her rope- that she heard Theos's voice.

-35-

Stop. Give it up. Let go.

The words woke Leiala in the night, jolting her from her sleep. Her heart was pounding in her chest and her shirt clung to her sticky, sweaty back. The words made her pulse quicken, made her want to vomit.

It wasn't a suicidal voice- she knew, because she'd had those uninvited visiting voices. The liquid amber of the voice that silkily promised that all her problems would disappear if she slipped into nonexistence. This voice was highly persuasive, Leiala knew from experience- until she was tempted into walking just to the start of that path. And then, abruptly, the thorns and felled logs and dragons lying in wait immediately came before her in a frightening reminder of what she'd been tempted to do.

So why did the words inspire such terror? She lay perfectly still, her furnace of a body cooling as she threw off the comforter that seemed to be suffocating her. How was it that the idea of letting go, just giving up on all that she had worked so hard to accomplish- felt impossible?

You've worked years, Leiala, YEARS, to get to the place that you're in now. You know how hard you had to work to make it here. Are you really going to give it all up? If you change your mind, it will take monumental effort to get back here. You might never make it back.

And that, Leiala agreed, was the problem. This second voice seemed to give life to the fears she clung so tightly to- what would happen to her if she stopped trying?

She didn't know. She couldn't remember *not trying*. Couldn't remember allowing whimsy and chance and divine circumstances to influence her plan. She remembered brief spells of time in which she had attempted to adopt a bit more flexibility, and the chaos that had ensued. Other people might be able to procrastinate or put in moderate effort and achieve satisfactory results, but Leiala didn't believe that these rules also applied to her. When she'd loosened her grip just a bit, things had deteriorated quickly.

She'd gotten a B in a class, ruining her perfect GPA.
She'd gone up a pants size.
She'd missed her employer matching potential on her 401k plan.

Filed away in the deepest recesses of her mind were these limited past experiences that seemed to overwhelmingly influence every decision she made.

If she didn't count her calories, she would get fat. FAT. Morbidly obese.
If she skipped a run, she would lose her entire foundation and struggle even to make it a mile.

If she didn't put one hundred percent effort in one hundred percent of the time, she would disappoint everyone and reveal herself as a giant, inexcusable, unlovable fraud.

And there was the issue, the fear that even Leiala couldn't see. Fear no longer supplied her with these thoughts- these responses were cast out of years' worth of memories and illogical thought patterns. They paralyzed Leiala, and yet she could not let go.

***

"She is totally missing it!" Fear worried, exclaimed, as he watched Leiala with mounting frustration. "I don't think she's going to be able to pull herself out of this. She's approaching this like she approaches everything else- she's trying to be perfect even in her recovery. She is SO clueless!"

“She won’t be able to pull herself out of it,” Yeshua agreed. “She can go to therapy and spend time reading her Bible and receiving encouragement from her community and she can change her actions...but until Matsar is banished, she will not be free.”

“So let’s get him out of there!” Fear announced, charging forward with fist clenched in determination.

“He will go,” Yeshua said slowly without offering any details.

“How?” Fear pressed. “Leiala doesn’t even see that he’s there. She has no idea that she has a parasite literally clawed into her back.”

“She will realize,” Yeshua answered. “His grip has already loosened a bit- have you noticed?”

Indeed, Fear had- it was not dramatic, but Matsar’s grip on Leiala was not the ironclad attachment it had once been. But Matsar was not going to go without a fight. Fear had watched his evident agony and torment when Leiala spent time in prayer, in the Word, or in worship. Matsar writhed like a fish on a hook, covering his ears at what Pneuma had explained sounded like bloodcurdling, high-pitched shrieks coming from Leiala every time she spent time with Theos.

Leiala could hear during those times- Matsar was so distracted in preserving his sanity that he could not consume and monopolize Leiala’s thoughts. In these moments, she felt peace- but it was quickly stripped of her as she walked back out into the world, departing from Theos’s presence. For Matsar was nothing if not an aggressive, ruthless opponent- his frustration and outrage doubled over the trauma he’d experienced, he came back with a vengeance, convincing Leiala that she’d just imagined the peace and that there was not actually anything to be done about her situation. The attacks were rampant, incessant, a volley of rocks trebucheted past any defenses Leiala had been able to muster during her time spent with Theos.

It made Fear wonder if her time spent with Theos was a total waste- until he remembered the army that was growing in her name. Leiala couldn't see it- if she was blind to the existence of Matsar, she had no chance whatsoever of realizing that which was materializing in the alternative realm- but there was an army of Theos's workers congregating on her behalf. Every prayer uttered brought another worker to her defense, another soldier who began training for battle. Prayers whispered by others brought workers, too- Leiala now had thousands of workers prepared to fight solely for her benefit.

They did not do anything that Fear could see- he waited with expectation, wondering when these workers would descend upon earth to reclaim Leiala for their kingdom. They were waiting on Theos's word, he knew- but if it were up to Fear, the intervention would have taken place a long time ago.

"Expectancy, not expectation," Pneuma counseled him. "You're expecting Theos to act in a certain way, at a certain time, with a certain outcome. Theos is ruler because He is wiser, He has greater capacity for wisdom and knowledge and truth than you could ever hope to hold. He doesn't respond in the way you might imagine Him to- and that's a blessing for everyone. Wait with expectancy- He *will* show up, and His glory will be made known in Leiala's life- but stop trying to foretell or plan what that might look like."

Fear hadn't said anything. He quietly digested this statement, the words immediately finding their mark on the core of his heart.

"He never works how you might expect," Yeshua chimed in, chuckling. "It's almost a game to him. He answers the pleas and prayers of His children, but in the most unexpected ways."

"The tapestry," Fear acknowledged, thinking of the great multitude of threads swirling and dancing, woven into unique patterns even as he spoke.

"Theos is a great artist," Yeshua agreed.

***

Leiala woke up feeling no different than she did on most Sundays. She felt anxious in the same ways, she felt worry over the same problems. She had learned techniques with which to combat these feelings, and she knew that she was to act in a certain way no matter how she might feel.

The degree to which she felt unsettled varied from day to day: some days, she felt safe, relaxed- she wondered why certain unknown elements bothered her. But other days, the scope of the feelings that hit her threatened to overcome her entirely- it took courage simply to get out of bed. This was one of many reasons why Leiala made it a point to get out of bed early in the morning to start her day- if she did not, she ran the risk of succumbing to despair that was greedy and fat, an insatiable beast whose appetite could not be satisfied.

This particular Sunday felt somewhere in between- there was no real anxiety, but no real anticipation or excitement for the day's events. She had plans to meet her sister for church, and while she took notes on the sermon and participated in the worship, there was no revolutionary pull on her soul.

She sat with her sister after the service, the two of them chatting and encouraging one another as the masses thronged out of the sanctuary. When the crowd had thinned, they made their way out, coming into stride next to an eccentric woman. One who interjected into their conversation when she heard the topic of discussion, and who proceeded to pray a blessing over her sister. Leiala smiled and joined into the prayer, her hand gently resting on her sister's shoulder. And then, the woman asked if she could pray for Leiala.

It felt a bit like an afterthought, but Leiala knew the state of her forlorn soul, and she was not in a position to turn down any prayer. So she said yes.

***

Electricity sparked through the air and sent Fear running to the west end.

It was happening- it was time. He knew it was happening. He couldn't explain how he knew, but he *knew*.

"When? Where?" Fear breathlessly proclaimed as he screeched to a halt, mouth hanging wide open.

There, in front of him, stood a legion of Theos's workers. Trained, experienced, fierce soldiers- armed for battle. The size and level of weaponry varied from worker to worker, but every worker possessed the gritty, hardened look of determination and a righteous white light that seemed to light up the unsheathed swords held firmly. Fear had never seen such an army, and it struck him dumb. Every worker, with feet firmly planted, facing Theos, the master commander, situated at the front of the pack. He had no need for a pedestal or a platform- His very stature and presence were awe-inspiring and tremendous.

Theos raised his right hand, and in perfect unity, the army took a knee, humbled before their leader as they waited expectantly for His word. Fear felt his mouth run dry, and he could not even bring himself to pick his feet up and move to the side- he was rooted in position and doubted even a tornado could displace him.

Theos's hand remained upright for a long moment- long enough for Fear to watch as Leiala verbally identified her struggle for control, a statement that mercifully led the wise woman to proclaim the presence of a spirit of control in Leiala's life.

Fear's fingers began to tremble and the blood in his veins seemed to gush through him with the energy of a thousand racehorses. Matsar- he had been identified. Leiala could see that which had been so carefully hidden from her, and she was about to cast him off. Fear leaned forward, the weight shifting to the tips of his toes. The army was poised and ready, and so was Leiala.

It wasn't as dramatic as Fear had imagined it might be. Yeshua had been wise to warn him to retrain his expectant mind to instead anticipate expectancy. With a single wave of Theos's right hand, the righteous army descended to earth. Fear was left in the wake of a colossal wind which forced him to blink once before he watched with wide-open eyes as the army struck Matsar from Leiala's back.

It was a single motion, one that hardly necessitated the legion of workers that swooped to Leiala's defense. But maybe that was the point- the army that had rallied was so extraordinary that there never was any chance for Abaddon in the first place.

His eyes remained glued to the scene on earth, to Leiala freed from the nasty, surreptitious beast. Fear watched her with interest- she didn't seem to realize that which had just taken place. She'd been freed- *freed*! Why wasn't she jumping and dancing with joy?

"It's not always an electric moment," Pneuma explained. "But it doesn't make it any less real."

"When will she know?" Fear asked, trying to hide the disappointment from his voice. He'd expected a big to-do, a dramatic showdown that hadn't materialized.

"Soon," Pneuma explained, a bemused smile on His face. "We won, Fear," He reminded the character. "Don't look so upset."

"Yes," Fear agreed, trying to muster more positive feeling. "We did win. Leiala's been set free- I'm glad that's over."

"Over?" Pneuma was quick to chirp. He studied Fear's innocent face and shook His head slowly. "Oh no, it's not over. It's just beginning."

This time, Fear couldn't hide his knee-jerk reaction.

"You're joking," Fear asked, the wretchedness of his voice cutting through the air sharply.

"I am most certainly not," Pneuma told him seriously. "Leiala's battle is just beginning, despite what you might imagine."

Fear stood mute, disappointed and distraught beyond belief.

“This was a great victory,” Pneuma went on in an attempt to lift Fear’s spirits. “And this awakening will take Leiala to a level of awareness and strength and power that will startle even her. But it’s nowhere near over.”

“There will be more,” Fear said quietly, voicing the words in the hopes that their message might sink in.

“Many more,” Pneuma agreed. “But not all to this extent. Leiala’s been marked,” Pneuma reminded him. “She’s destined to do great things, to go to dark places that others might not willingly go to.”

“And Abaddon won’t let that happen without a fight,” Fear finished, putting two and two together.

“Not a chance,” Pneuma confirmed. “She’s much more equipped for the battles to come, Fear. And her journey is about to become far more interesting. You’re going to see a boldness to Leiala, a passion, an edgy, raw nature that’s been lying dormant for a long time.” He said the words with an unrestrained smile on His face, a sign of encouragement that brought genuine hope.

“More than just the red lipstick?” Fear asked, finding his humor again.

“Far, far more than just her new proclivity for red lipstick,” Pneuma chuckled. “This girl who has hidden in desperate fear from all things slightly edgy is about to become the edgiest of them all.”

Here, Fear had to laugh. He couldn’t fathom this to be true- he’d spent his entire life following and influencing a girl who worshiped that which was cautious, conservative, and safe. But he’d seen the seeds of this promise, and he’d watched over the past year as she’d walked herself headfirst into the raging storm, first in a futile attempt to take all things on in her own power, and now with the renewed strength and divine inspiration that came from Theos’s blessing.

***

Monday morning was quiet. Leiala smiled as she remembered Sunday, the peaceful ebb and flow of the afternoon following church. It had been a good day, she reflected- and there was no "but" or baleful charcoal cloud that tarnished the experience.

By Tuesday morning, Leiala realized that something was different. She wasn't just going through the motions of how she was supposed to behave, according to her therapist and the Bible and words of wisdom spoken to her by those who loved her- she was actually operating from a different place. She hadn't recognized it at first, because she wasn't working so hard to attribute each experience of her day to a specific event or thought or future implication. She was just....*living*.

She'd let go. For all the fear and trepidation and terror that this simple statement had generated, she'd somehow crossed over the threshold without any monumental efforts of her own.

The revelation brought warmth, peace- she was filled with overwhelming gratitude. Even in the present moment, she knew that her hardships were not over, that her story would include far more trials and anxious moments and seemingly-insurmountable challenges. But she knew now where they came from, and this awareness brought along with it a new battle plan.

It wasn't up to her. If it were up to her, she would fail. Every. Single. Time. She *couldn't* do it- that was the point. She was never going to be able to do it, and with every flailing, grasping hand desperately reaching for control, she sunk deeper and deeper into the quicksand, farther and farther from rescue.

But she'd been rescued.

New hope sprang forth within her soul: the long trek through the desert had left her blistered and parched and cracked, but now she sat quietly amongst lush, decadent foliage, kelly-green grass that carpeted hillsides split by babbling brooks and dotted with exultant wildflowers. In the same way her soul had felt tormented, she now felt pervasive, indescribable peace, peace that assured her that no matter what her future held, it would be lovely.

This final thought alone brought tears of joy to Leiala's eyes, made her giggle out loud. She never could have imagined it to be possible- that the deepest desire of her heart could be sidelined, no longer the solo feature film dominating all airtime in the theaters, but a hope that was gently pocketed, safely set aside for the time being. It didn't matter, Leiala realized- and this time, she believed it! It wasn't spoken shrilly, with hunger and desperation that it would become true. It simply *was*.

On some level, Leiala was aware that her life was just beginning. She'd had a multitude of experiences that had enriched her life and that had taken her to wondrous places- but the freedom and purpose that now burned in her soul whispered to her that the greatest things were yet to come. Hope, redemption, beauty, and grace- they were all on the horizon. All she had to do was receive.

Author's Note

This wasn't a book I was planning to write. It doesn't fit in with the genre of books I've written in the past. It's been a few years since I published my last book, and I felt the itch to write again. To *really* write! It frustrated me, because I wasn't sure where the urge was coming from, and I wasn't sure what I was supposed to be writing about.

The itch wouldn't leave, and one night I found myself sitting in Starbucks with my laptop open, a blank document before me. The blinking cursor on the screen seemed to punctuate my uncertainty and lack of direction- what was I supposed to write? So I did what I always do in these types of situations- I stopped thinking and just started doing. I made my fingers begin typing even as I had no idea what words would come forth. I typed the thoughts in my head, the questions I had, and the confusion I felt. And the story began to surface.

By the third chapter, the fog had cleared, and inspiration came on thick. As with all my books, I never knew what would happen next- I just sat down, wrote a chapter, and then packed up my things and left.

This story means a lot to me because it doesn't follow the format or sequencing of any other project I've worked on. The emphasis isn't on the events themselves, but on Leiala's interpretation of them- what is *really* happening to her as all of these events unfold? Certain periods of her life receive more airtime than others- because certain periods of our life serve to influence, mold, and shape us more than others.

There's another reason this story is so dear to me, and that's because this is very much a story inspired by my own life's journey. Writing has always been an escape for me- a way to transfer my emotions and creativity into something outside of myself. In the past, that's been accomplished through the composition of fantastical narratives that allowed me to enter into a magical, fictitious world that offered solace during challenging periods of my life. This was very different.

In putting my story (or parts of it) down on paper, I gave myself permission to revisit and assess those moments (or seasons) of my life that most influenced and shaped me. Giving names and motives and personalities to the emotions and demons allowed me to sort through my feelings and thought patterns and to fight back through my writing. It exposed lies for what they were: **LIES**, and it brought truth and light to the center-stage when it felt buried underneath mountains of garbage.

I'm overwhelmingly thankful and grateful to God for speaking directly to my heart during this time of writing: guiding me to see, to understand, and to accept the unseen. My prayer is that this story also touches you, and that it gives you pause: I pray that it brings to the surface your own demons and lies and insecurities that have been planted by the enemy so that you might be hidden from truth and God's infinite, overwhelming love.

As we walk through life together and struggle alongside one another, I would love to hear your story. How are you being molded and shaped in this present moment? What (and who!) are you allowing to influence you?

For we wrestle not against flesh and blood, but against principalities, against powers, against the rulers of the darkness of this world, against spiritual wickedness in high places.
Ephesians 6:12

So as we all work to do the best we can with the hand we've been dealt, be kind. Be kinder than you think others deserve. I'm going to say it again: *be kind*. Everyone is fighting a battle- we see some, and others go unseen. Sometimes, the invisible battles can be the hardest to face- *especially* because others don't see the weapons being used against you, can't understand how it feels to wage war against something you can't touch. In these difficult times, it's important to remember that despite what you might feel or perceive as reality, you are ***never*** alone.

Written with love,
Alyssa

P.S. I would truly love to hear from you! If you have a story to share, a prayer request, a question- anything really!- you can reach me here: abhuckleberry@gmail.com.

Made in the USA
San Bernardino, CA
01 August 2017